KU-303-396

R. D. Wingfield, who is married with one son and lives in Basildon, Essex, is a prolific writer of radio crime plays and comedy scripts, some for the late Kenneth Williams, star of the 'Carry On' films.

His crime novels featuring DI Jack Frost are *A Touch of Frost*, *Frost at Christmas*, *Hard Frost*, *Night Frost* and *Winter Frost*. The series has been successfully adapted for television as *A Touch of Frost* starring David Jason.

Also by R.D.Wingfield

FROST AT CHRISTMAS
A TOUCH OF FROST
HARD FROST
WINTER FROST

and published by Corgi Books

NIGHT FROST

R.D. Wingfield

CORGI BOOKS

NIGHT FROST
A CORGI BOOK : 9780552145589

Originally published in Great Britain by
Constable & Co. Ltd

PRINTING HISTORY
Constable edition published 1992
Corgi edition published 1992

15 17 19 20 18 16 14

This book is set in 10pt Monotype Plantin by
Phoenix Typesetting, Burley-in-Wharfdale, West Yorkshire.

Corgi Books are published by Transworld Publishers,
61–63 Uxbridge Road, London W5 5SA,
a division of The Random House Group Ltd.

Addresses for Random House Group Ltd companies outside
the UK can be found at: www.randomhouse.co.uk
The Random House Group Ltd Reg. No. 954009.

Printed and bound in Great Britain by
Cox & Wyman Ltd, Reading, Berkshire.

The Random House Group Limited makes every effort to
ensure that the papers used in its books are made from trees
that have been legally sourced from well-managed and credibly
certified forests. Our paper procurement policy can be found
at: www.randomhouse.co.uk/paper.htm.

Sunday

The old lady's name was Mrs Haynes – Mary Haynes, but no-one had called her Mary for years, not since her husband died. She was seventy-eight years old and she stood on the doorstep trembling with fear.

She had just come back from the churchyard. She went there every Sunday, weather permitting, to tidy up her husband's grave and put fresh flowers in the cut glass vase that had once stood on the dark oak sideboard they had bought the first year they were married and which was now in the unused back room. Today, when she reached the churchyard the vicar was waiting for her, his face grim. 'I'm afraid you must prepare yourself for a shock, Mrs Haynes.'

When she saw what they had done to the grave she thought she was going to pass out. The headstone she had saved for so carefully was desecrated with purple painted graffiti. A crudely drawn skull and crossbones and words she couldn't bring herself to repeat defaced her husband's name. The vase had been hurled against the headstone and smashed to pieces.

The vicar was most sympathetic. He and his curate had been comforting distraught mourners all day. Vandals had left a trail of broken headstones, graffiti and strewn wreaths in a mindless moronic orgy of destruction. The police had been informed, he assured her, and had promised that the cemetery would be kept under constant observation in the hope of catching the perpetrators in the act.

She couldn't remember the journey home, her mind in a whirl at what had happened. Such a relief to creak open the front gate. But at the tiny porch another shock. As she fumbled in her purse for the key she noticed that the porch doormat had been moved. She was ever so careful how she replaced it when she hid the spare door key and there was no doubt it had been moved.

Hands shaking, she lifted the corner of the mat. The key wasn't there. Someone had taken it. Perhaps even used it to get inside. She stepped back and looked up at the house. Was it her imagination, or had the bedroom curtains shivered as if someone had just twitched them shut?

Her gloved hand clutched her chest to hold the hurt of her fluttering heart. She needed help. Anyone's help. A light was on next door where that awful young man with the motor bike lived. She staggered across and pressed the door bell. She could hear it ringing inside the house. No-one came. She pressed it again.

Upstairs in the bedroom, the man with the knife smiled to himself and patiently waited.

Monday morning shift

Rain slashed across the windows blurring the view of the dreary houses on the opposite side of the street. Liz Gilmore, kneeling on the settee, stared out moodily. It hadn't stopped raining since they moved into this poky little house two days ago. Married three years and all they'd ever lived in was a succession of rented police accommodation. 'I hate this lousy town,' she announced.

She had never wanted to come to Denton. When the promotion came through she was hoping he'd be posted to somewhere exciting, somewhere with a bit of life – theatres, clubs, decent shops . . . not this boring little backwater.

Her husband, Detective Sergeant Frank Gilmore, twenty-four, stockily built with dark, close-cropped hair, checked his watch for the eighth time. He wished Liz would stop her moaning. He had so much on his mind. 8.45. In a quarter of an hour he would be meeting his new Divisional Commander to take up his first assignment as a newly promoted detective sergeant. He wanted to keep his mind clear. First impressions were important. Denton was a one-eyed town, but it was the first step on the ladder leading to dizzy heights. 'It won't be for long, Liz.'

She flicked back her blonde hair and picked up the local newspaper, the Denton *Echo*. The front page was dominated by a photograph of upturned, smashed and graffiti-desecrated headstones. *Graveyard Vandals Strike Again*, screamed the headline. *Vicar Suspects Black Magic Coven*. 'Black magic coven,' she muttered. 'If I knew where it was, I'd join it. Probably the only bit of excitement in this dead-and-alive hole.'

He faked a smile. Liz seemed to delight in shocking people with her outrageous remarks. 'Any other news?'

' "Denton crippled by flu epidemic",' she read, then tossed the paper to one side. 'Graveyards, flu, poky rooms and non-stop rain. This town is just one bag of laughs!'

Again he consulted his watch. Timing was important. He didn't want to turn up too early. That smacked of in-security. A newly promoted detective sergeant shouldn't appear insecure. He wanted to breeze in at a minute to nine and be shown directly to the Divisional Commander's office. 'I'll have to leave soon.'

'Let's have a look at you.' She stood up and studied him, removing an imaginary speck of fluff from his new charcoal grey Marks and Spencer's suit. An approving nod. 'You'll pass.' And then she was the old Liz, pressing close to him, her arms holding him tight. 'I'm sorry I'm such a bitch sometimes.'

'You're not!' he assured her, his arms round her.

She winced. 'Your pen is sticking in me.' She un-buttoned his jacket and he could feel her hot, burning body and the arousing smell of her perfume. Good old Liz. Her timing lousy as always.

'You smell nice,' she purred, nuzzling her nose against his chin.

He frowned uneasily. At her insistence he had put on that expensive Chanel aftershave she had bought him for Christmas, but he knew it was the wrong thing. He pulled away. 'I really must go. I'll be late.'

'And you will be back at six? None of this working all the hours God sends stuff?'

He smiled. He was now on surer ground. The Denton Divisional Commander's office had sent him an itemized timetable, detailing almost minute by minute his itinerary for the coming week. Denton was clearly a well organized, efficiently run station. Today, after his meeting with the Divisional Commander, he was to be taken around the station and introduced to the personnel and the various departments. Then his new boss, Detective Inspector Allen, was taking him on a tour of the district to familiarize him with the area. After lunch in the canteen (1.15-2.15) he was off to visit the local Forensic Laboratory. At 5.30 precisely, a car would collect him up and return him to his home (e.t.a. 5.55 p.m.). 'I'll be back by six,' he assured her.

One last lingering kiss and he put on his mac and

dashed through the rain to his car. Liz flopped back on the settee and flicked through the paper again. She barely gave a glance to the item at the bottom of the front page: *Hope Dies For Missing News Girl*.

Denton Police Station didn't look the model of efficiency Gilmore had been led to expect. The lobby was unattended, the floor wet from a hasty mopping and reeking of disinfectant. Somewhere a phone was ringing and no-one answered it. Leaning against the counter, snorting with impatience, a middle-aged man waited. He raised his eyebrows to the ceiling as Gilmore entered, inviting him to share his disgust at the treatment meted out to rate-paying members of the public. 'My car's been pinched. They won't accept details over the phone that's too bloody easy. You have to take time off from flaming work, hire a cab because you've got no car and come down in person and fill in a damn form.'

A balding, uniformed sergeant with a mournful face came in. This was Bill Wells, pushing forty, tired and fed up. Today should have been his rest day. 'Right, Mr Wilkins. Details have been circulated.'

'So what happens now?'

The sergeant shrugged. 'It was probably taken by joy-riders. If a member of the public reports it abandoned somewhere, we'll let you know so you can collect it.'

'And that's the limit of the help I get from the police? If someone happens to spot it, you'll pass on the message. Brilliant. Aren't the police going to look for it?'

'Of course we are,' the sergeant told him, 'but we do have more important things on our plate.' He nodded towards the poster on the wall behind him. The poster displayed a black and white photograph of a child in school uniform standing by a bike. The heading read: *Missing – have you seen this girl?*

The man snorted his contempt as he stamped out. 'If I've got to wait for you to find that poor little cow, I'll wait for ever.'

Wells stared stony-faced at the man's retreating back, then opened a door to yell, 'Can't someone answer that damn phone,' before turning his attention to Gilmore. 'Can I help you, sir?'

'Detective Sergeant Gilmore to see Mr Mullett.'

Behind Gilmore the lobby door opened again and two men and a woman came in, shaking umbrellas. One of the men unbuttoned his raincoat to reveal a clerical collar. 'Appointment with Mr Mullett,' he announced.

'Yes, vicar. He's expecting you,' Wells told him.

'My appointment's at nine,' hissed Gilmore, waving his itinerary as proof.

'Then you'll have to wait.' The sergeant brushed past him to escort the trio through the swing doors to the Divisional Commander's office.

Fuming, Gilmore checked his watch. A minute to nine. The one thing he knew about his new Divisional Commander was that Mullett was a stickler for punctuality and, because that fool of a sergeant had let the newcomers through first, he was going to be late reporting for duty on his very first day.

He slumped down on the hard wooden bench and prodded a puddle of disinfectant-smelling water with his shoe. The hands of the wall clock clunked round with monotonous regularity, marking out the number of minutes he was going to be late. He shifted his gaze to the missing girl poster. *Paula Bartlett, aged 15, dark hair, pale complexion, height 5' 3". Last seen September 14th, in the Forest Lane area.* September 14th! Some two months ago!

She wasn't a particularly pretty-looking kid, but perhaps the photograph didn't do her justice.

The swing doors clicked together as the sergeant returned. Gilmore sprang to his feet. 'My appointment with Mr Mullett . . .'

'You'll have to wait.' Wells had no time for jumped-up newly promoted constables.

Gilmore felt he had to report to someone. He consulted his itinerary. 'Tell Inspector Allen I'm here.'

'He's off sick. Everyone's off flaming sick.' The internal phone buzzed. 'No, Mr Mullett, Mr Frost isn't in yet. Yes, I did tell him nine o'clock. Yes, sir.' He hung up.

Rain blew in from the lobby doors as a scruffy figure in a dripping mac pushed through. He peeled a sodden maroon scarf from his neck and wrung it out. 'It's peeing down out there,' he announced, then his nose twitched. 'Disinfectant and perfume. This place stinks like a tart's slop-bucket.'

'The disinfectant is from the cleaners,' the sergeant informed him. 'We had drunks throwing up all over the place last night. And the poncey scent is from the new boy's aftershave.' He jerked his head at Gilmore, who scowled back. 'Mr Mullett's been asking for you.'

'He's always asking for me. I think he fancies me. He likes a bit of rough.' He unbuttoned his mac to expose a crumpled blue suit with two buttons missing. The red tie beneath the frayed shirt collar had a tight, greasy knot and looked as if it had been put on by being pulled over his neck like a noose. He turned to Gilmore and held out a nicotine-stained hand. 'I'm Detective Inspector Jack Frost.'

Gilmore shook the proffered hand, his mind racing. A detective inspector! This rag-bag was a detective

11

inspector? A joke, surely? But no-one seemed to be laughing. 'You'll be working with me,' continued Frost.

Now that just had to be a joke. He waved his itinerary. 'I've been assigned to Mr Allen.'

'All been changed – Allen's got the pox,' said Frost.

'He's down with flu,' corrected the station sergeant. 'Half the damn station's down with it, most of the others are on sick leave following Friday's punch-up and the rest of us silly sods are dragged in on their rest day and working double shifts.' The internal phone buzzed.

'If it's Mullett . . .' said Frost, backing towards the exit doors.

It wasn't Mullett. It was Control for the inspector. 'The Comptons – the couple receiving the hate mail. They've had a fire – someone's tried to burn their summer house down.'

'On my way,' said Frost, banging down the phone. He jerked his head at Gilmore. 'Come on, son. If you like rigid nipples you're in for a treat – the lady of the house is a cracker.'

'But I'm supposed to report to the Divisional Commander,' Gilmore protested.

'You can do that when we get back.'

The internal phone rang. This time it was Mullett.

Frost grabbed Gilmore's arm and hurried him out into the rain.

Frost's old Ford Cortina was tucked out of sight, round the corner from the station car-park where, hopefully, Mullett wouldn't spot it. While Gilmore waited in the pouring rain which was finding its way through his new raincoat, Frost cleared the junk from the passenger seat, including two mud-encrusted wellington boots which he tossed into the back of the car. 'In you get, son.'

12

Gilmore scrubbed pointedly at the seat with his handkerchief before risking its contact with his brand new suit. His head nearly hit the windscreen as Frost suddenly slammed the car into gear and they were away.

'Where are we going?' he asked, hastily clicking the buckle of his seat belt as the car squealed into Market Square, shooting up spray as it ploughed through an unexpectedly deep puddle.

'A little village called Lexing – about four miles outside Denton.' A blur of shops zipped past then the engine was labouring and coughing as it clawed up a steep hill and there was a smell of burning oil. Frost sniffed and frowned. 'Do you know anything about engines, son?'

'No,' said Gilmore, firmly. There was no way he was going to mess up his new suit poking under the bonnet of Frost's filthy car. They were now passing a heavily wooded area, with sagging, rain-heavy bushes.

Frost jerked a thumb. 'Denton Woods. Right over the far side is where that schoolgirl went missing. She was doing a newspaper round, but never finished it. Her bike and her undelivered papers turned up in a ditch, but no trace of the kid.'

'Had there been trouble at home? Could she have run away?'

'Don't know, son. It was Mr Allen's case until he conveniently got the bloody flu. Now I'm lumbered. We'll have to start reading through the file when we get back.' He scratched a match down the dashboard and lit up, then remembered he hadn't told Gilmore about the case they were driving to. 'Married couple, in their mid-twenties, live in a converted windmill. Some joker's been frightening the life out of them.'

'How?' Gilmore asked.

'Lots of charming ways. Sending fake obituary notices

– tombstone catalogues and things like that. They even had an undertaker call on them last week to collect the husband's body. His poor cow of a wife went into hysterics.'

The car was now jolting and squelching down a muddied lane and the smell of burning oil was getting stronger. Frost wound down the window to let in some air, then pointed. 'There it is!' Looming up before them, imperfectly seen through the Cortina's mud-grimed windscreen, was a genuine old wooden windmill, its sails removed, and painted a smart designer black and white.

Gilmore leant forward and craned his neck to take it all in. He was impressed. 'That must have cost a few bob?'

Frost nodded. 'Rumour has it that the Comptons paid close on a quarter of a million for the place. With the slump in the housing market it's worth a lot less now.'

The car scrunched up the gravel driveway which led to a white-framed, black front door outside which a police car was already parked. Alongside the drive ran a lawn, once immaculate, but now a muddy, churned-up, tyre-grooved mess a-slosh with dirty water. Their job done, firemen were clambering into a fire engine ready to drive off. In the middle of the lawn the Fire Investigations Officer, rain bouncing off his yellow sou'wester, was gloomily poking through a jumble of sodden ashes and burnt, paint-blistered wood, all that was left of the summer house. Frost paddled over to him, cursing as water found the holes in his shoes and ruefully remembering his wellington boots snug and dry in the back of the car. Gilmore stayed put on the path. He wasn't ruining his shoes for a lousy burnt-out summer house.

Frost flicked his eye over the smouldering remains. 'I could have made a better job of putting it out by peeing on it.'

14

The fire officer straightened up and grinned. 'We didn't stand a chance, Jack. The wood was soaked with petrol. We got here twelve minutes after the call, but it had almost burnt itself out by then.'

'Petrol?' Frost picked up a chunk of wet burnt wood and sniffed it. It smelled just like wet burnt wood. He tossed it back on the pile and watched the fire engine drive away.

'No doubt about it. I'm still checking, but it was probably set off by some crude form of fuse – a candle or something. I'll be able to tell you more when I find it.'

'You know me,' said Frost. 'If it's crude, I'm interested.' He squelched back to the drive.

Gilmore hammered at the front door while Frost scuffed moodily at the gravel path and tried out the rusty bell on an old-fashioned, woman's bicycle which leant against the wall. The door creaked open on heavy, black, wrought iron hinges and a scrawny, leathery-skinned woman in her late sixties, carrying a mop and bucket, scowled out at them. She wore a man's cap, pulled right down over her hair, and a drab brown shapeless dress, tied at the waist with string.

Frost nodded towards the bucket. 'No thanks, Ada – I went before I came out.' He introduced her to Gilmore. 'This is Ada Perkins, the Swedish au pair.'

The woman grunted. 'You're not half as funny as you think you are, Jack Frost.' She jerked a bony thumb towards a door at the end of the passage. 'There's a policeman in the kitchen drinking tea.'

'Then let's start in the kitchen,' said Frost.

It was a spacious, no-expense-spared kitchen, fitted out in solid oak with marble worktops, burnished copper cookware on the walls and miniature hand-operated

15

water pumps instead of taps over the sink. A black Aga disguised to look like an old coal-fired cooking range breathed the warm crunchy smell of baking bread. Black-moustached PC Jordan, twenty-six, his tunic unbuttoned, was seated at a scrubbed pine designer table drinking tea from a thick designer mug. He jumped up to attention as the detectives entered, but Frost waved him to sit and dragged up a chair alongside him. Gilmore did the same.

'I suppose you want some tea?' said Ada and, without waiting for their reply, poured two teas from a brown teapot, pushed the sugar bowl across, then shuffled out, muttering something about having work to do.

Frost found a tea towel and dried his wet hair. 'This is Frank Gilmore.'

'Hi, Frank,' said Jordan, offering his hand.

The hand was ignored. 'Detective *Sergeant* Gilmore,' came the icy correction. 'And button up that jacket.' Start as you mean to go on. Don't let the lower ranks get too familiar or they'll walk all over you.

Frost passed round his cigarettes, then asked for a report. Jordan, stifling his resentment at Gilmore's snub, flipped open his notebook. 'I got the call from Control at 9.23. I arrived at 9.34. The fire brigade was already here so I left them to it and went straight in to Mrs Compton.'

'Mrs Compton?' interrupted Frost. 'Not the husband?'

'He's away on business,' said Jordan.

A smile traversed Frost's face. 'Good. Then I won't have to watch him fondling her bloody body . . . What's she wearing this morning?'

'That pink shortie nightie,' said Jordan. 'The one she wore the first time.'

Frost whooped with delight. 'The shortie – wow!

16

That's the one that barely covers her bum. I must try and drop something on the floor for her to pick up.' Then he remembered the serious business of the day and nodded for Jordan to continue.

'She got up just after nine, picked the post up from the mat, made herself a cup of tea and went into the lounge. The first letter she opened was this.' Jordan pushed across a transparent plastic bag. Inside it was a sheet of cheap quality A4 paper on which were pasted letters cut from a glossy magazine to form words.

Frost read it, his face grim, then passed it across to Gilmore. The message was short and chillingly to the point. THE NEXT THING TO BURN WILL BE YOU, YOU BITCH.

'Where's the envelope?' demanded Gilmore. This case was looking a little more worthy of his attention now. Jordan handed over another plastic bag containing a manila envelope, 9 inches by 4 inches. The address, typed in capitals, read: MRS COMPTON, THE OLD MILL, LEXING. It bore a first-class stamp and had been posted in Denton the previous evening. He motioned for Jordan to continue.

'Next she heard this roaring sound from outside. She opened the lounge curtains and saw the summer house on fire, so she dialled 999.' He closed his notebook.

Frost drained his mug and dropped his cigarette end in it. 'This is getting nastier and nastier. It started off with heavy-breathing phone calls, now it's death threats. Right, Jordan. Nip down to the village and ask around. Did anyone see anything . . . any strange cars lurking about . . . someone stinking of petrol.' As the constable left, he stood up. 'Buttock-viewing time,' he told Gilmore. 'We're going to chat up Mrs Compton.'

Gilmore followed him out of the kitchen, along the waxed wooden-floored passage and into the lounge, a large, high-ceilinged room which had a rich, rustic, new-sacking smell from the dark chocolate-coloured hessian covering its walls.

Jill Compton, standing to receive them, looked much younger than her twenty-three years. She wore a gauzy cobweb of a baby doll nightdress which hid nothing, and over it a silken house-coat which flapped open so as not to spoil the view through the nightdress. Her hair, fringed over wide blue eyes and free-flowing down her back, was a light, golden corn colour. She wore no make-up and the pale, china doll face with a hint of dark rings around the eyes gave her a look of vulnerability. She smiled bravely. 'I'm sorry I'm not dressed.'

'That's quite all right, Mrs Compton,' said Frost, and there was no doubting the sincerity in his voice. 'It's a sod about your summer house.'

'It could have been the house,' she said, her voice unsteady. 'Did you see that letter?'

Before Frost could answer the front door slammed and a man's voice called, 'Jill – I'm home! Where are you?'

'Mark!' She ran out to meet her husband.

'Damn!' grunted Frost. 'The buttock-squeezer's back!'

Mark Compton was twenty-nine and flashily good-looking. Fair-haired, a bronzed complexion, although slightly overweight from good living, he looked like a retired life-guard out of *Neighbours*. Gilmore hated him instantly for his looks, his money, his perfectly fitting silver-grey suit, his arm around Mrs Compton, but most of all for his hand caressing her bare arm.

'A letter? My wife said there was a letter threatening to kill her.'

18

Frost showed it to him. His face went white. 'Why are we being persecuted like this?' He sank down into a leather armchair. His wife dropped down on his lap and snuggled up to him.

'That's what I want to know,' said Frost. 'Why?' He and Gilmore were sitting, facing the Comptons, in a large leather settee. He fumbled for his cigarettes. 'Whoever's doing this must have a reason.'

'Reason?' said Compton 'There's no bloody reason. It's the work of a maniac.'

'We've been receiving a spate of complaints about poison pen letters. "Did you know your wife's been having it off with the milkman?" – that sort of thing. I'm wondering if it could be the same bloke.'

'We've had death threats, Inspector, not stupid poison pen letters.'

'Run through the main course of events again,' said Frost. 'Just for the benefit of my new colleague here.'

Mark Compton slipped his hand under Jill's house-coat and gently stroked her bare back. 'OK. As you know, we run a business from this place . . . Jill was on her own one night when this bugger phoned.'

'What sort of business is it?' interrupted Gilmore.

'Dirty books,' said Frost.

Compton glowered. 'We're fine art dealers,' he corrected. 'Mainly rare books and prints, a small proportion of which might be termed erotica, and manuscripts, but not many. There's over a quarter of a million pounds' worth of stock upstairs.'

Gilmore whistled softly to show he was impressed. 'Safely locked up, I hope?'

'We couldn't get insurance if it wasn't,' Compton replied icily. 'Your Crime Prevention Officer has given us the once-over and was quite satisfied. We've got a

19

sophisticated alarm system with automatic 999 dial-ling. If anyone tried to break in, they'd set off the alarm at your police station.'

'Books and manuscripts,' said Gilmore, 'and a wooden building. I shouldn't think the insurance company were too happy about that?'

Mark Compton pointed to metal roses dotting the ceiling. 'Automatic sprinklers in every room, a condition of the policy.'

'So not too much danger from fire?'

'An ordinary fire, perhaps, but if some stupid bastard starts pouring petrol all over the place like they apparently did with our summer house . . .'

Frost's head came up sharply. 'How did you know that, sir?'

'The fireman outside told me. It's not a state secret, is it? I am entitled to know the methods maniacs use to destroy my property.'

Frost smiled and switched his attention to the woman. 'Tell us about the phone calls.'

The recollection made her shudder. 'It started about two weeks ago. The phone kept ringing in the middle of the night. Every time I answered it, the caller hung up. It was frightening. This place is so isolated. I was terrified.' Again she shuddered. Her husband moved his hand up to cup and squeeze her breast in reassurance. In case Gilmore hadn't spotted this, Frost drew it to his attention by a sharp dig in the ribs with his elbow. Gilmore pretended not to notice and, trying to keep his eyes well above breast level, he asked Jill to continue.

'The next morning a black Rolls Royce came up the drive. It was a hearse, with a coffin in the back!' She was shaking uncontrollably. Mark squeezed her tighter and she clung to him. At last she was able to continue. 'Two men dressed all in black got out and knocked. They said they were undertakers and had come to collect the body of my husband. I think I screamed.'

'Some stupid, sick bastard's idea of a joke,' cut in Compton angrily. 'Fortunately I came home a couple of minutes later. Jill was having hysterics. Then the phone rang. The Classified Ads section of the local paper checking details of my obituary notice which had just been phoned in. Apparently I had died suddenly as the result of a tragic accident. Just imagine if Jill had taken that call.' She blinked up at him and buried her face in his chest. 'Later that day, just to complete this hilariously funny sick joke, a firm of monumental masons sent me a quotation for my headstone. That was when I called in the police . . . not that it did us any damn good. The next day our ornamental pond was full of dead fish. They'd been poisoned. The maniac had poured bleach in. Then he phoned me.'

Gilmore's head shot up. 'Phoned you?'

'He said, "Dead fish first, dead people next." Then he hung up.'

'Did you recognize the voice?' asked Gilmore.

'Of course I didn't recognize it. Would we be sitting here wondering who it was if I did?'

Gilmore flushed. It would almost be worth his job to smack the smug bastard one in the mouth. 'Can you describe the voice, sir?'

'It was obviously disguised. Very soft, almost a whisper. You couldn't tell if it was a man or a woman.'

'Anything else?'

'Things came through the post – newspaper cuttings, obituaries of people called Compton, or reports of killings or sudden deaths with the victim's name crossed out and our name written in. Charming little things like that.'

'Right,' said Gilmore. 'Whoever is doing this must hate you. Any suggestions?'

'Don't you think we've racked our brains, trying to think of something?' barked Compton. 'There's no rhyme nor reason behind this. I keep telling you, this is the work of someone with a sick mind.'

'Sick minds or not, sir, they've got to have a reason for picking on you in the first place.'

Jill Compton caught her breath and her eyes widened as if a thought had suddenly struck her. 'Mark . . . that man who tried to pick a fight with you!' She rose from his lap and sat on the arm of the chair.

Her husband frowned. 'What man?'

'In London – the security system exhibition.'

A scoffing laugh. 'That was over a month ago.' To the detectives he said, 'A bit of nonsense. It's got nothing to do with this.'

Then why did you look guilty when she mentioned it? thought Frost. 'Let's hear about it anyway, sir. Suspects are pretty thin on the ground at the moment.'

'It's got nothing to do with this,' insisted Compton. 'We'd gone up to London for an antiques fair at the Russell Hotel. This security system exhibition was on at the same time at a different hotel – I forget the name . . .'

'The Griffin,' his wife reminded him.

'That's right . . . Anyway, Guardtech, the firm that fitted up the alarm systems here, had sent us an invitation, so we looked in for a couple of hours. I was in the bar. Jill had gone off somewhere.'

'I was powdering my nose,' she told him.

'Well – whatever. This woman comes up to me and asks for a light. Suddenly, her drunken lout of a husband staggers over and accuses me of trying to take his wife away from him. I didn't want any trouble, so I turned to go. He swings a punch at me, misses by miles and falls flat on his face. It turned out he was a salesman for Guardtech security systems. Their sales manager came over and apologized. Said this chap was insanely jealous of his wife and had been knocking back the free booze all day, just spoiling for a fight with anyone.'

'Do you remember his name?' asked Gilmore, hopefully. Compton shook his head.

'His name was Bradbury, darling,' said his wife, looking proud that she could supply important information. 'Simon Bradbury.'

'Something like that,' grunted Compton begrudgingly. 'But you're wasting your time going after him. He lives in London.'

While Gilmore scribbled the name in his notebook, Frost stood up and wound his scarf round his neck. 'We'll check him out, anyway. If anything else happens, phone the station right away.'

Mark Compton's mouth dropped open in disbelief. 'You're just walking away? For God's sake, man, my wife's life has been threatened. I want round-the-clock protection.'

Frost shrugged apologetically. 'I'll get an area car to make a detour from time to time, just to keep an eye on the place, but we haven't got the resources for twenty-four-hour surveillance.'

Compton's voice rose to a shout. 'Bloody marvellous! Well, let's make one thing clear. If the police won't do anything, then I will. If he lays one finger on my wife, and I catch the bastard, I'll kill him with my bare hands, and that's a bloody promise.'

The Fire Investigations Officer was sitting in the back seat of the Cortina waiting for them. He declined a cigarette, pleading a sore throat. 'I think I'm coming down with flu, Jack. Half the watch are off with it.'

'Tell me what you've found and then push off,' said Frost. 'I don't want to catch it from you.'

The fireman passed across a plastic envelope. Inside was a chunk of burnt wood with a snail's trail of a dirty grey waxy substance dribbled over it. 'Candle grease from an ordinary household candle. And I've found several scraps of burnt cloth. My guess is that the fire was set off by a stump of candle burning down to some inflammable material – possibly rags soaked in petrol.'

Frost handed the envelope back. 'How long would a fuse like that take to burn down?'

The fireman scratched his chin. 'Depends on the length of the candle, but I shouldn't think they'd use a full one, not in that situation. Too much risk of it toppling over or getting blown out. The more reliable way is just to use a stump, the shorter the better and then you're talking an hour – maybe a lot less.'

'But if they did use a full-length one?'

'Four and a half hours top whack.'

Frost chewed this over and stared up at the black-clouded sky through the windscreen. 'How good is that sprinkler system in The Mill?'

'Damn good.'

'Even if petrol was used again?'

'It would definitely keep it under control until we got here.' His nose wrinkled and his eyes widened as he dived into his pocket for his handkerchief, but too late. His violent sneeze rocked the car.

'Thanks a bunch,' grunted Frost. 'Flu germs are all we bleeding need.'

*   *   *

24

The Cortina bumped down the puddled lane on its way back to Denton. An agitated Gilmore, concerned about his delayed meeting with the Divisional Commander, was fidgeting impatiently, willing the inspector to drive faster. Frost seemed to be driving by remote control, his mind elsewhere, his cigarette burning dangerously close to his lip. They were approaching the gloomy Denton Woods before Frost spoke. 'What did you think of Jill Compton?'

'A knock-out,' admitted Gilmore.

Frost wound down the window and spat out his cigarette. 'Did you see how he was groping her? I thought she was going to get his dick out any minute.' He shook another cigarette from the packet straight into his mouth. 'When you get a chance, son, find out where Compton was last night and if there's any way he could have started that fire.'

'Compton?' Gilmore was incredulous. 'Why should he destroy his own property?'

'I don't know, son. I don't like the sod. He's a bit too bloody lovey-dovey with Miss Wonder-bum for my taste – almost as if he wants to shout out for our benefit how devoted he is.'

Gilmore was unimpressed. 'I thought he was genuinely devoted.'

'Maybe so, son. I'm probably way off course as usual, but check anyway.' The car was now speeding down the hill leading to the Market Square. 'I'll drop you off at the station. If Mullett asks, you don't know where I am.'

The radio belched static, then Control asked for Mr Frost to come in please. 'What's your position, Inspector?'

Frost looked through the window at the row of shops and the turning just ahead leading to the police station.

25

A bit too close to Mullett for comfort. 'Still at The Mill, Lexing, investigating arson attack.'

'Would you call on Dr Maltby, The Surgery, Lexing. One of his patients received a poison pen letter this morning and tried to kill himself.'

'On my way,' replied Frost, spinning the car into a U-turn.

'Is Detective Sergeant Gilmore with you?' asked Control. 'Mr Mullett wants to see him right away.'

'Roger,' said Frost.

'He also wants to see you this morning without fail,' added Control.

'Didn't get that last bit,' said Frost. 'Over and out.' He slammed down the handset and turned off the radio.

Lexing was a small cluster of unspoilt houses and cottages, nothing later than Victorian. Perched on the hill to the north was the mill they had just visited and leaning against the front door of Dr Maltby's cottage was the same bike they had seen outside the Comptons'. And, sure enough, it was Ada Perkins who let them in.

'What did the doctor say, Ada?' asked Frost confidentially. 'Are you pregnant or is it just wind?'

'Not funny,' she snapped. 'I've just done the hall so wipe your muddy boots.'

She ushered them into the surgery. Maltby, a grey-haired, tired-looking man in his late sixties, wearing a crumpled brown suit, was seated at an old-fashioned desk and was furtively stuffing something that chinked into his top drawer and slamming it shut as he popped a Polo mint in his mouth. The waft of peppermint-tinted whisky fumes hit Gilmore as Frost introduced him.

'This is Dr Maltby, son. He's got the steadiest hands in the business. He can take a urine sample and hardly spill a drop.' In spite of this build-up the hand that Gilmore shook didn't seem at all steady.

Maltby squeezed out a token smile. 'I'm not much fun this morning, Jack. I've been up half the night – patients are dropping like flies from this damned flu epidemic. And now this. I said someone would kill themselves if you didn't stop these poison pen letters and now it's happened.'

'Calm down, doc,' said Frost, scraping a match down the wooden wall panelling. 'Just give me the facts, and slowly – you know what a dim old sod I am.' He slumped down in the lumpy chair reserved for patients and wearily stretched his legs, puffing smoke at the 'Smoking Can Kill' poster.

'Ada found him,' said Maltby.

'Found who, doc? Don't forget I've come in in the middle of the picture.'

'Old Mr Wardley,' said Ada. 'He lives next door to me. I do his cleaning once a week when I've finished at The Mill. I got no reply when I knocked so I used the spare key he gave me. No sign of him downstairs. "That's strange," I thought. "That's very strange." So I called out, "Mr Wardley, are you there?" No answer.'

'Get to the punchline, Ada,' prompted Frost, impatiently.

'I went upstairs and there he was on the bed, fully dressed.'

'I'm glad his dick wasn't exposed,' said Frost.

She glowered, but carried on doggedly. 'His face was deadly white, his flesh icy cold, just like a corpse. So I dashed straight over to the doctor's and he came back with me.'

Frost cut in quickly and poked a finger at Maltby. 'Now your big scene, doc.'

The doctor rubbed his eyes and took over the narrative. 'He'd swallowed all the sleeping tablets in his bottle. He was unconscious, but still alive. I phoned for an ambulance and got him into Denton General Hospital. I think he'll pull through.'

'Good,' nodded Frost. 'I like happy endings. So, in spite of your big build-up, no one's actually killed themselves?'

'Not for the want of trying,' said Maltby.

'Was there a suicide note?' asked Gilmore.

'I didn't see one,' said the doctor.

'So why did you say it was suicide? It could have been accidental.'

'You don't accidentally take an overdose of sleeping tablets at nine o'clock in the morning with all your clothes on,' Maltby snapped irritably.

'All right,' murmured Frost. 'Show me the poison pen letter that made him do it.'

'We couldn't find the letter,' said Maltby, 'but this was on his kitchen table.'

He handed the inspector a light blue envelope bearing a first-class stamp which had missed the franking machine and had been hand-cancelled by the postman. The name and address were typewritten. Frost checked that the envelope was empty before passing it over to Gilmore who compared the typing with that on the envelope received that morning by Mrs Compton. Gilmore shook his head. 'Different typewriter.' Frost nodded. He knew that already. He also knew that the envelope and the typing were identical to the two poison pen letters in the file in his office. 'An empty envelope, doc. Why should you think it was a poison pen letter? Why not a letter from the sanitary inspector about the smell on the landing?'

A pause. But it was Ada who broke the silence. 'If you

28

don't want me any more, doctor, I've got lots to do.' She clomped out of the room.

As the door closed behind her, Maltby unlocked the middle drawer of his desk and took out a sheet of white A4 typescript. 'This came in an identical envelope.'

He handed it to Frost who read it aloud. '"Dear Lecher. Does your sweet wife know what filthy and perverted practices you and that shameless bitch in Denton get up to? I was watching again last Wednesday. I saw every disgusting perversion. She didn't even draw the bedroom curtains . . ." Bleeding hell, this is sizzling stuff,' gasped Frost. He read the rest to himself before chucking the letter across to Gilmore. 'What's cunnilinctus, doc – sounds like a patent cough syrup.'

'You know damn well what it is,' grunted the doctor. He looked across at Gilmore who was comparing the typing with that on the envelope addressed to Wardley. 'The same typewriter, isn't it, Sergeant.'

'Yes,' agreed Gilmore. 'The "a" and the "s" are both out of alignment. How did you come by it, doctor? It wasn't addressed to you, was it?'

'I should be so bloody lucky,' said Maltby. 'One of the villagers received it and asked me to pass it on to the police. For obvious reasons he doesn't want me to tell you his name.'

'We've got to talk to him,' insisted Frost. 'We need to find out how the letter writer discovered these details.'

Maltby shook his head. 'I'm sorry, Jack. There's no way I can tell you.'

Frost stood up and adjusted his scarf. 'Well, we'll let our Forensic whizz kids have a sniff at the letter and envelope, but unless people are prepared to co-operate, there's not a lot we can do.'

'You're going to do something, though?' insisted Maltby.

'We'll have a look through Wardley's cottage and try and find the letter. I'll have a word with him in the hospital. How old is he?'

Maltby flicked through some dog-eared record cards. 'Seventy-two.'

'I wonder what he's been up to that made him try to kill himself.' At the door he paused. 'What do you know about the Comptons, doc?'

'Seem a loving couple,' said Maltby, guardedly.

'Yes,' agreed Frost, 'too bloody loving. They were nearly having it away on the dining table while we were there. Know anyone who might have a grudge against them?'

Maltby shook his head. 'Ada told me what's been happening. I can't think of anyone.' The phone rang. He lifted the receiver and listened, wearily. 'Right,' he said. 'Keep her in bed. I'll be right over.'

Back in the car Frost gave the volume control on the radio a tentative tweak. '. . . Mr Frost report to Mr Mullett urgently.' Hastily he turned it down again. 'I get the feeling its going to be a sod of a day, son.'

Monday afternoon shift

Police Superintendent Mullett, Commander of Denton Division, gave his welcoming smile and nodded towards a chair for Gilmore to sit down. They were in Mullett's spacious office with its blue Wilton carpet and the walls, with their concealed cupboards, panelled in real wood veneer. A striking contrast to the dark green paint and beige emulsion decor of the rest of the station.

He turned the pages of Gilmore's personal file and nodded his approval. This was exactly the sort of man they wanted in the division, young, efficient and ambitious. He looked up as Station Sergeant Bill Wells tapped on the door and walked briskly in.

'Mr Frost has gone home, sir,' Wells announced. 'I phoned his house, but there was no answer.'

Mullett tugged the duty roster from his middle drawer. Just as he thought, Frost was clearly marked down for afternoon duty.

'He was on duty all last night and most of this morning, sir,' explained Wells. 'He's probably grabbing some sleep.'

Mullett sniffed his disapproval. What was the point of having duty rosters if they were blatantly ignored? The envelope from County marked *Strictly Confidential* glowered up at him from his drawer as he replaced the roster. Frost was really in trouble this time.

'I want to see the inspector the minute he gets in, Sergeant . . . the very minute.' Let Frost try to wriggle out of this one.

'I've left instructions, sir. I'm off home myself now.' Wells yawned loudly and rubbed his eyes to show how tired he was.

Again Mullett snatched up the roster and jabbed his finger on the afternoon shift which showed that Wells was the station sergeant on duty until six o'clock. He studiously consulted his gold Rolex wrist-watch. Half-past three!

'I'm on again at eight o'clock tonight, sir,' explained Wells. 'I'm filling in for Sergeant Mason. He's down with the flu.'

Mullett flapped a hand impatiently. He didn't want all

31

the fiddling details. 'If you must alter all the shifts around, Sergeant, do me the courtesy of letting me know.' He grunted peevishly as his red biro neatly amended the roster. 'I can't run a station in this slipshod fashion.'

Wells bristled. There he was, working all the hours God sent, doing double shifts, and all this idiot was concerned with was his lousy duty roster. 'This virus thing is making it impossible, sir. We need more men.'

'We have one extra man,' beamed Mullett, nodding towards Gilmore. 'And I'm sure, like me, he would like a cup of tea.' He flashed his teeth expectantly.

'Tea?' spluttered Wells. 'I've got no-one I can spare to make tea, sir. As you know, the canteen's closed . . .'

Mullett didn't know the canteen was closed and he wasn't interested. 'Two teas,' he said firmly, 'and if you can find some biscuits . . . custard creams would be nice.' What a sullen look the man gave him as he left. He would have to speak to him about it. He swivelled his chair to face Gilmore. 'I'm having to plunge you straight in at the deep end, Sergeant. You'll be working split shifts with Mr Frost, so you're on again tonight.'

'Tonight?' echoed Gilmore in dismay.

'That presents no difficulties, I hope?'

'No, sir. Of course not.' God, Liz would raise hell over this.

'Good. One other thing.' Mullett cleared his throat nervously and hesitated as he carefully picked his words. 'If, when you are working under Mr Frost, you notice anything that you feel should be brought to my attention, you will find I have a very receptive ear.' He lowered his eyes and began fiddling with his fountain pen.

Gilmore pulled himself up straight in his chair. 'Are you asking me to spy on the inspector, sir?'

Mullett looked pained. 'If you consider that what I

have suggested constitutes spying, Sergeant, then of course you will forget I ever said it.' He closed the green cover of the detective sergeant's personal file. 'You are promotion material, Sergeant, but to promote you, I need a vacancy.'

He stared hard at Gilmore. Gilmore stared back, holding Mullett's gaze, then gave a tight smile and nodded.

They understood each other.

They were still smiling smugly at each other when Wells crashed in with the tea.

'This will be your office.' Detective Constable Joe Burton, stocky, twenty-five years old and ambitious, tried to keep the resentment out of his voice as he showed the new detective sergeant around. Gilmore stared in amazement. The poky room he was expected to share with that scarecrow, Frost, was a complete shambles with papers and files everywhere but in their proper place, dirty cups perched on the window ledge and the floor littered with cigarette stubs and screwed-up pieces of paper that had missed the target of the waste bin. 'And this is your desk,' added Burton.

The spare desk, the smaller of the two, was awash with papers and ancient files. Gilmore's jaw tightened. His first job would be to put this pigsty into some semblance of order. The internal phone rang. At first he couldn't locate the instrument which was buried under a toppled stack of files on Frost's desk.

'Control here,' said the phone. 'Got a dead body for you – probable suicide. 132 Saxon Road. Panda car at premises.'

Gilmore scribbled down the details. He could fit it in on his way home. He told Burton to come with him.

On their way out to the car-park, they passed Mullett

33

who was talking to a scowling Sergeant Wells. 'You should be off duty, Gilmore.'

'Possible suicide, sir. Thought I'd better handle it personally.'

Mullett beamed. 'Keenness. That's what I like to see. A rare commodity, these days. All some people think of is getting off home.' His pointed stare left Sergeant Wells in no doubt as to who he was referring to.

Wells kept his face impassive. 'Crawling bastard!' he silently told Gilmore's retreating back.

Rain hammered down on Frost's blue Cortina as it slowly nosed its way down Saxon Road, a street of two-storey terraced houses in the newer part of Denton. He spotted a police patrol car at the far end and parked behind it. One last drag at his cigarette, then out, head down against the rain, as he butted his way up the path to number 132.

A worried-looking woman opened the door. Behind her, the bitter sound of sobbing. She looked enquiringly at the scruffy figure on the doorstep who was fumbling in the depths of his inside pocket. 'Detective Inspector Frost,' he said, showing her a dog-eared warrant card.

She peered doubtingly at the card. 'I'm just a neighbour. Do you want to see the parents?' She inclined her head towards the back room from which the sobbing continued unabated.

'Later,' he said. And he wasn't looking forward to it.

Up the stairs to the girl's bedroom where a white-faced uniformed constable stood outside. This was PC John Collier, twenty years old. Collier, still very green and usually working inside the station with Wells, had been pitched out on patrol because of the manpower shortage. He hadn't yet got used to dead bodies.

The bedroom door opened, releasing a murmur of

angry voices. DC Burton came out. He seemed relieved to see the inspector and carefully closed the door behind him.

'What have we got?' asked Frost, shaking rain from his mac.

'Suicide, but our new super-sergeant is treating it as a mass murder.'

'He's new and he's keen,' said Frost. 'It'll soon wear off.'

The bedroom was small, neat and unfussy, with white melamine furniture and pink emulsioned walls. A glowering Gilmore was watching Dr Maltby, red-faced and smelling strongly of alcohol, who was pulling the sheet back over the body on the single bed. Gilmore scowled at Frost's entrance. He'd asked for a senior officer. He didn't expect this oaf. 'I thought you were off duty,' he muttered.

'They dragged me out of bed. So what's the problem?'

Gilmore opened his mouth to speak but the doctor got in first. 'There's no problem, Inspector. It's a clear case of suicide.' He jerked his head towards a small brown glass container on the bedside cabinet. 'Overdose of barbiturates. She swallowed the lot.' He glared at Gilmore as if daring him to contradict.

'You don't look very happy, Sergeant,' observed Frost, wondering why the man had requested a senior officer to attend a routine suicide.

'There was no suicide note,' Gilmore said.

'It's not obligatory,' snapped the doctor. 'You can commit suicide without leaving a note.' He was tired and wanted another drink. What he didn't want was complications. 'It's suicide, plain and simple.' He moved out of the way so the inspector could get to the body.

'I'm glad it's simple,' said Frost, pulling back the sheet,

'I'm not very good when things are complicated.' Then his expression changed. 'Oh no!' he said softly, his face crumpling. 'I never realized it was a kid.'

'Fifteen years old,' said Gilmore. 'Everything to live for.'

She lay on top of the bed. A young girl wearing a white cotton nightdress decorated with the beaming face of Mickey Mouse. Over the nightdress was a black and gold Japanese-style kimono. Her feet were bare, the soles slightly dirty as if she had been padding about the house without socks or shoes. A Snoopy watch on her left wrist ticked softly away. It seemed wrong. Almost obscene. Mickey Mouse and Snoopy had no place with death.

Frost gazed down at her face, trying to read some answers. A pretty kid with light brown hair gleaming as if newly brushed, spread loosely over the pillow. Gently, as if afraid to wake her, Frost touched her cheek, flinching at the hard, icy cold feel of death. 'You silly bloody cow,' he said. 'Why did you do this?'

He switched his attention to the bedside cabinet. Standing on top of it was a bright red, twin-belled alarm clock, its alarm set at 6.45, a pair of ear-rings, a Bic pen, an empty, brown pill bottle and, over to one side away from the bed and almost on the edge of the cabinet, a tumbler with an inch of water remaining. Frost crouched to read the label on the pill container. *Sleeping Tablets prescribed for Mrs Janet Bicknell.*

'They were prescribed for the mother,' Gilmore explained. 'There were about fifteen or so left. The kid got them from the bathroom cabinet.'

Frost sank down on the corner of the bed and lit up a cigarette. 'Any doubts it's a suicide, doc?'

'If the post-mortem shows a lethal dose of barbiturates

in her stomach, no doubts whatsoever. If you could speed things up, Jack, I'd like to get off home. I've had one hell of a day.'

'Right,' said Frost. 'How long has she been dead?'

'Rigor mortis hasn't reached the lower part of the body yet. That and the temperature readings suggest she's been dead some nine to ten hours.'

Frost checked his watch. It was now a few minutes past five. 'So she died between seven and eight o'clock this morning?'

'She was still alive at half-past seven, this morning,' interjected Gilmore.

'Then she was dead pretty soon after,' snapped the doctor. His head was throbbing and Gilmore was getting on his damn nerves.

'Slow down,' pleaded Frost. 'Let's take it step by step, starting with her name.'

Gilmore opened up his notebook and read out the details. 'Susan Bicknell, fifteen years old. In the fifth form at Denton Comprehensive.'

'And who found the body?'

'Her stepfather, Kenneth Duffy.'

'Stepfather?'

'Yes. Her father died two years ago. Her mother married again in March.' Gilmore paused, then added significantly, 'He's a lot younger than the mother.'

'Ah,' said Frost. 'I'm getting the scenario . . . teenage girl, randy young stepfather. But let's get the doc out of the way first. I don't want to shock him with our rude talk.'

'I've got nothing more to tell you,' said Maltby, dropping a thermometer in his bag and snapping it shut. 'You'll have my written report today. Any joy with our poison pen writer?'

'No,' Frost told him. 'I'll go and see Wardley in hospital when I get a chance.' The doctor lurched towards the open door. A curse as he appeared to miss his footing on the stairs.

'He's drunk!' hissed Gilmore.

'He's tired,' said Frost. 'The poor bastard is overworked. He never refuses a call day or night and people take advantage of him.' He whispered something to Burton who chased after Maltby and called, 'Give us your keys, doc. I'll drive you home.' Maltby handed them over without a murmur.

'Follow on in the Panda and take Burton back to the station,' Collier was told. Frost lit up another cigarette. 'So what's on your mind, son?'

'The suicide note's missing,' said Gilmore.

'What makes you think there was one?'

Gilmore steered the inspector across to the bedside cabinet. 'One ballpoint pen.' He pointed. On the floor, by the bed, was a pad of Basildon Bond writing paper. 'One notepad.'

'So she had the means to write a suicide note,' said Frost. 'But it doesn't follow she wrote one. I don't have to do a pee just because I pass a gents' urinal.'

'Look at the glass with the water in,' continued Gilmore. 'Right on the edge of the cabinet. If she was lying in bed when she took the pills, she'd have replaced the glass on the side nearest to her. If she took them before she lay on the bed, she'd have put the glass somewhere in the middle.'

'I'm sure this is all significant stuff,' Frost said, 'but I'm such a dim sod I can't see it.' He wandered over to the window and opened it to let out the smell of tobacco smoke. In the darkened street below, the street lights were just coming on.

Gilmore sighed inwardly. He knew the man was thick, but surely he didn't have to explain every detail. 'I'm saying the glass was moved by someone else. I'm saying she left a suicide note and weighed it down with the glass. The stepfather found the body, saw the note and because it implicated him, he destroyed it. There's two sets of prints on the glass. I'm laying odds they're the girl's and the stepfather's.'

Frost squinted at the glass. 'Anything else?'

'Yes,' said Gilmore. 'I've got a feeling about the step-father. He's hiding something. I just know he is.'

Frost nodded. Feelings and hunches were things he knew all about. His eyes slowly traversed the room. Yes, there was something wrong. He could sense it too. 'All right, son, let's go and have a chat with the stepfather.' He pitched his cigarette out of the window and closed it, then took one last look at the still figure on the bed before covering her with the sheet.

They were in the lounge, a large, comfortable room with heavy brown velvet curtains drawn across a bay window. From the other room the heart-breaking sound of sobbing went on and on. Frost stared gloomily at the blank screen of a 26-inch television set and wished they could get this next part over. He looked up as the stepfather, Kenneth Duffy, a dark-haired, boyish-looking man in his late thirties, came in.

Duffy's eyes were red-rimmed and his cheeks glistening wet. He had been crying. Drying his face with his hands, he dropped heavily into an armchair opposite the two detectives. 'My wife's too upset to talk to you.'

'I quite understand, sir,' murmured Frost, sympathetically. 'I know you've already explained everything to my colleague, but I wonder if you'd mind telling me. I understand you're a van driver with Mallard Deliveries?'

'Yes.'

'And it was you who found Susan?'

'Yes.' His voice was so low they had to lean forward to catch what he was saying. 'I found her.'

'What time would this be?'

'Time? This afternoon . . . just after four. She was on the bed. I touched her. She was cold.' He broke down and couldn't continue.

Frost lit a cigarette and waited until Duffy was ready to go on. 'Tell me what happened this morning. Right from the beginning.'

'Susan always got herself up . . . made her own breakfast. She had a half-term holiday job in the new Sainsbury's supermarket . . . shelf-filling and sometimes helping out on the check-out. She had to clock in at eight and left the house at half-past seven. I'd wait until I heard the front door slam, then I'd get up.'

'You wouldn't come down until after she had gone?'

'I don't start work until 8.30. We'd only get in each other's way.'

'I see,' said Frost, wondering if there was more to it than that, if Susan was deliberately avoiding being alone with her stepfather.

'I heard her going up and down the stairs this morning, but now I think of it, I never heard the slam of the front door. She always slammed it when she went out. Today she must have gone back upstairs to her bedroom. I came down a little after 7.30, washed, dressed and went to work.'

'And you didn't notice anything out of the ordinary?'

'No. There was nothing to suggest she hadn't gone to work.'

'You didn't look in her bedroom before you left?' asked Frost, looking for somewhere to flick his ash.

'I had no reason . . . but in any case, she hated people going into her room when she was out. So I went to work and my wife went to work and Susan was upstairs dying.' Again he broke down.

'So what made you go into her bedroom at four o'clock this afternoon?' asked Frost.

'I'd finished early and was home just before four. I phoned Susan at Sainsbury's to remind her about the groceries we needed and they told me she hadn't been in to work all that day. I suddenly remembered I hadn't heard that front door slam. I went upstairs and looked in her bedroom.' He knuckled the tears from his eyes. 'I'm sorry,' he said. 'I'm so sorry.' He was apologizing for crying. Frost gave a sympathetic nod and made a mental note to check with Duffy's firm about him finishing early.

'Have you any idea why Susan should want to take her own life?'

'There was no reason – no reason at all.'

'Was she worried about anything?'

'She seemed a bit edgy over the last couple of days. We thought something had gone wrong at school . . . a row with a friend or something . . . nothing serious.'

'Did she have a boyfriend?'

'Stacks of them – no-one steady.'

'She must have had some reason for killing herself,' Frost insisted. 'Family trouble, perhaps? Girls don't always get on with their stepfathers.'

'We got on fine,' insisted Duffy. 'She was happy at home . . . doing well at school . . . everything was right for her.'

'If everything was right,' said Frost, 'she'd still be alive.' He stared at Duffy until the man had to turn his head away. 'We couldn't find her suicide note.'

The knuckles of Duffy's hands whitened as he gripped

hard the arms of the chair to try to stop his body from shaking. 'There wasn't one.'

'My colleague here is pretty certain there was.'

'If there had been a note, I'd have found it.'

'Of course,' said Frost, treating Duffy to an enigmatic smile. 'Of course you would.' He studied the glowing end of his cigarette, then casually asked, 'Was she pregnant?'

'Pregnant? Girls don't kill themselves these days just because they're pregnant.'

'It depends who the father is,' snapped Gilmore.

Duffy's head came up slowly, angry patches burning his cheeks. He sprang to his feet, fists balled. 'What are you suggesting? What filth are you bloody suggesting?'

Frost stepped between them and pushed Duffy back into the chair. 'We're suggesting nothing, Mr Duffy. The post-mortem will tell us if she was pregnant, in which case we might want to talk to you again.'

'I'd like to talk to Susan's mother,' said Gilmore.

'No!' Duffy leapt from the chair and stood by the door to bar their way.

'It's all right, sir,' said Frost. 'It won't be necessary.' He jerked a thumb at Gilmore. 'Let's go, Sergeant.'

Gilmore glared at Frost. Right, you sod. Mullett wants the dirt on you, I'll find it for him. With a curt nod at Duffy, he followed the inspector out. The sobbing from the kitchen was much softer, weaker. The mother had cried herself to exhaustion.

Outside in the car they watched as a hearse pulled up to collect the body for the post-mortem. Two undertakers in shiny black raincoats slid out the coffin.

'Well?' asked Gilmore, impatiently. 'What do we do about it?'

'We do nothing,' said Frost. Before Gilmore could protest, he explained. 'Look, son, just on a hunch and

42

without any evidence, you expect me to believe that Duffy's been having it away with his unwilling, fifteen-year-old, schoolgirl stepdaughter.'

'Yes,' replied Gilmore, biting off each word, 'that's exactly what I expect you to believe.'

Frost took a long drag at his cigarette. 'If it's any consolation, son, I agree with you all the way. I reckon he put Suzy up the spout and that's why she killed herself and that's why stepdaddy destroyed the suicide note. But we could never prove it. She never made a complaint and now she's dead.' He wound down the car window and jettisoned his cigarette end into the gutter. 'There's sod all we can do about it.'

'You want proof?' said Gilmore, his hand on the car door handle. 'I'll get you proof. Let me go and talk to the mother. She must have noticed something.'

'No!' Frost grabbed Gilmore's hand and pulled it away from the handle. 'You do not breathe a word of this to the mother. Don't you think the poor cow's suffered enough? Let it drop, son. That's the end of it.'

Gilmore stared at the rain. 'So the bastard gets away with it?'

'Yes,' agreed Frost. 'The bastard gets away with it.' He started the engine.

The undertakers were sliding the coffin into the back of the hearse.

The light in the upstairs bedroom window went out.

The rain bucketed down.

Monday evening shift

The internal phone grunted and gave its peevish ring. Automatically Wells picked it up and said, 'No, sir, Inspector Frost hasn't come in yet . . . Yes, sir, the minute I see him.' He banged the phone down and stamped his feet to try and restore his circulation. It was freezing cold in the lobby. The central heating had broken down and wouldn't be repaired until the following day at the earliest. How he envied all those lucky devils who were down with the flu and were tucked up in their nice warm beds and didn't have to put up with Mullett bleating every five minutes. He consulted the wall clock. Twenty to ten. Only ten lousy minutes of the shift gone. Still, it was only half a shift. Sergeant Johnnie Johnson was to relieve him at two. So only another four freezing hours of this.

A roar of poncey aftershave as the new chap, Detective-newly-promoted-to-bloody-Sergeant Gilmore marched up to the desk. 'Where's Inspector Frost?'

'No idea,' beamed Wells, delighted to be so unhelpful.

Gilmore scowled at the clock. Frost was ten minutes late already. 'How do I get a cup of tea?'

'You make it yourself. The canteen's closed. The night staff are all down with flu.'

Gilmore scowled again. Detective sergeants didn't make the tea. He would find DC Burton and get him to do it. As he turned to go he bumped into a woman wearing a red raincoat with the hood up over her head. 'Sorry,' he muttered, stepping out of her way.

'Yes, madam?' asked Wells. Then he recognized her

44

and his voice softened. 'What can we do for you, Mrs Bartlett?'

'I've got to see Inspector Allen. It's very urgent. I've news about Paula . . .'

Gilmore stopped dead. Paula? Paula Bartlett? Of course, the girl on the poster, the missing school kid. 'Perhaps I can help, madam. I'm Detective Sergeant Gilmore. I'm handling the case in Mr Allen's absence.'

She looked up at him, eyes blinking behind heavy glasses, a dumpy woman in her early forties. Her usually pale face was flushed with excitement. 'Wonderful news. Paula's alive. I know where she is.'

'Mrs Bartlett . . .' began Wells guardedly, but Gilmore took her by the arm and drew her away to one of the benches. 'Where is she, Mrs Bartlett?'

'In a big house, overlooking the woods.'

His hand shaking with excitement, Gilmore scribbled this down.

'Where did you get this information from?' called Wells from the desk.

Gilmore scowled. He was handling this. He didn't want any interference from the sergeant.

She turned towards Wells. 'From Mr Rowley. He's a clairvoyant.'

Gilmore's heart sank. 'A clairvoyant?'

She nodded earnestly. 'He phoned us. He told us things about Paula that no-one would know. He said he suddenly had this mental picture of Paula in a tiny room . . . a tiny attic room. She was being held prisoner. He described the room, the house, everything.'

'I see,' said Gilmore. He stood up. 'If you'll excuse me for a moment.' He crossed over to Wells and lowered his voice. 'Do we know a clairvoyant named Rowley?'

'No,' grunted Wells. 'But we know a nut-case called

45

Rowley who thinks he's a clairvoyant. He spots the girl in about fifty different places every bloody week.'

'Shit!' said Gilmore. He returned to the woman, who was waiting expectantly. 'I don't think you should raise your hopes too high,' he began, but she was in no mood for pessimism.

'Paula's alive,' she said simply. 'You're going to find her and bring her back to me. I've got the full details here.' She pressed a sheet of folded notepaper into his hand.

The lobby doors crashed open and Frost barged in. 'It's peeing cats and dogs out there,' he announced, tugging off his scarf and flapping rain-water all over the papers on Wells' desk. 'Oh heck!' He had spotted Mrs Bartlett walking across the lobby with Gilmore. He turned quickly and pretended to be studying a 'Foot and Mouth Restriction Order' poster on the wall. It was cowardly, but he couldn't face her. He felt like a cancer specialist trying to avoid a terminally ill patient anxious for reassuring news. There was no reassuring news. The girl was dead. He knew it.

'Everything all right, Mrs Bartlett?' called Wells.

'Yes, thank you,' she smiled, pulling the red hood over her hair. 'This gentleman here is going to bring Paula home for me. I've got her room all ready.' She gave Gilmore a look of such implicit trust, he didn't have the heart to contradict her. He opened the lobby door and watched as she crossed the road in the rain to hurry home and wait for her daughter.

'Poor bitch,' murmured Frost. 'She comes in two or three nights a week.'

'You might have warned me,' Gilmore snapped angrily to Wells.

'You never gave me the chance,' said Wells happily. To Frost he said, 'Mr Mullett wants to see you.'

'Sod Mr Mullett,' said Frost.

46

'That's what I say,' said Wells, 'but he still wants to see you.'

In direct contrast to the arctic conditions in the rest of the station, Mullett's office was a hothouse with the thermostat on the 3-kilowatt convector heater set to maximum. But the heat did nothing to soften the expression on his face which was pure ice as he waited for Frost, who was already nearly a quarter of an hour late.

A half-hearted rap at the door. Unmistakably Detective Inspector Frost. Even his knock was slovenly. Mullett adjusted his chair to dead centre, straightened his back and curtly said, 'Enter!'

The door opened and Frost shuffled in. What a mess the man looked. The shiny suit with the loose buttons, creased and crumpled where it had received a soaking from last night's rain and had then been dried over a radiator. His tie was secured with a greasy knot that looked impossible to undo and Mullett was sure that the shirt was the same one the inspector had been wearing for the past six days. Why was this flu virus perversely selecting all the best men for its victims and leaving the rubbish unscathed?

Frost flopped into a chair. 'Take a seat,' said Mullett a split second too late. His lips tightened as he unlocked the middle drawer of his desk and removed the envelope from County HQ.

Frost watched warily, wondering which of his many transgressions had come to light. He adjusted his face into a pre-emptive expression of contrition and waited.

'I've never been so humiliated and ashamed in all my life,' began Mullett.

No clue here. Mullett had used these opening remarks many times before.

'That an officer in Denton Division – *my* division – should be detected in forgery.'

Forgery? Frost's mind raced. He had often forged Mullett's signature on those occasions when his Divisional Commander's authorization had been required and Frost knew it would not be forthcoming. But the last occasion was months ago.

Mullett pulled out a wad of papers from the envelope and detached the *Strictly Confidential* County memo. The rest he pushed across to the inspector.

Frost's heart dropped with a squelch into the pit of his stomach. He recognized them immediately. His car expenses. His bloody car expenses, back like an exhumed corpse to accuse him

'Ah – I can explain, Super,' he began, frantically trying to dream up an excuse that would satisfy Mullett.

But Mullett was in no mood for explanations. He snatched up the receipts for the petrol Frost was claiming to have purchased during the month. 'Forgeries!' he snapped. 'Twelve different petrol stations, but identical handwriting. *Your* handwriting, Inspector.' He waggled the receipts under Frost's nose and Frost could see that someone in County had done the Sherlock Holmes with his expense claim and had ringed in red ink all the similarities in the handwriting of the various receipts.

'Flaming hell!' gasped Frost. 'Here we are, down to less than half-strength, working double shifts, and some lazy sod in County has got the time to go through a few lousy petrol receipts.' He tossed the expense claim back on the desk. 'If I was you, sir, I'd damn well complain.'

'Complain?' shrieked Mullett. 'I'm in no position to complain. One of my officers, an inspector, fiddling his car expenses . . .'

'I wasn't fiddling,' said Frost. 'I lost the proper receipts and had to make copies.'

'Copies! They weren't copies. They were forgeries . . . and not even good forgeries at that!'

Frost switched off his ears as Mullett ranted on, his face getting redder and redder, his fist pounding the desk at intervals. He wasn't interested in what Mullett was saying, he was only concerned at what Mullett intended doing about it. This could be the chop, the heaven-sent opportunity his superintendent had been dreaming about for years. Then something Mullett was saying penetrated his filtering mechanism.

'This could have been the end of your career in the force, but much against the grain, I have interceded on your behalf with County . . .'

Interceded. Bloody hell, thought Frost. What's the catch?

Mullett stuffed all the receipts back into the envelope and gave it to Frost. 'Resubmit your expense claim, but this time with proper, genuine petrol receipts and nothing further will be said.'

Frost sat stunned. This was too good to be true. He slipped the envelope in his inside pocket. 'Right, Super, leave it to me.' He rose, ready to take his leave before Mullett came to his senses.

'This is your last chance, Inspector. One more slip-up – just one – and . . .' But he was talking to an empty room. Frost had gone.

Mullett sighed deeply. He unfolded the *Confidential* memo from County and read it again. It pointed out that he, as Divisional Commander, had signed Frost's expense claim, certifying that he had checked it and found it correct. How on earth was he expected to check everything he had to sign? It was most unfair. And what was more unfair was that in getting himself off the hook, he had to get Frost off as well. Damn. He returned the memo to his middle drawer and locked it, then phoned Sergeant Wells saying he wanted a briefing meeting with the night shift in ten minutes.

The murmur of conversation stopped abruptly and everyone sprang to their feet as Mullett marched into the Briefing Room. He frowned. There seemed very few people in attendance. A quick count . . . eight in all, six men and two WPCs. No sign of Frost. He raised his eyebrows at Wells, querying the small turnout.

'This is all there is, sir,' he was told. 'Two more down with flu, plus Bryant and Wilkes still in hospital after the pub punch-up last week. Collier's on the desk in the lobby standing in for me.'

'And Mr Frost?'

'I did tell him, sir.'

Mullett's lips narrowed. Typical. Well, he certainly wasn't going to wait for him. He looked around the room. The new man, Gilmore, smartly turned out, was in the front row. Next to him, a sullen DC Burton, all brawn and no brains. Burton was a good man to have at your side in an emergency, but he would never progress beyond the rank of DC.

Mullett shivered and rubbed his hands together briskly. It was damn cold in here. 'Sit down, everyone, please. Well, what we lack in quantity, I'm sure we more than make up for in quality.' He let the half-hearted ripple of laughter die. 'Firstly, I'm sorry to tell you that Mr Allen has suffered a set-back and will not be returning to duty for some time . . .' His brow furrowed in annoyance as the door crashed open and Frost burst in.

'The bloody canteen's shut,' announced Frost, looking round in puzzlement. 'What's everyone doing in here?' Then he spotted Mullett. 'The briefing meeting! Sorry, Super . . . I forgot . . .'

Mullett waited until Frost had found himself a seat right at the back. 'I was just telling everyone the sad news about Inspector Allen.'

'Sad news?' echoed Frost, genuinely misunderstanding. 'Bloody hell, he's not coming back, is he?'

When the laughter subsided Mullett gave a tolerant smile. 'He won't be back for some time. I was about to explain that, in the meantime, you would be taking over his cases. Our resources are going to be spread very thinly, so I don't want any wasted effort. We've got two people tied up in the Murder Incident Room on this Paula Bartlett case. What's the current position?'

'It's more or less fizzled out,' said Frost, striking a match down a filing cabinet. 'I can't see any progress there until the body turns up.'

'Good,' smiled Mullett, ticking off the first item on his pad. 'Then on the basis of your assessment, Inspector, I'm closing down the Incident Room pro tem. This will release much-needed personnel to more urgent duties.' He beamed as if that solved everyone's problems, then frowned as he reached the next item on his list. 'Another senior citizen burglary, over the weekend, Inspector?'

Frost looked up. 'That's right, Super. Old lady living alone. He got away with about £80 in used fivers.'

'Correct me if I'm wrong, Inspector,' said Mullett, 'but this would be the sixteenth such break-in in three weeks, the victims all senior citizens?'

Frost gave a vague shrug. 'I haven't been counting, but you're probably not far out.'

'I am exactly right,' snapped Mullett. 'Sixteen – all

senior citizens, most of them robbed of their life savings. What are we doing about it?'

'What the hell can we do about it?' replied Frost. 'He leaves no clues and nobody sees him. It doesn't give us much to go on.'

'What does he take?' asked Gilmore. 'If it's jewellery, have we got all the local fences covered?'

'Good point!' agreed Mullett.

'Of course I've got the fences covered,' replied Frost. 'Even a dim old twat like me thought of that. If anyone tries to sell any of the loot, I'll be contacted. But he takes very little jewellery. He concentrates on cash – used notes. Many of these old people mistrust banks. They keep wads of banknotes in the house. They stick it in the wardrobe or in the middle drawer of the dressing table under the condoms and the leather knickers. They think no-one will find it there – but it's the first place he looks.'

'You say there's been no clues,' said Mullett. 'I understand people have spotted a blue van in the vicinity. That should give you something to go on. There can't be that many blue vans in Denton.'

'Sixteen burglaries,' said Frost. 'In two instances, we found neighbours who claim they saw a van parked in the vicinity late at night. One thought it was a small blue van, another a biggish van, dark-coloured, could have been blue.'

'But it's a lead,' insisted Mullett. 'Do a check on all blue vans.'

'Do you know precisely how many blue vans there are in the Denton area alone?' asked Frost, producing and waving a small notebook.

Mullett flapped a hand. He didn't want to know, which was a relief to Frost as he had no idea himself, although he was fully prepared to pluck an astronomical figure out of thin air if Mullett called his bluff. 'It doesn't matter how many there are, Inspector. We've got a computer. It can churn out the information in seconds.'

'But the computer can't check through it and knock on bloody doors and question people,' said Frost. 'That's what us poor sods would have to do and it could take weeks – months – and still lead nowhere.'

Mullett gave Frost a vinegary smile. 'It's easy to be negative, Inspector. I offer suggestions, you offer objections. I'm getting a lot of flak from the press on this one. I want him caught now. That's your number one priority. We haven't got many men, but take as many as you like.' He frowned with annoyance as Sergeant Wells' hand kept flapping, trying to attract his attention. Not more of the man's moans, he hoped. 'Yes, Sergeant?'

'With respect, sir. It's all very well saying Mr Frost can have as many men as he likes, but I've still got a night shift to run and I've hardly any men to do it. This flaming flu epidemic doesn't seem to have hit the criminal fraternity yet.'

'I'm well aware of that, thank you, Sergeant, which brings me to my next point. We're under strength so some things will have to go by the board. We are going to have to turn a blind eye to many of the minor crimes, even . . .' and he flashed a paternal beam in Gilmore's direction, '. . . suicides which look slightly doubtful. We will not go out of our way to look for trouble. I don't want any arrests for drunkenness, rowdiness, soliciting, illegal parking, loitering – anything minor like that. We just haven't got the time or the manpower.' He smiled at Wells. 'So that should lighten your load quite a bit, Sergeant.'

'Yes, sir,' mumbled Wells, doubtfully.

'Fine,' said Mullett, closing his notepad and turning to go. Then he remembered one other item. 'Oh –

Inspector Frost. I had a visit from the vicar of All Saints and Councillor Vernon this morning. They are very worried at this current wave of mindless vandalism in the cemetery. There was another incident over the weekend. How are the patrols going?'

'What patrols?' asked Frost.

'The anti-vandalism patrols I asked you to organize. I sent you a memo.'

'I never got it,' said Frost hastily. It was probably buried somewhere in his in-tray together with all the other stupid rubbish Mullett kept sending him.

'And I spoke to you personally about it.'

'Ah – so you did,' agreed Frost, vaguely remembering Mullett chuntering something about graveyards, 'but as you so rightly said, Super, we can't waste time on these piddling trivialities.'

Mullett gave Frost a pitying shake of the head. Hadn't the man any common sense? 'There's no such thing as a piddling triviality when a member of the town council is involved, Inspector. See to it right away – the vulnerable time seems to be between ten and midnight.'

'I've got no-one to send,' said Frost.

'Then attend to it yourself, Inspector. These are difficult times, so we act as a team. We've all got to pitch in.' Mullett looked at his watch and yawned. It had been a long day and it was freezing cold in the Briefing Room. Time for him to get home to bed.

Monday night shift (1)

Rain dripped down the upturned collar of Frost's mac. 'How long have we been here?' he asked peevishly.

Gilmore wriggled his watch free of his sleeve. 'Five minutes.'

Frost hunched his shoulders against the cold, penetrating drizzle and wound his scarf tighter around his face to blunt the teeth of the wind chewing on his scarred cheek. As he stamped his feet to try and bring some feeling to his frozen toes, his wet socks squelched in his shoes. 'This is all a bleeding waste of time,' he muttered, rasping a match on a weather-eroded headstone. The match spluttered, then flared to show the moss-blurred inscription:

George Arthur Jenkins
Born and Died
Feb 6th 1865
Suffer the little children to come unto me

'There's one poor little sod who never drew his old age pension,' he muttered moodily, letting the wind extinguish the match.

The sky was black and heavy with rain and the graveyard looked as lonely and as miserable as a graveyard should look at half-past ten on a cold, wet night. They were in the old Victorian section among weather-eroded angels who wept granite tears over the graves of long-dead children, and where overgrown grass straggled over the crumbling headstones and collapsed graves of their long-dead grief-stricken parents. Through the rain, way over on the far side, Frost could see the serried ranks of stark white marble marking the modern section, where the recently deceased slept an uneasy, decaying sleep. One of the cold marble headstones marked the grave of Frost's wife. He hadn't visited it since the funeral.

Detective Sergeant Gilmore, shutting his ears to Frost's constant moanings, was squinting his eyes, trying to focus through the lashing rain to something over to the left, near an old Victorian crypt. Was it the wind shaking the ivy, or could he see someone moving about?

Frost peered half-heartedly in the direction of Gilmore's pointing finger and grunted dismissively. 'There's sod all there. It's the wind.' He perched himself on the infant Jenkins' headstone and sucked hard at his cigarette. 'How long have we been here now?'

'Eight minutes,' replied Gilmore.

Frost ground his cigarette to death against the headstone and stood up. 'That's long enough. We're going.'

'But Mr Mullett said . . .'

'Sod Mr Mullett,' called Frost, scurrying back to the car. 'If anyone wants to vandalize graves in this pissing weather, then good luck to them.'

Gilmore stared hard across the ranks of marble. The wind rattled the ivy again. There was someone there, he was sure of it. But a cloud crawled across the moon and it was too dark to see. When it passed, there was nothing.

The pub was packed, thick-fogged with eye-stinging smoke, and very noisy. Disco music belted out and voices were raised to overcome it. A group of teen-aged girls, clutching vodka and limes, were shrieking with high-pitched laughter at the punchline of some dirty joke. No-one took any notice of the disc jockey framed by flashing disco lights up on the small stage, who was chewing a microphone to announce the next number. In counterpoint to the throbbing beat of the disco, a drunken Irishman in the far corner was singing 'Danny Boy' in a high tenor voice to a fat lady in black who had tears in her eyes.

Gilmore was edgy. His very first night on duty in Denton and they had disobeyed Mullett's express orders. He decided he would choke his drink down and tell Frost he was going back to the cemetery, as ordered by his Divisional Commander, and would continue the surveillance on his own if necessary.

By waving a £5 note Frost managed to grab the attention of the barman who lip-read his order. As he waited, he let his professional eye wander over the throng. The girls with the vodkas were silent, poised ready to shriek anew as the next joke reached its climax. The drunken Irishman had fallen in mid-song and was face down on the table while the fat lady, no longer tearful, thumbed through his wallet.

The main doors were still swinging behind someone who had left hurriedly and Frost recalled a face, a blur in the crowd that had seemed alarmed at the entrance of the two detectives. It was a face he should know, but couldn't place. He shrugged. What the hell. They were here for a drink, not to feel the collar of some petty crook.

The barman pushed the two lagers across and was back from the till with Frost's change when the bar phone rang. He answered it, then, holding the receiver aloft, yelled, 'Is there a Mr Frost here?'

Frost swapped worried glances with Gilmore. Who knew they were here? Flaming hell, had Hornrim Harry sent his narks after them to report on their every movement? Gingerly, he took the phone and pressed it tight against his face, his finger jammed in the other ear to deaden the background noise. The caller was mumbling and he couldn't hear what the man was saying. 'You'll have to speak up,' he shouted and then, as clear as a bell, he heard the words 'dead body'. 'Say that again?'

'Seventy-six Jubilee Terrace. Upstairs bedroom. The old girl's dead. I think the husband's killed her.'

'How did you know I was here? Who's this speaking?'

A click as the caller hung up. Frost swore to himself and slid the phone back across the counter. If it was someone's idea of a joke, it wasn't a very funny one. And that voice. He knew it. It went with the face he glimpsed leaving the pub as they came in. The harder he tried to remember, the further it slipped out of his grasp.

'Trouble?' Gilmore asked anxiously. It was always trouble with Frost. If it was Mullett who had phoned, he'd make it quite clear that he had obeyed Frost's orders under protest.

Frost scooped up his change. 'Knock back your drink, son. I might have another corpse for you to look at.'

The man on the bike tucked his head down against the rain as he took the short cut through the cemetery after his meeting with the vicar. This damn rain seeping through his mac wasn't going to do his cold any good and he hoped he wasn't in for a dose of this flu thing that everyone seemed to be catching. Row after row of headstones slipped silently past as he pressed down on the pedals. Graves and tombs didn't frighten him, not even at this hour of night, but he would still be happier once he was out through the cemetery gates and on to the main road.

And then he nearly lost control of the bike as a sudden sound reverberated around the churchyard. A funeral bell. His head swivelled as he tried to locate the source. There! It was coming from the old Dobson vault! Someone had broken in and was tugging at the rope inside, tolling the bell installed some 150 years ago by old William Dobson who was terrified of being buried alive and wanted to be able to summon help should he awake in his coffin.

Through the rain he could see a light bobbing. He yelled and someone burst from the crypt, and hared off into the darkness.

He turned his bike and pedalled for all he was worth back to the vicarage where he called the police.

Jubilee Terrace was a cul-de-sac of Edwardian terraced houses and would soon be torn down when the next phase of the new town development was reached. Number 76, the fanlight still showing a light, was the end house standing next to a high brick wall which guarded an electricity sub-station. The rain had eased off slightly and the reflection of a lamp standard shimmered in a large puddle where the drain was blocked.

Gilmore knocked at the door and waited, his fingers drumming impatiently on the porch wall. No-one came. He knocked again louder this time.

The door to number 74 opened and a shirt-sleeved man looked out. 'No use knocking there, mate. The old git's as deaf as a post.'

'Actually, it's the lady of the house we want,' said Frost. 'Do you know if she's in?'

'She's got no choice . . . she's bed-ridden. Never goes out.'

'I heard she was dead,' said Frost.

'Dead? You must have the wrong house, mate. He may be deaf but he makes a lot of noise. These walls are paper thin. I can hear them talking and rowing – if my luck's out, I can even hear him gobbing down the sink.'

'I'm not sure I've got their names right.'

'Maskell – Charlie and Mary – he's Charlie, she's Mary.'

'Oh, *he's* Charlie!' Frost pretended to make an alteration in his notebook, then, as soon as the man went in he dropped to his knees and squinted through the letter-box. A dimly lit hall papered in dreary, dark chocolate brown.

'How can she be dead if he's heard them talking?' protested Gilmore. 'This has got to be a wind-up.'

'You're probably right, son,' grunted Frost, still at the letter-box. Then his nose twitched and he knew it wasn't a wind-up. The bad breath of decay. He could smell death.

The detective sergeant took his turn to sniff then shook his head. 'It's damp and stuffy, that's all.'

'It's more than that, son.' He gave one more knock which shook the front door. Noises inside, but no-one came. 'Let's try the back way.'

A lowish wall muddied their trousers as they clambered over to land with a splash in a small back yard, a few square feet of puddled concrete containing a dustbin and an outside toilet, its gaping door hanging from one hinge. Ever the optimist, Frost tried the back door, but it was locked and bolted. A downstairs sash window, curtains drawn and no light showing, defied the efforts of Frost's penknife.

'Let's leave it,' said Gilmore, edging back to the wall. They were trying to break into someone's house just on the say-so of an anonymous phone call.

But Frost wasn't listening. He had now transferred his attention to the upstairs window. Difficult to tell from that angle, but it appeared to be open at the bottom. 'Keep watch, son. Give a yell if anyone comes.' He climbed up on top of the dustbin which seemed ideally sited for the purpose and heaved himself up on the outside toilet roof and then to the sill.

Yes, a gap at the bottom he could get his hand under. For a moment he hesitated. It all seemed too good to be true; the dustbin conveniently placed and the window invitingly open. But there was no turning back now. He lifted the window and dropped inside.

A pitch dark room. The torch he pulled from his pocket was on the blink, but its faltering light enabled him to steer a tiptoeing course through a maze of booby-trapped junk ready to topple at any moment – an old treadle Singer sewing machine, cardboard boxes gorged with useless items too good to throw away, the frame of a push bike and an old-fashioned pram from the late 1930s in pristine condition which, for some reason, made him think of the baby's grave in the churchyard.

Cautiously, he turned the door handle. The door whined open.

A landing from which stairs descended to the hall. To his right a door with a crack of light showing from inside. He moved towards it. From downstairs came the sound of someone lumbering about and talking in the overloud voice of the deaf. Crockery clattered. The old boy was making tea or something.

The smell hit him as soon as he opened the door. And then he saw her. On the bed. An old woman, her head propped up with pillows. She didn't move. She couldn't move. She was a shrivelled, mummified husk and had been dead for many months.

Shit! Just what he bloody wanted! He rammed a cigarette in his mouth, but didn't light it, then steeled himself to walk across and lift the discoloured bed sheet which made a tearing noise as it parted from the body. The stains on the bedding weren't blood. No signs of injury anywhere. There was something round the mouth. Mouldering food and a brown dribble of something still sticky. On a rickety card table alongside the bed was a cup of cold scummy tea and a plate of congealed food. Shit and double shit. He now knew what it was all about and wanted to get out of the room and back in the car and as far away as possible. The bloody cemetery was preferable to this.

Before he could get to the door he heard someone coming up the stairs. The old boy, talking away to himself.

He spun round, frantically looking for another way out. There was a window behind thick, drawn curtains which belched death-scented dust. He parted them to scrabble at the window catch. But it was rusted in and wouldn't budge.

A clatter of crockery then a tap at the door. 'Your supper, love.'

Frost pressed himself tight against the wall, hoping the opened door would conceal him. The old man, tall and stooped, came in. A tray holding a bowl of soup and a plate of bread and butter rattled in unsteady hands. He frowned at the food on the card table then turned angrily to the husk in the bed. 'You didn't eat it!' he shouted. 'I cooked it for you and you didn't eat it.' Then his voice softened. 'You know what the doctor said. You've got to eat to keep your strength up.' He exchanged the old tray for the new and picked up a spoon. 'You must try and eat some of this, love. It's full of goodness,' and he spooned soup over the gaping mouth, dabbing with a handkerchief as it dribbled down the shrivelled chin. He was deaf. He didn't hear the thud of Frost's footsteps down the stairs and into the street.

In the car, Gilmore listened incredulously, his face creased in disgust. 'And he's still bringing her food? Flaming hell!'

'The poor old sod won't accept her death,' said Frost, sucking thankfully at a cigarette.

Before Gilmore could reach for the radio to inform the station, Frost's hand shot out to stop him. 'Forget it, son. We don't want to get involved.'

A shocked Gilmore said, 'You can't just drive away and do nothing about it.'

'We're not supposed to be here,' said Frost. 'We're supposed to be tomb-watching.'

'But she's dead. He's probably still drawing her pension.'

'Big bloody deal,' grunted Frost. 'I'll try and live with it.' And then the car radio which had been pleading urgently for attention to an empty car, tried again.

'Control to Mr Frost. For Pete's sake come in, please . . . over.'

Frost snatched up the handset. 'Frost.'

'At flaming last, Jack!' It was Bill Wells, the station sergeant. 'Where are you?'

Frost looked out of the window on to Jubilee Street. 'On watch at the cemetery, as ordered,' he replied, trying to sound puzzled at such an obvious question.

'No, you're not, Inspector. If you were, you'd see the place was crawling with bloody police cars.'

'Ah yes . . . there does seem to be some commotion at the far end,' said Frost, signalling for Gilmore to put his foot down and get the damn car back to the cemetery at top speed. 'What exactly has happened?'

'Vandals breaking into a crypt.'

Right. 'I'll check it out and call you back.' He switched off hurriedly and urged Gilmore not to heed the approaching red traffic light.

There was only one police car at the graveyard, its blue flashing beacon reflecting eerily off the rain-soaked marble markers. Gilmore parked tight behind it.

'There!' pointed Frost.

Ahead of them, right off the main path, was the Victorian crypt they had spotted earlier, an ugly little building, looking like a small, ivy-covered boiler house and guarded by tall, sharply spiked, cast-iron railings. Two marble angels with naked swords stood sentry on each side of the entrance gate where a uniformed officer, PC Ken Jordan, was talking to an old man in a flat cap who was supporting a push bike. Jordan left the man to meet the two detectives.

'Who's the old git with the running nose?' asked Frost.

'He's George Turner, the churchwarden. He phoned us.' Jordan filled them in on what had happened. 'I've had a quick look around. No sign of anyone.'

'Ah well,' said Frost, anxious to get back in the car and the dry, 'I'll leave you to handle it.' He jerked his head to Gilmore. 'Come on, son.'

But Gilmore was rattling the heavy iron gates. They were held firm by the lock. 'So how did he get in?'

'There's a couple of broken railings round the back,' said Jordan.

'Show me,' demanded Gilmore. They followed Jordan to the rear of the crypt. Next to a stand-pipe supporting a dripping tap, two of the cast-iron railings had been broken away leaving a gap wide enough to squeeze through. They squeezed through, Frost reluctantly bringing up the rear, and marched round to the entrance to the crypt.

The door, solid oak some 3 inches thick, bore a crudely sprayed skull and crossbones in still-wet purple paint. It should have been secured by a heavy duty padlock and hasp, but the screws fixing it had been prised out of the door jamb and the door yawned open.

'Vandals!' bawled Turner. 'I'd horsewhip them till they screamed for mercy.'

'Ah well,' said Frost, fumbling for a cigarette, 'not much harm done.'

'What I want to know,' continued Turner, 'is where were the police who were supposed to be on watch? Something should be done about them. They should be taught a lesson.'

Frost nodded his agreement. 'They should be flogged until they screamed for mercy, then castrated without an anaesthetic.'

'Aren't you going to look inside?' asked Turner. 'They might have done some damage.'

'Right,' grunted Frost, without enthusiasm.

The old man leading, and guided by Jordan's torch, they went in, down two steps to the stone-floored chamber.

Jordan's torch prodded the darkness. It was a very small chamber with some six ornate, black-painted Victorian coffins stacked on stone ledges along the walls on each side. From the roof the bell rope was still quivering.

'I've never been inside a crypt,' observed Gilmore. 'I thought it would be bigger.'

'What for?' asked Frost. 'They aren't going to get up and bleedin' walk around, are they?' His nose twitched. 'What's that smell?'

'I can't smell anything,' said Turner, 'but then I've got a cold.' To prove it he foghorned into a large handkerchief.

'It smells like a corrugated iron urinal in a heat-wave,' Frost said. 'When did you bung the last corpse in?'

'The crypt hasn't been used since 1899,' he was told.

'It's coming from over here,' said Jordan, his torch sweeping the floor.

'There!' called Frost, grabbing the torch and directing it towards the far corner. The light bounced off a large, bulging bundle wrapped in black polythene sheeting, criss-crossed with 2-inch wide brown plastic adhesive tape and tied with cord.

'That didn't ought to be here!' said Turner.

As they dragged it to the centre of the floor it trailed foul-smelling liquid. Frost bent down and prodded it gently with his finger. The bundle felt cold and squelchy and the stench of putrefaction belched out. Frost's penknife slashed open the plastic sheeting. So strong and sickening was the smell that they all had to retreat back to the door to inhale the clean, rain-washed night air.

They steeled themselves to go back in. Holding his breath, Frost cut the slit bigger and peeled back some of the plastic. A gas-bloated putrefying face looked up at him.

PC Jordan gagged, his hand shaking so much that he nearly dropped the torch. Frost snatched it from him and handed it to Gilmore. 'If you're going to throw up, Jordan, do it outside. It stinks enough in here as it is.' Gladly, the constable charged up the steps. 'Are you all right, Sergeant?'

Fighting hard to control his stomach, Gilmore nodded. If the inspector could stand it, so could he.

Jordan returned, white and sweating, wiping his mouth. 'I hope you haven't desecrated someone's grave?' said Frost sternly. Jordan didn't answer. He hadn't looked and he just didn't care.

'Nip upstairs,' Frost told Gilmore, 'and radio through to the station. Tell Sergeant Wells we've found a body in the churchyard. When he stops peeing himself laughing and saying, "But the churchyard is full of bodies," tell him "ha-bloody-ha" from me and I want a doctor, Forensic, Scene of Crime Officer and a gross of air fresheners.'

The mobile generator grunted and coughed before chugging away contentedly, and the Victorian vault was bathed in electric light for the first time in its life. Duck boarding had been placed down the centre of the steps and over the floor and footsteps clacked as they crossed it. Frost stood outside, keeping well out of the experts' way as they measured and photographed, took samples and dusted for prints. The body remained tied up in the sheeting awaiting the arrival of the police surgeon.

A cursing as someone stumbled unsteadily down the path. Frost grinned to himself, happy to see that Dr Maltby was still on duty and not that jumped-up, toffee-nosed sod, Slomon.

'Welcome to the boneyard, doc.'

Maltby waved his bag and lurched over. 'What have you got for me this time?'

'Body in a sack. It's past its best.'

'Aren't we all,' said Maltby, following the inspector down the stone steps. 'Any progress with my poison pen writer?'

'Give us a chance, doc,' pleaded Frost. 'I've been tripping over corpses all day.'

Maltby dropped to his knees and bent over the body. 'Well, he's dead,' he announced.

'I should hope he is,' grunted Frost. 'If I smelt like that, I wouldn't want to live.'

Gilmore snorted his disgust. Frost seemed to thrive on bad taste remarks.

'By the way, Jack,' said the doctor casually as he gently prodded the puffy flesh through the torn opening in the plastic, 'you know that dead girl – the suicide . . .'

'What about her?' asked Gilmore.

Pointedly addressing Frost, the doctor continued. 'Tear up the report I did on her. I'm writing a new one.'

'What was up with the old one?' asked Frost.

'I missed something. The morgue attendant tipped me the wink. He spotted it when he undressed her.' He stood up and wiped his hands on a towel from his bag. 'This one's been dead at least eight weeks – possibly longer.'

'What did the morgue attendant find?' asked Gilmore. He knew there was something dodgy about that suicide.

Maltby's head twisted to the detective sergeant. 'There were marks on her buttocks – weals – about a week old, fading but still visible. She'd been quite severely beaten with a whip or a cane. And there were needle marks on her left arm.'

Gilmore's eyebrows shot up. 'And you missed it?' He pulled the inspector to one side. 'Surely you're not going to let him get away with this?'

'When you've made as many balls-ups as I have, son, you don't hesitate to help fellow sufferers,' Frost told him.

Maltby snapped his bag shut. 'I can't tell you any more about this one unless you unwrap it.'

'Might be best to wait for the pathologist,' suggested the man from Forensic who had been hovering, ears flapping. 'You know how fussy he is about bodies being left untouched.'

'Sod the pathologist,' snapped Frost. 'It'll be hours before he gets here. Cut it open.'

'I'll do it,' said Forensic, cutting through the cord to preserve the knots.

'Must preserve the knots, doc,' Frost explained. 'The murderer might be a Boy Scout.'

'We don't yet know it's murder,' commented Forensic pedantically, as he delicately sliced through the plastic sheeting.

'Bleeding hard to commit suicide and then tie yourself up in a parcel,' sniffed Frost.

Forensic moved away. 'All yours, doctor.'

As Maltby laboriously peeled aside the black plastic which tried to cling to the moist, rotting flesh, both Forensic and Gilmore found it necessary to move nearer the door and the sweet night air.

'Bloody hell!' exclaimed Frost. 'It's a woman.'

Gilmore forced himself to look. He saw the the bloated body of a female, stark naked, hunched in a foetal position, knees bent to breasts and trussed with string which bit deep into wet, oedematous flesh. The hair, stained and discoloured, looked dark, almost black.

'She's wearing shoes!' cried Frost. He bent over. No tights or stockings, just flat-heeled brown shoes, tightly laced over swollen naked flesh. 'I want photographs.'

The doctor moved to one side to let Ted Roberts, the burly Scene of Crime Officer, take photographs, then began a close, careful examination, gently forcing open the mouth, then scrutinizing the neck. 'She's in too bad a condition, but I'd guess at manual strangulation.' His examination continued downwards. He asked for the string to be cut so he could see the lower part of the body. He parted the legs slightly. 'Dear God!' he exclaimed, visibly startled at what he saw.

The lower stomach and genital area was a mass of blackened and charred weeping flesh.

Frost dropped on his knees beside the doctor and gasped. 'Look at this, Gilmore. Some bastard's burnt her.'

A fleeting glance was enough for Gilmore who stood well back, willing his stomach to keep calm while camera motors whirred and flash tubes crackled.

Maltby's nose scraped the blackened area. 'To do this sort of damage you'd need a blow-lamp.'

'Bloody hell!' said Frost. 'Was it done before or after death?'

The doctor shook his head. 'I don't know. I hope it was after.'

No longer hunched up, she looked smaller than Frost had first thought. 'How old is she, doc?'

'Young,' Maltby told him, again exploring the mouth. 'Fifteen . . . sixteen.'

'Fifteen!' echoed Frost. 'And dead eight weeks?' His head sank. 'There ought to be a mole on the right shoulder, doc. Have a look, would you.'

Maltby moved some strands of hair and nodded.

'Shit,' cried Frost. 'Shit and double shit!'

This putrid mess of tortured flesh was the missing newspaper girl.

They had found Paula Bartlett.

'I didn't see what he looked like,' the church warden told Frost. 'He just dashed off into the dark.'

'Was he tall, short, fat, thin . . .? You must remember something. It's bloody important. He'd just dumped a girl's body in there.'

70

'Just a dark shape, that's all I saw.' Then he hesitated. 'I think there might have been more than one of them.'

'More than one?' yelled Frost. 'Blimey, you kept that up your bloody sleeve.'

'As I was pedalling up, I thought I heard voices – men's voices.'

'So why didn't you tell us this before?' demanded Gilmore.

'Because I didn't think it was important. I thought we were dealing with vandals, not a flaming murder. I didn't hear what they were saying and I didn't see anyone else.'

'You're a fine bloody help,' moaned Frost. 'A body dumped right under your nose and you see damn all! We're looking for one or more men with no description.'

'Don't you blame me for the shortcomings of your lot,' snapped Turner, picking up his bike. 'If the police were doing their job, they'd have caught them. They were supposed to have two men on watch for vandals . . . so where the hell were they? Boozing in some pub, I imagine.'

Frost went cold. He hadn't considered this aspect. 'Bleedin' hell, son,' he muttered to Gilmore. 'I've just given Mullett my head on a platter.'

By the time the pathologist and his secretary arrived, some forty minutes later, Forensic and Maltby had left and the mortuary squad were waiting outside, shuffling their feet impatiently, anxious to pick up the remains and get out of the rain. The pathologist was in a foul temper, furious that Frost had disturbed the body before he had a chance to see it and angry to learn that Maltby, who had been most rude to him after a clash of medical evidence in a recent court case, had done a detailed examination. 'If I'm called in no-one, but no-one – let alone jumped-up general practitioners – touches one hair

71

of the corpse, do you hear? All this clumsy handling has probably destroyed vital clues.'

'Anything you say, doc,' said Frost in his 'couldn't care less' voice.

'And don't call me doc,' snapped the pathologist, pulling on a pair of long, almost transparent rubber gloves.

Frost left him to it, wandering up the steps for a smoke. PC Jordan's personal radio spluttered. Control wanting a word with Mr Frost. 'How's it going?' asked Sergeant Wells.

'The pathologist's just turned up with his blonde secretary. They both went down the crypt and he started putting some rubberware on, so I discreetly left them to it.'

Wells gave a guarded laugh. 'Mr Mullett's at my side, Inspector. He wishes to speak to you.'

Frost waited apprehensively. He certainly didn't want to speak to Mr Mullett.

The superintendent was bubbling over with fury and was almost shouting incoherently. 'You disobeyed my orders, my express orders. Your incompetence has made us a laughing stock, an absolute laughing stock . . .'

Frost turned the volume down and let the superintendent rant away unheard. He couldn't think of any way he could get out of this foul-up. His head turned as Gilmore emerged from the crypt.

'Preliminary report from the pathologist. The body wasn't dumped there tonight. It's been in the crypt for at least six or seven weeks.'

Six or seven weeks? Frost frowned as he worried this through. So the kid must have been hidden there almost immediately after she was killed. So it *was* vandals Turner saw running away. They had nothing to do with the girl. The grin returned to his face as he turned up the volume of the radio where Mullett was still in full flow.

'. . . If you had been doing your damn job you'd have caught the murderer in the act of dumping the damn body . . .'

'Hold on, Super,' Frost interrupted. 'How could I have caught him in the act of dumping the damn body tonight when it's been stinking the flaming vault out for eight weeks?'

So knocked off balance was Mullett by Frost's explanation that he completely forgot that his orders had been disobeyed and ended up by apologizing. 'Forgive me if I was too hasty, Inspector . . . the strain of work, you know.'

'You're forgiven, Super,' said Frost grandly.

'The family will have to be informed, of course.'

'It's half-past midnight,' said Frost. 'I was thinking of leaving it until the morning.'

But Mullett was adamant. 'The press have already got hold of the story. The family mustn't learn of it through the media.'

Frost groaned. Mullett was right, of course. 'Right, sir. We're on our way.'

The Bartlett house was in darkness, but a low-wattage light burnt hopefully in the porch.

Even as they walked up the drive to the front door, Frost kept hoping the girl's parents would be out, preferably staying with friends in some other division so that someone else would have the pleasure of breaking the news. But an upstairs light clicked on to dash his hopes. Sleeping fitfully, the Bartletts must have been awakened by the slam of the car door.

It was the mother who opened the door, a dressing gown over her nightdress. Ignoring Frost, she looked over his shoulder to Gilmore, the young man she had seen earlier. 'It's about Paula, isn't it?'

73

His face grim, Gilmore nodded.

'You've found her? I knew you would. I told you you'd find her. Thank God!' She was weeping with happiness.

Flaming hell! thought Frost. This is an unmitigated balls-up. That bleeding clairvoyant, I could tear his dick out by the roots.

Behind the woman, her husband, a sad-looking man, read the message in Frost's expression, a message his wife was refusing to see. He moved forward and put his arm around her. She looked at him puzzled, not understanding why he wasn't rejoicing with her . . . and then she looked at Frost again. And then she knew.

'Do you think we might come in?' asked Frost.

They were in Paula's bedroom where everything had been left exactly as it was on the day she went missing. The bed was made, blue pyjamas folded neatly on the pillow and the alarm clock, wound each day ready for her return, set to ring at 6.45 so she wouldn't be late for her paper round. From downstairs the heart-tearing wail of Mrs Bartlett, her grief for her daughter sounding uncannily like that of the mother of the fifteen-year-old who had killed herself. It reminded Frost that they had to visit the mortuary to see the marks on Susan Bicknell's body. He felt in his inside pocket for something to jot a reminder down on and felt an unfamiliar wad of papers. His car expenses. Something else he had forgotten about. How the hell was he going to find the time to get the proper copies made that bloody County were demanding? He stuffed them back in his pocket and forgot about them again.

'What are we doing here?' asked Gilmore.

'I don't know,' said Frost wearily. 'I just wanted to have a think away from all the bloody crying.' He looked around the room. Everything plain and simple, just like the dead girl. No posters, no pop records. On the bedside cabinet was a framed photograph of her mother and father. A small bookcase held some children's books, her school textbooks, a Collins Concise Encyclopedia and a Pocket Oxford Dictionary. Inside the bedside cabinet, standing on its end, was a black and green Adidas nylon holdall. He unzipped it and looked inside. Some gym clothes, a track suit and a couple of exercise books. He stuffed it back again. On the floor by the cabinet was a wastepaper bin. The bin contained a crumpled Milky Way wrapper and a small cardboard carton that had once held a lipstick.

'You're right, son,' he said. 'We're wasting our bloody time here.'

He opened the door and they went downstairs.

The crying went on and on.

They let themselves out.

Monday night shift (2)

Sergeant Wells stared glumly at the cold scummy tea left in the cup, palmed two aspirins into his mouth and flushed them down in a shuddering swallow. It was just a headache. He envied those lucky devils who had gone down with the flu virus and were tucked up in their nice warm beds, leaving mugs like him to do the extra duties they were being paid for. He had been on duty since half-past nine, no-one to help him, the heating on the blink, no canteen and Mullett demanding cups of tea or coffee every five minutes.

'Two teas and a fairy cake, please, Sergeant.'

Wells jerked two fingers up at Jack Frost who came bouncing in with that aftershaved ponce, Gilmore.

Frost ambled over and pulled out his cigarettes. 'Bleeding cold in here, Bill. It was warmer down the crypt.'

'Only the people who matter get heat. It's like St Tropez in Mullett's office. And he wants to see you.'

'He can't get enough of me,' said Frost, trotting off to the inner sanctum.

'Gilmore!' Wells called as the detective sergeant headed for the office. 'Your wife phoned about two hours ago. Wanted to know when you were coming home.'

'Thanks,' said Gilmore. 'If she phones again . . .'

'If she phones again,' cut in Wells, '*you* talk to her. I'm off in fifteen minutes.' In any case, he wasn't acting as messenger boy for a lousy jumped-up ex-detective constable.

It wasn't cold in Mullett's office. The 3-kilowatt heater purred happily, and Frost had to fight to keep awake in the hot room as he gave the Divisional Commander a brief update, sparing none of the details.

'Burnt with a blow-lamp?' gasped the shocked Mullett. 'That's depraved . . . You kept it from the parents?'

'Yes,' said Frost. 'And I want it kept from the press – that and the fact she was wearing shoes.' There'd be the usual spate of nutters coming up with false confessions based on details they'd read in the papers.

'And the pathologist is quite certain the body wasn't placed in that crypt tonight?' asked Mullett, reluctant to let the inspector off the hook.

'The poor little cow was dumped weeks ago . . . that's why she's stinking to high heaven now.'

Mullet winced and moved his chair back slightly. Frost's description of the advanced state of decomposition had been so graphic, he was sure he could smell it. Or perhaps the stench was clinging to that dirty old mac Frost insisted on wearing. Frost took a cigarette end from behind his ear and pushed it into his mouth. He struck a match on his fingernail. Mullett sighed deeply. This case would get extensive press and TV coverage. He daren't risk exposing this slovenly, foul-mouthed lout to the media as typical of the Denton constabulary.

He cleared his throat. 'I have decided to take full executive control of this case, Inspector.'

The lighted match paused an inch from the end of the cigarette. 'Executive control?'

'Yes. You will be responsible for the day-to-day routine, but under my direct control. Do you understand?'

I do all the work and get the bollockings when things go wrong, and you take all the credit when they go right, thought Frost grimly. 'Yes, I understand,' he said aloud.

'I've promised the Chief Constable an early result. This must be our number one priority. What do you need to achieve an early result?'

'A lot of bloody luck and some more men.'

'We can't have any more. Normal schedules will have to go by the board. Everyone will have to follow my lead – work that little bit harder, push themselves to the limit.' He yawned and glanced at his watch. Time he was back home and in bed. 'Everyone must pitch in. We're all one big team.' He gleamed white teeth at Frost in a crocodile smile as he stood up and slipped on his overcoat.

The phone rang. Mullett answered it and passed it over to Frost. The pathologist. He had a heavy schedule for the morning, so he was doing the post-mortem on the newspaper girl in an hour's time.

'I'll be there,' Frost said, yawning.

'Good,' nodded Mullett, moving to the door. 'Well, I must try and snatch a few hours' sleep so I can be fresh for the morning. Report to me tomorrow at nine and we'll go over our plan of campaign.' He clicked off the heater and, when Frost had left, turned out the light and locked the door.

As he passed through the lobby he saw Wells moodily staring at the clock. The wretched man was always clock-watching. He would have a word with him about it in the morning. He responded with a curt nod as the sergeant called good night to him.

Miserable sod, thought Wells. It was 2.59 a.m. Sergeant Johnnie Johnson, who had the morning shift, was coming in three hours early to relieve him. Usually Johnnie was early, arriving a good five minutes before the start of the shift, but Wells wasn't worrying yet. He began stuffing away his pens and notepads in the drawer to leave a clean desk for his relief. The phone gave a timorous, half-hearted ring. 'Denton Police, Sergeant Wells speaking.'

'Hello, Bill. It's Doreen.'

The cold tea curdled in his stomach. Doreen. Johnnie Johnson's wife. What the hell did she want at this time of the morning?

'It's John, I'm afraid, Bill. We've had to have the doctor in.'

That bloody hypochondriac! A headache and he thinks he's got a brain tumour. 'Oh dear, Doreen. Nothing serious, I hope?'

'The doctor thinks it's this flu virus that's going around.'

One sniffle and the bastard's down with flu . . . typical. 'Terribly sorry to hear that, Doreen.'

'. . . so he won't be able to come in to work tonight, I'm afraid.'

'Of course not. We wouldn't expect him to. You tell him to stay away until he is really fit.' He slammed the phone down. 'Skiving bastard!' Leaving the lobby unattended, he dashed off to Jack Frost's office to have a moan.

Gilmore was on the phone as the sergeant came in. He had rung Liz, hoping there wouldn't be an answer, but she was still awake, staring at the clock and complaining about being left on her own for most of the day and half the bloody night. It was three o'clock, and he was overdue for a meal break. He told her he was on his way and she said she'd rustle up a quick meal for him. Not that he felt like eating at this time of the morning, but he didn't want another row. He was shrugging on his overcoat when Frost bowled in and immediately Wells started his moaning.

'It's not on, Jack. I was supposed to be relieved. I've already done a double-bloody-shift. I'm not fit myself, but I stagger in. And what thanks do I get?'

'Bugger all,' said Frost cheerfully, not really listening. 'You can't slope off yet, Gilmore,' he called. 'Post-mortem on the girl in a hour.'

'In an hour?' croaked Gilmore, dropping into his chair with a crash. He reached for the phone to dial Liz before she started cooking.

'And Mullett doesn't give a damn,' continued Wells.

Frost moved some files from his chair to the floor and sat down. 'His door, like his bowels, is always open, Sergeant.'

'Sod Mullett!' snorted Wells.

'The lobby phone's ringing,' said Gilmore, trying to concentrate on what Liz was saying.

'And sod the phone,' snarled Wells, stamping back to the lobby.

Frost had a half-hearted forage through his in-tray which was filled to overflowing, but was thankfully interrupted by a phone call from Forensic. A preliminary report on the black plastic sheeting used to wrap Paula Bartlett's body. It was made up of black plastic dustbin sacks, the standard Denton Council issue for refuse collection, of which more than two million had been issued to households over the past twelve months. Further tests were under way.

'Thanks a lot,' said Frost, gloomily. 'That's narrowed it down to the whole of bleeding Denton.'

'Actually it doesn't,' said Forensic. 'Nearly all the councils in this part of England use an identical sack.'

'Just when I thought it was going to be easy,' Frost said, hanging up. 'I'll be in the Murder Incident Room,' he yelled to Gilmore who was doing a lot of listening on the phone and didn't appear to be saying much.

Two people only in the Murder Incident Room. DC Burton, a phone pressed tightly to his ear, his pen scribbling furiously, and WPC Jean Knight, a redhead in her mid-twenties who was waiting for the computer to finish a print-out.

'Couple of odds and ends from Forensic,' called Burton, waving his sheet of paper.

Frost ambled over and poked a cigarette into Burton's mouth, then offered the pack to the redhead who declined with a smile. 'I know all about the dustbin sacks, son. I'm applying for two million search warrants.'

Burton grinned. 'We can do a bit better than that, sir. Firstly, the padlock. Forensic reckon those screws were prised out at least twice before within the past couple of months and then hammered back.'

Frost's cigarette drooped as his mouth fell open. 'Twice before?'

'Yes, sir. Someone could have got in on two or more different occasions, or it could even have been twice on the same day.'

'Forensic always seem to think they're being bloody helpful,' said Frost. 'Now I'm more mystified than ever.' He looked up as Gilmore came in. 'Did you hear that, son? The padlock to the crypt had been forced at least twice.'

'Oh?' said Gilmore, not really taking it in. His ear was still sore from the phone and his mind was full of Liz's moans and complaints.

'There's more,' announced Burton. 'Forensic found a footprint.'

'Ah,' said Frost. 'So we're looking for a one-legged man.'

'It wasn't exactly a footprint,' continued Burton patiently. 'It was more a clump of mud that had fallen from the sole of a shoe.'

'Where did they find it?' asked Gilmore, stifling a yawn.

'Top step, just inside the crypt door. Forensic reckon it was some eight weeks old which makes it round about the time the body was dumped.'

'How the hell can they tell it's eight weeks old?' asked Gilmore.

'Don't ask!' pleaded Frost. 'Just accept it. You'll be none the wiser if they explain. OK, Burton. We've got a bit of mud. How does that help?'

Burton pulled his notes towards him. 'There were traces of copper filings and lead solder in the mud.'

Frost worried away at his scar with a nicotine-stained finger. 'Copper filings and solder?' If it had any significance, he couldn't see it.

'A plumber!' called WPC Jean Knight from the computer. 'They put central heating in my flat last week. They were forever sawing up lengths of copper tubing.'

'A homicidal plumber!' said Frost doubtfully. He ambled across to the shelf of telephone directories and pulled out the Yellow Pages for Denton and district. There were some fifteen pages of plumbers – nearly three hundred firms. 'At least it's less than two million,' he observed.

'There'll be more names under "Central Heating",' Burton reminded him.

There were nearly two hundred entries under 'Central Heating', although some of these were also entered under 'Plumbers'.

'The gas company does central heating,' added Jean Knight. 'They'd employ plumbers as well.'

'I'm losing interest already,' said Frost.

'It might not be a plumber at all,' added Gilmore. 'It could be someone, like Jean, who's had central heating installed and that's how the filings and solder got on their shoes.'

'It might be a man with a length of copper tubing soldered on the end of his dick who'd popped into the crypt for a Jimmy Riddle,' said Frost unhelpfully. Then he stopped dead and a smile crept over his face. 'Or it might be a lot easier than we think.' Excitedly he expounded his theory, the cigarette in his mouth waggling as he spoke. 'We're not looking for any old plumber. Our killer didn't stagger into the cemetery with a gift-wrapped body just on the off-chance he'd find somewhere to hide it. He knew the crypt was there and he knew he could get into it. Now I've lived in Denton most of my life and I never knew we had a Victorian crypt in the churchyard . . . did any of you?'

Burton and the WPC shook their heads. 'I visit cemeteries as infrequently as possible,' said Burton.

'Me too,' said Frost. 'I only go in one if I can't find anywhere else to have a pee. But our plumber knew where to find it and knew he could get in it.' He jabbed a finger at Gilmore. 'How?'

Gilmore shook his head. He had no idea.

'Right, son, let me mark your card. What was alongside the crypt, by the broken railings?'

'A stand-pipe and a tap,' said Gilmore, beginning to see what the old fool was getting at.

'Exactly, sergeant. And they looked fairly new. So who would have installed them?'

'A plumber,' said Gilmore, 'and he'd know how to get in through the broken railings.'

'And he'd know how to use a blow-lamp,' added Burton.

Frost chucked an empty cigarette packet into the air and headed it against the wall. 'Another case solved. Get in touch with the vicar, find out who did the work, then bring him in for routine questioning and beating up.' He yawned and looked at his watch. Nearly an hour to kill before the post-mortem. He was about to suggest sending out for some Chinese takeaway when the phone rang. Control for the inspector. Another burglary at a senior citizen's home – old lady of eighty-one.

'Damn!' muttered Frost. He could have done without this tonight.

'There's worse to come,' said Control. 'The intruder beat her up. She's not expected to live.'

Clarendon Street. Lights blinked out from quite a few of the houses where the occupants had been wakened by the police activity. Outside number 11 was an empty area car, its radio droning and no-one to listen, and behind that, an ambulance, engine running, rear doors open. As Gilmore parked the Cortina on the opposite side of the street, two ambulance men carrying a stretcher emerged from the house, closely followed by a uniformed constable. By the time they crossed the road the ambulance was speeding on its way to the hospital.

'Anyone at home?' yelled Frost down the passage.

A door at the head of the stairs opened. 'Up here, Inspector.' Tubby Detective Sergeant Arthur Hanlon beckoned them in.

A bedroom, its bed askew in the middle of the floor, the sash window open and Roberts, the Scene of Crime Officer, bending, engrossed in dusting the bottom edge of the frame for fingerprints. There were fragments of a smashed blue and white vase on the floor and the top centre dressing table drawer gaped open, its riffled contents spewing out.

By the dressing table a hooked-nosed woman in her mid-forties wearing a quilted dressing gown was talking earnestly to PC Jordan.

The scene was familiar. This burglar seldom varied his technique. A quick in and out job. Straight for the dressing table to grab indiscriminately whatever jewellery was instantly available, then, starting with the top centre drawer, he looked for the 'cleverly hidden' cache of notes which couldn't be trusted to the bank and which were nearly always at the back of the top centre drawer. Then out again, the whole operation lasting a maximum of five minutes. A familiar scene, but this time with a difference. There was blood everywhere, on the floor, on the bedding and on the curtains.

'How's the old girl?' asked Frost.

'Not good,' said Hanlon, honking loudly into a handkerchief and dabbing a sore-looking nose. 'Stab wounds and a possible fractured skull. The ambulance men don't think she'll regain consciousness.'

'Damn,' muttered Frost, but his eyes were looking over Hanlon's shoulder at the SOC man, who was offering an irresistible target. 'Excuse me a moment.' Frost tiptoed over and accurately jabbed a nicotined finger at the seam of the tight trousers. 'How's that for centre?' he roared.

Roberts shot up, hitting his head on the window sill. He spun round angrily, only to grin when he saw Frost. 'It's you, Inspector. I might have guessed.'

Gilmore raised his eyes to the ceiling in exasperation. A potential murder investigation and the fool was indulging in schoolboy games. Well, someone had to act responsibly. 'What happened?' he asked Hanlon.

'The victim is Alice Ryder, a widow aged eighty-one. She occupies the top half of the house, a Mr and Mrs Francis live downstairs. Mr Francis is on night work – that's the wife over there.' Hanlon nodded towards the woman with Jordan. 'She found the old lady.' Sensing their eyes on her, the woman came over, anxious to relate her part in the drama.

'I woke up about quarter-past three to go to the toilet and I noticed her light was still on. I was worried, so I went up to check. Her telly was going full blast and her bedroom door was open. I looked in . . .' She paused, shuddering at the recollection. 'There she was, on the floor and blood everywhere. I couldn't get to the phone quick enough. She was terrified of anyone breaking in . . . she must have had a premonition.' She wrapped her dressing gown tighter around her. It was cold in the room with the window open. 'That's all I can tell you.'

'You didn't see who it was who did it?' asked Gilmore.

She gave him a thin smile. 'I'd have mentioned it if I had – just in case it was important.'

'Sarcastic cow!' seethed Gilmore when she had gone.

'I thought she was quite nice,' observed Hanlon, who was irritated at the way the new bloke kept trying to take charge.

'I didn't like her nose,' said Frost, 'or her dressing gown.' He nodded to the SOC officer. 'Surprise me. Tell me that this time he left fingerprints.'

Roberts shook his head. 'He wore gloves, as always.'

'Consistent bastard!' snorted Frost. 'All right, Ted, paint me a word picture. Let's have a reconstruction.'

'Right,' said Roberts. 'The old lady was in the front room watching the telly. Our intruder gets in through the bedroom window, but this time he was unlucky. She'd stuck that blue and white vase on the window ledge and as he clambered in, he knocked it over and it fell to the floor. The old lady heard it, came charging in to see what it was, so he went for her with this . . .' Roberts clicked open his 'evidence case' and pulled out a sealed, transparent polythene bag. Inside the bag was a black-handled kitchen knife, its blood-smeared blade honed to razor sharpness. 'It was on the floor, by the bed.'

'You're saying he had this knife in his hand when the old girl came charging in?' When Roberts nodded, Frost shook his head. 'I can't buy that, Ted. If I was climbing through windows I wouldn't want a lethal thing like that in my hand . . . I could cut my dick off.'

'He wouldn't carry it in his hand when he was climbing. He'd have it in a tool bag.'

'All right,' said Frost. 'I'll pretend to accept that for the moment. Then what happened?'

'He stabs her, but she puts up a fight. He drops the knife in the struggle, punches her repeatedly in the face then finishes her off by smashing her skull in with a cosh or something.'

Frost's finger prodded away at the scar on his cheek as he worried this over. 'I can't believe it's the same bloke who did all the others. He's never resorted to violence before.'

'He hasn't been disturbed before,' offered Hanlon. 'His other victims were damn lucky they never heard anything.' He sniffed and dabbed his nose. 'I think I've got the flu.'

'No, you haven't,' said Frost firmly. 'We're too busy. Do we know what's been taken?'

Jordan stepped forward. 'Same as all the others. Bits and pieces of of jewellery – Mrs Francis has given me a description – and money. Mrs Francis doesn't know how much, but says the old lady always kept a fair amount of cash by her – a couple of hundred at least.'

'I want this bastard,' said Frost. 'People who kill for a couple of hundred lousy quid are dangerous.' He looked at the bed, knocked askew with splodges of blood all over the pillows and sheets. Someone must have heard or seen something. 'Get as many men as you want from Bill Wells and start knocking on doors.'

'I've already asked. He says he can't spare anyone until the next shift.'

'He's bloody well going to have to. We're not going to wait for her to die, Arthur, she might sod us about and linger. We're going to anticipate. This is a murder enquiry as of now. I want a team knocking on doors, I want Forensic, I want someone by the old girl's bedside night and day in case she can give us a description. If I've forgotten anything, I want that as well.'

While Hanlon radioed the station, he ambled over to the open window and looked out on to a small, rain-puddled yard. Below him was the dustbin used by the man to gain entrance. It reminded him of the yard in Jubilee Terrace and the mummified corpse. What a bloody night this had turned out to be. First the mummy, then Paula Bartlett . . . Paula . . . Flaming heck! The autopsy! He daren't be late for that. He was in enough trouble with the pathologist as it was.

He checked his watch. Ten to four. They could just do it if they ignored fiddling details like adverse traffic lights. 'I've got to leave you to it, Arthur. Just solve the case and tie it all up before the end of the shift.' He dashed across to the door. 'Come on, Gilmore. We've got an autopsy to watch and ten minutes to get there.'

At four o'clock on a cold, dark, rainy morning, the mortuary lights gleamed across the driveway to the hospital and bounced off the black, supercilious shape of the pathologist's Rolls Royce. Frost's mud-coated Cortina shuffled in and parked alongside. 'Don't forget . . . ours is the one on the left,' he reminded Gilmore.

The night porter, a gangling twenty-year-old with an embryonic moustache, snatched a cigarette from his mouth and dropped it to the floor as the two detectives walked in. He thought it was that toffee-nosed pathologist who had already rebuked him for smoking on duty.

'Midnight matinée,' said Frost, flashing his warrant card. 'Paula Bartlett.'

'We should get paid double for handling bodies in that condition,' complained the porter, leading them through to the autopsy room which was in darkness apart from the end table where the overhead lights poured down on a mass of decomposing and charred flesh that was once a fifteen-year-old schoolgirl. 'Dockers get dirty money, so should we.' He opened a side door and called, 'Police are here, doctor.'

'Overture and beginners, doc,' yelled Frost, perching

himself on a stool for a good view. Gilmore, not so eager, moved back out of the splash of light.

The pathologist, his faithful secretary in tow, entered, scowling. He found nothing about his job amusing. The smile would be wiped off Frost's face when he read a copy of the report he was sending to his Divisional Commander complaining that the inspector had allowed every Tom, Dick and Harry to maul the body before he had had a chance to see it.

'Do you reckon he sleeps with her?' whispered Frost to Gilmore as the secretary adjusted the lights over the end autopsy table to her master's satisfaction. 'It must be off-putting, banging away at someone, knowing you're shaking up her stomach contents and her internal organs.'

Gilmore pressed further back into the blackness, not wanting to get involved in Frost's coarse asides.

While the porter turned on the extractor fan above the autopsy table, the pathologist allowed his secretary to help him on with his green gown and heavy plastic apron. He fiddled with a control under the perforated table top and as water gurgled and trickled, he pulled on a pair of rubber gloves and flexed his fingers. He was ready.

First, he carefully examined the body from top to bottom, without touching any part of it. 'Body of a female in advanced state of decomposition,' he intoned. Miss Grey's pencil zipped across the page of her notebook. He eased open the mouth with a spatula and shone a small torch inside. 'Age about . . .'

'We know how old she is, doc,' Frost told him. 'I even know her birthday. What I don't know for sure is how she died.'

The pathologist's eyes flashed. 'Don't interrupt!'

'Sorry, doc,' said Frost, quite unabashed, 'but we're

operating at half-strength and I've got lots to do. Could you just give me the headlines? I'll read all the boring bits in your report.'

'I don't cut corners. Aged around fifteen.' He snapped his fingers and demanded: 'Dental records!' Miss Grey passed him across a small typed card with marked diagrams. He studied it then handed it back. His spatula clicked on the teeth checking extractions and fillings. 'From the dental record I can identify the body as that of Paula Bartlett, aged fifteen years and two months. Some traces of blood in her mouth.' He wiped the mouth with a swab and dropped it into a container held out by his secretary.

'She anticipates his every move,' Frost whispered to Gilmore. 'I bet he doesn't have to tell her when to thrust or withdraw.'

Gilmore couldn't even pretend to smile.

Frost fidgeted with impatience as the pathologist plodded on, the swollen neck now receiving his painstaking scrutiny, fingers carefully prodding and probing.

'Dr Maltby said death was due to manual strangulation,' prompted Frost. Why was this man so bloody slow?

'If I was one of Dr Maltby's patients,' murmured the pathologist, his nose almost touching the neck, 'I'd insist on a second opinion on everything he told me.' To his secretary he said, 'Signs of manual pressure applied to neck.'

'Ha!' exclaimed Frost. 'So that's what killed her.'

'I'll tell you what killed her when I have completed the autopsy,' said Drysdale, crushingly. 'For all I know, there are eight bullet wounds in the stomach. Just keep quiet.'

Frost gave his watch a pointed stare, sighed deeply then went outside for a smoke. Gilmore was happy to join him. Even with the extractor fan working full blast, the atmosphere in the post-mortem room was foul and would worsen when Drysdale used the scalpel to open the body up.

The porter brought them two mugs of tea and gratefully accepted a cigarette from the inspector. Through the swing doors they could see the autopsy proceeding. A bone saw screamed and Gilmore turned his eyes away, his teeth gritted against the noise.

'Perhaps we could browse while we wait,' requested Frost. 'Have you got a Susan Bicknell in stock?'

The porter flipped open his ledger and ran a nicotine-stained finger down the entries. 'Suicide? Came in this afternoon? This way.'

They followed him to the refrigerated section. On a small side table near the door was a polythene bag containing a folded Mickey Mouse nightdress, a black and gold kimono and, separately wrapped, a Snoopy watch. Snoopy's paws pointed to 4.29. 'Her things,' announced the porter laconically, jerking his thumb.

He stopped in front of one of the bank of metal drawers, checked the name tag and pulled it open. Sliding on rollers, a sheeted body silently emerged. When the sheet was removed the girl was seen to be naked. A red label tied to her big toe seemed an obscene addition as if some joker had put it there for a laugh. Needle marks were clearly visible on her left arm.

The porter folded the sheet and stared down in disapproval. 'I hate seeing them so bloody young.'

'Give my colleague a hand to turn her over,' requested Frost.

Gilmore hesitated, then steeled himself and complied. He wasn't prepared for the hard coldness of the flesh and nearly let her fall back. The porter gave him a scornful look. 'She can't hurt you. She's dead. Bloody hell . . . look at that!'

Now she was turned, they could see it. All across her buttocks, fading but still visible, deep, criss-cross lines of red weals and smudges of pale yellow bruises. They were the marks left by a thrashing, a vicious thrashing, from a whip or a cane. At least twelve weals could be counted. Frost winced. 'It hurts just to look at it. Who the hell could have done this?'

'That bloody stepfather,' snapped Gilmore. 'I'd like to meet him on a dark night.'

A firm shake of the head. Frost couldn't buy that. 'She was fifteen years old, for Pete's sake. She'd never submit to that.'

A sniff from the porter who offered his worldly-wise opinion. 'I reckon she was kinky. Perhaps she enjoyed being beaten.'

'Maybe, but not as hard as this. She'd have been yelling blue murder after the first cut . . . and yet she took more than twelve of them.'

'She could have been into bondage as well,' offered Gilmore. 'Strapped down while it was done to her. Some women like that.'

Frost's eyebrows shot up. 'Blimey, Gilmore, what sort of women do you go out with? I never have such luck. I only have to blow in their ear-hole and they think I'm a pervert.'

'When you've quite finished your voyeurism . . .' The pathologist glowered disapproval, his gown stained and carrying the taint of the grave into the clean coldness of the refrigerated section.

Back to the autopsy table where the body had been crudely stitched and the secretary was writing out neat labels for jars of removed organs. 'She was trussed up and put inside the plastic sack within three or four hours of being killed,' said Drysdale watching Gilmore note this information down. 'Cause of death manual strangulation.'

'That's what Dr Maltby said,' beamed Frost.

Ignoring him, Drysdale plunged on. 'The killer's two hands went round her throat like this.' Obligingly, his secretary allowed herself to be used for a demonstration and stood still as he grabbed her throat, sinking his thumbs deep into her larynx. 'The girl would have struggled desperately, fighting for her life. I imagine she grabbed his wrists, trying to break his grip but her killer, his hands still tight round her throat, swung her from side to side and smashed her head against a wall, probably hard enough to make her lose consciousness.' He swung Miss Grey from side to side as illustration, but spared her the banging of the head. She looked disappointed as he released his grip, but carried on labelling jars of human offal.

Indicating blood-matted hair and a discoloured area on the scalp Drysdale invited them to inspect the damage.

'If she struggled, doc,' asked Frost, 'wouldn't she have marked him . . . scratched him . . . gouged out chunks of flesh?'

A tight smile. 'If you're hoping for pieces of tell-tale flesh under her fingernails, I must disappoint you, Inspector.' He lifted the girl's misshapen right hand and displayed the fingernails. They were bitten down to the quick.

'Damn,' said Frost.

Carefully Drysdale lowered the hand to its original position. 'Clear evidence of sexual intercourse just before she died.'

Frost nodded glumly. He had expected this. 'Rape?'

'I think so,' replied the pathologist blandly.

'You *think* so?' echoed Gilmore, incredulously. 'You only *think* so .

'There is evidence of bruising that could suggest intercourse took place against her will . . .'

'Then she was raped,' cried Gilmore.

'If I might be allowed to continue,' grated Drysdale. 'The girl was a virgin. She could have submitted willingly, but have been tensed instead of relaxed. This might account for the bruising. Equally, she could have been raped. There is no magic way of knowing at this stage.'

'If she submitted willingly, doc,' said Frost, 'there would have been no real need to have wrung her neck afterwards.'

'That', snapped Drysdale, 'is in your province, Inspector Frost, not mine. I give the medical facts. It's up to you to speculate.'

Frost nodded ruefully. 'Then give me some facts on the way the bastard burnt her so I can speculate how to catch the sod.'

'I was coming to that,' said Drysdale testily. 'As you can see, the genital area is badly charred. In my opinion this occurred very soon after death, within an hour, say.'

'Dr Maltby thought it could have been done with a blow-lamp.'

Drysdale frowned. 'For once, Dr Maltby might have been right. To do that sort of damage you'd need something like a blowtorch.'

'But why would anyone do it, doc? Is it a new kind of sexual perversion?'

'I've come across something like this once before. A murdered rape victim, a thirty-eight-year-old prostitute. She was found in some bushes near a railway embankment. The lower part of the body was badly burnt where her killer had doused paraffin over her and set it alight.

It seems he had heard about genetic fingerprinting. You've probably read about it.'

'No,' said Frost. 'I only read comics and dirty books.'

'There's a newly developed technique,' lectured Drysdale, 'that allows us to determine an individual's genetic fingerprint from traces of body fluid – semen, say.'

Frost's mouth dropped open. 'You mean a dick print instead of a fingerprint?'

The pathologist winced. 'I wouldn't put it as crudely as that, Inspector, but yes, by DNA testing we can positively identify the donor of a semen sample.'

'So if I produced a suspect . . .' began Frost, hoping Burton had traced the plumber.

'If you produced a suspect, we could either positively incriminate him, or positively eliminate him, but he would have to supply us with a blood sample for comparison.'

'I'll get a blood sample for you,' said Frost. 'And if he won't give us one voluntarily, I'm sure we can arrange for him to fall down the station stairs.'

The pathologist's smile wavered. Like many people, he never knew when Frost was being serious or when he was joking. 'Unfortunately, Inspector, it wouldn't work with this poor girl. Even without the burning, the advanced stage of decomposition of the body precludes any possibility of carrying out the test.'

'This bastard's having all the luck,' moaned Frost. 'Anything else, doc?'

Drysdale made a mental note to include in his complaint to the Divisional Commander his displeasure at the way Frost chose to address him. 'Yes.' He held out his hand and clicked his fingers. Miss Grey gave him a large sealed jar full of squishy, lumpy brown unpleasantness dotted with green. 'The stomach contents. She hadn't had time to digest her last meal before she died.'

Frost screwed his face and turned his head. 'Tell me what it is, doc, so I can make a point of not ordering it.'

'Something with chips and peas. You'll get a detailed analysis some time tomorrow. My report will be on your desk by noon.'

'Do you feel like eating, son?' asked Frost as they climbed back into the car. 'Something with chips and peas?'

'No,' said Gilmore. All he felt like doing was going to bed and sleeping the clock round.

Five o'clock. Cold, raining steadily and still dark.

Tuesday morning shift (1)

They got back to the station at 5.15. A less than happy Sergeant Bill Wells was still on duty wearing his greatcoat against the cold of the unheated lobby.

'Still here?' asked Frost.

'Yes, still bloody here. But I'm going home at six on the dot whether anyone relieves me or not. I've had it up to here.' His hand indicated a point well above his head. He spun round to Gilmore. 'And I've got enough to do without keeping on answering calls from your bloody wife demanding to know when you're coming home.'

'When did she phone?' Gilmore asked.

'Do you mean the first time, the second or the third? The last one was ten minutes ago.'

Gilmore hurried off to the office to use the phone and Wells accepted a cigarette from Frost. 'She sounded well

96

sozzled, Jack,' he confided. 'You could smell the gin over the phone.'

'They've not been married long,' said Frost. 'She's suffering from night starvation.'

'Tough!' grunted Wells, pulling his phone log over. 'Couple of messages for you. Jill Knight phoned from the hospital. The old lady is still in intensive care. Doubtful if she'll regain consciousness. And Arthur Hanlon says one of the neighbours spotted a blue van parked at the back of Clarendon Street just before midnight.'

'Clues are pouring in thick and fast,' said Frost, trotting off down the corridor.

In the office Gilmore was making apologetic noises down the phone. 'I know, love . . . I'm sorry. What time will I be back?' He clapped his hand over the mouthpiece and looked enquiringly at Frost.

'Let's pack it in now,' said Frost. 'Grab a few hours' sleep and be back about twelve.'

Gilmore nodded his thanks and assured Liz, cross his heart, he'd be with her in fifteen minutes.

On the way out Frost pushed open the door to the Murder Incident Room. Burton was slumped by the phone, half asleep. Frost gave him a shake. 'Come on, son. I'll take you home.'

Burton smothered a yawn. 'I've located the firm that did the work at the cemetery, but I won't be able to get the plumber's name and address until their offices open at nine.'

'That's what I want,' mused Frost. 'A nine to five job, an expense account with no limit and a sexy secretary with no knickers.' He sighed at the impossibility of his dream. 'Leave a note for your relief to follow it through. Let's go home.'

*   *   *

The Cortina was juddering down Catherine Street, Gilmore fighting sleep at the wheel, Frost slumped with his eyes half closed at his side and Burton yawning in the back seat. They passed a row of shops; one, a newsagent's, had its lights gleaming. Burton in the back seat stirred and peered through the car window. 'That's where Paula Bartlett worked.'

'Pull up,' yelled Frost. Gilmore steered the car into the kerb. The name over the shop read *G. F. Rickman, Newsagent.* 'Let's chat him up,' said Frost. With a searing scowl at Burton for not keeping his big mouth shut, Gilmore clambered out after him.

George Rickman, plump and balding, was deeply engrossed in a study of the Page Three nude in *The Sun*. On the floor in front of the counter, stacked in neat piles, were the newspapers he had sorted and marked ready for the kids to take out on their rounds. The shop bell tinkled to announce a customer, old Harry Edwards from round the corner for his *Daily Mirror* and some fifty pence pieces for the gas. While he was serving Harry, the bell sounded again and two men he hadn't seen before came in: one, in his early twenties, looking tired and irritable; the other, older, wearing a crumpled mac. They hovered furtively by the door, obviously waiting for the shop to empty before they approached. Rickman smirked to himself. Dirty sods. He knew what they were after.

Harry shuffled out and the two men sidled across. Warning them to wait with a movement of his hand, Rickman darted over to the shop door and squinted through the glass to make sure no-one else was coming, then lowered his voice. 'Who sent you – Les?'

'Yes,' replied Frost, equally conspiratorial, wondering what the hell this was all about.

'You can't be too careful,' said Rickman, unlocking a door behind the counter. He ushered them through. 'Some of this stuff's dynamite.' He clicked on the light. The room was full of shelved books and magazines with lurid covers of naked, sweating, entwined men and women. In boxes on a table were stacks of soft porn videos.

'Les said you had something special,' suggested Frost, signalling to Gilmore, who was fumbling for his warrant card, to hold his horses.

Rickman leered and tapped the side of his nose knowingly. He unlocked a cupboard. More videos, this time in plain white boxes with typed labels.

'There's everything here,' he said proudly. 'All tastes catered for – men with men, women with women, with kids, animals . . . any permutation you want. Fifty quid a time – return it undamaged and I'll allow you twenty-five quid off your next purchase.'

'I don't know that I've got that much money on me,' said Frost, reaching for his inside pocket.

'I take Access . . . American Express . . . any card you like.'

'What about this one?' asked Frost.

Rickman stared at a warrant card. His jaw dropped. 'Shit!' he said.

A ting from the shop bell and a boy's voice called, 'Papers ready, Mr Rickman?'

'By the counter. Take them and go.' He waited until the bell signalled the boy's departure. 'Look, officer. I'm sure we can come to some understanding.' He brought out his wallet and pulled out two £50 notes.

'Give the gentleman a receipt for a £100 bribe,' said Frost, holding out his hand for the money. 'I'll read you the numbers.'

Hastily, Rickman stuffed the banknotes in his pocket. 'You misunderstand me, Inspector.'

'I hope I do,' replied Frost. 'You're in enough bloody trouble as it is.' He read some of the labels on the videos and shuddered. They were very explicit.

Rickman fumbled for a handkerchief and dabbed sweat from his face. 'I don't usually indulge in this sort of stuff. Harmless soft porn, yes, but not the hard stuff. I met this bloke in a pub . . .'

Frost cut him short. 'Save your fairy tales for the officer down the station.' He sent Gilmore to the car to radio for someone to collect Rickman and the books and videos.

'You try and do people a good turn and this happens,' moaned Rickman. 'What bastard shopped me?'

'We've been watching this shop for months,' lied Frost. He had taken an instant dislike to the podgy newsagent. Some of the videos involved schoolgirls. He wondered if Paula Bartlett was tied in with this in some way. He stared at the fidgeting Rickman and slowly lit a cigarette. 'We've found her, you know.'

'Found who?'

'Paula.'

'Paula Bartlett . . . my news girl?'

Frost nodded.

'Is she . . .' He steeled himself to say it. 'Is she dead?'

Another nod.

'Oh, that's terrible.' His face was screwed tight in anguish.

'Yes,' said Frost. 'And you should see what the bastard did to her. It would make a good video for you to sell.'

The shop bell tinkled again as Gilmore returned. He'd also asked Bill Wells to phone his wife and say he would be late, but had got short shrift from the sergeant.

Frost sat on the corner of the ice-cream cabinet. 'Tell me about Paula.'

'A really nice, sweet kid,' said Rickman.

'They're always nice when they're dead,' said Frost. 'Tell me what she was like while she was still alive.'

Rickman shrugged. 'She was a nothing. A dull kid. A bit of a pudding. Never laughed. Hardly ever spoke. Did her work. That was all.'

Again the shop bell quivered and rung and an old woman shuffled in. 'We're closed,' said Frost, taking her by the arm and steering her out into the street. He reversed the *Open/Closed* sign and rammed home the bolts.

'Tell me about the day she went missing.'

'I've already told all this to the other detective . . . the ferret-faced bloke. An absolutely normal day. She left as usual to go on her round and that was the last I saw of her.'

'Had she complained about men molesting her . . . or following her?' asked Gilmore.

'Not to me, she didn't. She hardly spoke a bloody word to me.'

Frost ambled over to the counter and glanced at the paper Rickman had been reading. He studied the naked Page Three girl, his cigarette drooping dispassionately. 'How was young Paula set up? Well stacked, was she?'

'No different to most of the other girls. They mature so bloody quickly these days . . . see them at fifteen you think they're twenty. Mind you, Paula didn't flaunt it. She used to wear loose woolly cardigans and things like that.'

'Did she go out with any of the newspaper boys?'

'No. Between you and me, I don't reckon she'd ever been with a boy or knew anything about sex.'

Frost raised his eyebrows. 'Why do you say that?'

'Something that happened three months ago. I'm in the

101

shop sorting out the papers for the rounds. Only two of the kids were in, Diana Massey and Jimmy Richards.'

'Who are they?' asked Frost.

'They were both in Paula's class at school – both just turned fifteen. Anyway, I'm sorting out the papers when I realize they've both gone missing. Well, not that I mistrust anyone, but I keep the day's takings in that other back room there until I can get to the bank, so I sticks my head round the door and what do you think I saw?'

'Tell me,' said Frost.

'Diana's on the floor, jeans round her ankles, he's on top of her, jeans ditto and they're having it away on a stack of *Radio Times*. Fifteen flaming years old. Didn't even stop when I yelled at them.'

'I don't think I would, either,' observed Frost.

'Anyway, I hears a gasp behind me. I turned around and there was Paula Bartlett. She was staring at them horrified. She dropped her papers and just ran out of the shop. It was obvious to me she didn't know what the hell they were up to. Innocent, that's what she was.'

'If our plumber lets us down, we'd better check out this Jimmy Richards,' said Frost. 'He might have acquired a taste for innocent newspaper girls.'

While Gilmore was noting down the address, an area car drew up outside and two uniformed officers rattled the door handle. Frost let them in. 'Stack of pornographic gear in the back,' he told them. 'Take it and our friend here down to the station and charge him under the Obscene Publications Act.'

Back to the car. Gilmore slammed the door, hoping this would wake up Burton who didn't deserve to sleep after causing all this trouble, but to no avail. He was fastening his seat belt when the damn radio called for the inspector.

Frost reached for the handset as Gilmore slumped back wearily, waiting for the worst.

'Can you do a quick job for me, Inspector?' asked Sergeant Wells.

'No,' replied Frost. 'Gilmore's got to get home. He's left his wife on the boil.'

'It's on your way, Jack. Probably a false alarm. Number 46 Mannington Crescent. A pensioner, Mrs Mary Haynes. She lives there on her own, but yesterday's milk is still on the doorstep and her cat's miaowing like mad inside. The milkman's phoned us. He thinks something might have happened to her. Take a look, would you?'

'This is uniform branch stuff,' snapped Gilmore.

'The only spare car is loaded down with your filthy books,' Wells snapped back.

Frost sighed. 'OK, Bill. We're on our way.'

The houses in Mannington Crescent were just waking up. A milk float was outside number 46. They parked behind it and Frost shuffled over to the milkman and flapped his warrant card.

Relieved at their arrival, the milkman blurted out the details. 'Might be nothing in it, but she's usually so regular. She'd never go away and leave her cat and it's miaowing like hell in there and yesterday's milk is on the step.'

'Couldn't she have run off with the lodger?' yawned Frost, following the man to the doorstep.

'She's seventy-eight years old!' said the milkman.

'Well – hobbled off with the lodger, then?'

'She hasn't got a lodger,' said the milkman.

Frost yawned again. 'Another brilliant theory shot up the arse.' He moved to one side to let Gilmore tackle the door.

Gilmore jammed his finger in the bell push.

'The bell don't work,' said the milkman.

Gilmore hammered at the knocker.

'I've already tried that,' said the milkman.

Ignoring him, Gilmore hammered again. Silence. A look of smug triumph on the milkman's face. 'What did I tell you?'

Across the road a fat woman in a shortie nightie called, 'Milkie! You haven't left me any milk.' The milkman signalled he was coming over and she waddled back into her house, acres of fat bottom wobbling below the hem of her nightdress.

Frost winced. 'It must be my day for horrible sights. You'd better carry on with your round, Milkie. Thanks for phoning.'

'What do you think?' asked Gilmore, who was staring at the Cortina, where Burton, oblivious to all this, was still asleep on the back seat.

Frost looked up and down the street, hoping to see the reassuring sight of a uniformed constable who would take the responsibility from him, but no such luck.

The downstairs window was heavily curtained and held firmly closed by a security catch of some kind. Frost did his letter-box squinting routine, seeing only an empty passage with a pot plant drooping dejectedly on a side table. There was an open purse on the side table, a small bunch of keys alongside it. He straightened up wearily. It looked bad. The old dear certainly wouldn't leave the house without her purse and her keys. 'We'll have to break in.'

Gilmore picked up the bottle of milk from the step and used it to smash one of the coloured glass door panels. He put his hand through and turned the lock. They stepped inside.

The first door they tried led to the kitchen. From

a dark corner two green eyes flashed, then a plaintive mew. Frost took some milk from the fridge, slopped it into a saucer and watched the cat's frantic lappings. He tried the back door, but it was firmly bolted on the inside. Gilmore looked in the other downstairs room, a musty-smelling, rarely used lounge.

The cat finished the milk and waited expectantly, its tail swishing. Frost topped up the saucer. 'Hundred to one she's upstairs, son. Dead in bed. Nip up and take a look.' As Gilmore's footsteps thudded overhead, Frost found a tin opener on the draining board and opened a tin of Felix which he emptied on a plate for the cat.

A sudden yell from Gilmore sent him running. 'Inspector! Up here. Quick!'

She was on the bed. She had been knifed repeatedly in the stomach and her throat was a gaping, open wound. The body was cold. Ice cold.

'I know you've got no-one to send,' Frost told a complaining Sergeant Wells, 'but I want four of them.' He pressed the handset against his chest so he couldn't hear the sergeant insisting this was impossible. 'I can't manage with less than four. I need people knocking on doors before everyone leaves for work. Over and out.' He clicked the switch, cutting off Wells in mid-moan and returned to the house.

Gilmore was waiting for him in the bedroom, anxious to show him a mess of blood on the carpet, hidden behind the open door. A lot of blood. On the floor, a crumpled heap that was her best black coat. 'He was hiding behind the door. He slashed her as she came in to hang up her coat, then dumped her on the bed.'

Frost nodded glumly. Gilmore was probably right, but knowing where he killed her wasn't going to help them catch the bastard. 'Sod that bloody milkman,' he said. 'We could have been in bed and asleep by now.'

Burton thudded up the stairs. He had been sent out to knock on doors. 'Two things, Inspector. A woman across the road says the old lady visited Denton Cemetery every Sunday afternoon to put flowers on her husband's grave. She saw her leave about three. The bloke next door – a Dean Reynold Hoskins – says the old lady knocked him up on Sunday afternoon just after five, all agitated. She reckoned someone had nicked her spare front door key which she kept hidden under the mat in the porch, but when Hoskins looked, there it was.'

'Have you checked to see if it's still there?'

Burton nodded and held up a bagged key. 'Hoskins called her a silly cow and went back to his own house. She kept ranting on about it not being in the same place she'd left it.'

'The poor bitch was right,' said Frost. 'There's no sign of forcible entry, all doors and windows are internally secured. The killer must have let himself in through the front door. He was already in the house.'

Gilmore grunted begrudgingly. He couldn't fault the inspector's logic.

'Right,' continued Frost. 'He got in after she went off to the graveyard at three. He wouldn't have hung about after slicing her up, so we can assume he left fairly soon after five. Knock on more doors. People usually go deaf and blind when there's been a crime but someone must have seen or heard something. And ask if it was general knowledge that she secretly kept a spare key under the mat.'

'Right,' said Burton, swaying slightly.

The poor sod's dead on his feet, thought Frost. 'I've got some more men coming soon, Burton. You can go home when they arrive.'

The detective constable shook his head. 'I can hold on for a while, sir.'

Stifling a yawn, Frost wished there was someone to tell him to go home. He wouldn't refuse. He turned his attention to Gilmore who was waiting to speak.

'I've checked her purse,' Gilmore told him. 'Empty except for a membership card for All Saints Church Senior Citizens' Club and a hospital appointment card. Nothing else in the house appears to be disturbed or taken.'

'A few quid,' said Frost. 'I can't believe the bastard ripped her up for the few quid in her purse.' He let his gaze wander around the bedroom, which smelt stalely of blood and lavender furniture polish. He lit a cigarette and added the smell of tobacco smoke. On the wall above the veneered walnut dressing table hung a framed black and white wedding photograph, the bride in white and the groom in morning dress amidst a snow shower of confetti. That same bride was now in funeral black, eyes wide open and staring up at the yellowing ceiling. Her dress and the bed-cover were rusted with gummy gouts of dried blood.

'That must be her grave-visiting dress,' muttered Frost. Something brushed against his legs. The cat. He leant down and scratched its neck, then put it outside. Crossing to the window he twitched aside the curtain and looked down on the empty street where black clouds kept the morning dark. His head was buzzing. So much to do and he didn't really feel he was capable of handling it.

An area car nosed into the street and stopped outside the house. PC Jordan and two disgruntled-looking detective constables who had thought their shift was over climbed out. A second car brought Roberts, the SOC officer, with his cameras and flash-guns, and hardly had this pulled up when a green Honda Accord brought the two men from Forensic. Gilmore led them all up to take turns to view the body before sending the constables to join Burton, knocking at doors.

'Find out if anyone saw a blue van,' bellowed Frost as they left.

'You haven't touched anything?' asked one of the Forensic men.

'I haven't even touched my dick,' said Frost, giving his well-worn, stock reply.

The door knocker thudded. 'The doctor's here,' called Gilmore, pushing Maltby up the stairs.

'Bit of fresher meat for you this time, doc,' said Frost as a bleary-eyed Maltby, his face flushed, squeezed between the Forensic men into the tiny bedroom.

'I might have guessed it would be you again,' growled Maltby, who seemed to be in a sour mood.

'Three bodies in one shift,' agreed Frost. 'I'm beginning to suspect I'm on *Candid Camera.*'

The doctor grunted and bent over the body. His examination was brief.

'She's dead.'

'I worked that out myself,' said Frost. 'I offered her a fag and she wouldn't reply. When did she die?'

Maltby took a pad from his bag and scribbled something down. 'You've sent for the pathologist, I understand?'

'That's right, doc.'

'Then let him answer your questions. He gets paid a lot more than I do. Found out who's been sending those poison pen letters yet?'

'Blimey, doc,' moaned Frost. 'It was only six hours ago when you last asked me. I haven't even had a pee since then.'

Maltby blinked at the inspector. His eyes didn't seem to be focusing properly. 'Hours ago? Is that all?' He felt for a chair and sat down heavily.

'Are you all right, doc?' asked Frost with concern.

'Yes, yes, of course I'm all right.' He grabbed the inspector's arm and pulled him down, dropping his voice and engulfing Frost in Johnnie Walker fumes. 'Did you know Drysdale's put in a complaint about me, just because I examined that body in the crypt before he did? He phoned me especially to tell me.'

'The man's a bastard, doc,' soothed Frost. He nodded towards the bed. 'How long has she been dead?'

Maltby lurched over to the corpse and prodded the flesh. 'Rigor mortis has come and just about gone. Some time Sunday evening, say. Anything else you want to know, ask Drysdale.' With a sharp snap he closed his bag and bustled off. 'God's here,' he bellowed from half-way down the stairs. A burble of exchanged frigid conversation and the pathologist swept into the bedroom accompanied by his secretary. He stared pointedly at the Forensic men who took the hint and retired downstairs.

'Was that Dr Maltby who just brushed past me?' he sniffed.

Frost nodded.

'And he's been mauling the body about, I suppose?'

'He never touched it,' said Frost. 'He didn't want to spoil your pleasure. If you could speed it up, doc.'

Drysdale gritted his teeth at the 'doc', but his eyes gleamed when he saw the body. He took off his long, black, expensive overcoat and handed it to his secretary. She, in turn, passed the coat over to Frost who screwed it into a ball, dumped it on a chair and sat on it. He shook a cigarette from his packet.

'Please don't smoke,' snapped Drysdale, glad to have the chance of putting this oaf in his place. Methodically he examined every inch of the body, murmuring the results of his findings to the secretary whose pen translated the great man's words into the loops and whirls of Pitman's shorthand.

After fifteen long minutes, ignoring Frost's repeated and over-loud signs of impatience, he straightened up to deliver his verdict. 'She's been dead approximately thirty-six hours.'

'That's what Dr Maltby said,' grunted Frost.

The pathologist smiled thinly. 'Delighted to have my opinion confirmed by such an expert. The pattern of the bloodstains indicates she was standing upright when she was attacked. The killer would have come at her from behind . . .'

Frost wriggled in the chair. The overcoat buttons were biting into him. 'He was waiting for her behind that door, doc. There's a couple of lovely blood puddles there if you want to have a paddle.'

Drysdale allowed himself a brief look, then carried on. 'The killer would have clamped his hand over her mouth – you can see the thumb pressure mark on the left cheek?' He moved away to allow Frost to inspect this if he wished, but Frost declined with a flick of his hand. He didn't need a pathologist to point out something he had noticed as soon as he entered the bedroom.

The pathologist shrugged. 'The killer then stabbed her three times in the abdomen with a knife. The blade would be single-edged, non-flexible, about 6 inches long – and – and razor sharp.'

'Something like a kitchen knife, doctor?' asked Gilmore who had returned after giving instructions to the door-knocking team.

'Could very well be,' accepted Drysdale.

'There was a similar attack last night . . . an old lady in Clarendon Street. He left a knife behind.'

'Clarendon Street?' barked Drysdale. 'Why wasn't I called?'

'You can have first crack at her as soon as she dies,' replied Frost, 'but at the moment she's still alive.' He related the details.

'If you let me examine the knife,' said Drysdale, 'I'll do some tests to confirm whether it could be the same weapon used to inflict these wounds.'

Frost scribbled a reminder about the knife on his discredited car expenses. 'I'll get it sent over. Carry on, doc. I'm sure you and your secretary want to get back to your bed . . . er, beds.'

Not noticing Frost's lewd wink to Gilmore, Drysdale continued. 'The killer jerked back her head, pushed the tip of the blade into her throat just there.' His thumb pointed to the left-hand side of the gaping wound. 'He twisted the knife so the blade was horizontal – that's why the wound is much wider at that point, then slashed open her throat from left to right.'

Frost yawned openly. The pathologist was making a damn meal of this. She was stabbed from behind and dumped on the bed. He'd deduced that himself within seconds. 'Would he have got blood on his clothes?'

'Yes. Possibly on his upper left arm, but almost certainly a considerable amount of blood from the throat would have gushed on to his right hand – the knife hand – and the sleeve of his coat or whatever he was wearing. He also stepped into the pool of blood when he carried the body across to the bed. You can see the imprints on the carpet.'

'You mean the ones Forensic have ringed round in chalk? Yes, we did spot them, doc.'

'How did blood get there?' asked Gilmore, pointing to a patch of discoloration on the left-hand sleeve of the black dress. 'That doesn't fit in with any of the wounds.'

Annoyed that he had missed it, the pathologist studied the mark. 'That's where he wiped the blade clean of blood.' He straightened up. 'That's all I can tell you for now, Inspector. You'll have a full report when I have completed the post-mortem.' He looked around the room. 'Has anyone seen my overcoat?'

The body had been carefully placed in a cheap coffin and man-handled down the narrow staircase for transport to the mortuary. The Forensic team had departed with their spoils and Frost, alone in the empty bedroom, sat moodily dragging at a cigarette and staring down at bare floorboards. All the bedding had been stripped from the bed and the carpet and underfelt removed for examination.

He stubbed out his cigarette in one of the little glass dishes on the dressing table. The young bride in the photograph, her face wreathed in smiles, beamed down happily through the shower of confetti to the stripped, bleak room where she died, alone and terrified.

He wandered downstairs, his feet clattering on the bare wood where the stair carpet had been taken away for examination. Gilmore and Burton and two of the uniformed men were in the kitchen drinking tea. 'Any joy with the neighbours?'

'No reply from most of the houses,' said Burton, handing him a mug. 'Probably gone to work. We'll have to try again tonight. Three people saw someone suspicious hanging around yesterday afternoon.'

Frost's head came up hopefully. 'Did you get a description?'

'I got three descriptions,' Burton ruefully admitted. 'All different. One medium build, darkish hair who may or may not have a beard aged between thirty and fifty. He was walking up and down the street just after two, staring at windows. The next was a skinhead on a motor bike who kept going round and round the block and the third was a West Indian in a dark suit.'

'And what did the West Indian do to arouse suspicion?' asked Gilmore.

'He just walked by, Sarge, minding his own business. I don't think the lady I spoke to liked West Indians.'

Frost sipped his tea. It was lukewarm. 'It'll be a waste of time, but check them out anyway. Have we traced any relatives, or anyone who might be able to tell us if anything's been pinched apart from her purse money?'

'Not yet,' answered Gilmore. 'I'll check with that senior citizens' club she belonged to. They might be able to help.'

'Good. What sort of woman was she? Did she get on well with the neighbours?'

Burton shook his head. 'A cantankerous old biddy by all accounts, always finding something to complain about. No-one liked her much.'

'We'll have to find out what she's been complaining about recently. Perhaps someone resented it enough to kill her.' He looked around. 'Where's the moggie?'

'The RSPCA bloke has taken it away,' Gilmore told him.

'I expect the little bleeder will have to be put down,' gloomed Frost, swilling down the dregs of tea and pulling a face as if it were bitter medicine. 'Tell me something to cheer me up.'

'Forensic found a few alien prints dotted about,' offered Gilmore. 'One looked very hopeful.'

'It'll be from the sanitary inspector or her family planning adviser, anyone but the killer.' He stood up and stretched. 'I'm too tired to think straight.' He glanced across to Gilmore who was grey with fatigue. 'Let's call it a day. We'll have a couple of hours' kip, then back to the station at noon.'

Noon! The detective sergeant sneaked a look at his watch. That would give him about three hours' sleep if he was lucky. He hoped Liz wouldn't be awake, waiting up for him, spoiling for a row.

He sat tense in the car as Frost drove him back after dropping off Burton, expecting every radio message to be the one sending them out on yet another case. But none of its messages were for them, although one call rang a familiar bell. 'Neighbours complaining of strange smells coming from 76 Jubilee Terrace.'

'Must have been your aftershave,' muttered Frost as the tyres scraped the kerb outside 42 Merchant Street. He had to shake Gilmore awake.

The house was quiet when Gilmore got in. A plate of cold, congealed food stood accusingly on the dining room table. His supper. He scraped the food into the waste bin and dropped the plate in the sink.

Upstairs, Liz was sleeping. Even in repose her face was angry. He undressed and crawled into bed beside her, moving carefully for fear he would wake her and the row would start. Almost immediately he plunged into an uneasy sleep, full of dreams of bodies bleeding from knife wounds and all looking like Liz.

Frost slammed the car into gear and headed for home and bed. He nearly made it.

'Control to Mr Frost. Come in, please!'

The plumber. The suspect in the Paula Bartlett case. Able Baker had picked him up. They were holding him at the station.

'On my way,' said Frost, spinning the wheel for an

114

illegal U-turn, deaf to the shouts from a minicab driver who had to brake violently to avoid a collision.

Tuesday morning shift (2)

Superintendent Mullett strode briskly into the station, pausing only to remove and shake the rain from his tailored raincoat. At 9.30 in the morning the lobby had a tired, slept-in look, which reminded him that he wanted to have a few words with Frost to ascertain his progress with the Paula Bartlett case.

'Mr Frost in yet, Sergeant?'

'No, sir,' replied Wells, barely managing to camouflage a yawn. 'He's out on another fatal stabbing – an old lady in Mannington Crescent.'

Mullett's forehead creased in anguish. 'Oh no!'

'Nasty one by all accounts,' continued Wells. 'Stomach ripped and throat cut.'

'Send the inspector to me the minute he comes in, Sergeant. Do you know if he left a report for me on the Paula Bartlett case? I've got a press conference at two.'

'I haven't seen one, sir.'

Mullett sighed his annoyance. 'How can I answer press questions if I'm not kept informed? It just isn't good enough.'

'We're all overworked, sir,' said Wells.

'Excuses, excuses . . . all I hear are excuses.' His eyes flicked from side to side, doing a brisk inspection of the lobby. 'This floor could do with a sweep, Sergeant.'

'Yes, sir,' agreed Wells, swaying slightly from side to

side, trying to give his impression of a loyal, dedicated policeman almost dead on his feet from overwork. 'The thing is, with this flu epidemic . . .'

'We mustn't use that as an excuse to lower standards, Sergeant. This lobby is our shop window. The first thing the public see when they come in. A clean lobby is an efficient lobby . . . it inspires confidence.' He paused and stared hard at the Sergeant. 'You haven't shaved this morning. A fine example to set the men.'

In vain Wells tried to explain about the double shift and that his relief sergeant was down with the virus, but Mullett wasn't prepared to become involved in the trivial details of station house-keeping. 'Excuses are easy to make, Sergeant. Those of us fortunate enough to escape the flu virus must work all the harder. Standards must be maintained.'

Waiting until the door closed behind his Divisional Commander, Wells permitted himself the luxury of an impotent, two-fingered gesture.

'I saw that, Sergeant!' rasped the unmistakable voice of the Chief Constable.

Wells spun round, horrified, then flopped into his chair, almost sweating with relief. Grinning at him from the lobby doorway was Jack Frost who had been hovering in the background, waiting for Mullett to leave.

'You frightened the flaming life out of me, Jack.'

'The man of a thousand voices but only one dick. So what's been happening?'

'Well, I've been working all bleeding night . . .'

'Excuses, excuses, Sergeant . . . give me the facts, man.' He pushed a cigarette across and lit it for Wells.

'Rickman's given us a statement.'

'Who's he?'

'The porno video merchant. Says he bought them from

a man in a pub . . . didn't know his name. We've released him on police bail.'

'What about my plumber?'

'Interview Room number two.'

'Thanks,' said Frost, making for the swing doors. He paused. 'This floor could do with a sweep, Sergeant.'

'I'll get you a broom,' grinned Wells. The internal phone rang. Bloody Mullett again. Wells' expression changed. 'The canteen's closed, sir. I haven't got anyone who can make your tea.' He jiggled the receiver, then slammed the phone down. Not interested in excuses, Mullett had hung up.

Outside the interview room an excited Detective Sergeant Arthur Hanlon ran forward to meet Frost. 'We could be on to something here, Jack.' He opened the door a crack so the inspector could see inside. A fat, balding man with shifty eyes in his mid-forties was slouched in a chair. He wore dark blue overalls over a beer belly.

'He's guilty,' said Frost. 'Never mind a trial, just hang him.'

Carefully closing the door, Hanlon continued. 'Bernard Hickman, forty-four years old, married, no children. The day Paula went missing, Hickman was supposed to be working in the cemetery, installing that new stand-pipe by the side of the crypt. His time sheet says he started work at eight, but the vicar is positive he didn't arrive until gone nine.' He opened a folder to show Frost the time sheet.

'Where does he live?'

'63 Vicarage Terrace, Denton.'

Frost chewed this over. The area where Paula went missing was north of Denton Woods. Vicarage Terrace was some four or five miles to the south. 'Has he got a motor?'

'Yes. It's in the car-park.'

Then Hickman could have driven and forced the girl into his car, raped and killed her and got to the cemetery by nine. But what was he doing north of the woods in the first place? The cemetery was in the opposite direction.

'It wasn't a chance encounter,' suggested Hanlon. 'It was planned. He'd seen the girl before and lusted after her. He knew where she'd be and waited for her.'

'Lusted after her?' said Frost, doubtfully. 'Why her? The poor cow was a pudding.'

'There's no accounting for taste, Jack. Some men lust after the ugliest of women.'

Frost looked reproachful. 'That's no way to talk of the Divisional Commander's wife.' Hanlon froze in mid-laugh, alerting the inspector to danger.

'Inspector!'

And there was Mullett charging down the corridor. Please don't let him have heard, pleaded Frost as he slid into his guileless smile. 'Sir?'

'Where's your report for me on the Paula Bartlett case? I've got a press conference at two.'

'Just about to interview a suspect now,' said Frost, jerking his head at the interview room.

Mullett's eyes gleamed. 'A suspect? Already? Marvellous. That's just marvellous. If we can tie this up in time for the press conference . . .' He beamed at the two men, then his expression hardened as Hanlon took out a handkerchief and blew his nose loudly. 'I hope you're not going down with this flu thing, Hanlon?' he snapped accusingly. 'We're enough men short as it is.' He turned on his heel and stamped off down the corridor.

'You can't even blow your blinking nose, now,' moaned Hanlon.

'Don't breath your filthy germs over me,' said Frost. 'Let's question our suspect.'

Hickman shifted his position in the hard, uncomfortable chair and stared unblinkingly at the nervous young uniformed constable, forcing him to look away. He smirked to himself, proud of his small triumph. 'I could smash you with one hand,' he leered.

'Not if we handcuffed you first and gave him a truncheon,' said a voice.

The tubby bloke had returned with a grotty-looking man in a shiny suit.

'Detective Inspector Frost,' announced the man, dropping into the chair opposite Hickman. 'Like to ask you a few questions.'

'I'd like to ask you one,' said Hickman. 'Why am I here? Or is it a state secret?'

'You're here,' Frost told him, 'because we're investigating a very serious matter. I hope we can eliminate you from our enquiries, but if we can't, you're in dead trouble. So just answer my questions.'

'Then ask,' said Hickman. 'Let's get this bloody farce over.'

'September 14th. I want to know everything you did. From when you got up, to when you went to bed.'

'That's over two months ago. How the hell can I remember that?'

'Perhaps this will jog your memory,' said Frost, pushing over a sheet of paper.

Hickman took the time sheet and stared at it in disbelief. 'So this is what it's all about? I fiddle an hour on my time sheet and the bastards call in the flaming Flying Squad! They can stuff their job . . .'

'Your firm didn't call us in,' Frost told him, 'and it's a darn sight more serious than fiddling your time sheet. Tell me what you did on that day.'

'I was working at All Saints Cemetery, fitting a new stand-pipe. They were extending the burial section so the old piping had to be rerouted. On that day – it was a Thursday, I think – I'm ready to drive to work when the flaming car dies on me. I fiddle about with it – no joy. So I have to call in a mobile mechanic and walk to work. I got there an hour late, but it wasn't my fault so why should I let the firm have the benefit?'

'We'll want the name and address of the mechanic.' said Hanlon.

'I've got it at home. Anyway, I worked until half-past twelve, nipped across to the pub for lunch, came back for more work and finished at six.'

'So you were at the cemetery from nine until six,' checked Frost. 'Then what?'

'In the pub for a few more drinks, home for dinner, then back to the pub until closing time. Supper at eleven, then bed, a bit of the other, and sleep.'

'How can you be so sure about the bit of the other?' asked Frost with genuine interest.

'I'm a creature of habit. Every night without fail whether she wants it or not.'

Frost lit a cigarette and dribbled smoke from his nose. 'How old is your wife?'

'Forty-two.'

'Ever fancied a younger bit of stuff?'

'Like bleeding hell, I have,' giggled the man. 'Trouble is, they never fancy me.'

'Big chap like you,' said Frost, 'that shouldn't be a

problem. You could force them to do what you wanted – whether they wanted to or not.'

Hickman's eyes narrowed. 'I don't think I'm getting your drift.'

From a green folder Frost removed a colour photograph and slid it across the table. 'Do you know her?'

Hickman stared down at the serious, unsmiling face of Paula Bartlett. 'Never seen her before . . .' Then he recognized her. 'Bloody hell! It's that kid!' Then he realized the implication and sprang up, sending the chair flying. 'Just what the flaming hell are you accusing me of?'

A nervous PC Collier moved forward to restrain the man and was relieved when Frost waved him back. Frost snatched up the photograph and thrust it under Hickman's nose. He spoke slowly and calmly. 'I've just come from her post-mortem. I haven't yet plucked up the courage to tell her parents what's been done to her. So, no matter how loudly you scream and shout and bluster, you're going to answer my bloody questions. Now sit down!'

His face sullen, Hickman pushed the photograph away and lowered himself into the chair.

'That's better,' said Frost, beaming disarmingly. 'Now tell us why we found fingerprints all over the inside of the crypt which match the fingerprints on your time sheet.' No fingerprints had been found inside the crypt, but Hickman wasn't to know.

'The crypt? Is that where you found her?' He leant back in his chair and smirked. 'If I wanted to rape someone, I'd pick somewhere more romantic than a flaming coffin store.'

Frost's eyes narrowed. 'Who said she'd been raped?'

'I'm not stupid. What have you been asking me questions about sex for if she hadn't been bloody raped?'

'And what were you doing in the crypt in the first place?'

'About eleven o'clock we had this dirty great bleeding thunderstorm. Didn't last long but it was bucketing down. There was no cover and I was getting drenched. I thought the crypt was a tool shed or something, so I forced out the screws with a claw hammer and stood inside the door. When the rain stopped, I hammered the screws back in and went on with my work.'

'What do you think, Jack?' asked Hanlon while Hickman's statement was being typed, ready for his signature.

'I've got an awful feeling the sod's innocent. We'll have to let him go for now, but check every bit of his story out. I want confirmation that his car was up the spout that day, witnesses who saw him working in the bone yard that day, and I want you to find out if it was peeing down with rain like he said.'

'He knew about the rape,' said Hanlon.

'He thought she was raped in the crypt,' said Frost, 'but she was already dead and bagged when she was dumped there. He's our only suspect, but I don't think he did it – so let's go and wipe the smile off our Divisional Commander's face.'

Mullett pulled his overflowing in-tray towards him and flicked through the contents. No sign of the promised amended car expenses from Frost but a complicated-looking batch of multi-coloured forms from County requesting a detailed inventory of the station. He shook his head in dismay. County did pick the worst possible time for their returns. A tap at the door. He straightened his back, smoothed his hair and called, 'Enter.'

A disgruntled-looking Sergeant Wells came in with

Mullett's cup of tea which he banged down rather heavily on the desk. 'Could I have a word with you, sir?'

Mullett's face fell. No more moans from the sergeant, he hoped. Everyone was overworked, but the solution was to buckle down and do that little bit extra, not keep whining about it all the time. He forced a creaky smile and pointed to the chair for Wells to sit.

The phone rang. Mullett glared at it, then frowned at Wells. He had specifically asked that all his calls be held. Wasn't there anyone capable of obeying a simple order? 'Mullett,' he snapped, but immediately his expression changed, his back went straighter than straight and his free hand was adjusting his tie. The caller was the Chief Constable. 'How are we coping, sir? Well – you've seen our manning figures . . . Yes, I appreciate Shelwood Division are in the same position as us . . . I see, sir . . . Well, if Shelwood can cope, then so can we . . .'

Wells gave a silent groan. The Chief Constable was playing Denton off against neighbouring Shelwood, knowing both Divisional Commanders were at daggers drawn in rivalry, each striving to be next in line for promotion.

Mullett swarmed on. 'Yes, sir, this epidemic has hit us pretty badly too, but thanks to . . .' and he gave a modest cough, 'good leadership, marvellous team work and . . .' He raised his voice and shot a significant glance across to Sergeant Wells. '. . . uncomplaining co-operation from the full team, we're coping extremely well.' He swivelled his chair around and lowered his voice. 'Sorry if I sound a mite ragged, sir, but I've been up half the night. You've heard we've found Paula Bartlett's body?'

'Stinking to high heaven and raped.'

Mullett cringed. He hadn't heard Frost come in. He spun his chair round and signalled frantically to the inspector to be silent. 'Apparently the poor child was sexually assaulted, sir, although I don't have the full details at the moment.' He glared to let Frost know whose fault this was. 'However, we do have a suspect . . .'

'No, we don't,' called Frost. 'I've let him go.'

Mullett clamped his hand over the mouthpiece and his eyes spat fire. 'Keep quiet,' he hissed. Back to the phone. 'Events seem to be moving faster than I thought, sir. I'll come back to you.' He smiled sycophantically until the receiver was safely back on its rest, then the smile snapped off. 'You will not make comments when I am on the phone,' he snarled at Frost.

'Sorry, Super. I didn't want you to make a prat of yourself with the Chief Constable.'

The inspector didn't sound sorry and Mullett was irked to note the lighted cigarette wiggling in the man's mouth. He expected people to ask permission before smoking in his office. In Frost's case that permission would have been refused, but that wasn't the point. However, he would see what Wells wanted first.

'Sergeant Johnson is still away. I'm doing double shifts and I'm on again tonight, sir. It's getting a bit much.'

Mullett tried to look sympathetic. 'Don't talk to me about double shifts, Sergeant. It goes without saying that no-one works harder than I do . . .' He paused. He thought he heard a snort of derision from Frost. But the innocent look on the man's face suggested he was wrong. 'If Shelwood Division can cope without extra help, then so can we.' He raised a hand to silence the sergeant's protest. 'A little extra uncomplaining effort and we'll come out with flying colours. If you've got any problems, any worries, come straight to me. My door is always open.' He beamed at the sergeant. 'Perhaps you'd close it as you leave.'

Wells opened his mouth to reply, but thought better of it and accepted his dismissal. He resisted the temptation to slam the door behind him.

Without waiting to be asked, Frost slid into the vacated chair and yawned loudly, not bothering to cover his mouth. What a pig the man is, thought Mullett. 'How are you coping?' he asked.

'We're not coping,' said Frost. 'We're struggling and sinking bloody fast.'

'Shelwood . . .' began Mullett.

'Sod Shelwood Division,' chopped in Frost. 'Shelwood haven't got three major murder enquiries on the go.'

Mullett breathed on the lenses of his glasses and polished them carefully. With his glasses off, the blurred image of Frost didn't look quite so scruffy. But when he replaced them, there was the man, creased, crumpled and slovenly in sharp focus. 'The reason we are not coping, Inspector, is because of sloppiness and inefficiency.'

'You're doing your best, sir,' said Frost generously.

Mullett glared. 'No-one can accuse me of inefficiency, Frost. I prepare the rotas, but no-one sticks to them. I never know who is on duty and who isn't. We've got to organize ourselves . . . allocate the tasks, use our resources to the best advantage. I've prepared new duty rosters.' He pushed a neatly typed list across the desk. 'And they will be strictly adhered to. I will not tolerate any deviation . . . any excuses.'

Frost picked up the roster and studied it. Like most of Mullett's edicts, it was beautifully laid out, but would be impossible to adhere to.

'We'll all have to work that little bit harder,' cajoled the superintendent, 'but it won't be for long. Mr Allen will be off the sick list next week and you'll hand the Paula Bartlett case back to him. Other men are coming off the sick list all the time.' He flashed his 'be reasonable' smile. 'It will only be for a few days.'

Right, you sod, thought Frost. We'll play it your way. He yawned and heaved himself up. 'I see from the roster I'm off duty, so I'll slope off home and get some kip.'

'Wait!' Mullett waved him back to his chair. 'I need an update on the cases you are working on.' He listened distastefully as Frost spared him none of the gory details of the stabbing and the post-mortem. 'One victim's still alive – so it's only two murders.'

'She's eighty-one,' said Frost, 'and her skull's fractured. The hospital don't reckon she'll pull through. I'm anticipating on this one.'

Mullett clenched his fist angrily. 'Catching this swine must be our number one priority, even to the exclusion of other cases.' He pulled his notepad towards him. 'I'm holding a press conference at two on the Paula Bartlett case. No joy with your plumber?'

'Not unless we can pick holes in his story, and I don't think we will.'

'A pity,' said Mullett pointedly, as if it was Frost's fault. 'Have you told the parents yet that she was raped? I don't want them to find out from the media.'

Damn! thought Frost. He'd completely forgotten this aspect. 'No, sir. I don't want to sod up your nice new roster, so as I'm off duty I'll leave that for you.'

The Parker pen doodled in the air and dotted an imaginary 'i'. 'I'd do it willingly, Inspector. But you've got their confidence. They don't want a stranger breaking such bad news. I'll leave that in your capable hands.'

Frost smiled his 'you bastard!' smile. 'Of course, sir.'

Mullett studied his list. 'Only one case demands urgent attention. This maniac with the knife. He's got to be caught before he kills again. That's the case we deploy our manpower on. The rest can go on the back burner until we're back to full strength.'

'But what about Paula Bartlett?' protested Frost. 'She's been murdered and raped – do we stick her on the back burner?'

Mullett nodded emphatically. 'She's been dead for over two months. The trail's gone cold. Waiting a week until Mr Allen returns is sensible and won't make the slightest bit of difference.' At Frost's continued hesitation, he added, 'It's a question of priorities, Inspector. Face facts! We haven't the manpower to handle more than one major investigation. By concentrating our resources, I'm looking forward to an early arrest.'

Frost pulled a cigarette stub from behind his ear and poked it in his mouth. 'I'll give it a whirl,' he muttered doubtfully. He wasn't happy at back-pedalling on the school kid. His every instinct screamed for him to go all out to find the bastard responsible. But Hornrim Harry was right for once. They didn't have the resources for more than one big case and they weren't going to get any help from County.

'Good man!' Mullett smoothed his moustache with his two forefingers. 'But we must keep a high profile with the public. We mustn't let them know we are marking time on the Bartlett case.' His eyes gleamed and he snapped his fingers triumphantly. 'I've got it! There's a video somewhere that Mr Allen had made when the girl first went missing. I'm sure we could get the TV companies to run it again.' The video showed a Paula Bartlett look-alike, wearing similar clothes and riding the identical bike along the route of Paula's newspaper round. It was hoped it would jog someone's memory, but it hadn't been successful. As Paula did her round every day, same route, same time, there was much confusion in the minds of people who had come forward as to the actual day they had seen her. The usual reports of strange men in slow-moving dark cars, but none of the leads had led anywhere.

'If it didn't work when memories were fresh, I can't see it working two months later,' said Frost, 'but I'll arrange it if you like. I could do an appeal to the public.'

'Leave it all to me,' cut in Mullett hastily. 'You've got far too much to do.' There was no way he was going to let Frost appear on TV, slouching in front of the cameras in that terrible suit, retrieving half-smoked cigarettes from behind his ear. He beamed at Frost. 'See the parents, then go and get some sleep. And remember, we concentrate only on vital things. Nothing else matters.'

Frost had almost reached the door when Mullett called him back, waving the complicated inventory return from his in-tray. 'You might fit this in when you have an odd moment, Inspector.'

Frost's gave the return a dubious stare. 'It doesn't look vital to me.'

Mullett's smile didn't waver. 'Shouldn't take you long, now that I've lightened your work load. County want it back this week.'

County can bleeding want, thought Frost morosely as he walked back to his office. He buried the inventory return in his in-tray, screwed up the new duty roster and hurled it at the waste bin, then kicked shut the door and sank wearily into his chair. In two minutes he was fast asleep.

Tuesday afternoon shift

Frost, cold and stiff from an uncomfortable sleep, staggered into the Murder Incident Room where Gilmore and Burton, seated at adjacent desks behind mounds of green folders, barely gave him a glance. They were transferring details from the folders on to roneoed forms which were then collected by WPC Jill Knight who fed them into the computer for collation.

A large-scale map of Denton, well-studded with coloured pins, had been fixed to the wall alongside the computer and Frost wandered over to take a look at it. The pins marked the scenes of all the recent senior citizen burglaries. On the far wall hung the map compiled by Inspector Allen showing the route of Paula Bartlett's last paper round. A newly added black thumb tack pin-pointed the crypt where the body was found. A beefy little blonde WPC brought in another armful of green folders and dumped them on the desk.

'You seem to have things well organized,' said Frost.

'Someone had to do it,' grunted Gilmore who was in a sour mood. A little over three hours' sleep and then treated to a dose of Liz whining and moaning at being left on her own so much and then, when he reported for duty, he had found Frost sprawled asleep in his office without having done a damn thing about getting the Murder Incident Room set up.

'Thanks,' acknowledged Frost. Organization was not his strongest point. 'Well, the good news is that according to Mr Mullett's new roster, we're all off duty until tonight.

The bad news is, we're far too busy to sod about with his rubbish.' He wandered across to Burton and Gilmore, both occupied with their green folders. 'What's all this in aid of?' He dropped a cigarette on each desk, then poured himself a mug of tea from Burton's thermos.

Gilmore looked up from his folders. 'I'm initiating a computer program. What it does . . .'

Frost's hand shot up. If it was to do with computers, then he didn't want to know. 'Please don't explain how it works, son, then I won't have to pretend I understand what you're talking about.'

But Gilmore explained anyway. 'We're feeding the computer with details from all the recent break-ins and burglaries and attacks involving senior citizens to see if we can build up some sort of pattern . . . why did the burglar pick on them, and so on.'

Frost peered over Jill Knight's shoulder, watching the cursor fly across the monitor screen, leaving a complicated trail of facts and figures. 'Any pattern emerging so far?'

'A lot of the victims seem to belong to senior citizens' clubs,' she told him.

'Perhaps that's the sort of club that senior citizens join,' said Frost, unimpressed. He flicked through a file half-heartedly, then pushed it away and jabbed a finger at Burton. 'You were going to check with the vicar about Mary Haynes.'

'I left a report on your desk,' protested Burton.

'You know I don't read reports. Tell me what it said.'

'She'd been a member of the church senior citizens' club for nearly six years. No relatives as far as the vicar knows. She kept herself to herself, never invited anyone back to her place and didn't have any close friends.'

'That wouldn't have been worth reading a report for,' commented Frost moodily.

'There's more,' continued Burton. 'She visited her husband's grave at the cemetery on Sunday . . .'

Frost's head shot up. The cemetery. That reminded him. 'Get the car out – we've got to give her parents the good news that their daughter was raped.'

'If I could finish,' said Burton. 'Her husband's grave had been vandalized . . . swear words sprayed on with an aerosol. She had a row with the vicar about it. She was always having rows. I've started a list of people she quarrelled with, but it's all trivial stuff.'

'Follow it through anyway,' said Frost. 'Did anyone spot our famous blue van?'

'No-one so far.'

A sudden thought. Something else he had forgotten. 'Damn! We should have asked dry-cleaners to look out for bloodstained clothing.'

'Already in hand,' said Gilmore, smugly.

A messenger entered with a large envelope and a package for Frost. He ripped it open. The post-mortem reports from the pathologist, beautifully typed by his loyal secretary on expensive paper. Frost flipped open the first and skipped through it. It was for the suicide, the kid in the Mickey Mouse night-shirt, Susan Bicknell. Drysdale's usual thorough job. He hadn't missed the marks of the beating, but reported them without comment. His sole concern was the cause of death which was confirmed as barbiturate poisoning, probably self-inflicted. Signs of recent intercourse, but she was not pregnant.

He gave the file to Gilmore who studied it grimly. 'She didn't kill herself because she was up the spout, son.'

'Then why did she?'

'We'll probably never know.' Frost opened up the other folder. 'I hope everyone's had their lunch – because it's stomach contents time.' He quickly read the typed sheet. 'Isn't science wonderful? She's been dead two months, yet they can tell us she died within half an hour of knocking back chicken and mushroom pie, chips and peas and – wait for it – a dollop of brown sauce.'

The plump blonde WPC pulled a face. 'I had that for dinner yesterday.'

'If you get raped and strangled, we'll know there's a connection.' He studied the report again. 'Paula must have had another meal. She'd never have eaten all that for breakfast.'

'She was a growing girl,' suggested Burton. 'You'd be surprised what kids eat these days.'

'She died within half an hour of eating,' Frost reminded him. 'The meal wasn't fully digested. I saw it. I can show it to you if you don't believe me.' At Burton's shuddering refusal, he continued. 'If she had eaten it at home, she would have to be dead by half-past seven.'

'We've got a witness who saw her at 8.15,' said Burton.

'Either the witness is lying, or mistaken, or Paula had another meal. A hot, cooked meal.' He opened up the package. 'I hope this isn't the bloody stomach contents.' They backed away as he plunged his hand inside but it was a polythene bag he pulled out. Inside were the shoes found on the body. He gave them to the blonde WPC and asked her to send them to Forensic. And that reminded him. 'Bloody hell – I forgot to ask Forensic to send Drysdale the knife from last night's stabbing.'

'Already done,' said Gilmore. What an inefficient lout the man was.

Frost nodded his thanks. Naked, but wearing shoes. Ate a hot meal. You couldn't force a kid to eat. She must have gone willingly with her killer and that tended to rule the bald plumber out. But Mullett said they shouldn't spend time on this case. Leave it for whizz-kid Allen. Sod Mullett. He'd do things his way. 'Come on, the pair of you,' he told Gilmore and Burton. 'Let's drive over the route she took for her paper round.'

There were a number of strange cars in the car-park. Of course. Mullett's press conference must be in full swing. Mullett would be telling them all about the suspected rape and he hadn't broken the news to Paula's parents yet. 'We'll call on them first,' he said. 'Let's get it bloody over.'

Burton waited in the car and watched Gilmore and the inspector make the short dash through the rain to the Bartletts' house. The girl's father, who answered their knock, was stooped and grey-faced and seemed to have aged some ten years since the previous night. He showed them into the living-room where his wife sat staring into empty space. She forced a ghost-smile of greeting. Frost stood uneasily by the door, not knowing how to begin.

'Would you like a cup of tea?' Mr Bartlett asked them.

'We'd love one,' Frost replied, hoping the mother would leave the room to make it. He wanted her out of the way while he broke the news of the sexual assault to her husband. But she sat, staring, unseeing, and didn't move.

Her husband touched her shoulder. 'Tea for you, love?' She shook her head.

Frost left Gilmore to keep the woman silent company and followed the man into the kitchen. Bartlett filled an electric kettle from the tap. 'She's been like this ever since we heard.'

'There's something I must tell you,' said Frost. He

steeled himself to deliver the blow. The father steeled himself to receive it. 'Your daughter was sexually assaulted before she died.'

The hand holding the kettle shook violently, splashing water all over the tiled floor. Gently, Frost took it from him and guided him towards a chair. Sobs racked the father's body.

His face sharing the man's pain, Frost could only watch and wonder what the hell to say next. The sobbing brought Mrs Bartlett into the kitchen. She cradled her husband's head in her arms and held him tight. 'What is it, love?' But head bowed, tears streaming, he couldn't answer. She looked enquiringly at Frost who had to force the words out again.

'I had to tell him that . . . that Paula was raped.'

Husband and wife clung together, clutching each other like young lovers, saying nothing, their closeness consoling each other. Ignored by them both, Frost fidgeted and wished he was miles away. 'If it's any consolation,' he told them, 'your daughter was a virgin.' Why the bloody hell did he say that? What possible consolation could it be that your daughter was a virgin before some bastard raped and choked the life out of her? He became aware that the father, his tears now of anger, was shouting at him.

'Of course she was a virgin. She was only fifteen. A kid. She'd had no bloody life . . .' And then he was sobbing again.

Hastily, Frost excused himself. 'I'll be in the other room.' In the living-room Gilmore, uncomfortable in a too-low chair, raised an eyebrow in query. 'I sodded it up,' Frost told him. 'It's the wailing bleeding wall out there.' He flopped into a chair. No sign of an ashtray, but he had to have a smoke. He lit one up, offering the pack to Gilmore who declined.

Barely two puffs later the woman was back, her eyes red. She seemed surprised that they were still there. He pinched out the cigarette and stood up. 'Two more things, Mrs Bartlett.' She looked apprehensive. What further horrors could he inflict? 'It's just that we're repeating the video made when Paula first went missing. It'll be shown on the television news tonight.'

She nodded, relieved that it was nothing worse.

'And – just for the record. Can you tell me what Paula ate on that last morning?'

'Cornflakes and toast.'

'You're sure? She wouldn't have cooked herself anything?'

'Oh no. I was down here with her . . . cornflakes and toast. That's all she ever had for breakfast.' As they moved to the front door, she clutched the inspector's arm. 'When can we put her to rest?'

At first he didn't understand what she meant, then realized she was asking about the funeral. 'Not for a while, love,' he said.

'I'd like to see her,' said Mrs Bartlett, her eyes blinking earnestly behind her glasses.

'No, love,' said Frost firmly.

'Please . . .' She gripped so tightly, it hurt.

He gently disentangled her fingers from his sleeve. 'She wouldn't want you to see her as she is now, Mrs Bartlett.'

'I don't care how she looks. She's my daughter. She's my daughter . . .!'

Her shouts followed them to the car. With the car door closed she stood in the doorway, still shouting, but they could only hear the rain thudding on the car roof. Then her husband appeared and led her back into the house.

'That wasn't an unqualified success, was it?' sighed Frost, sticking the cigarette end back in his mouth. 'She had cornflakes for breakfast, Burton. What do you deduce from that?'

'That you were right, sir. She must have had another meal after she was abducted,' replied the detective constable.

'Precisely.' He scratched the match down the car window. 'You're a fifteen-year-old virgin, Burton. You've been abducted and taken somewhere. Would you have an appetite for chicken pie, peas and chips?'

'It depends how long I'd been without food. She might have been held for hours without having anything to eat.'

Frost thought this over and nodded. 'Cooked food, so it's got to be indoors. And if he's keeping the girl hidden there for any length of time, he's got to be alone in the house. Lastly, to get her from his car to the house, he must be pretty certain he won't be seen. Which means the house has got to be remote.' He blew the end of his cigarette and watched it glow. 'The schoolmaster who usually gave her a lift. Is his house remote?'

Burton nodded. 'It's all on its own – miles from anywhere.'

'Then we've got the bastard.'

'What are you suggesting?' asked Gilmore who was feeling left out of the discussion. This was typical Frost, plucking a suspect from thin air, then forcing the facts to fit.

'I'm suggesting that bloody schoolmaster met her in his car and took her back to his house.'

'The schoolmaster was at his wife's funeral that day,' Burton reminded him.

'This was around eight in the morning. The funeral wouldn't have been until ten at the earliest.'

'But he didn't have to go in the car and fetch her,' said

Burton. 'She was due to call at his house with the paper anyway.'

'He was impatient,' said Frost, stubbornly. 'Burning for a bit of the other and couldn't wait.'

'So impatient,' scoffed Gilmore, 'that he gives her chicken pie, peas and chips at eight o'clock in the morning before he has it away with her and then trots off to his wife's funeral.'

Frost sank down in the car seat and expelled smoke. 'All right, so that's shot that theory up the arse. But I'd still like to have a word with this schoolmaster. Do you know where he lives, Burton?'

Burton nodded.

'Then take us there. Follow the route the girl went. Point out the houses where she delivered. Show me where her bike was found.'

Burton backed out of Medway Road and cut through some side streets. Gilmore tried to orientate himself, but soon got lost. And then, after a few minutes, the area looked familiar and the car was splashing through Merchant Street. He looked up as the house flashed by, noting that the bedroom curtains were still drawn. Liz would be sleeping, making sure she would be fully refreshed, ready to renew her moaning when he finished his shift. God, what a cynic he was becoming. How he hated this lousy little town.

The car juddered over cobbles as it negotiated a steep hill, then cut through the market place, empty of shoppers in the heavy rain. The houses they passed became fewer and further between and soon they were skirting the woods.

'She made her first deliveries here,' said Burton as they crawled past a small, walled estate of some forty houses and maisonettes built by the New Town Development

Corporation. 'You don't want to see the individual houses, do you?'

'No,' replied Frost, 'just a general outline of the route.'

They left the estate and drove on to the Forest View area where old Victorian properties had been converted into flats, then they headed away from the wood, along bumpy lanes flanked by hedges, past little clusters of old cottages. Burton slowed down and stopped outside a green-roofed bungalow. 'She made her last delivery there – the *Daily Telegraph* and a photographic magazine. The lady of the house saw Paula pedalling away down the lane about a quarter past eight. That was the last time she was seen alive.'

Frost stared at the bungalow, then signalled for Burton to drive on. The car sloshed in and out of puddles and turned into an even narrower lane where overgrown branches on each side slashed spitefully at the car as it squeezed through. Burton braked. 'This is where we found her bike and the abandoned newspapers.'

They climbed out and stood looking down at a deep ditch running beneath an overhanging hedge. The ditch was brimful and covered with a thick layer of emerald green scum, through which the wheels of an upturned supermarket trolley protruded.

'The bastard must have been waiting for her just about here,' said Burton.

Frost nodded glumly. He had hoped that visiting the actual locale would give him some magic flash of inspiration. He stood in the pouring rain, looking down into the green slimy water, and decorated it with his discarded cigarette end.

Back in the car he asked Burton where the girl's bike was. 'Locked up in the shed at the station. The

138

two newspapers she didn't deliver are in the exhibits cupboard.'

'Only two more houses,' said Burton, as the car bumped into an extra deep puddle which sent a spray of dirty water all over the windscreen.

'Mind what you're doing,' barked Gilmore, who hadn't had a chance to put Burton in his place for some time.

Burton's knuckles whitened on the steering wheel, but he controlled his temper. He pointed up a small side lane which crawled up to a two-storeyed house standing on its own. 'That's called Brook Cottage. They would have had the *Sun* but she never made it.'

Brook Cottage looked a mite dilapidated. They could hear a dog barking as they passed.

The lane widened and passed through empty scrub land. After some minutes a red-bricked house lurched up in front of them. It was an old, solid-looking property and stood alone in extensive grounds. A shirt-sleeved man was working in the garden seemingly oblivious to the pouring rain. 'She finished her round here,' announced Burton as he switched off the engine. 'The man in the garden is Edward Bell, Paula's schoolteacher.'

Frost crushed his cigarette in the ashtray, then turned up the collar of his mac. 'Let's have a word with the bastard.'

The man, wrenching up weeds from the heavy soil, gave a cry of pain as the sharp thorns of a hidden bramble pierced his palm. He stared angrily at the bright red globules welling from the punctures. The damned briar was everywhere. As fast as you cleared it from one section it appeared somewhere else. Well, if it thought it was going to defeat him, it was making a damn mistake. He tore up a thick clump of grass and wrapped it round the briar as

139

protection then pulled and tugged, swearing out loud as the bramble resisted. It took a great deal of effort but at last he tore it free of the rain-sodden earth and hurled it on to the growing pile of garden refuse. His hand was sticky with blood and rain and sweat. He sucked salt and moved on to the next section, only dimly aware of the sound of slamming car doors and approaching footsteps.

'Mr Bell?'

'Eh?' He straightened up and eased the pain in his back. There were two men, one dark-haired, young and neatly dressed, the other older, hair starting to thin, wearing a crumpled raincoat that had seen better days. The younger one held up a piece of plastic bearing a coloured photograph. 'Police, Mr Bell.'

'Is it about Paula?' he asked. 'Has she been found?'

'Let's talk inside,' said the scruffy man.

The house was cold and unwelcoming. They passed through the kitchen, its sink and draining board stacked with dirty saucepans and crockery. On top of the fridge stood a half-bottle of lumpy milk. The room was a mess. It reminded Frost of home.

Muttering apologies for the untidiness, Bell opened one door, decided against it and took them into a musty-smelling lounge. Rain streamed down the patio window, blurring the view of the garden beyond. A miserable room. Frost would be glad to get out.

'Not too cold for you, is it? I haven't had the heating on. I suppose I should, but it seems pointless . . .' Bell's voice trailed off.

'This is fine, sir,' said Frost without conviction, winding his scarf tighter. He and Gilmore sat side by side on the beige Dralon settee, facing Bell who was squatting on a footstool, dripping rain on to the pink carpet.

Bell, who wore a rain-blackened checked shirt and

baggy corduroy trousers, was in his late thirties. Thin and nervous-looking, his face was framed by unstyled light brown hair and a few tufts of a scraggy beard. A hint of dark rings around his eyes suggested he hadn't been sleeping too well.

Unaware of Frost's scrutiny, Bell unwrapped the blood-stained handkerchief, studied his palm, then wrapped it again. Suddenly he remembered the reason for their calling.

'Paula's been found, you say? That's splendid. How is she?'

Frost's eyes flicked to Gilmore, who sat impassive. This was too naïve. Surely Bell must have heard about the discovery of the girl's body? 'Don't you read the papers, sir?'

'Papers?' He shook his head. 'They don't deliver papers here any more. The parents won't let their children do it.'

'Don't you listen to the radio? Or talk to your colleagues?'

'It's half-term and I've been too busy in the garden these past few days to listen to the radio. So what has happened?'

'Paula is dead, sir,' said Frost bluntly, carefully watching Bell's reaction. The man jerked back as if he had been hit, then his face crumpled.

'Oh no. That poor child. Oh no!' His grief and shock at the news seemed genuine.

Without taking his eyes from the teacher, Frost slowly lit a cigarette. 'She was murdered, sir. Raped and murdered.'

Bell stood up. He took the soiled handkerchief from his hand and stuffed it into his pocket. Nervously, he paced the room. 'She was only fifteen.'

'Kids mature earlier these days,' said Frost. 'They have

sex earlier, they get raped earlier, they get murdered earlier.' He exhaled smoke and watched it disperse. 'What sort of girl was she?'

The man dropped back on the footstool and thought for a moment. 'Quiet. Didn't mix much. An excellent scholar.'

'Why did you start giving her lifts to school?' asked Gilmore.

'It was her parents' request. Her newspaper round took her some five miles in the opposite direction. Sometimes the papers would be late which could make her late for school and they didn't want her to miss any of her lessons. I would meet her at the top of the lane and give her a lift from there.'

'What did you do about her bike?' This from Frost.

'It was one of those folding ones. I put it in the boot. She could then cycle home when school was over. This is all in your files . . . I made a full statement to that other officer.'

'What sort of things did you talk about when you drove her to school?' asked Gilmore. 'Did she mention boy friends, or crushes on any of the masters, or anything?'

Bell shifted his position to face the sergeant. 'We hardly passed more than a few words. She was a quiet girl, and that suited me. When I'm driving, I like to concentrate, not talk.'

'Was she a teaser?' asked Frost.

His pale cheeks showed two red spots. 'How the hell should I know?'

'In the car, sir, you and her, close. The old knees rubbing together . . . flashes of elasticated knicker leg and tender young thigh all juicy and throbbing?'

Bell's lip curled contemptuously. 'I find you offensive, Inspector.'

Through a haze of cigarette smoke Frost beamed at him. 'You're not alone in that, sir. But I found it offensive when I saw what that sod had done to that kid, so just answer my questions.'

Bell stood up and towered angrily over the inspector. 'I hope you're not suggesting I am involved in this poor child's death?'

'Let's just say you're quite high on my list of suspects.' In fact, thought Frost, you're my one and only bloody suspect, so if it isn't you, I'm nowhere. 'Can you tell me your movements for the morning she went missing?' His raised hand halted Bell in mid-protest. 'I know you've told it all to the other bloke, but I'd like to hear it first-hand.'

'It was the morning of my wife's funeral. The hearse arrived from the undertakers at 9.30. The interment was at ten. I got back home a few minutes before noon.'

'So, before the funeral, you were alone in the house until 9.30?'

'No. My wife's parents were here. They'd travelled down from Berwick for the funeral and stayed with me overnight.'

'Oh.' Frost tried not to sound disappointed. 'They'd confirm this, of course?'

'I think you'll find they've already given statements to Inspector Allen.'

Frost groaned inwardly. Why the hell hadn't he done his homework? 'I've only just skimmed through the files, sir.' Skimmed! He hadn't even opened them. 'Your morning paper hadn't arrived by the time you left for the funeral. Didn't that worry you? Didn't you wonder why?'

'I didn't give it a thought, Inspector. The only thing on my mind was the funeral.'

143

'Of course, sir.' Damn, thought Frost. There goes my best suspect. All he was left with now was the plumber. Which reminded him. 'Did it rain during the funeral?'

'There was a sudden cloudburst,' said Bell. 'We all got drenched.'

And damn again, thought Frost. Now I haven't even got the plumber. He poked another cigarette in his mouth and lit up. The smoke curled and drifted and he followed it with his eyes, watching as it was drawn to the fireplace, some of it wafting up to the mantelpiece. In the centre of the mantelpiece a clock in Chinese black lacquer, long unwound, had stopped at ten past eight. Something poked out from behind it. A light blue envelope, the address typed. It looked very similar to the one sent to old Mr Wardley.

A sharp cough to catch Gilmore's attention and a jerk of the head to direct him to the clock. Silently, Gilmore sidled over and pulled out the envelope. He raised his eyebrows and nodded. The typing was identical.

Bell, staring out at the rain-soaked garden, saw nothing of this extended mime show.

'One final thing,' said Frost casually. 'What did the poison pen letter say?'

Bell stiffened, then slowly turned. He saw the envelope in Gilmore's hand and snatched it from him. 'You've no right . . .'

'We've every bloody right,' snapped Frost, standing and holding out his hand. 'The letter, please, sir.'

Bell stared at him, knuckles white, body stiff with fury. He almost threw the envelope at the inspector. 'You bastard!' he hissed. 'You lousy bastard.'

'Sticks and stones,' reproved Frost, mildly. He unfolded the sheet of cheap typing paper. The typed message said, simply, *Fornicator*.

'Terse,' murmured Frost, passing the message to Gilmore. 'Why should anyone accuse you of that, sir?'

'It's none of your damn business.'

'In a murder enquiry, sir, everything is my damn business.'

Bell walked back to the window and again stared at the puddled garden blurred out of focus by the curtain of rain crawling down the pane. He wouldn't look at Frost. He spoke to the glass. 'If you must know, my wife had been ill for a very long time. We were not able to live together as husband and wife. There was a woman in Denton . . .'

'Do you mean a tart?' asked Frost, bluntly.

His back stiffened. 'Yes, she was a prostitute. Someone must have been spying on us, hence the letters. Filthy letters. I burnt the others. This one came on the day of the funeral.' He covered his face with his hands and his body shook. 'The day of her funeral.'

On the way back to the car they detoured. There was the remains of an old bonfire at the end of the garden. Quite a large bonfire. Frost poked at the rain-sodden ashes with his foot. Bits of twigs, stalks and dried leaves. No burnt remains of buttons or the charred remnants of clothes stripped from a schoolgirl's body. He added his cigarette end to the heap.

'We're wasting our time here,' said Gilmore.

'Maybe,' muttered Frost, looking back to the house where a thin, bearded figure was watching them from the patio window. 'But my philosophy in life is never to trust bastards with thin straggly beards.'

Burton started the engine as Frost slid into the passenger seat beside him. 'Back to the station, Inspector?'

'One more call, son. Let's check with the headmaster of Bell's school. I want to find out if there's been any complaints of Hairy-chin teaching advanced anatomy to the senior girls.'

'We shouldn't be doing this,' protested Gilmore from the back seat. 'You're forgetting – Mr Mullett said we should drop this case and concentrate on the stabbings.'

'Mr Mullett says lots of stupid things, son. The kindest thing to do is ignore him.'

As Gilmore had predicted, calling on the headmaster was a waste of time. The man, stout and pompous, was outraged that such an accusation could be levelled at any member of his staff. Mr Bell had an excellent record, was highly regarded, and didn't the inspector realize that the poor devil had recently lost his wife?

Frost felt like retorting, didn't the headmaster know that while his wife was dying, his excellent schoolmaster was having it away with a tart in Denton? But he held his tongue and took his leave.

'Yes, son,' he said, before Burton could ask. 'Back to the station.' And they nearly made it. Another couple of minutes and they would have been in the car-park when Control called.

'Calling all units,' said the radio. 'Anyone in the vicinity of Selwood Road? Over.'

Before Frost could restrain him, Burton had snatched up the handset. They were a minute away from Selwood Road.

'Eleven Selwood Road. Old-age pensioner living on her own. Neighbour reports she hasn't been seen all day, her newspaper's still in the letter-box and her milk is still on the step.'

The neighbour who made the phone call, a sharp-faced little busybody of a man wearing a too-big plastic mac, was hovering in the street and scurried over to the car as they pulled up. 'Are you the police?'

146

'More or less,' grunted Frost.

'I live next door,' said the man, darting in front of them like an over-enthusiastic terrier as they made their way across to the house. 'She always goes out during the day. I watch her through the window. She didn't today. And none of her lights are on, her milk is on the doorstep. She's an old-age pensioner, you know.'

'Thanks,' muttered Frost, wishing the man would go away.

'I'm an old-age pensioner too, but you'd never think it, would you?'

'No,' said Frost unconvincingly. 'Never in a million years.' The old sod looked at least eighty. They were now at the door, which was painted a vivid green.

'Are you going to break in?' asked the neighbour, pushing between them. 'Only the council have just repainted these doors.'

Frost leant on the bell push.

'No use ringing if she's dead!'

'Nothing good on telly?' asked Frost pointedly, hammering at the door with the flat of his hand.

'You could get over my garden fence if you liked,' offered the man, 'but she always keeps her back door locked.'

Frost moved the man out of the way so he could have a look through the letter-box.

'You won't see anything. Her morning paper's stuck in there.'

Frost tugged at the paper, but it was wedged fast.

'You won't shift it, I've tried.'

Frost gave a savage yank and the newspaper came free.

'You've torn it,' reproved the man pointing to a thin corrugated tongue of paper that had caught on the side of the letter-box.

147

'If she's dead, she won't mind,' said Frost, peering through the flap. All he could see was solid dark. He sent Burton for the torch.

'I've got a torch,' said the neighbour, 'but it doesn't work.'

Burton returned from the car with the flashlight. Frost shone it through the letter-box. He caught his breath. The beam had picked out a crumpled heap at the foot of the stairs. A woman. And there seemed to be blood. Lots of blood.

'Kick the door in, son . . . quick!'

At the second kick there was a pistol shot of splintering wood and the door crashed inwards. Frost found the light switch as they charged in. She was lying face down, her head in a pool of blood. He touched her neck. There was a pulse. She was still alive. Burton dashed back to the car to radio for an ambulance. Gilmore helped Frost turn her on her back, while the neighbour brought a blanket from the upstairs bedroom to cover her.

Her eyes fluttered, then opened. She seemed unable to focus. Frost knelt beside her. 'What happened, love? Who did it?' He turned his head away as the stale gin fumes hit him.

'I fell down the bleeding stairs,' she said.

Tuesday night shift (1)

Liz was in bed asleep when Gilmore arrived home late in the afternoon and was still asleep at eight o'clock when he staggered out of bed, tired and irritable, ready for the evening shift of Mullett's revised rota. He was clattering about in the kitchen, frying himself an egg and Liz came eagerly downstairs. She thought he had just come home and was furious to learn he'd been working when he should have been off duty and was now starting on another night shift.

'You said it would all be different when they made you a sergeant. You said you'd be able to spend more time with me. It's Cressford all over again.'

'It won't always be like this,' said Gilmore, wearily, cursing as the yolk broke and spread itself all over the frying pan.

'How many times have I heard that before? It's never been any damn different.' She moved out of the way so he could reach a plate, not helping him by passing one over.

Gilmore buttered a slice of bread. 'Could you give it a rest? I've had a lousy day.'

'And what sort of a day do you think I've had? Stuck in this stinking little room.'

'You can always go out.'

She gave a mocking laugh. 'Where to? What is there to do in this one-eyed morgue of a town?'

'You could mix . . . make friends.'

'Who with?'

'Well – some of the other police wives . . .'

'Like his wife . . . that old tramp – the one who's supposed to be an inspector?'

'His wife is dead.'

'What did she die of – boredom?'

Gilmore rubbed a weary hand over his face. 'That old tramp, as you call him, has got the George Cross.'

'So he should. You deserve strings of bloody medals for living in this dump!'

He opened his mouth to reply, but the door slammed and she was back in the bedroom. He pushed the egg to one side, he couldn't eat it. He was pouring his tea when a horn sounded outside. Frost had arrived to pick him up.

Outside the rain had stopped and a diamond-hard moon shone down from a clear sky. Frost shivered as Gilmore opened the car door to enter. 'It's going to be a cold night tonight, son.' He turned the heater up full blast and checked that all the windows were tightly closed.

'Yes,' agreed Gilmore. 'A bloody cold night.'

Bill Wells tugged another tissue from the Kleenex box and blew his sore, streaming nose. His throat was raw and he kept having shivering and sweating fits. And the damn doctor had the gall to say it was just a cold and he hadn't got the flu virus. A couple of aspirins and a hot drink and he'd be as right as rain in a day or so. His pen crawled over the page as he logged the last trivial phone call which was from a woman who had nothing better to do than to report two strange cats in her garden.

The log book page fluttered as the main door opened. Without raising his eyes, Wells finished the entry, blotted it, then forced a polite expression to greet the caller. Then his jaw dropped. 'Bleeding hell!' he croaked.

A small, bespectacled man wearing a plastic raincoat stood in the centre of the lobby. When he had Wells' attention, he parted the raincoat. He was wearing nothing underneath it.

'Oh, push off,' groaned Wells, slamming his pen down. 'We're too bloody busy.'

Defiantly, the man stood his ground, holding the mac open even wider. Another groan from Wells. 'Collier,' he yelled. 'Come and arrest this gentleman.'

The lobby door swung open again as Frost bounded in, a disgruntled-looking Gilmore at his heels. He glanced casually at the man, did a double take and stared hard. 'No thanks, I've got one,' he said.

'When you want a flasher,' moaned Wells, 'you can't find one. When you don't want one, they come and stick it under your nose.'

There were extra staff in the Murder Incident Room where the phones were constantly ringing.

Frost looked around in surprise. 'What's going on?'

Burton, a phone to his ear, noted down a few details, murmured his thanks and hung up. 'It's the response to the Paula Bartlett video. It went out on television again tonight. We're flooded out with calls from people who reckon they saw her.'

'After two months they reckon they saw her,' grunted Frost. 'When the video went out the day she went missing, no-one could remember a damn thing.' He picked up one of the phone messages from a filing basket. A woman reporting seeing Paula in the town two days ago. Frost flicked it back in the basket. 'A waste of bloody time.'

'Excellent response to the video,' boomed Mullett, sailing in and beaming at all the activity.

'Just what I was saying, Super,' lied Frost. 'How did the press conference go?'

'Very well,' smirked Mullett. 'I recorded an interview for BBC radio. They hope to repeat it in *Pick of the Week.*'

'Are you sure they said "pick"?' Frost enquired innocently.

There was the sound of stifled laughter and people in the room seemed desperate to avoid Mullett's eye. One of the WPCs had a fit of the giggles and was stuffing a handkerchief in her mouth. Mullett frowned, uneasily aware he was missing out on something, and not sure what. He didn't see the joke, but he smiled anyway. He remembered the messages he had to deliver. 'Who's been telexing the Metropolitan Police about someone called Bradbury?'

'Simon Bradbury?' asked Gilmore eagerly. 'That was me.'

'Who's Simon Bradbury?' Frost asked.

'The computer salesman. The bloke who picked the fight with Mark Compton. I thought he might be the one who's been sending the death threats.'

'You could be on to something, Sergeant,' said Mullett, handing Gilmore the telex. 'The Metropolitan Police know Bradbury. He's a nasty piece of work and he's got form.'

Bradbury had been involved in drunken brawls, had served two prison sentences for assault and had been fined and disqualified for drunken driving. There was an arrest warrant out on him for beating up a barman who refused to serve him. He had defaulted on police bail and was no longer at his last known address. Full details and a photograph were following.

Gilmore rubbed his hands. 'Sounds like our man, Super. I could have a result on this case very soon.'

'Excellent,' beamed Mullett. 'Results are something we are very short of at the moment.' He glared significantly at Frost then looked around the room where the phones were still ringing non-stop. 'Anything interesting on the Paula Bartlett video?'

'Yes,' sniffed Frost. 'Proof there's life after death. She was still being seen delivering papers up to last week.'

Mullett forced a smile. 'Ah well. Carry on with the good work.' He turned to leave and was nearly hit by the door as Sergeant Wells burst in.

'Urgent message for Mr Frost from Fingerprints,' panted Wells. 'The senior citizen killing . . . Mary Haynes. One of the prints in the bedroom. It's someone with previous.'

'Who?' asked Frost, pushing Mullett to one side.

'Dean Ronald Hoskins. Collier's pulling out his file.'

On cue, a panting Collier rushed in waving a buff folder. Wells snatched it and skimmed through the details. 'Dean Ronald Hoskins, aged twenty-four. Three previous – burglary, breaking and entering and assault with a knife.'

'A knife,' hissed Mullett, snatching the file from Wells. 'By God, we've got him.' He was so excited he could hardly hold the file still. He couldn't wait to phone the Chief Constable . . . 'Sorry to disturb you at your home, sir,' he would begin modestly, 'but a bit of good news I thought you'd like to know . . . Denton Division triumph yet again . . . another murder solved within twenty-four hours . . . watertight case . . . prints . . . full confession . . .'

His soaring flights of fancy were abruptly grounded by Frost who had rudely snatched the file and was now staring at it, a cigarette sagging from his mouth. 'Bloody hell! He didn't have to travel far to kill her. He lives next door.'

'I interviewed him,' said Burton. 'It was Hoskins who told us about the key under the mat.'

Mullett was now bubbling with excitement. 'Bring him in. Take all the men you need.' He pulled open the door. 'I want a result on this one, Inspector. Let's see if we can't give the Chief Constable some good news for a change.'

The patrol car followed Frost's Cortina as far as the road adjoining Mannington Crescent. Two uniformed men got out and sprinted to the rear of number 44 where they climbed the back fence into the garden, blocking Hoskins' retreat that way.

Gilmore coasted the Cortina around the corner, parking it at the end of the street where he switched off the lights and waited for the uniformed men to radio that they were in position. Next to Gilmore sat Burton. In the rear seat were Frost and WPC Helen Ridley, the beefy little blonde, who had changed into plain clothes and was spoiling for a fight.

Most houses in the street showed lights, the exception being number 46, the murder house with its drawn curtains and a heavy padlock securing the front door. From next door, number 44, an overloud hi-fi belted out heavy metal.

'Jordan to Inspector Frost,' whispered the radio. 'We are in position – over.'

'Right,' grunted Frost. 'We're moving in.'

They climbed out of the car and casually sauntered up to the front door of number 44 which seemed to be pulsating as the wham of an electronic bass boomed from inside. Frost lifted the knocker and beat out a rhythmic rat-tat-tat. The others pressed tight against the shadow of the porch. The music blared out louder as an inside door was opened. Footsteps along the passage and a man's shadow against the frosted glass of the front door.

'Yeah? Who is it?'

Frost muttered something unintelligible.

'What?' yelled the voice from inside.

Frost muttered again.

'Just a minute . . . can't hear a bloody word you're saying.' The latch clicked. As the front door opened, Frost moved quickly out of the way and Gilmore pounced, pinning to the wall a man in patched jeans and a washed-out red vest. A potted plant on a stand toppled and crashed to the floor, spilling earth all over the lino. Gilmore tried to yell 'Police!', but the man suddenly sprang forward, his palm clamped under the detective's chin, fingers clawing for his eyes. Gilmore swung him round and crashed him against the opposite wall.

'Let him go, you bastard.' A girl wearing a black T-shirt and very little else raced down the passage slashing at the air with a kitchen knife.

'Police,' spluttered Gilmore, trying to hold Hoskins with one hand and ward the girl off with the other. He had done it all wrong. The knife blade was whistling perilously close to his ear, but the hallway was so narrow, it prevented Burton and the WPC getting past to the girl.

Snorting like a stallion on heat, the little WPC charged into the fray, sending the men crashing to the floor and leaping over them to grab the girl, spin her round and jerk her wrist up high into the small of her back. The WPC's foot hooked round the girl's ankle and sent her toppling.

Frost stepped back and lit a cigarette. As usual, he was superfluous.

'Get this bloody dyke off of me,' screamed the girl, face down in earth and potted plant with the WPC kneeling on her back and twisting her knife arm to near breaking point.

'Drop the knife,' hissed the WPC.

'I've dropped, it, I've dropped it,' screeched the girl.

'I've got it,' said Frost, picking it up.

Reluctantly, the WPC relaxed her grip and dragged the girl to her feet. Gilmore, panting away, now had Hoskins facing the wall in an arm lock. With his free hand he fumbled in his pocket for his warrant card. He stuck it under the man's nose. 'Police. Are you Dean Ronald Hoskins?'

'Yes. How many of you are there?'

'There's two more of the sods in the garden,' the girl told him. 'Who are we supposed to be – Bonnie and bleeding Clyde?'

'Well, you're certainly not Di and bleeding Charles,' said Frost. 'Can we go somewhere comfortable?'

'There's nowhere comfortable in this bloody shithouse,' said the girl.

'You don't have to live here,' Hoskins snarled at her. 'You can pack your carrier bag and go whenever you like.' He nodded towards the far door. 'In there.'

The room housed a settee that doubled as a bed, a hi-fi unit with two shaking, throbbing speakers spewing out heavy metal, a black and white television set and a motor bike which was leaking oil on to bare floorboards.

Frost kicked at the hi-fi flex, yanking the plug from the power point. The music died abruptly and the resulting silence took some adjusting to. He opened the window to the garden and yelled for Jordan and the other uniformed man to come in. 'Search this place from top to bottom. Bag all clothing for forensic examination.'

'Have you got a warrant?' demanded the girl.

Frost smiled sweetly. 'I don't understand these technical terms, love.' He found himself a chair, shook off the dubious pair of underpants it contained and sat down. He pointed to the settee, indicating they too should sit. With an energetic shove the WPC helped them comply.

Frost drew on his cigarette. Their heads moved simultaneously, watching his every move like a rabbit watching a snake. Smoke dribbled from his nostrils. He fanned it away. 'My colleague thinks you might be able to help him with his enquiries.' He nodded for Gilmore to take over.

Gilmore stared at each of them in turn, holding their gaze and forcing them to break away. 'You know why we're here.'

'I've got no bleeding idea,' snapped the man. 'You come bursting in here with that bloody lesbian . . .'

'A woman's been murdered next door and you don't know why we're here.' Gilmore thrust his face to within an inch of Hoskins 'Why did you knife her? A poor old lady who never did anyone any harm.'

'Knife her?' exclaimed Hoskins incredulously. 'Me?'

'Don't give me that innocent crap. You've used a knife before.'

'Only in self-defence.'

'This was in self-defence,' snapped Gilmore. 'She caught you robbing her house. She would have gone to the police. So, in self-defence, she had to be silenced.'

'Oh, marvellous,' sneered the girl. 'The police are bleeding baffled so they arrest the poor sod next door just because he's got a police record.'

'Not just because he's got a police record, love,' said Frost. 'It's because the poor sod next door left his finger-prints all over the murdered woman's bedroom.'

The girl's head snapped round to Hoskins. 'You stupid bastard! You never told me you touched anything.'

'That's right, you mouthy cow!' snarled Hoskins. 'Sign my bleeding death warrant!'

Gilmore gave a yell of triumph. 'Caution them,' said Frost, 'and take them down to the station.' He went out to see how the search for the knife and for bloodstained clothing was getting on. The bedroom was a pigsty. Jordan and WPC Ridley were stuffing unwashed clothing into a black plastic dustbin sack, the same type of sack Paula Bartlett's body was found in.

'Nothing yet,' Jordan told him. Frost nodded glumly. Outside through the window, he could see two police officers sifting through the contents of the dustbin. Something told him that this wasn't going to be as easy as Gilmore seemed to think.

*   *   *

157

The interview room was cold. The heating engineers had managed to restore heat to the basement cells, but wouldn't get round to this floor until the morning. So it was cold. But Hoskins was sweating. The girl, now wearing a thick sweater, sat by his side. Gilmore had wanted the pair questioned separately, but Frost favoured having them together.

Gilmore switched on the tape recorder, announced the details of the time and who was present, then dragged a chair across and sat facing them.

'I want to make a statement,' said Hoskins.

'You're on the air, so go ahead.'

'I never touched her. Like I told the other cop, the old girl knocked at our door moaning that someone had got into her house with the spare key, but when I looked, the key was there all the time, so I left her to it. After a while, I got worried about her, so I went back and knocked, but got no answer. I thought I'd better check, just in case, so I used her spare key from under the mat to get in. I called, "Are you all right, Mrs Haynes?" Dead silence. Funny, I thought. I called again. Nothing. So I nipped upstairs just to make sure she's all right and, Christ! There she was on the bed and blood everywhere. I couldn't get down them bleeding stairs fast enough.' He turned to the girl to verify his story.

'Dean was as white as a sheet when he came in,' she confirmed, 'and he was sick as a bloody parrot down the sink.'

'What time was this?' Gilmore asked.

'About eleven o'clock Sunday night.'

'And you didn't think of calling an ambulance, or the police?'

'Ambulance? She was dead – I could see that.'

'Police then?'

158

'What – a bloke with a record inside a dead woman's house? That's as good as a signed confession to you lot. I'd have been in Death bleeding Row within the hour.'

Gilmore flicked through his notes. 'You told the other officer it was five o'clock Sunday when Mrs Haynes rang your bell.'

'That's right.'

'And you were so worried about her, you waited six hours before knocking to see if she's all right?'

'Well, at least I did go and knock. Other people wouldn't have bothered.'

'I don't believe you,' said Gilmore.

'I don't expect you to,' said Hoskins, loud and clear to the microphone. 'But it's the gospel truth.'

Gilmore frowned as the door opened and the little blonde WPC hovered, waving something – a large brown envelope. He'd give her a mouthful for interrupting at a crucial moment. It was Frost who spoke to her, keeping his voice low, then he called Gilmore over. Murmurs of excited conversation while Hoskins looked on worried, straining his ears in vain, wondering what it was about.

The two detectives returned, Gilmore carrying the envelope which he shook over the table. Five banknotes fluttered out, a £20 note, a £10 note and three £5 notes, all crisp and brand new. Hoskins tried to look puzzled. 'Guess what we found hidden behind one of your chair cushions,' said Gilmore. He picked up one of the notes and sniffed delicately, then smiled. 'Smell it. Lavender!' He looked across to the girl. 'Hardly your style, is it, love?' He waggled the note under Hoskins' nose. 'The old girl's purse reeked of it!'

Hoskins pushed Gilmore's hand away. 'It's my giro money,' he muttered.

'Of course it is,' said Gilmore, 'but just in case you're telling me a porky, I'll check the numbers with the post office where Mrs Haynes drew her pension. If they tally, Sonny Jim, you're for the high jump.' He pushed the money back into the envelope. He felt much happier now. Hoskins was beginning to squirm and the girl looked worried. Frost seemed fidgety, no doubt annoyed that the new boy was scoring all the goals.

Hoskins took a deep breath. 'All right, I'll tell you the truth. It is her money, but she lent it to me. I needed some spares for my motorbike.'

'Lent it?' scoffed Gilmore. 'She wouldn't have lent you forty-five pence, let alone forty-five quid.'

'She bloody lent it to me,' insisted Hoskins. 'And I was very grateful, that's why I went in later to check she was all right.'

Frost leant forward. 'She gave you everything she had in her purse. How was the poor cow going to manage?'

'I intended paying her back in a couple of days. She said she could wait.'

'When did you borrow it?' asked Frost.

'When she thought she'd lost her spare key. I saw her purse in her hand so I asked her.'

'Do you mind if I continue, sir?' asked Gilmore with an edge to his voice that would slice through tempered steel. He didn't want Frost taking over just when victory was within grasp.

Frost's hand waved him to silence. 'Indulge me, Sergeant.' He puffed cigarette smoke down over the seated man. 'All right, Hoskins, let's pretend she lent you the money. And let's pretend you were so full of gratitude that you were worried about her and decided to see if she was all right at eleven o'clock at night. When you knocked, were the lights on in her house?'

Hoskins paused for a moment. 'No.'

'So when you got no reply, from a house with all the lights out, you thought it was your duty to investigate it – to use her spare key and nose around inside?'

'That's right.'

'It never occurred to you that at eleven o'clock at night the most obvious answer was that this seventy-eight-year-old woman might be in bed, asleep?'

Hoskins' mouth opened and shut, then he shook his head. 'No. It didn't occur to me at the time.'

Frost gave a weary sigh. 'Don't waste my time, son. Of course it occurred to you. You were banking on it. You wanted her to be in bed and asleep.'

'I don't know what you're talking about,' Hoskins muttered to the floor.

'You stupid little git. You're going to talk yourself into a life sentence.' He stood up and started to button his mac. 'I don't think you killed her, but if you're sticking to that story I'm charging you with murder and your girlfriend as an accessory.'

Hoskins, his face set, stared stubbornly down at the ground.

'If you don't tell them the bleeding truth, then I will,' said the girl. 'They're not nicking me for something I didn't do.'

Hoskins took a deep breath. 'All right . . . scrub everything I said. This is now the gospel . . .'

Frost sat down again and waited. Gilmore was scowling, arms folded, itching to take over the reins of the questioning.

'Yes, I was going to do the place over – nip in, grab what I could and get out quick. I knew where the spare key was, so I waited until eleven o'clock when I thought the old girl would be asleep. I let myself in. Her bag was

161

on the hall table, so I nicked the money from her purse. Then I crept upstairs. The first door I tried was her bedroom. Christ, when I saw her smothered in blood, it frightened the shit out of me. My feet never touched the flaming stairs as I came down. I took the money, but I never bleeding killed her.'

'I believe him,' said Frost when they were back in the office.

'Well, I don't,' said Gilmore. He was furious. He'd have got a bloody confession to murder if the old fool hadn't butted in.

'Mind you,' added Frost, 'if Forensic find her blood all over his clothes, I'm prepared to change my mind.'

Tuesday night shift (2)

'Woman on the phone for you,' yelled Wells as they crossed the lobby. 'A Mrs Compton.'

'Old Mother Rigid Nipples!' exclaimed Frost, as Gilmore took the phone.

'Mr Mullett wasn't too pleased you're only charging Hoskins with petty theft,' Wells told him.

'Mr Mullett's happiness is rather low on my list of priorities,' grunted Frost, pushing through the swing doors and nearly bumping into an irritable-looking Mullett on his way out.

'Car expenses,' barked Mullett.

'Be on your desk first thing tomorrow, Super,' called Frost, instantly regretting his folly. The expenses, much scribbled on, were still in his pocket and there wasn't a hope in hell of getting the amended receipts by the morning. Ah well, he philosophized, a lot could happen between now and then. Mullett could get injured in a car crash and break both his legs. But he popped the bubble of this optimistic fantasy. The bastard would hobble in on crutches if it meant catching him out.

A quick look in at his office. Exactly as he had left it, cold and untidy. Protruding from under an empty, unwashed mug was a memo headed *From The Office Of The Divisional Commander*. It bore the single word *Inventory???* ringed in red and underlined several times in Royal Blue by Mullett's Parker pen. He ferreted through his in-tray and dug out the inventory return, hoping it wouldn't look so complicated as at first sight. It looked even worse, so he reburied it even deeper.

The door slammed to punctuate an angry Gilmore's return. 'That damn Sergeant Wells!' He flung himself into his chair.

Frost stifled a groan. He had enough troubles of his own. 'What's the matter now, son?'

'That phone call from Mrs Compton. Her husband's away and she's alone in the house.'

'It sounds a bloody good offer,' said Frost. 'We'll flip a coin to see who has the first nibble.'

Gilmore's scowl cut even deeper. 'It's not funny. She's had another threatening phone call. The bastard told her tonight will be her last night on earth. She's frightened out of her wits. I've told Sergeant Wells I want a watch kept on the house tonight and he says he can't spare anyone.'

Frost picked up the internal phone. 'I'll have a word with him.'

At first Wells dug his heels in. He wasn't going to let any jumped-up, know-nothing, aftershave-smelling detective sergeant tell him how to organize his own men. And did the inspector know how many men he had available to cover the whole of Denton – the *whole* of bloody Denton? Four! Two in cars, two on foot. The others had to be kept in to answer the flaming phones which were ringing non-stop after that stupid Paula Bartlett video on television. Frost put the phone down on the desk and let Wells rant on, while he lit up another cigarette. When the whining from the ear-piece stopped, he picked up the receiver and made a few sympathetic sounds with the result that Wells now grudgingly admitted that perhaps he could spare one man and one car to keep a spasmodic watch on The Old Mill, but he couldn't guarantee one hundred per cent coverage.

'You're a prince, Bill,' said Frost. 'Your generosity is exceeded only by the size of your dick.' He hung up quickly before Wells could change his mind then twisted his chair round to tell his sergeant the good news, but if he expected thanks, he was disappointed.

'What a bloody way to run a station,' snarled Gilmore, stamping out of the room.

The office was too cold to stay in for long so Frost sauntered along to the Murder Incident Room where the temperature wasn't much better. Two WPCs and one uniformed man, all well wrapped up against the cold, were beavering through the senior citizen burglary files and answering the spasmodic phone calls that were still coming in following the TV broadcast. Another WPC was slowly working through the vast computer print-out of light vans and estate cars, either blue or of a colour which could be mistaken for blue under street lamps. 'Mr Mullett's orders,' she explained.

'You don't need to tell me,' sniffed Frost. 'Anything stupid and useless, it's always Mr Mullett's orders.'

Even if a blue van was involved, it could well have been repainted but still be registered under its original colour.

He dipped into the filing tray and read a couple of the messages. Paula was still being sighted. A woman had spotted her in France, and a man was positive that Paula was the same girl who had delivered his paper that very morning.

At a corner desk, DC Burton, a sandwich in his hand, was reading the *Sun*. He stuffed it away hastily as Frost approached and busied himself with the senior citizen files. 'On my refreshment break, sir,' he explained. He accepted a cigarette. 'Hoskins and the girl have been charged. We're holding them in the cells overnight pending the result of the forensic examination.'

Frost nodded and plonked himself down on a chair. 'I want to get filled in on the Paula Bartlett case, but I'm too bleeding lazy to read through the file. Start right from the beginning.'

'September 14th,' said Burton. 'She was on her paper round. Left the shop at 7.05.'

'Hold it,' interrupted Frost. 'Five past seven? Her parents said she usually started her round at half-past seven.'

'That was when her teacher gave her the lift. She would have had to cycle to school that day, so she gave herself more time.'

Frost blew an enormous smoke ring and watched it wriggle lazily around the room. 'I'm still listening.'

'At five o'clock her parents are expecting her home from school. By half-past five they're phoning around and are told she hadn't been to school at all that day. At ten past six they phone us.'

'And two months later, we found her,' commented Frost, wryly.

Burton grinned patiently. 'Anyway, we sent an area car. They got details of her delivery route from the paper shop and followed it through with the customers. As you know, she never made the last two houses.' He heaved himself from his chair and crossed to the large-scale wall map. 'Her last delivery was here at around 8.15.' His finger jabbed the map. 'Her next delivery should have been Brook Cottage . . . here. She never made it.'

Frost joined him at the map which was studded with yellow thumb tacks marking Paula's progress. 'She was doing her round half an hour earlier than usual?'

Burton nodded.

'Then unless the bloke who abducted her knew that, it must have happened by chance – he saw her, acted on impulse and grabbed her.'

Burton destroyed that theory. 'She'd been doing it half an hour earlier for the previous four days, sir. Mr Bell stayed away from school when his wife died, so Paula didn't get her lift in.'

'Whoever it was, he must have had a car. He either bundled her in and dumped the bike, or it was someone she knew and trusted. Someone, perhaps, with a wispy beard who offered her a lift. The bike went in the boot and he dumped it later.'

A tolerant smile from Burton. Inspector Allen had reasoned all this out months ago. 'If she was picked up in a car, sir, it couldn't have been by Mr Bell. He never left the house before the funeral. His wife's parents confirm it.'

'He's still got a wispy beard,' said Frost, 'and I don't trust the sod.' He returned to his desk. 'Right. She's reported missing. What happened from there?'

'Mr Allen took over the case at 20.15. The area between Grove Road and Brook Cottage was searched. At 23.32 we found her bike and her newspaper bag with the two undelivered papers, dumped in the ditch. The ditch was dragged in case the girl was there as well. It was then too dark to continue so it was resumed at first light with the search area extended to include part of the woods. Mr Allen had all known sex offenders, child molesters, flashers and the like brought in for questioning.' He pulled open a filing cabinet drawer jam-packed with bulging file folders – the results of the questionings.

Frost regarded them gloomily. Far too many for him to read through.

'There's more,' said Burton, tugging open a second drawer.

Frost winced and kneed them both shut. 'Say what you like about Mr Allen, but he's an industrious bastard. I take it he cleared them all?'

'Yes.'

'Then that's good enough for me.' He struck a match down the side of the filing cabinet and lit up another cigarette. 'Where's the bike?'

Burton led him to the freezing cold evidence shed in the car-park and unlocked the door.

The bike, swathed in dimpled polythene, was leaning against the wall. Burton pulled off the covering and stood back. A neat little foldable bike in light grey stove-enamel with dark grey handle-grips and pedals. Frost stared at it, but it told him nothing. He waited while Burton replaced the dimpled polythene, then followed him back to the Incident Room.

'Let's see the physical evidence.'

Unlocking a metal cupboard Burton took out a large cardboard box that had once held a gross of toilet rolls and dumped it on the desk. Then he pulled a bulging box-file down from the shelf and handed it to the inspector. 'The main file.'

Frost opened it. From the top of a heap of papers a serious-looking Paula Bartlett regarded him solemnly through dark-rimmed glasses. The school photograph provided by the parents when she first went missing, which was used for the 'Have You Seen This Girl?' poster. There were many more photographs, including those taken at the crypt and at the post-mortem. Frost shuddered and dug deeper, pausing to examine the flashlight enlargements showing the handlebar of the bike poking through the green scum of the ditch. 'Any prints on the bike?'

'You've already asked me, sir. Just the girl's and the schoolmaster's.'

Frost paused. Why did little buzzes of intuition whisper in his ear every time the schoolmaster was mentioned?

The rest of the file consisted of negative forensic reports on the bike and the canvas newspaper bag, plus statements from Paula's school friends – no, she had never talked of running away; no, she wasn't worried or unhappy about anything; no, she had no boyfriends. In the early days of the investigations, as no body was found, it was hoped that she had dumped her bike and, like so many kids of her age, run away from home. There were reports from various police forces who had followed up sightings of Paula look-alikes, teenage girls on the game or sleeping rough. A few missing teenage girls were restored to their families, but the Bartletts just waited, and hoped, and kept her room ready exactly as she left it.

He closed the file and handed it back to Burton, then pulled the cardboard box towards him. Inside it, loosely folded in a large transparent resealable bag, was the black, mould-speckled plastic rubbish sack, Paula's shroud, ripped where the knife had cut through to reveal her face.

'A rubbish sack,' commented Burton. 'Millions of them made. No clue there.'

'Tell me something I don't know,' gloomed Frost, taking the next item from the box. A canvas bag which had held the newspapers. The stagnant smell of the scummy ditch in which it had been immersed wafted up as he examined it. He slipped his arm through the shoulder strap. The bag was too high and uncomfortable. Paula was much smaller than he was. What the hell does that prove? he thought. He shrugged off the strap and put the bag on top of the rubbish sack. Next were the brown, flat-heeled shoes, the stained laces still tied in a neat double bow.

'Naked, raped and murdered, but still wearing shoes,' muttered Frost. 'It doesn't make sense.'

'What's going on?' Gilmore was staring pointedly at Burton. 'I thought I told you to go through the senior citizen files.'

'He's helping me,' said Frost. He held up the shoes. 'Why was she wearing shoes and sod all else?'

'She tried to get away,' offered Gilmore, not very interested. Mullet had told them to forget the Paula Bartlett case. 'She put on her shoes so she could make a run for it, but he came back and caught her.'

'She'd been raped,' said Frost. 'She was terrified. If she wanted to run, she'd bloody well run barefoot. She wouldn't waste time putting on shoes and tying them both with a double bow.'

'Then I don't know,' grunted Gilmore, moving away and busying himself with the senior citizen files, making it clear that he knew where his priorities were, even if others didn't.

The brown shoes refused to yield up their secrets, so Frost put them to one side and took out the last item in the box, a large plastic envelope which held the two undelivered newspapers, the *Sun* and the *Daily Telegraph,* each folded in two so they would fit the canvas bag.

Frost slipped them from the envelope. The same stagnant smell as the bag, both papers yellowed and tinged with green from their immersion. With great care he unfolded the *Sun* which the soaking in the ditch had made slightly brittle. Scrawled above the masthead in the newsagent's writing was the customer's address, *Brook Ctg*. He turned to page three and studied the nude dispassionately. She too was stained green. 'There's a green-tinged pair of nipples to the north of Kathmandu,' he intoned, closing the paper, careful to ensure it settled along its original folds.

He nearly missed it. It caught the light as he was returning it to the envelope. A quarter of the way down the back page, running across the width of the paper. A roughened, corrugated tongue-shaped tear an eighth of an inch wide and barely a quarter of an inch long. He pulled out the schoolmaster's *Telegraph* and scrutinized the back and front pages. Nothing on that, so back to the Sun. It was telling him something, but he didn't know what. 'What do you make of this, Burton?'

Burton made nothing of it.

'Come and look at this, Gilmore,' called Frost.

Making clear his resentment at being dragged away from more important work, Gilmore took the newspaper, gave it a cursory glance and handed it back. 'A bit of damage in the handling,' he said.

No, thought Frost. Not damage in the handling. It was more than that. A faint bell began to tinkle right at the back of his brain. The drunken fat woman earlier that day. Her paper was jammed tight in the letter-box. He'd had to pull it out and he'd torn it. A very similar tear to that on the back page of the undelivered *Sun*. Or was it undelivered? Hands trembling, he took up the newspaper and gave it a second, loose fold. The rough corrugated tongue ran exactly down the line of the new fold.

Frost felt his excitement rising. 'Did Mr Allen notice this?'

'I don't know, sir. Why, is it important?'

'It could be bloody important, son. The papers are folded once so the girl can fit them in the canvas bag. But they have to be folded again so they can be poked through the letter-box.' Frost pointed to the tear. 'I'd stake my virginity that this paper has been pushed through a letter-box and then pulled out again.'

The DC took the paper and twisted it in the light to examine the abrasion. It was possible. Just about possible. 'But we know it *wasn't* delivered,' he said.

'Who lives at Brook Cottage?'

Burton pulled the details from the folder and read them aloud. 'Harold Edward Greenway, aged 47. Self-employed van driver. Lives on his own. His wife walked out on him a couple of years ago.'

This was getting better and better. Frost rubbed his hands with delight. 'Has he got an alibi for the day the girl went missing?'

Burton turned a page. 'According to his statement he had no jobs lined up, so he stayed in bed until gone eleven, then pottered about the cottage for the rest of the day. He never saw the girl and he didn't get a paper.'

'And we believed him?'

'We had no reason to doubt him, especially when we found her bike and the papers in the ditch.'

Frost sat on the corner of the desk and shook out three cigarettes. 'OK. Try this out for a scenario. Harry boy lives all on his own. Wife's been gone for two years and his dick's getting rusty through lack of use. One morning, what should come cycling up his path but a nice, fresh, unopened packet of 15-year-old nooky with his copy of the *Sun*. She rolls it up and pokes it through the door. The sexual symbolism of this act hits him smack in the groin. He invites her in, or drags her in, or whatever. She can scream if she wants to, there's no-one for miles to hear. Afterwards, when all passion's spent and she's screaming rape, he panics, and strangles her.'

Burton, caught up with Frost's enthusiasm, could see where the plot was leading. 'Greenway puts the newspaper back in the bag, dumps it with the bike in a ditch and we all think she never made the delivery.'

Even Gilmore looked impressed. 'It's possible,' he decided reluctantly, 'but it still doesn't explain the shoes.'

'Sod the shoes,' said Frost, hopping down from the desk. 'Let's get our killer first, then get explanations.' He stuffed the papers back into the plastic envelope and handed it to Burton. 'Tell you what you do, son. Send both newspapers over to Forensic. Tell them our brilliant theory and get them to drop everything and make tests.'

'And then come back and get down to these bloody files,' called Gilmore. 'We're never going to get through them at this rate.'

The stack of folders didn't seem to be getting any lower. Gilmore ticked off the squares on the roneoed form and dropped it into the filing basket ready for the girl on the computer. Something sailed past his nose. It was a paper aeroplane which attempted to soar upwards before losing heart and nose-diving with a thud to the ground at his feet. He bent down and picked it up. The paper looked familiar. He unfolded it. One of the roneoed forms. He turned suspiciously to Frost who grinned back sheepishly.

'Sorry, son.'

Frost was bored. He'd been staring at the same robbery folder for the past forty minutes. He was dying for an excuse to get out of the station, but the phone stubbornly remained quiet. 'About time Forensic came back to us on those newspapers.'

'They've only had them five minutes,' said Gilmore.

'How long does it bloody take?' asked Frost peevishly, pulling the phone towards him and dialling the lab.

'Give us a chance, Inspector,' replied Forensic testily. 'We've got half our staff down with this flu virus thing. We're still working on the clothing and other items collected from 44 Mannington Crescent. Negative so far.'

'That old rubbish can wait,' said Frost. 'It's not important. Get cracking on those newspapers.'

A scowling Gilmore looked up. 'We're supposed to be concentrating on the senior citizen murders and you're telling Forensic it can wait?'

Frost was saved from answering by the phone. WPC Ridley from Intensive Care, Denton Hospital. Alice Ryder, the old lady with the fractured skull, had regained consciousness.

The moon, floating in a clear sky, kept pace with the car as they raced to the hospital. Frost, puffing away nervously in the passenger seat, was willing the old dear to stay alive until they could question her. A detailed description of her attacker would be worth a thousand of those lousy forms they had been filling in for the computer. A detailed description! He was kidding himself. She was eighty-one, concussed and dying. The bastard had attacked her in the dark. The poor cow would tell them sod all.

The dark sprawl of the hospital loomed up ahead. 'Park there, son.' He pointed to a 'Hospital – No Waiting' sign by the main entrance and was out of the car and charging up the corridor before Gilmore had a chance to switch off the ignition.

Gilmore pushed through the swing doors in time to see the maroon blur of Frost's scarf as he darted down a side corridor. With a burst of speed, he caught up with him. 'Straight ahead,' panted Frost, indicating a small flickering green neon sign reading 'Intensive Care'.

The night sister looked up angrily and glared them to silence. She nodded grimly at Frost's warrant card. 'Mrs Ryder is over there.' A jerk of her head indicated a curtained-off corner.

'How is she?' asked Frost.

'She's dying, otherwise I wouldn't let you near her.' As they moved across, she added, 'Not too many of you. Send the WPC out.'

They slipped through the curtains. A concerned WPC Ridley was bending over the bed talking quietly. She looked up with relief at Frost's appearance. 'Her eyes are open, sir, but I don't think she's really with us.'

'Take a break, love,' said Frost flopping down in the chair alongside the bed. Gilmore stood behind him. The old lady, a small frail figure, seemed unaware of their presence. She lay still, her head barely creasing the plumped hospital pillow, an irregular bubbling sob marking her shallow breathing. Her face was a dull grey against the starkness of the turban of bandages around her head. Taped to her cheek, a thin, transparent tube ran into her left nostril. Another tube descended from a half-filled plastic bag on an iron stand and dripped fluids through a hollow needle to a vein on her wrist. Her hand, a yellow claw, was trembling and making tiny scratching noises on the bed-cover.

Everything was clean and white and sterile and Frost felt gritty and dirty and out of place. He leant forward. 'Mrs Ryder?'

Her red-rimmed eyes stared blankly up at the ceiling. She gave no sign that she had heard him. Her head was twitching slightly as if trying to shake off the tube fastened to her nose which was clearly uncomfortable and worrying her.

Why can't they let the poor cow die in comfort, thought Frost. He brought his face close to hers. 'Mrs Ryder, I'm a police officer. If I'm to get the bastard who did this to you, I need your help.'

No response.

'A description, Mrs Ryder – anything. If you can't talk, blink. A blink means yes. Do you understand?'

If she understood, she didn't respond.

Undeterred, Frost plunged on. 'The man who attacked you. Was he tall?' He waited. No response. 'Short? Fat? Thin?'

Her breath bubbled. Her fingers drummed. Her eyes, unblinking, were fixed on the ceiling.

Frost slumped back in his chair. Why was he hassling her? She wasn't going to tell him anything, so why not let the poor cow die in peace. He dug his hands in his pocket and felt his cigarettes. No chance of a smoke in here. The night sister would have him out on his ear.

'Let me try,' said Gilmore, but before Frost could answer the old lady made a choking sound. 'I'll get the sister,' said Gilmore, trying to open the curtains.

'No!' hissed Frost, grabbing his arm. 'Wait!'

The old lady was attempting to raise her head, but the effort was too much. Her eyes fluttered wildly and her lips quivered. She was trying to speak, but the words wouldn't come. Frost brought his ear right down to her mouth and felt the hot rasp of her faint breath on his face.

'Try again, love. I'm listening.'

One word. Very faint. It sounded like 'stab' but he wasn't sure if he heard it correctly. 'I know what he did, love. Can you describe him? Did you get a good look at him?' He kept his voice down. He didn't want the sister running in to order him out.

She nodded.

'Was he taller than me?'

Her lips moved, then her eyes widened and there was a choking noise at the back of her throat. And then she was still . . . dead still, the fingers no longer drumming.

The old girl was dead. Damn and sodding blast. She'd told him nothing. He dragged back the curtains. 'Nurse!'

He signalled for WPC Ridley to take over and hustled Gilmore out of the ward.

In the corridor outside he fumbled in his inside pocket to make a note of what the old lady had said and found he had pulled out those damn car expenses, the ones he had promised Mullett he would hand in tomorrow morning. Well, he'd have to think of yet another excuse for the Divisional Commander to disbelieve. Something was scribbled on one of the phoney petrol receipts. The name 'Wardley'. He racked his brains, but it meant nothing. 'Who's Wardley?'

Doesn't the old fool remember anything, thought Gilmore. 'He's the old boy who attempted suicide after he got the poison pen letter.'

Frost grinned. Something else to delay their return to the cold, dreary station. 'I promised the doc I'd have a word with him. Come on, son.'

Gilmore almost lost Frost in the labyrinth of corridors. Denton General Hospital was originally an old Victorian workhouse, but had been added to and rebuilt over the years. Frost darted up dark little passages, across storage areas and up clanking iron staircases to get to the ward where Wardley was lying. The staff nurse in her little cubicle with the shaded lamp greeted Frost as an old friend. She wasn't too keen on the idea of waking Wardley up, but Frost assured her it was essential.

Wardley, a little man of around seventy-five, his thinning hair snow white, was sleeping uneasily, turning and twitching and muttering. Frost shook his shoulder gently. Wardley woke with a start, mouth agape. He looked concerned as Frost introduced himself.

'Have you come to arrest me?' he croaked in a quavering voice.

'Attempted suicide isn't a crime any more,' said Frost, dragging a chair over to the bed. 'Besides, for all we know, it was an accident.'

Wardley frowned. 'You know it was suicide. I left a note.'

'Did you? We couldn't find it.'

The old man pulled himself up. 'It was on the bedside cabinet. My note . . . and that letter. How could you miss them?'

Frost scratched his head. 'They might have fallen under the bed. We'll look again later. Suppose you tell me what the letter said?'

The old man shook his head and his hands gripped and released the bedclothes. 'Terrible things. I'm too ashamed.'

'Blimey,' said Frost, 'I hope I can do things I'm ashamed of at your age.'

'It happened a long time ago, Inspector.'

'Then it doesn't bloody matter,' said Frost. 'Tell me what it said.'

A long pause. Someone further down the ward moaned in his sleep. A trolley rumbled by outside.

'All right,' said Wardley at last. 'It goes back thirty years – before I came to Denton. I lived in a little village. It was miles away from here, but I'm not telling you its name. I ran one of the classes in the Sunday school.' He paused.

'Not much sex and violence, so far,' murmured Frost. 'I hope it warms up.'

Wardley pushed out a polite, insincere smile and immediately switched it off. 'There were these two boys in my class. One was twelve, the other thirteen. After the class they would come back with me to my house. We would chat, watch television. All innocent stuff.' His voice rose. 'As God is my witness, Inspector, that's all it was.'

'What else would it be?' soothed Frost, thinking to himself, You dirty old bastard!

'One of the boys told lies about me. Filthy lies. I was called up before the Sunday school superintendent. I swore my innocence on the Bible, but he didn't believe me. I was forced to resign.' He stopped and studied the inspector's face, trying to read signs that he was being believed now.

'Go on,' murmured Frost.

'I couldn't stay in the village. People whispered and pointed. I had to move. So I came to Denton. After thirty years I thought it was all over and done with. And then I received that awful letter.'

'What did it say, Mr Wardley?'

'Something like "What will the church say when I tell

them what you did to those boys?" I'm a churchwarden, Inspector. It's my life. I couldn't face it happening all over again. If it gets out, I won't fail next time.'

Gilmore asked, 'Is there anyone in Denton, or locally, who could have known about your past?' Wardley shook his head.

'These two boys you messed about with,' Frost began, stopping abruptly as Wardley, quivering with rage, thrust his face forward and almost shouted.

'I never touched them. It was all lies. I swore on the Bible.' So loud did he protest that the staff nurse hurried anxiously towards the bed, only turning back when Frost gave her a reassuring wave.

He rephrased his question. 'The boys who lied, Mr Wardley. I want their names. And the name of the Sunday school superintendent, and all the people from your old village who would have known about this. We've got to check and see if any of them have moved to Denton.'

He left Gilmore to take down the details and went down to the car where he could smoke and think. Why on earth was he wasting time on this poison pen thing when he was way out of his depth with more important cases?

The car lurched to one side as Gilmore climbed in. 'Where to?' he asked, trying to get comfortable in the sagging driving seat.

His reply should have been 'Back to the station,' but he couldn't face going back to that cold Incident Room and wading through those endless, monotonous robbery files. 'Wardley's cottage. Let's have another look for that letter.'

'We shouldn't be wasting time on this,' moaned Gilmore. 'And how are we going to get in?'

'Dr Maltby will have a key,' said Frost, hoping this was true.

Frost was in luck. Maltby did have the key. He sat them in his surgery while he went upstairs to fetch it. 'Watch the door,' hissed Frost, darting for the doctor's desk.

'What are you doing?' asked Gilmore, horrified, watching the inspector methodically opening and closing drawers.

'Looking for something,' grunted Frost, busily opening a locked drawer with one of his own keys.

A creak of a floorboard above, then footsteps on the stairs.

'He's coming,' croaked Gilmore, wishing he could run and leave Frost to face the music.

'Got it,' crowed Frost, waving a blue envelope. He glanced at it and stuffed it back, quickly locked the drawer, then slid back into his seat just as the door opened and Maltby came in with the key to Wardley's cottage.

'What the hell was that about?' asked Gilmore when they were outside.

'The poison pen letter the doc gave us yesterday. He wouldn't tell us who it was sent to, so I sneaked a look at the envelope. Sorry to involve you, son, but you've got to grab your chances when they come.'

'So who was it addressed to . . . anyone we know?'

Frost grinned. 'Mark Compton. Mr Rigid Nipples.'

Gilmore's eyebrows shot up. 'What?'

'Doesn't it make you hate the swine even more . . . married to that cracking wife and having it off every Wednesday with a female contortionist in Denton?' He halted outside the door of a small, dark cottage, pushed the key in the lock and they went in.

They started in the bedroom, with its iron-framed single bed, and worked downwards. Everything inside the bedside cabinet was taken out. Frost showed mild interest in some loose tablets he found in the drawer, then seemed to lose interest. The cabinet was pulled away from the wall in case the note and the letter had fallen behind it. The bed likewise was moved, exposing a rectangular patch of fluffy dust. Even the bedclothes were stripped and shaken.

Gilmore, watched by Frost from the doorway, crawled all over the room on his hands and knees, looking in corners, behind curtains. He even stood on a chair and looked on top of the wardrobe. 'Nothing here,' he said, brushing dust from his jacket.

A quick poke around in the bathroom and then downstairs. Again Frost didn't seem inclined to join in the search, but let Gilmore do it while he sat on the arm of a chair, smoking and flipping through some bird-watching magazines he'd found in the magazine rack then looking all the way across the room at some nail holes in the wallpaper through a pair of high-powered binoculars he'd taken from a shelf.

'It would be quicker with two,' said Gilmore.

'When you get fed up, we'll go,' said Frost. 'The letters aren't here. I'm only staying because you seem so keen.'

Gilmore glowered. 'All right,' he admitted. 'I'm fed up.'

'We'll have a word with Ada next door,' said Frost.

You're messing me about, thought Gilmore as he followed the inspector to the adjoining cottage with its black-painted door and shining, well-polished brasswork. A quick rat-tat-tat at the brass knocker and the door was opened by Ada Perkins, her sharp pointed chin thrust forward belligerently. 'Oh, it's you, Jack Frost. I thought I could hear heavy feet plonking about next door.'

'And we thought we could hear the sound of an ear-hole pressed against the wall,' replied Frost. 'We'd like a couple of words . . . preferably not "piss off".'

With a loud sniff of disapproval she showed them into a spotlessly clean, cosy little room where a coal fire glowed cherry red in a black-leaded grate and where chintz curtains hid the damp and depressing weather outside. In the centre of the room stood a solid oak refectory table draped in a green baize cloth on which was a quantity of different coloured wine bottles bearing white, hand-written labels.

'Not interrupting an orgy, are we?' asked Frost.

She ignored the question and pointed to the high-backed wooden chairs by the table. 'Sit down!'

While Gilmore fidgeted, and kept consulting his watch, anxious to get back to his files, Frost settled down comfortably and warmed his hands at the fire. He picked up one of the bottles and pretended to read the label. 'What's this? "Cow's Dung and Dandelion. A thick brown wine, sticky to the palate." That sounds good, Ada.'

She snatched the bottle. 'It's *Cowslip* and Dandelion, as well you know. I'm sorting out my home-made wine.' She turned to Gilmore, who was drumming his fingers impatiently. 'Would you like to try some?'

Gilmore shook his head curtly. 'We're not allowed to drink while we're on duty.'

'This isn't alcoholic,' Frost assured him. 'This is home-made.' He beamed at Ada. 'Perhaps just a little sip – to keep out the cold.'

From the top of the matching solid oak sideboard, she produced two of the largest wine glasses Gilmore had ever seen and, after giving them a quick blow inside to shift the dust, banged them down on the green baize. She filled them to the brim, and slid them across. 'Try that.'

Gilmore lifted his glass and eyed the cloudy contents with apprehension. 'That's more than a sip.'

Frost told him, 'You've got to have a lot to get the full

benefit,' and raised his glass in salute to Ada who waited, arms folded, for their verdict. 'Cheers!' The wine tiptoed down his throat as smooth as silk, tasting of nothing in particular, then, suddenly, the pin slipped from the hand grenade and something exploded inside him, punching him in the stomach, making him gasp for breath and firing little star shells in front of his eyes. 'Gawd help us!' he spluttered as soon as the fit of coughing stopped.

'What's it like?' whispered Gilmore who hadn't plucked up the courage to try his yet.

'Delicious,' croaked Frost, his throat raw and stinging as if he had swallowed a glass of hot creosote. Quickly he covered his glass as Ada offered a second helping. 'If you're trying to get us drunk so you can have your way with us, Ada, forget it. I lust after your body, but all I want at the moment is the letters.'

Her expression hardly changed as she rammed the cork home in the bottle. 'What letters?'

Pausing only to slap the coughing, red-faced Gilmore on the back, Frost said, 'The poison pen letter and the suicide note.'

She stared blankly, as if mystified.

'You don't have to be a bleeding Sherlock Holmes to deduce you've got them, Ada. Wardley left them on his bedside cabinet. You were the first one in. They were gone by the time the doc arrived a couple of minutes later. Don't sod me about. I want them.'

Her lips tightened stubbornly. 'Did Mr Wardley say you could have them?'

'Yes, Ada. And he also said if you didn't hand them over, I was to give you a clout round the ear-hole.' He held out his hand. She hesitated, then took a folded sheet of notepaper from her apron pocket and thrust it at him.

Frost was slowly becoming aware that he was beginning

to feel a trifle light-headed. Everything in the room was starting to blur slightly round the edge. It took a great deal of effort to bring the typed letter into focus. Thank God he'd refused a second glass of Cowslip and Dandelion.

'Give it to me,' said Gilmore impatiently. He unfolded the note and read it aloud. '"Dear Lecher. What would the church say if I told them about you and the things the boys said you did?"'

'Is that it?' asked Frost, sounding disappointed.

Gilmore nodded. 'Typed on the same machine as the others. The "a" and the "s" are out of alignment.'

'It all looks out of alignment to me,' muttered Frost, wishing he hadn't made such a pig of himself on Ada's lethal brew. He squinted up at the blurred outline of the woman. 'And where's his suicide note, Ada?'

Stubbornly, she folded her arms. 'I burnt it.' At Frost's angry exclamation, she explained, 'Suicide is a mortal sin. Mr Wardley is a churchwarden. I wanted people to think the overdose was an accident.'

Frost pulled himself to his feet and waited to give the room a chance to steady itself. 'I wish you hadn't done that, Ada.'

She walked with them to the front door. 'Think yourself lucky I kept the poison pen letter. I was in two minds whether to burn that as well.'

'Thanks for the wine,' said Frost. 'I only felt sick for a little while.' A cold, swirling mist was waiting for them outside. Its chill dampness embraced them, sobering Frost instantly and making him shiver.

Gilmore edged the car out of the village and headed for Denton. Up on the hill, looking down on them, The Old Mill, a dark blur in the mist. No lights showed. 'Old Mother Rigid Nipples has gone to bed,' Frost murmured. 'Her husband's probably got one of them stuck up his nose right now.'

'Her husband's away,' grunted Gilmore, trying to spot the area car that was supposed to be watching the place, but there was no sign of it.

As they drove back, the radio was pleading for all available patrols to help break up a fight between two gangs of youths outside one of the town's less reputable pubs. 'Steer clear of there,' said Frost, not wanting to get involved.

And then the radio was calling them. 'Can you get over to The Old Mill right away?' asked a harassed-sounding Bill Wells. 'I had to call Charlie Alpha away to help with this pub fight. Mrs Compton's seen someone prowling about the grounds.'

Tuesday night shift (3)

The smell of burning oil from Frost's clapped-out Cortina grew stronger as Gilmore roared the car up the hill. 'I can see the sod!' yelled Frost. A hunched shape was moving across the lawn towards the house. Gilmore braked violently, slewing the car across the gravel driveway, and flung open the door. The sound of breaking glass shivered the silence, followed by the shrill urgency of an alarm bell.

'There he goes!' said Gilmore as something darted back across the lawn and was swallowed by shadow. 'I'll cut across that field, round to the side of the house. You nip that way to the end of the lane and cut him off as I flush him out.' Frost, his running days long past, listened without enthusiasm, and was still fumbling with his seat belt as Gilmore streaked away into the darkness.

The radio called to report that the alarm at The Old Mill was ringing. 'Yes, we know,' said Frost.

Gilmore, out of breath, was clinging to a tree, sucking in air for dear life as Frost eventually ambled over. Frost lit a cigarette and pushed a mouthful of smoke in the sergeant's direction. Gilmore fanned it away and, at last, between gasps, was able to croak, 'Where were you?'

Frost ignored the question. 'Did you see him?'

Gilmore's head shook in tempo with his panting. 'No. I told you to head him off.'

'I must have misheard you,' said Frost. 'Let's go to the house and see what he's done.' He spun round abruptly as a figure crashed towards them out of the black. 'Who the hell's this?'

'Did you get him?' It was Mark Compton, flourishing a heavy walking stick.

'He was too fast,' panted Gilmore. 'We thought your wife would be here on her own.'

'That's probably what that swine thought,' snapped Compton. 'I changed my schedule. I've just got in.' He led them back to the house and through to the lounge where curtains billowed from a jagged hole in the centre of the large patio window. Glass slivers glinted on the carpet. The cause of the damage, a muddied brick, probably from the garden, lay next to what looked like a bunch of flowers. Frost picked it up. It wasn't a bunch of flowers.

'My God!' croaked Compton.

It was a funeral wreath of white lilies, yellow chrysanthemums and evergreen leaves. Attached to it was an ivory-coloured card, edged in black. A handwritten message neatly inscribed in black ink read simply, and chillingly, *Goodbye*.

'The sod doesn't waste words, does he?' muttered Frost, passing the wreath to Gilmore. He stared out at the empty, dead garden, then pulled the curtains together. The night air had crept into the room and that, or the wreath, was making him feel shivery. 'Did you see anything of the bloke who did it?'

'No. Jill said she'd heard someone prowling around, but I couldn't spot anyone. I thought she'd imagined it, then the glass smashed, then the damned alarm. I saw someone running away, but that was all.'

'And you've no idea who it might be?'

'I've already told you, no.'

Frost scuffed a splinter of glass with his shoe. 'He's going to a great deal of trouble to make his point. He must really hate you . . . or your wife.'

'There's no motive behind this, Inspector,' insisted Compton. 'We're dealing with a nut-case.'

'Mark!' His wife calling from upstairs.

'I'm down here with the police.'

Gilmore pushed himself in front of the inspector. 'A quick question before your wife comes in, sir. Simon Bradbury – the man you had the fight with in London . . .'

'Hardly a fight, Sergeant,' protested Compton.

'Well, whatever, sir. It seems he's got a record for drunkenness and violence . . . and now we learn that his wife – the lady you obliged with a light – has given him the elbow. Any reason why he might believe you were the cause of her leaving him?'

Compton's face was a picture of incredulity. 'Me? And Bradbury's wife? I lit her damn cigarette over four weeks ago and that is the sum total of our relationship. You surely don't think Bradbury's responsible for what's been happening here? It's ridiculous!'

'The whole thing's bloody ridiculous,' began Frost

gloomily, quickly cheering up as the door opened and Jill Compton entered in a cloud of erotic perfume and an inch or so of nightdress. Her hair hung loosely over her shoulders and while Frost didn't know how breasts could be called 'pouting', pouting seemed a good word to describe Jill Compton's breasts as they nosed their way through near-transparent wisps of silk.

She smiled to greet Frost then she caught her breath. 'Oh my God!' She had seen the wreath. Her entire body began to tremble. Mark put his arms round her and held her tight. 'I can't take much more of this,' she sobbed.

'You won't have to, love,' he soothed. 'We'll sell up and move.'

'But the business . . .'

'You're more important than the bloody business.' He was squeezing her close to him, his hands cupping and stroking her buttocks, and Frost hated and envied him more and more by the second.

From somewhere in the house a phone rang. It was 00.39 in the morning. Everyone tensed. The woman trembled violently. 'It's him!' she whispered. Her husband held her tighter.

'I'll take it,' Frost barked. 'Where's the phone?'

Mark pointed up the stairs. 'In the bedroom. We switched it through.'

Frost and Gilmore galloped up the stairs, two at a time. The bedroom door was ajar. Inside, the room held the sensual smell of Mrs Compton. Frost snatched up the onyx phone from the bedside table and listened. A faint rapid tapping in the background. It was the sound of typing. At this hour of the morning? And indistinct murmurs of distant voices. Frost strained to listen, trying to make out what was being said. There was something familiar . . . Then a man's voice said, 'Hello

. . . is there anyone there?' and he flopped down on the bed in disappointment. The caller was Sergeant Wells.

'Yes, I'm here,' replied Frost. 'Sorry if I'm out of breath. I'm in a lady's bed at the moment.'

'Got a treat for you, Jack. Another body.'

'Shit!' said Frost. The only body he was interested in just now was Mrs Compton's. 'What's the address?' He snapped his fingers for Gilmore to take it down.

'The body's out in the open. It was dumped in a lane at the rear of the corporation rubbish tip.'

'Ah,' said Frost. 'Sounds like a job for Mr Mullett. I'll give you his home phone number.'

'Don't mess about, Jack. Jordan and Collier are waiting there for you. Could be foul play, but I've got my doubts.'

'Collier? You're pushing that poor little sod in at the deep end?'

'I had no-one else to send. Both area cars are ferrying the wounded down to Denton Casualty after the pub punch-up. There's blood and teeth all over the floor down here.'

'Excuses, excuses,' said Frost, hanging up quickly. 'Why do I always get the shitty locations? Rubbish tips, public urinals . . . I never get knocking shops and harems.' Well, he was in no hurry for this one. He stretched himself out on the bed and inhaled Jill Compton's perfume. 'Nip down and tell the lady of the house I'm ready for her now,' he murmured to Gilmore. 'And ask her to wash her behind. I don't fancy it with her husband's sticky finger-marks all over it.'

'Don't you think we should hurry?' asked Gilmore.

'I can't work up much enthusiasm about a body in a rubbish dump.' Reluctantly, he hauled himself up from the soft, still warm bed and had a quick nose around.

Other people's bedrooms fascinated him. His own was cold, cheerless and strictly functional, a place for crawling into bed, dead tired, in the small hours, and out again in the morning to face a new day's horrors. But here was a bedroom for padding about, half-undressed, on the soft wool carpeting, and for making love on the wide divan bed with its beige velvet headboard. By the side of the bed, a twin-mirrored, low-level dressing table where pouting-breasted Jill Compton would splash perfume over her red-hot, naked body, before sprawling on the bed, her hair tumbled across the pillow, awaiting the entrance of her rampant, adulterous sod of a husband.

He shook his head to erase the fantasy and walked across to the wide window to look out, across the moonlit garden. The wind had dropped and everything was quiet and still. 'Any chance the bloke we saw could have been the husband?'

'The husband?' Gilmore's eyebrows shot up. What was the idiot on about now? 'Smashing his own window? Scaring the hell out of his own wife?'

'I just get the feeling there's something phoney about this.'

'I don't share your opinion,' sniffed Gilmore. 'And in any case, there was no way it could have been the husband. He was with his wife when the window was smashed.'

'Then I'm wrong again,' shrugged Frost.

Downstairs, husband and wife were in close embrace, the shortie nightdress had ridden up to pouting breast level and hands were crawling everywhere.

Frost scooped up the wreath and passed it over to Gilmore. 'We'll see ourselves out,' he called.

They didn't hear him.

Police Constable Ken Jordan, his greatcoat collar turned up against the damp chill, was waiting for them at the lane at the rear of the sprawling rubbish dump. The lane was little more than a footpath with rain-heavy, waist-high grass flourishing on each side. In the background the night sky glowed a misty orange.

'Blimey, Jordan, what's that pong?' sniffed Frost, in-haling the sour breath of the town's decaying rubbish. 'It's not you, I hope?'

Jordan grinned. He liked working with Frost. 'Pretty nasty one this time, sir. The body's a bit of a mess.'

'I only get the nasty ones,' said Frost. 'Let's take a look at him.'

They followed Jordan, stumbling in the dark, as he led them down the narrow path, the wet grass on each side slapping at their legs. 'The old lady died, sir – at the hospital. I suppose you know.'

'Yes,' said Frost. 'I know.'

The lane curved. Ahead of them sodium lamps gleamed and flickering flames of something burning bloodied the haze. The tip was perimetered by 9-foot high chain link fencing, giving it the appearance of a wartime German prisoner of war camp.

Behind the wire fence, towering proud through streamers of mist, rose mountains of black plastic rubbish sacks and chugging between them, pushing, scooping and rearranging the landscape, a yellow-painted corporation bulldozer splashed through slime-coated pools of filthy water. As it demolished heaps of rubbish, rats scampered and scurried, their paws making loud scratching sounds on the plastic sacking. The smell was stale and sickly sweet like unwashed, rotting bodies.

Frost wound his scarf around his mouth and nose as

he nodded towards the bulldozer. 'I didn't know they worked nights.'

'It's this flu virus,' explained Jordan. 'Half of the work-force are off sick and the rest have to do overtime to keep ahead. It was the bulldozer driver who spotted the body.'

'Then sod him for a start,' said Frost.

'This way, sir.' Jordan led them off the path, trampling a trail through the lush, sodden grass to where a pasty-faced PC Collier stood uneasily on guard over rusting tin cans and a tarpaulin-covered huddle.

Frost lit up a cigarette and passed around the packet. Everyone took one, even Collier who didn't usually smoke. Frost looked down at the tarpaulin and prodded it with his foot. 'I can't delay the treat any more.' He nodded to Collier. 'Let's have a look at him.'

Collier hesitated and didn't seem to want to comply.

'You heard the inspector,' snapped Gilmore. 'What are you waiting for?'

Keeping his head turned well away, Collier fumbled for the tarpaulin and pulled it back.

Even Frost had to gasp when he saw the face. The cigarette dropped from his lips on to the chest of the corpse. He bent hurriedly to retrieve it, trying not to look too closely at the face as he did so.

Jordan, who had seen it before, stared straight ahead. Gilmore's stomach was churning and churning. He bit his lip until it hurt and tried to think of anything but that face. He wasn't going to show himself up in front of the others.

The body was of an old man in his late seventies. There were no eyes and parts of the face were eaten away with bloodied chunks torn from the cheeks and the lips.

'The rats have had a go at him,' said Jordan.

'I didn't think they were love bites,' said Frost. He straightened up. 'Still, we're lucky the weather's cold. Did I ever tell you about that decomposing tramp in the heat-wave?'

'Yes,' said Jordan hurriedly. Frost was fond of trotting out that ghastly anecdote.

'Did I tell you, son?' said Frost, turning to Gilmore. 'The hottest bloody summer on record. I can still taste the smell of him.'

'Yes, you told me,' lied Gilmore.

The dead man, the exposed flesh yellow in the over-spill of the sodium lamps, lay on his back, lipless mouth agape, staring eyeless into the night sky. He wore an unbuttoned black overcoat, heavy with rain, which flapped open to reveal a blue-striped, flannelette pyjama jacket which bore the bloodied paw marks of the feeding rats. The pyjama jacket was tucked inside dark grey trousers which were fastened by a leather belt.

'Do we know who he is?'

'Yes, Inspector.' Collier came forward. 'It's that old boy whose daughter-in-law reported him missing from home last week. He was always walking out and sleeping rough.'

'I bet the poor sod has never slept as rough as this,' observed Frost. 'Sergeant Wells said you think it's foul play?'

'His face looked battered, sir,' said Collier, pointing, but not looking where he was pointing.

Frost haunched down, slipped a hand beneath the head of the corpse and lifted it slightly. He dribbled smoke as he stared long and hard at the mutilated face, then stood up, wiping his palm down the front of his mac. 'That's just where the rats have been tucking in, son. There's no other marks . . . see for yourself.'

'I'll take your word for it, sir, if you don't mind,' said Collier.

Jordan's personal radio squawked. He pulled it from his pocket. Sergeant Wells wanted to speak to Inspector Frost urgently.

Frost took the radio. 'Everything's bloody urgent,' he moaned.

'Fifteen Roman Road, Denton,' said Wells tersely. 'Mrs Betty Winters, an old lady living on her own. A neighbour's phoned. He reckons he saw a man breaking in through the front door. The intruder is still in the house. Sorry about this, but I've got no-one else to send.'

'On our way,' said Frost, stuffing the radio back in Jordan's pocket. 'Jordan, come with us. Collier, stay here and wait for the police surgeon.' At the young PC's look of dismay at being left alone with the body, he added, 'You can handle it, son. If death isn't due to natural causes, let me know right away.'

With Jordan driving they made it to Roman Road in three minutes, coasting past number 15 and stopping outside the public telephone box where a middle-aged man emerged and hurried over to them. 'It was me who phoned,' he announced. 'I knew he was up to no good the minute I saw him. I thought he was going to pee in the porch. They do that, you know – dirty sods. You put your empty milk bottles out . . .'

'What did he look like?' cut in Frost as the man drew a breath.

'A big, ugly-looking sod. I couldn't get to that phone quick enough. Stinks of urine in that phone box. When they're not peeing in your porch or your milk bottles they're peeing in the phone box . . .'

'Are you sure he's still inside?' asked Gilmore.

'Positive.'

'Is there a back way out?'

'Through the gardens and over the rear wall. But I don't think he's got out that way. You'd hear next-door's bloody dog barking . . . bark, bark, bark, all bleeding night.'

'Go with the gentleman, Jordan,' said Frost, anxious to get rid of the verbose neighbour. 'Get into the garden over his fence and block the escape route.'

As soon as Jordan radioed through that he was in position, Frost did his letter-box squinting act. Utter blackness. A quick examination of the front door. No sign of a forced entry, so if there was an intruder, how did he get in? Hopefully he looked under the porch mat for a spare key. Nothing.

'Shall I smash the glass panel?' offered Gilmore.

'No,' grunted Frost, poking his hand through the letter-box and scrabbling about until his fingers touched something. A length of string looped at the end. He gave the string a tug. There was a click as the door knob was pulled back. Cautiously he pushed open the door, grabbing it as a sudden gust of wind threatened to send it crashing against the wall of the hall.

They tiptoed inside and Frost flicked the beam of his torch to show Gilmore how the string ran through staples and was tied round the door catch. 'The burglar's friend, son.' If the tenant forgot his key, he just had to pull the string. But so could anyone else who wanted to gain entry.

They held their breaths and listened. The house stretched and creaked and breathed and sighed. Then an alien sound from upstairs made Frost grab at Gilmore's sleeve, willing him to silence. A small click like a door closing. Signalling for the sergeant to stay by the front door, blocking that escape route, Frost padded along the passage and began creeping up the stairs.

Every stair seemed to creak no matter how carefully he placed his feet. At the top his torch picked out a small landing and two doors side by side. He clicked off the torch and slowly turned the handle of the nearest door.

Pitch black and a feeling of cold and damp. A hollow plop. Water slowly dripping from a tap. And a smell of sweat. Of fear. His thumb was on the button of the torch when he caught the metallic glint of a knife just as something hit him, sending his head smashing against the wall.

The torch dropped from his grasp as arms locked round him and dragged him down to the ground. Someone was on top of him, punching. There was hardly any room to move. His arm was trapped between his body and the wall, but he strained and wriggled frantically until he managed to free it. He reached up. Cloth. Flesh. Then a clawing hand clutched his face. He grabbed it, trying to tear it away while his other hand scrabbled in the blackness over cold, wet lino. Where was the damned torch?

He started to yell 'Gilmore!' when a fist crashed down on his face. He jerked up a knee, blindly. A scream of pain as his assailant fell back. His groping hand touched something metallic. The torch. Thankfully he grabbed it and swung it upwards like a club. A sharp crack and a groan as his attacker collapsed on top of him. Frost pushed and wriggled and managed to get on top.

Thudding footsteps up the stairs. 'Are you all right, Inspector?'

'No, I am bloody not!' panted Frost. 'I'm fighting for my bleeding life in here.'

Gilmore pushed in and fumbled for the light switch. They were in a small white-tiled bathroom. Frost, astride the intruder, was wedged between the wall and the bath.

His tongue took a trip round his mouth, prodding at teeth, tasting salt.

He stood up to get a better look at the unconscious man on the floor. His attacker was around twenty, fresh complexion, his hair black and cut short, dressed in grey slacks, a grey polo-neck sweater and a windcheater. Gilmore searched his pockets. No wallet, no identification. No sign of a weapon but over the sweater a heavy silver crucifix on a chain glinted like the blade of a knife.

The man on the floor groaned and stirred slightly.

'Hadn't we better get him to a doctor?' asked Gilmore.

Frost shook his head. 'He's only stunned.' Then he remembered the old lady who should have heard all the noise and be screaming blue murder. 'Let's find the old girl.'

She was in the bedroom. In the bed, eyes staring upwards, mouth wide open and dribbling red. The bedclothes had been dragged back, exposing a nightdress drenched in blood from the multiple stab wounds in her stomach. On the pillow, by her head, was a browning smear where her killer had wiped the blade clean before leaving.

While the little house swarmed with more people than it had held in its lifetime, Frost and Gilmore closeted themselves in the bathroom with their prisoner, now securely handcuffed. He lay still, apparently unconscious. A dig from Frost's foot resulted only in a slight moan. On the bath rack was an enormous sponge which Frost held under the cold tap until it was sodden and dripping, then he held it high over the man's face and squeezed.

The head jerked, and twisted, the eyes fluttered, then opened wide. He blinked and tried to focus on the piece of white plastic bearing a coloured photograph.

'Police,' announced Frost.

A sigh of relief as the man struggled up to a sitting position. 'In the bedroom – she's dead . . .' He winced and tried to touch his head and then saw the handcuffs. 'What's this? What's going on?'

'Suppose you tell us,' snapped Frost. 'What's your name?'

'Purley. Frederick Purley.'

'Address?'

'The Rectory, All Saints Church.'

'Are you trying to be funny?' snarled Gilmore.

Purley raised his dripping face to the sergeant. 'I'm the curate at All Saints Church. Please remove these handcuffs.' He tried to rise to his feet, but Gilmore pushed him down.

'Since when do curates break into people's houses in the middle of the night?' asked Frost.

'I only wanted to see if Mrs Winters was all right. I never dreamed . . .' His head drooped.

'Why did you think she wasn't all right?' asked Frost, dropping his cigarette end into the toilet pan and flushing it away.

'I'd been sitting with one of my parishioners – an old man, terminally ill – giving his daughter a break from looking after him. As I walked back I saw Mrs Winters' milk was still on the step. After that dreadful business with poor Mrs Haynes, I had to make sure she was all right.'

Gilmore's head jerked up. 'You knew Mrs Haynes?'

'Yes, Sergeant. I was with her on Sunday. Her husband's grave was vandalized. She was so upset.'

'It wasn't the poor cow's day,' said Frost. Then his eyes narrowed. 'There was no milk on the step when we arrived.'

'I brought it in with me. I put it in her fridge.'

198

Frost yelled down the stairs for the SOC man to check there was an unopened bottle of milk in the fridge and if so, to go over it for prints. Back to Purley. 'How did you get in?'

'There's a string connected to the front door catch. I've used it before . . . Mrs Winters is a cripple – she's under the hospital, chronic arthritis. She can't always get to the door.'

'Right,' nodded Frost. 'So what did you do next?'

'The hall was in darkness. I couldn't find the light switch, but I made my way upstairs. I tapped on her bedroom door. No answer. I went in and switched on the light and . . .' He shuddered and covered his face with his hands, 'and I saw her. And then I heard the door click downstairs. I thought it was the killer coming back. I switched off the light and hid in the bathroom. You know the rest.'

A brisk tap at the door. The SOC man came in holding a full pint bottle of red-top milk, shrouded in a polythene bag. 'This was in the fridge, Inspector. Two different dabs on the neck – neither of them the dead woman's.'

Frost squinted at the bottle. 'One should be the milkman, the other ought to be the padre here. Take his dabs and see if they match.' He ordered Gilmore to remove the cuffs.

Another tap at the door. 'The pathologist has finished,' yelled Forensic.

'Coming,' called Frost.

It was cold in the tiny ice-box of a bedroom with its unfriendly brown lino and the windows rattling where the wind found all the gaps. Drysdale buttoned his overcoat and rubbed his hands briskly. 'I estimate the time of death as approximately eleven o'clock last night, give or take half an hour or so either way.' He pointed to bruising on

199

each side of the dead woman's mouth. 'He clamped his hand over her face so she couldn't utter a sound, then he jerked back the bedclothes and stabbed her repeatedly – three times in the stomach and lastly in the heart. The wounds are quite deep. To inflict them he would have raised the knife above his head and brought it down with considerable force.' Drysdale gave a demonstration with his clenched fist. 'As he raised his hand, some of the blood on the knife splashed on to the wall.' He indicated red splatters staining the pale cream wallpaper.

'Would he have got any of that on himself?'

'Without a doubt,' said Drysdale, pulling on his gloves. 'Considerable quantities of blood spurting from the wounds would have hit his right arm and blood from the blade would have spattered him as he raised his arm to deliver the next blow.'

'No traces of blood in the bathroom waste-trap,' offered the man from Forensic, who was measuring and marking blood splashes on the wall, 'so he didn't wash it off before he left.'

'Dirty bastard!' said Frost. 'What can you tell us about the knife, doc?'

'Extremely sharp, single-edged, rigid blade approximately six inches long and about an inch and a quarter wide, honed to a sharp point.'

'The same knife that killed the other old girl – Mary Haynes?'

'It's possible,' admitted Drysdale, grudgingly. 'I'll be more positive after the post-mortem – which will be at 10.30 tomorrow morning. You'll be there?'

'Wouldn't miss it for the world,' replied Frost.

Gilmore was waiting for him at the head of the stairs. The vicar of All Saints had been contacted and had confirmed that his curate, Frederick Purley, had gone out to visit a terminally ill parishioner, and the SOC officer had confirmed that one of the thumb prints on the milk bottle belonged to the man in the bathroom.

Frost groaned his disappointment. 'The old lady died yesterday. So unless Purley killed her last night, then came back today just to put the milk in the fridge, we've lost our best hope for a suspect.'

He waited in the kitchen while Gilmore brought down the verified curate, who was vigorously rubbing his freed wrists, and who declined the offer of a doctor to look at his head on which a lump had formed nicely.

They sat round the kitchen table where the plates were already laid for the breakfast the old lady hadn't lived to enjoy. Frost utilized the egg cup as an ashtray. A rap at the door as PC Jordan entered.

'We've been all over the house, Inspector. No sign of forced entry anywhere. The back door's locked and bolted and all windows are secure. He came in through the front door.'

Frost nodded, then turned to Purley. 'Who else knew about instant entry with the old dear's piece of string?'

'Very few people, I should imagine. She wasn't a very friendly or communicative woman.'

'So how did you know her?'

'She used to be a member of our church senior citizens' club until her legs got too bad. I like to keep in touch.'

'Anything about her that would make her attractive to a burglar, padre? Was she supposed to have money, or valuables in the house?'

Purley shook his head. 'Not as far as I know.'

Frost scratched his chin. 'Was Mrs Haynes a member of your church club?'

'Yes, but an infrequent attender. She hasn't been for months.'

'What about a Mrs Alice Ryder?'

'Ryder?' His brow furrowed, then he shook his head. 'No. I don't recall the name.'

'We believe the same bastard killed them all,' said Frost. 'There's got to be a link.'

Purley gave a sad, apologetic smile. 'Then I'm afraid I don't know it.'

On the way back to the station they detoured to drop off the curate at the vicarage. As the car passed the churchyard Frost was reminded of the wreath dumped in the Comptons' lounge. He couldn't remember picking it up and was relieved when Gilmore jerked a thumb to the back seat where the wreath lay between a pair of mud-caked wellington boots.

'You might as well take the Compton case over, son. I'm not going to have much time for it.'

'Right,' said Gilmore, trying to keep the delight from his voice. A case of his own. He'd show these yokels how to get a result.

'You don't buy wreaths off the peg – they have to be ordered specially,' continued Frost. 'If I were you I'd get Burton to check with every florist in Denton.'

'That's what I intend to do,' said Gilmore.

As they crossed the lobby with the wreath, Sergeant Wells looked up from his log book. 'Who's dead?' he asked.

'Glenn Miller,' grunted Frost. 'It just came over on the radio.' He was in no mood for Wells' jokes.

'I'll tell you who is dead,' said Wells, anxious to impart his news.

Frost groaned, and walked reluctantly across to the desk. More cheer from Wells. The man was a walking

202

bloody obituary column. 'If it isn't Mullett, I don't want to know.'

Wells paused for dramatic effect, then solemnly intoned, 'George Harrison! Heart attack as he was going downstairs. Dead before he hit the bottom.' He leant forward to observe the effect this had on the inspector.

Frost's jaw dropped. Police Inspector George Harrison had only retired a few weeks ago after twenty-four years service. 'Bloody hell!'

'First you come round with the list for their retirement present,' said Wells, dolefully, 'next thing you know you're going round with the list for their wreath. You might as well collect both at once and be done with it.'

'Bloody hell!' said Frost again. The force was his life and retirement was the one thing he dreaded. The thought made him depressed. He jerked his head to Gilmore and headed for the stairs. 'Come on, son, let's get something to eat.'

'If you're going to the canteen, don't bother,' said Wells, happy to be the bearer of more bad news. 'It's shut.'

'Shut?' echoed Frost in dismay.

'The night staff are still down with flu. If you want anything, you've got to bring it in from outside.'

'And eat it in this ice-box?' moaned Frost, giving the dead radiator a kick. 'Sod that for a lark!' Then a slow grin crawled across his face. Somewhere in the building there was a room with comfortable chairs, a carpet and a 3-kilowatt heater. He pulled the car expense sheet from his jacket pocket and licked the tip of a stubby pencil. 'I'm taking orders for the all-night Chinky. Who wants curried chicken and chips?'

'I don't like this, Jack,' said Wells. 'If Mullett finds out . . .'

'He's not going to find out.' retorted Frost, peeping inside a foil container. 'Who ordered the sweet and sour?'

They were in the old log cabin, Mullett's wood veneer-lined office, Gilmore, Burton, Wells, and the four members of the murder enquiry team, the heater going full pelt, the room hot and steamy and reeking of Chinese food. The top of the satin mahogany desk was littered with foil containers and soft drink cans. Frost, in Mullett's chair, smoking one of Mullett's special cigarettes, was sorting out the food orders. 'Who wanted pancake rolls?'

Gilmore stood near the door, hovering nervously, his eye on the corridor, expecting any moment to see an irate Divisional Commander bursting through the swing doors.

'Come on, Gilmore,' called Frost. 'The chop suey's yours.'

Gilmore smiled uneasily and sat himself where he could still see down the corridor. He shuddered to think what discovery would do for his promotion chances.

'All we want is a disco and a few birds,' said Frost, spilling sweet and sour sauce on the carpet, 'and this job would be just about tolerable.' He swung round to Burton who was demolishing a double portion of sweet and sour lobster balls. 'Mrs Ryder died in hospital. Any news from Forensic on that knife the killer dropped?'

Burton swallowed hard. 'Nothing that helps much, Inspector. Their report's on your desk.'

'You know I don't read reports,' said Frost, dipping a chip in his curry sauce. 'What did it say?'

'An ordinary cheap kitchen knife of a standard pattern. No fingerprints, but traces of blood type O.'

Frost sniffed disdainfully. 'That's a coincidence – the victim was type O.' He peered suspiciously into his foil dish. 'This looks like stomach contents.' He sniffed. 'Smells like it, too.'

'Oh God, Jack,' shuddered Wells, pushing his food away from him.

Frost addressed the murder enquiry team. 'Any joy from the neighbours?'

'Most of them are in bed,' Burton told him 'We're going to have to go back first thing in the morning to catch the rest before they set off for work. Those we've spoken to hardly knew the old girl. She stayed in most of the time. No-one seemed aware of the string.'

'And no-one saw anyone suspicious hanging about,' added Jordan.

'Suspicious?' said Frost, pulling a piece of gristle from his mouth and flinging it in the vague vicinity of Mullett's wastepaper bin. 'This bastard isn't going to mooch about looking suspicious. He won't have a stocking mask on and a bleeding great knife poking out of his pocket. He's going to be inconspicuous. I want to know about everyone who's been seen going up and down the street – and that applies to the other two victims as well. I don't care if it's the road sweeper, the postman, doorstep piddlers or even a bleedin' dog – I want to know. People, vans, cars, the lot. We can then start comparing – see if anyone's been seen in all three streets.'

'The computer . . .' began Gilmore.

'The computer's a waste of time,' cut in Frost. 'I'm only going along with it to keep Hornrim Harry quiet. The only way to solve these cases is by good, solid detective work. By beating the hell out of some poor sod until he signs a fake confession.'

Gilmore faked a smile. 'It will be quicker with the computer, I promise you.'

'All right,' said Frost. 'I'll leave it to you.'

'What about a search team for the murder weapon?' asked Burton, wiping his mouth. 'He could well have chucked it.'

'Put a couple of men on it, but don't waste too much time. My gut feeling is that the bastard has kept it – ready for next time.'

The room went quiet. 'Next time?' said Wells.

'Yes, Bill.' He pushed the empty container away and fished out his cigarettes. 'I've got a nasty feeling in my water that he's going to kill again.'

Mullett's phone rang. A collective gasp and all eating stopped in mid-chew.

'It's all right,' assured Wells, 'I had the main phone switched through here.'

Frost picked it up. 'Mullett's Dining Rooms,' he said. Wells' eyes bulged with alarm until he realized the inspector had his hand over the mouthpiece.

The caller was a technician from Forensic reporting that he had extensively examined all the items removed from 46 Mannington Crescent, Denton and found nothing that would link them with the murder of Mrs Mary Haynes. As Frost listened he raised his eyes to the ceiling in despair. 'Sod clearing the innocent – what about nailing the guilty for a change? I asked you to drop that and check on those two newspapers as a matter of priority. No, I don't know who I spoke to. All right, all right.' He banged the phone back on its rest. 'He never got the message. Flaming Forensic. They're about as bloody efficient as we are. They can't start on the newspaper until tomorrow.'

'Well, it is two o'clock in the morning,' Wells reminded him.

'Then I'm bloody going home,' said Frost, not bothering to cover up a yawn. 'I've had enough for today. The rest of you, go home too. Grab some sleep and be back here by six. You can pinch some men from the next shift and start knocking on doors before people go off to work.'

'But Mr Mullett's rota . . .' began Wells.

'Sod Mr Mullett's rota. See you in the morning.'

He looked in his office on the way out. His in-tray was overflowing. He tugged the top paper from his tray. It was PC Collier's report on the dead body outside the refuse tip. He had almost forgotten about it. Natural causes – heart attack. Well, that was a relief. Clipped to the report was the SOC's photograph of the dead man *in situ*, sharp, clear and full of graphic detail. He showed it to Gilmore.

'I shall dream about that damn face tonight,' moaned Gilmore as they walked out to the car.

'I hope I don't,' said Frost. 'I want to dream of Mrs Compton.'

He did dream of Jill Compton. But she was eyeless and screaming and crawling with bloody-snouted rats. He woke up just before five in a cold sweat and couldn't get back to sleep again.

Wednesday morning shift

Police Superintendent Mullett stamped up the corridor to his office. He was angry. His sleep had been continually disturbed by calls from the media, and then from County, the Chief Press Officer, demanding his comments on a possible serial murderer in Denton, the brutal killer of three old ladies. When he had phoned the station to try to get some information from Frost, he was informed that, despite the rota, the inspector and his team had left for the night and calls to Frost's home indicated that the phone had deliberately been left off the hook. He finally managed to get the information required from Detective Sergeant Gilmore, but only after Gilmore's wife had been extremely rude over the phone, asking why her husband was expected to be at everyone's beck and call twenty-four hours a day.

Scooping up a fearsome stack of mail from his absent secretary's desk, he unlocked his office door, then paused, nose twitching, testing the air. What was that smell? A stale, rancid oniony aroma which reminded him of curry. He dumped the post in his in-tray and flung open the window. The curtains flapped wildly as the wind roared and drove in the rain. Below, in Eagle Lane, the noise of traffic was deafening. He hastily closed the window and returned to his desk where he reached for the internal phone to ask the station sergeant to come in with his morning report.

While he waited he flicked through the post, shuddering at a photograph of a mutilated body found outside Denton rubbish tip, then frowning at the totally inadequate, scrawled report from Frost – *Mrs Alice Ryder, victim of burglary assault, died in Denton Hospital – full report to follow. Mrs Betty Winters, aged 76, 15 Roman Rd, Denton. Murder by stabbing – full report to follow.* Mullett's frown deepened. As he knew from bitter experience, Frost's 'further reports' never materialized. The man's paperwork was hopeless. Which reminded him, where were those car expenses? He rummaged through his tray but, as expected, they were not there.

He looked up as Sergeant Johnson came in with the morning report and the mail from County. He greeted him with a smile. 'Good to see you back, Sergeant. Are you fit?'

208

'Well, actually, sir . . .' began Johnson, who was starting to feel a trifle light-headed and was wondering if he hadn't reported back to work too soon.

'Excellent,' cut in Mullett hastily. He didn't want a catalogue of the man's ailments. He'd had enough of moans from Sergeant Wells. 'Manning level?'

'Three men back from sick leave,' Johnson reported, 'but two more off – injured in that pub punch-up last night.'

'First class,' snapped Mullett, concerned only with the plus side of the arithmetic. 'We're winning, Sergeant.' He smiled as he signed the report and blotted it neatly. 'We'll soon be back to normal.'

'We're going to be very thin on the ground today as far as normal duties are concerned,' warned the sergeant. 'Mr Frost has commandeered most of my men for house-to-house enquiries – another old lady stabbed to death last night.'

'I know,' said Mullett bitterly. 'The press phoned me at three o'clock in the morning to tell me – and Mr Frost kindly scribbled a note for my in-tray.' He held aloft the piece of paper. 'County want us to tread very carefully with this one, Sergeant. A serial killer at large in Denton – could cause panic. It's vital I see the inspector the minute he comes in.'

'Sir,' said Johnson, taking the signed report.

The office door opened. Mullett hoped it was Frost, but it was his gum-chewing temporary secretary in a disturbing polo-necked sweater who wiggled in with the correspondence he had dictated yesterday. 'Sorry I'm late,' she said, dumping the poorly typed, heavily corrected letters on his desk, 'but we've run out of Snowpake. I had to buy some more. Oh – and this has just come.' She dropped the Denton *Echo* in front of him.

He snatched up the paper from her and stared goggle-eyed, mouth dropping with dismay at the screaming banner headlines. *Town of Terror – Granny Ripper Claims Third Victim!!! Terror spread like wild-fire amongst the senior citizens of Denton today as news of yet another brutal murder* . . . The phone rang. Still staring at the paper he groped for it. 'Yes?' he croaked. He jerked to attention. 'Good morning, sir . . . Yes, I've just seen the paper.' He clapped a hand over the mouthpiece and bellowed at Johnson, 'Find Frost. I want him here, now!'

To Johnson's surprise, Frost was already in his office, a wad of blank petrol receipts in front of him which he was filling in with different coloured pens. Sitting in the other desk was the new detective sergeant, looking disgruntled and also scribbling out petrol receipts.

'Hello, Johnny,' greeted Frost. 'Welcome back. We thought you were dying. We'll have to send the bloody wreath back now.' He indicated the withering floral tribute in his in-tray. 'Talking of wreaths reminds me of a joke.'

'Never mind jokes,' said Johnson, 'Mr Mullett wants to see you.'

'Sod Mullett,' said Frost. 'There was this woman . . .' He paused as DC Burton came in.

'Got a minute, sir?'

'Sure, son, but I've got a joke first. There was this woman . . .' He paused again as Detective Sergeant Arthur Hanlon, nose red and sore, poked his head round the door.

'Oh, if you're busy, Jack . . .'

'No – come in, Arthur. I've got a joke for you.'

Hanlon pulled a face. 'If it's the one about the man drinking the spittoon for a bet, you've told it to me.'

'A different one,' said Frost, beckoning him in. 'It's about the funeral of a woman who's had fifteen kids.' He frowned as the phone rang. Burton answered it.

'Forensic for you, Inspector. They say it's urgent.'

'Everything's bloody urgent!' He took the phone and in a strangulated voice said, 'Mr Frost will be with you in a moment.' He pressed the mouthpiece to his jacket. 'Where was I?'

'Fifteen kids,' reminded Johnson, anxious to get the story over so Frost could report to Mullett.

'Right. Funeral. Woman who'd had fifteen kids being buried. As the coffin's being lowered down into the grave, the vicar turns to the husband and says, "Together at last!" The husband says, "What do you mean, together at last? I'm still alive." "I wasn't referring to you," says the vicar. "I meant her legs." '

Gilmore sat stone-faced as Frost's raucous roar of mirth almost drowned the others. Old women butchered and the fool was cracking jokes! Frost raised the phone, poking his finger in his ear to shut out the laughter. 'Hello. Frost here. Sorry, I can't hear you. I think the Divisional Commander's throwing a party.' He flapped a hand for silence. 'That's better, I've shut the door. You were saying?' He listened. 'That's bloody marvellous. Check it out and let me know.' He hung up and beamed happily at Gilmore and Burton. 'Those newspapers we sent to Forensic. Nothing on the *Daily Telegraph*, but when they shoved the *Sun* under the microscope, not only were the Page Three girl's tits enormous, but they spotted tiny flakes of black paint and rust on the outside page.'

'Black paint and rust?' frowned Burton.

'If our luck's in, it's from Greenway's letter-box,' explained Frost. 'It could have rubbed off as the paper went in and out. Forensic are sneaking someone round

211

to his house to check. If the paint matches, we've got the bastard.' He rubbed his hands with delight and passed his cigarettes round.

Johnson was getting fidgety. 'Mr Mullett wants to see you, Jack.'

'I'm not ready for him yet.' He peeled off some blank petrol receipts. 'Fill these in for me, Johnny. Disguise your writing. Six gallons, eight gallons and four gallons.'

The sergeant's pen flew over the receipts. 'What crime am I committing?'

'Forgery,' said Frost, giving three blanks to Burton. 'Disguise your handwriting, son. Two lots of eight gallons and one of six.' He pushed two more blanks across to Arthur Hanlon. 'Five gallons and seven gallons, Arthur – and blow your nose, it's starting to drip.'

'Just tell me what I've done,' said Johnson, handing the completed receipts back.

Frost collected the balance from Gilmore and Burton and riffled through them. 'I lost all my receipts last month so I had to forge my car expenses. Some silly sod in County with nothing better to do spotted it. Mullett said I could get off the hook if I came up with the genuine ones.' He waved the receipts. 'These are them.'

'But they're still fakes,' insisted Johnson.

'But better fakes than the first lot. Besides, I didn't have time to go round all the flaming petrol stations asking for copies.' He turned to Hanlon. 'What's the latest on the house-to-house, Arthur?'

Hanlon handed over his two receipts. 'We've almost finished. The first of the results are going through the computer now.'

'Anything significant?' asked Gilmore.

Hanlon shrugged. 'One person thought they saw a blue van cruising down Roman Road late on the night of the

212

murder, another saw a strange red car. I'll check them out.'

After Hanlon squeezed out of the office, Frost remembered that Burton was still patiently waiting. 'Sorry, son, I forgot about you. What was it?'

'I've been checking all the florists about that wreath, sir. I traced the shop and found out who ordered it.'

Frost had to readjust his thoughts back to the Compton business. 'Who?' But before Burton could answer, Gilmore had leapt from his chair and was glowering angrily at the detective constable.

'This is my case, Burton,' he hissed. 'You report to me, not to the inspector.' He was in a lousy mood. Liz had been insufferably rude to the Divisional Commander when he'd phoned last night. Mullett was furious and it was pretty clear that his promotional chances were fast gurgling down the drain. How the hell could he report Frost's misdemeanours when the inspector involved him in them all . . . eating in Mullett's office, forging petrol vouchers. And now this cretin of a detective constable was going over his head.

Burton, taken aback by Gilmore's outburst, looked from the sergeant to the inspector.

'My fault,' said Frost. 'The sergeant is quite right. It is his case.'

'So who ordered the damn thing?' asked Gilmore, returning to his chair.

Burton flipped open his notebook. 'Mr Wilfred Blagden, 116 Merchants Barton, Denton.'

Gilmore smiled sarcastically. 'I suppose if I wait long enough you'll tell me who he is?'

The constable hesitated before deciding that the pleasure of smashing Gilmore's face in was marginally outweighed by the need to retain his job.

'He's an old man, eighty-one years old. His wife, Audrey, died last week.'

Gilmore still appeared mystified, but the penny dropped for Frost. 'The wreath was stolen from her grave?'

'Yes, Inspector. The old boy's very upset – wants to know what the police are doing about it.'

The police are sitting on their arses cracking dirty jokes, thought Gilmore. He waved Burton away with an irritated flap of the hand then skimmed through a report from Forensic reporting that the death threats to the Comptons had been cut from copies of *Reader's Digest*.

The office door crashed open and a flustered-looking Johnny Johnson burst in. 'Mr Mullett is screaming for you, Jack.'

Frost quickly checked through the newly forged car expenses, then stood up, moving the knot of his tie to somewhere near the centre of his collar. 'I'm ready for him now. Do I look innocent and contrite?'

'You never look innocent and contrite,' Johnson replied.

As he breezed through the lobby on his way to the old log cabin, he passed an old man sitting hunched on the hard wooden bench by the front desk. The man looked familiar, but Frost couldn't place him. He sidled over to Collier who was standing in for Johnny Johnson and jerked a thumb in query.

Collier leant forward, 'His name's Maskell.'

Frost clicked his fingers. 'Jubilee Terrace – Tutankhamun's tomb – mummified body?'

Collier nodded. 'He refuses to accept that his wife is dead. He keeps coming in to report her missing.'

Sensing their attention, the old man looked up. 'Her name's Mary. I left her in bed, but she's not there any more.' He cupped a hand to his ear so he wouldn't miss a word of their reply.

'She's dead, Mr Maskell,' said Collier.

But the old man refused to hear what he didn't want to hear. 'Her name's Mary Maskell – 76 Jubilee Terrace, Denton.'

Frost moved on hurriedly, leaving Collier to deal with him. He was half-way up the passage to Mullett's office when . . . 76 *Jubilee Terrace* . . . *Upstairs bedroom. The old girl's dead* . . . The tiny tape recorder at the back of his mind had been triggered into replaying, over and over, that mysterious phone call in the pub. How had the caller known about the old girl? Maskell wouldn't have let him in. She was upstairs and the bedroom windows were heavily curtained. The only way in would have been through the same window Frost had used. *Upstairs bedroom. The old girl's dead.* The voice. He knew that damned voice. He screwed up his face trying to squeeze his memory into action. Then it clicked. Wally Manson . . . Wally bloody Manson! He spun round and raced back to his office.

Johnny Johnson, gazing out of the window, saw Frost with the new bloke tagging behind, dashing across the car-park. The interview with Mr Mullett must have been a brief one, he thought. His internal phone rang. 'Yes, Mr Mullett?' His face froze. 'You're still waiting for him?' Through the window the Cortina belched smoke as it roared towards the exit. 'I think he's just gone out, sir.'

The grey Vauxhall Cavalier bumped up a side lane, stopping well short of the cottage. Tony Harding, a junior technician with the Forensic Laboratory, climbed out of the car and walked purposefully up the garden path of the isolated building, a clipboard in his hand. He hammered loudly at the door and took a pen from his pocket as if ready to conduct a market survey. The knocking rumbled through an empty house and awakened a dog in the back garden and started it yapping. Harding waited, then, to play safe, knocked again and called, 'Anyone in?'

With one last look around to make certain he was unobserved he knelt by the letter-box. The paint was black. Parts of it were flaking. With a pocket knife he gently scraped off a tiny portion into an envelope.

In half an hour he was back in the lab where the spectroscope was already set up.

'Who's Wally Manson?' asked Gilmore, swerving to avoid a road-crossing dog.

'Small-time villain who's been in and out of the nick most of his life. Stealing cars, shop breaking, receiving stolen goods, assault with a dangerous weapon. Wally's never turned his hand to burglary before, that's why I never reckoned him for those senior citizen larks. But it was definitely him who phoned me at the pub.'

Gilmore slowed down at the traffic lights. 'So what does that prove?'

'How did Wally know there was a date-expired corpse on the bed? Even the bloody neighbours didn't know. The only way he could have found out would be by doing what I did – climbing through the back window and sneaking into the bedroom.'

At last Gilmore twigged. 'He was going to rob the place?'

'That's what I reckon, son . . . and I bet he ruined a perfectly good pair of underpants when he saw the sleeping bloody beauty. Round the corner, here.'

This was part of the newer section of Denton, modern two-storey houses with front lawns in a street lined with sapling trees. 'Last but one on the right,' said Frost. Then he leant back and almost purred with satisfaction.

Parked outside the house was a battered van. It was a dark blue colour.

Belle Manson, Wally's wife, was a plump, bleached-haired woman of around forty with heavy ear-rings hanging, like tarnished brass curtain rings, from ear-lobes which looked as if they had been pierced with a 6-inch nail. She was on her knees, scrubbing the front doorstep, her over-sized breasts swinging in sympathy with the gyrations of her scrubbing brush. Without pausing in her labours, she scrutinized the two pairs of shoes plonked in front of her, one pair scruffy, unpolished, cracked and down at heel, the other so highly burnished she could see her fat face in them.

She didn't need to look up to see who it was. She'd seen those broken-down shoes many times before. The scrubbing brush worked vigorously at a stubborn spot in the corner. 'He's out. I don't know where he is. I don't know when he'll be back. I haven't seen him for days.'

'Thanks very much, Belle,' said Frost, stepping over the wet patch into the hallway. 'We'd love to come in.' She snorted annoyance and straightened up, flinging the scrubbing brush into the bucket and splashing Gilmore's trousers with dirty water in the process.

'You got a warrant?' she screamed.

'Would I come in without one?' asked Frost in a hurt voice, patting the forged car expenses in his inside pocket as he marched up the passage and into the kitchen.

'Yes, you bloody would,' she yelled, charging after him.

Frost drew a chair up to the formica-topped table and plonked himself down. He jerked his head for Gilmore

217

to have a quick look round for a lurking Wally.

'Where the hell do you think you're going?' she yelled as Gilmore clattered up the stairs.

'He wants to use your toilet,' Frost explained. 'He had curry for breakfast and it's given him the runs.'

Ear-rings and breasts quivering, Belle glowered. She flopped down in the chair opposite him. Frost gave her a friendly smile. 'You're looking well, Belle.'

'You're not,' she snapped. 'You're looking old and scruffy.' She waved away the offered cigarette. 'I don't smoke.' Then her face softened. 'Sorry to hear about your wife.'

'Thanks,' muttered Frost. An awkward silence. She'd thrown him off balance. He lit up and waited for Gilmore's return.

A kettle on the gas-ring rattled its lid and whistled. Belle heaved herself up and turned off the gas.

'Two sugars in mine,' said Frost.

'You've got the cheek of the bloody devil,' she snapped, banging three mugs on the table and hurling a tea-bag in each. Gilmore came in, shaking his head. Wally wasn't in the house. 'What did I tell you? I haven't seen him for days.' smirked Belle, filling the mugs from the kettle and slopping in milk. 'Help yourselves to sugar.' She slid the mugs over.

'So where is he, Belle?' said Frost, spooning out the dripping tea-bag and depositing it on the table.

'I've told you, I don't know.' She leant back to reach an opened box of Marks and Spencer's Continental chocolates from the dresser and wrenched off the lid. A chocolate truffle disappeared into her mouth and was washed down by a swig of tea.

'When did you last see him?' persisted Frost.

Her face contorted as she gave her impression of

thinking deeply. 'Last Friday. He goes away a lot on business. I hardly ever see him. He only comes back for you know what and that only lasts five minutes on a good day.'

Frost nodded sympathetically. 'We've got him down in our files as a quick in and out merchant, Belle.' His finger worried away at his scar. 'He doesn't take his van when he goes away, then?'

'His van?'

'The blue one outside.'

'Oh that,' sniffed Belle. 'No. It's broken down.' As she spoke, the front door slammed. Her head jerked round. She looked worried. Quick footsteps along the passage. At a sign from Frost, Gilmore was up out of his chair, standing by the door, ready to grab the newcomer.

'Mum, have you . . . Oh, sorry, I didn't know you were with clients.' It was a young girl.

Belle forced a smile. 'It's the police, Deidree . . . I was just telling them we hadn't seen your dad since Friday.'

Deidree Manson, fifteen years old, in a leather jacket and a short skirt, was a scaled-down replica of her plump mother, even down to small, curtain-ring ear pendants, but with sandy-coloured hair which had not yet made the acquaintance of the bleach bottle. She stared blankly at her mother. 'Dad? Oh yes . . . of course. We haven't seen him for days.'

Frost flicked ash into his tea mug. 'Clients? Are you back on the game, Belle?'

'Thank you very much!' mouthed Belle to her daughter. To Frost she said airily, 'I oblige the odd gentleman. Just for pin money.'

'Yes. Some of your clients are bleeding odd,' said

Frost, pushing his mug away. 'I hope you disinfect your crockery.' He swung round to Deidree. 'No school today?'

'Half-term,' she replied laconically, helping herself to a strawberry cream.

'What school do you go to?'

'Denton Modern.'

The same school as Paula Bartlett. Frost asked Deidree if she knew her.

Her tongue snaked out to catch a straying dribble of chocolate juice. 'She was in my class. Bit of a drip. Nose always stuck in a book. Had no interest in boys or sex or pop music or anything.'

'What about the teacher, Mr Bell?' asked Frost casually. 'What sort of a bloke is he?'

Deidree chomped and shrugged. 'Boring. I think Paula had a crush on him. Two drips together.'

A brisk rat-tat-tat at the door made Belle frown and consult her wrist-watch. She beckoned Deidree over for an enigmatic message. 'If it's "you-know-who" for "you-know-what", tell him it's inconvenient at the moment. Can he call back later?'

Frost watched Deidree's plump little bottom wriggle through the door and wondered how long it would be before she was invited to join the family business. 'We're going to have to search the place, Belle. Wally's been naughty.' He stood and signalled for Gilmore to follow.

Belle leapt up to block their path. 'I want to see your warrant, first.'

He pulled his car expenses from his inside pocket and flashed them under her nose. 'Satisfied?' Before she had a chance to examine them, they were back in his pocket.

'All right,' she nodded reluctantly. 'But don't make a mess – and don't pinch anything.'

A door in the hall led to the lounge. 'We'll start in here, son.' They were about to enter when there was a sudden angry burst of protestations from the disappointed client at the front door. 'If he won't go away,' called Frost, 'tell him I'll cut off his "you know what" and stuff it up his "he knows where".' Silence. The front door slammed.

It was a smallish room jam-packed with Belle's pin-money purchases of new furniture and dominated by an enormous 28-inch twin-speakered colour TV and a stereo video both housed in a mahogany-veneered, Queen Anne style cabinet. Frost nudged Gilmore and pointed. On top of the cabinet lay a familiar-looking box holding a video cassette. The box was white with a typed label which read: *Till The Blood Runs – Canings & Whippings*. The same title as one of the pornographic videos removed from the newsagent's. 'Belle!' he yelled.

'I know nothing about it,' said Belle as she waddled in. 'Something Wally brought home.' She looked at the label. 'Canings and Whippings? A bit too strong meat for my clients – it would give the poor old sods a heart attack. If you want to know about dirty videos, ask our Deidree. Some bloke wanted her to make one.'

The young girl was called in. 'Pornographic videos,' said Frost. 'Your mother says you were approached. Tell me about it.'

Deidree leant against the door frame and eased some toffee away from her back teeth with her finger. 'Nothing much to tell. We were coming out of a disco one night when this bloke came across from a posh car and asked me if I wanted to earn myself fifty quid posing in the nude with him for a video. I told him to stuff his video camera right up his arse.'

'I've always brought her up to be a decent girl,' said Belle proudly.

'What did he look like?' asked Frost. 'Would you know him again?'

'Old – about forty. Dressed to the nines – shirt and tie and all that stuff. Darkish hair. I might recognize him again, but I'm not sure.'

Frost dismissed them both with a flick of his hand. He couldn't waste time on this – porno videos were very low on his list of priorities. A quick search of the lounge revealed nothing. 'Right, son. Up the wooden stairs to Bedfordshire.'

He sat on Belle's soft-mattressed double bed with its plump purple eiderdown and watched Gilmore opening and shutting drawers. A packet of Hamlet cigars lay on the dressing table. Frost shook it hopefully. It rattled. There was one left. He lit it, stretched out on the bed and contentedly puffed smoke across to the detective sergeant.

'Excuse me,' said Gilmore huffily, annoyed that Frost wasn't helping. He leant over to tug open the drawer of the bedside cabinet. Packets of contraceptives . . . small aerosol cans. He seized one of the cans and showed it to the inspector. 'Look at this!'

Frost sat up and blinked at the label. 'Nipple Hardening Spray! I don't believe it.' He examined the can from all angles. 'This could make a man's thumb obsolete.'

'And this!' Gilmore flourished another can.

'Bloody hell, son, don't point it at me. It's the last thing I need at the moment. What else has she got?' Happy now to join in, he was soon rummaging through the various sex aids and stimulants.

The bedroom yielded nothing else of interest. The bedroom next door was Deidree's with its pop posters and record player. 'Leave it, son,' said Frost. 'Wally wouldn't have stuck any bent gear in here.'

'It still wouldn't hurt to look,' said Gilmore stubbornly, dragging out the wardrobe so he could see behind it.

'Whatever turns you on, son,' said Frost. He ambled over to the window and opened it so he could jettison the cigar. Below was the back yard, a miserable patch of concrete landscaped with oily rain-puddles, a couple of rusty, bottomless buckets, and two treadless car tyres. Car tyres! The blue van! He'd forgotten all about the bloody blue van. That was the next thing to search. He watched the cigar butt nose-dive to its death.

An excited shout from Gilmore had him spinning round.

Gilmore had found a crumpled bundle of blue cloth. He opened it out. A pair of men's jeans, grubby and thickly spattered with dried blood.

'Belle!' roared Frost, his bellow echoing down the stairs.

'Won't be a minute.' She was talking to someone, her voice low and urgent.

'I want you now!' he yelled.

'Coming.'

The front door clicked shut and as it did a bell shrilled a warning deep in his subconscious. From outside, an engine coughed, then roared into life. A van engine.

'Shit!' cried Frost, galloping down the stairs two at a time, Gilmore hard on his heels. At the bottom of the stairs was Belle, lumbering up very slowly, deliberately blocking their way. Frost almost pushed her over as they charged for the front door. Outside an empty street. A patch of oil where the van had been standing.

'Double shit!' howled Frost.

'There!' pointed Gilmore. Something blue disappearing round the corner trailed by a billow of exhaust.

The Cortina shuddered as they hurled themselves in and roared off in pursuit. Round the corner, but no sign of the van. Up to the main road. 'Which way?' asked Gilmore.

'Left,' said Frost. He had seen something blue jumping the lights. Drumming his fingers impatiently on the steering wheel, Gilmore waited for the lights to change. The blue van ahead was getting smaller and smaller in the distance.

What a foul-up, thought Gilmore. The van was there when they arrived, but they'd ignored it. 'That bloody fat cow,' he muttered. 'We ought to run her in for obstruction.'

'He's her husband, son,' said Frost, mildly. 'Your wife would have done the same to help you.'

Would she? thought Gilmore bitterly. She certainly didn't help me last night when bloody Mullett phoned. Before he could follow the thought further, the traffic lights flickered. He jammed his foot down, passing car after car after car. The blue van was getting bigger.

'Control to Mr Frost. Come in, please.'

Gilmore braked abruptly as an estate car shot out of a side turning right in their path.

'Control to Mr Frost. Come in, please.' repeated the radio.

'Shut your bleeding row,' said Frost to the radio as Gilmore swerved round the estate car. Frost twisted in his seat and jerked two fingers at the driver.

More traffic lights ahead. The blue van had stopped.

'Control to Mr . . .'

Frost snatched up the handset. 'Hold on, Control. We are . . . Shit!'

'Say again?' said Control.

'I said, "Tut tut",' muttered Frost bitterly and feeling like banging his head against the windscreen. The blue van they had been chasing had the name of a dress shop written on the side and was being driven by a woman. Gilmore glared poison darts at the inspector as if it was all his fault. Frost was philosophical. 'He'll turn up. He's got nowhere to go.' He was much more used to cock-ups than the sergeant. He raised the handset to his ear. 'Put out a call to all units. I want Wally Manson brought in. Last seen driving a blue Ford transit van about ten years old . . . I don't know the registration number, but you should be able to get it from the computer.'

'Will do,' said Control. 'Hold on, please. Sergeant Johnson wants to speak to you urgently.'

A rustling sound, then Johnson took over. 'Jack. Forensic have matched up the paint on the newspaper. It definitely came from Greenway's letter-box. Mr Mullett wants you back here right away.'

'My one aim in life is to gratify Mr Mullett's every whim,' replied Frost. 'We're on our way.'

Mullett was almost dancing with excitement. He waved the Forensic report at Frost. 'We've got him, Inspector. We've got him . . . and we can all take credit. A chance observation on your part, scientific skill and expertise from Forensic plus solid devoted team work under my supervision.' He lowered himself down into his chair and swung from side to side in smug satisfaction. Frost thought this was a good time to hand over the forged car expenses.

'Excellent,' said Mullett, giving them barely a glance as he signed them with a flourish of his Parker and tossed them into his out-tray. 'Things are really moving our way at last. How's the inventory going?'

'Almost finished it, Super,' said Frost, trying to remember where he had hidden the damn thing.

'Good,' beamed Mullett. 'I want this man Greenway picked up and brought in right now. How many men will you need?'

'The fewer the better, Super. He lives out in the wilds. If he spots half the Denton police force converging on his cottage, he might do a runner.'

'Very well, but don't let there be any foul-ups.' He was itching for Frost to go so he could pick up the phone and casually let drop to the Chief Constable that, despite the appalling manpower shortage, Denton Division had once again come up trumps. Then his euphoria crash-dived as he remembered what he had originally wanted to see Frost about. He snatched up the Denton *Echo* and jabbed at the headlines. 'Have you seen this? "Granny Ripper! Town of Terror!" What are we doing about it? The press are screaming for our blood and County are breathing down our necks.'

'I might be able to give you a quick result,' Frost said, filling him in on Wally Manson. 'We've sent the jeans over to Forensic.'

Mullett could hardly contain himself. Wait until the Chief Constable heard about this. 'I want Manson picked up and brought in,' said Mullett, scooping up the telephone and dialling.

'I'll make a note of it,' said Frost solemnly.

'Chief Constable, please,' said Mullett. He put his hand over the mouthpiece. 'That will be all, Inspector.' As the door closed behind Frost, he straightened his tie and smoothed back his hair. 'Oh, hello, sir.' He put on his weary voice. 'Sorry if I don't sound all that brilliant . . . lack of sleep, you know . . .' He gave a modest laugh. 'Someone's got to keep an eye on things, sir . . . Some double good news on the Paula Bartlett case and the senior citizen killings that I thought you should have right away . . .'

Wednesday afternoon shift

Harry Greenway dropped a tea-bag into a mug and drowned it with boiling water from the kettle. He felt uneasy. He didn't know why. On top of the fridge the portable radio was tuned into the local station where The Beatles were singing 'Eleanor Rigby'. Greenway pulled a face and switched it off. A miserable, lonely song about death. He wasn't in the mood for it. He was raising the mug to his mouth when his ears picked up the soft gentle click of a car door being carefully closed. Instantly, his hand shot out to the light switch. From the darkened kitchen he twitched back the curtains.

Two men were walking up the path, one middle-aged and scruffy, the other in his late twenties with the look of a thug. Greenway cupped his hand to the window pane to see better. The older man, a maroon scarf hanging unevenly round his neck had a scar of some kind on his cheek. He didn't recognize either of them, but they spelled trouble.

A half-hearted knock at the front door which sounded almost too deliberately reassuring. The dog at his feet, a nine-month-old Dobermann, sprang up and started to growl, then to bark. He grabbed its collar and shut it in the lounge where it barked even louder. Another knock, a little stronger this time. Greenway reached for the heavy walking stick he kept on the hall table as he cautiously opened up. The scruffy man was smiling apologetically.

'Mr Greenway? Sorry to bother you so late, sir. We called earlier, but you were out.' He held something up. Greenway's heart faltered and skipped a beat. It was a police warrant card.

'Police?' he stammered. *God, how had they found out?*

'Routine enquiry,' purred the man who he noted from the warrant card was Detective Inspector Frost. 'All right if we come in?' And without waiting to be asked, they were in the hall.

Routine enquiry? They don't send detective inspectors on routine enquiries, not even rag-bags like this one. He felt his hands trembling. He forced a smile of unconcern. 'I was just going to cook my dinner.'

'This won't take long, sir,' said Frost.

Hearing strange voices, the dog was barking and frantically scratching at the lounge door.

Greenway smiled. 'I'd better put Spike outside. He can get quite nasty with strangers.' They stood well back as he opened the lounge door and grabbed the Dobermann's collar as it leapt out. 'Find yourselves seats,' he called, dragging the snarling dog past them and into the kitchen.

'Thank you, sir,' said Frost, giving the dog a wide berth and following Gilmore into the lounge, a grotty room with a well-worn and sagging three-piece suite and old newspapers heaped on every chair. The settee had been dragged in front of the television set, at the side of which a waste bin overflowed with empty lager cans. Frost strode around, prodding, poking.

'Look at this!' Gilmore was holding up a girlie magazine with a picture of a busty blonde dressed in school uniform on the front cover.

But Frost was beginning to feel uneasy. 'He's taking a bloody long time putting that dog out . . . Shit!' He spat out the expletive at the growl of an engine starting up outside. Twice in the same flaming day! 'The bastard's done a runner!'

They dashed to the back door where a snarling Dobermann barred their way. Back along the passage and out the front door, just in time to see the rear lights of a delivery van disappearing into the dark.

Back in the car, bumping and jolting in hot pursuit, Frost fumed and castigated himself for letting the sod walk out so easily. Why hadn't he taken more men and posted someone at the back? If Greenway got away, he'd never hear the last of it from Mullett. 'Faster, son,' he urged Gilmore as the red rear-lights ahead shrunk to pinpricks.

'This car's not in the best of condition,' Gilmore retorted as the Cortina shook and shuddered in protest at the unaccustomed increased speed. A warning light on the oil gauge kept flashing and there was a hot metal burning smell. 'Hadn't you better radio Control for some back-up?'

Frost hesitated. Of course they needed back-up, but he was hoping they could get by without the station knowing what a twat he had made of himself. A teeth-setting grinding noise from the engine made up his mind. He radioed for help.

'Do you mean to say,' howled Mullett, snatching the microphone from Sergeant Wells, 'that you just let him drive off?' He had been hovering in Control, awaiting confirmation of a successful arrest.

'Just get me back-up – over and out,' muttered Frost, banging down the handset, aware that he had only delayed a Grade A bollocking from his superintendent.

'Where's the bugger gone?' The red lights had vanished. 'Look out,' he screamed as a dark shape loomed up in front of the windscreen.

Gilmore jammed on the brakes. The tyres screeched and the car slewed to a halt, throwing Frost heavily against Gilmore who almost lost control of the wheel. They had pulled up within inches of Greenway's delivery van.

'What's the silly bugger playing at?' asked Frost, all fingers and thumbs as he tried to release his seat belt. He was answered by Greenway blurring into vision at the side of the Cortina, swinging what they later realized was a long-handled sledge-hammer. A clanging thud which shook the car and nearly deafened them, then a splintering and shattering as the windscreen crazed into an opaque honeycombed sheet. When Frost finally managed to release the seat belt and leap from the car he was just in time to see the rear lights of the van dwindling into the distance.

'Shit!' yelled Frost yet again, after they had knocked out enough of the shivered windscreen to see where they were going. They limped off after Greenway, eyes streaming, faces stinging from the ice-hard punch of cold gritty air. Control had advised them that area car Hotel Tango was on its way to afford them assistance.

But they had lost too much time. The road was dead straight ahead and the van was nowhere to be seen. Turning his head to one side for protection against the slip-stream, Frost groped for the handset. 'We've lost him, I think. Last seen heading towards the motorway.'

'Hotel Tango receiving,' replied Simms. 'We are in position by motorway exit. Will block.'

'Bully for you, Hotel Tango,' said Frost, turning up his coat collar and sinking low in his seat to try and escape the worst of the slip-stream. He attempted to light a cigarette but the match died in its battle against the wind.

A gargle of squelch from the radio, then Hotel Tango, very excited. 'He's spotted us. He's skidded round. He's heading back in your direction. Am in pursuit.'

'There he is!' yelled Gilmore. Fast-approaching headlights flared and blinded and a horn screamed for them to get out of the way.

'Block him,' shouted Frost.

Not too happy about this, Gilmore spun the wheel, turning the car side on to the oncoming vehicle.

The headlights got nearer and nearer, the van's horn screaming and pleading. From behind came more headlights and the piercing wail of Hotel Tango's siren in pursuit.

'He's not going to stop!' screamed Gilmore, blinded by the dazzle of the headlights as he hit his seat belt release.

'Jump,' yelled Frost, thankful he hadn't refastened his seat belt after the last incident. He pushed open the door and dived out on to the road, rolling over and just regaining his feet as the van impacted, smashing into the car and sending it spinning. Tyres squealed and smoked. The van's engine raced impotently, then it started to back away. But the approaching police car was too close and Hotel Tango skidded to a halt, siren still blaring, blocking the road right behind the van.

Car doors opened and slammed. Two uniformed men emerged from the area car and approached cautiously from the rear. Gilmore, rubbing grazed elbows, advanced from the front. The cab door jerked open and Greenway leapt out, tightly gripping the sledgehammer which he brandished threateningly.

Crouching slightly, ready to leap, Gilmore edged nearer.

Greenway spun round, whirling the sledge-hammer above his head, his eyes wild and threatening.

'Drop that, you silly sod!' roared Frost. Momentarily distracted, Greenway jerked his head towards the inspector giving the two uniformed men the opportunity to risk a dash forward, but they were not quick enough. Greenway twisted round, swinging the hammer in a two-handed grip. As they backed away, Gilmore made his move, leaping on Greenway from behind, locking his arm tightly round the man's neck in a strangulating grip making him drop the hammer as he tried to prise Gilmore's arm away. A back elbow jab from Greenway almost paralysed Gilmore who cried in pain and slackened his hold which was enough for Greenway to dive to regain the hammer. He almost had it when he shrieked in agony as the heel of Frost's shoe stamped down on his hand with the inspector's full weight bearing down. 'You bastard!!'

'Naughty, naughty!' admonished Frost, only easing off his foot so Gilmore could pull Greenway's wrists behind him and snap on the handcuffs.

Gilmore stood up and brushed dirt from his grey suit then yanked his prisoner to his feet. 'You've broken my bloody hand,' whimpered Greenway. 'I want a doctor.'

'You'll want an undertaker if you don't shut up,' said Frost. 'It's police brutality week. Now get in that bloody car.' They all squeezed into the area car and drove back to the station. It was a silent drive. Greenway said nothing, just stared straight ahead. He didn't even ask what the charge was.

'Number 2 Interview Room,' called Wells as they marched their prisoner through the lobby.

'I want a doctor. The bastards have broken my hand,'

called Greenway, giving a good impersonation of a man in agony.

'Get him a doctor,' ordered Mullett, who was hovering excitedly in the background, grinning like a man with two dicks. 'We're going to play this one by the book.' He called the inspector over. 'The Chief Constable's thrilled to bits about this, Frost.'

'Then let's hope we don't disappoint the old git,' replied Frost. 'Our suspect's playing the injured innocent at the moment.'

'I've got a full Forensic team going over Greenway's cottage, inch by inch,' said Mullett. 'As soon as they come up with something, I'll let you know.' He squeezed Frost's shoulder. 'I have every confidence in you, Inspector.'

Then you must be bloody mad, muttered Frost under his breath as Mullett returned to the old log cabin. Whenever people expressed confidence, the doubts welled up.

'Shall I get a doctor?' asked Wells.

'Later,' said Frost. 'When I've finished with him. The odd jolt of pain might improve his concentration.'

Wednesday night shift (1)

Greenway twisted his head round to look at the clock high on the wall behind him in Interview Room number 2. Half-past nine. He resumed his sprawl in the chair and rubbed his injured hand. Opposite him, leaning against the mushroom-emulsioned wall, the young thug of a detective sergeant scowled down at him. Unblinking, Greenway scowled back.

'How much longer?' asked Greenway.

Gilmore said nothing.

'As long as that?' said Greenway in mock surprise. He turned to the little blonde WPC standing guard by the door. 'How long have I got to waste my time here, darling?'

WPC Ridley stared through him and didn't answer.

'Natter, natter, natter,' said Greenway. The door swung open and Frost breezed in, a bulging green case file under his arm. He chucked the file on the table, together with his matches and his cigarettes.

'Where's the doctor?' asked Greenway.

'He's putting someone's cat down at the moment,' said Frost, dropping into the vacant chair. 'He'll be along as soon as he can.' He poked a cigarette in his mouth and dragged a match along the table top. He lit up, then pushed the packet towards the prisoner.

'What's this?' asked Greenway with a sneer. 'The good guy and the bad guy routine?'

'No,' said Frost, grinning sweetly. 'We're both the bad guys. We both hate your guts.' He lit Greenway's cigarette. 'Make us hate you some more. Tell us all about it, blow by blow, thrust by thrust.'

Greenway spread his palms in mock bewilderment. 'Tell you about what? I haven't the faintest idea what this is all about.'

Frost puffed out a smoke ring and watched it drift up and curl around the green-shaded light bulb. 'If you don't know what it's about, why did you do a runner?'

'I panicked. I'm not used to the police barging into my house at night.' He stood up. 'If you're going to charge me, charge me. If not, I'm walking out of here.'

Gilmore pushed him back in the chair. 'The charge, as you bloody well know, is murder.'

A scornful laugh from Greenway. 'Murder?' His eyes flicked from Gilmore to Frost. 'Who am I supposed to have murdered?'

A damn good act, thought Frost, grudgingly. If I didn't have the forensic evidence I might start having doubts. He flipped open the folder and took out the photograph of Paula Bartlett, then steered it with his finger across to Greenway. 'Only fifteen. Must have been easy meat for a great hulking bastard like you.'

Greenway stared at the colour photograph with an expression of utter disbelief. 'The school kid? This is getting bloody farcical. I gave a statement to that other bloke . . . the miserable-faced git, Inspector Allen. She never even reached my place. I never got a paper that day.'

Gilmore moved his face forward close to Greenway's. 'Yes, you bloody did. She delivered the paper. On your own admission you were home that morning. You dragged her in . . . a fifteen-year-old kid, a virgin . . .'

'A fifteen-year-old virgin? There's no such thing!' smirked Greenway.

The detective sergeant's control snapped. He grabbed the man by the lapels, lifted him and slammed him against the wall. 'Don't come the funnies with me, you sod. I saw her body. I saw what you did to her.'

WPC Ridley coughed pointedly, reminding Gilmore that she was there to make notes of everything that happened between the detectives and the prisoner. Gilmore pushed Greenway away and wiped his hands down his jacket as if they were contaminated.

Greenway smouldered. 'I'm not answering any more questions.'

'Yes, you are,' said Frost, 'otherwise I might accidentally tread on your bad hand again.' He leant back, balancing the chair on its rear legs, and shot a column of smoke at the yellow ceiling. 'Let's talk about mitigating circumstances. Perhaps you didn't mean to kill her. What did she do – lead you on? Waggle it under your nose, then snatch it away?'

'I don't know what you're talking about,' yawned Greenway, feigning boredom. 'Whoever poked and killed that kid, it wasn't me. I like them older with big knockers – like that little policewoman there – not flat-chested schoolgirls.'

Frost's chair crashed down, the sudden noise almost making Greenway leap from his seat. 'Flat-chested, was she? When you stripped her off you saw she was flat-chested.' He jabbed a finger at Gilmore who was busy with his notebook. 'Underline that, Sergeant.'

'You don't have to strip anyone off to see if they're flat-chested or not,' sneered Greenway. 'That kid used to deliver here in the summer wearing only a T-shirt. You could see she had nothing.'

'You're quite right,' Frost agreed. 'She didn't have much to show when I saw her stretched out on the slab in the morgue. It didn't stop you raping her, though, did it?'

'Rape?' He snorted a hollow laugh. 'You must be bloody hard up for suspects.'

Frost pulled a sheet of typescript from the folder. 'This is the statement you gave to my colleague, Inspector Allen, the miserable-faced git. You say you're a self-employed van driver?'

'That's right.'

'You were asked to account for your movements for September 14th, the day Paula went missing.' He let his eyes run over the typed page. 'You said you didn't go out at all that day. Is that correct?'

'Bang on! There was no work for me.' Greenway flicked his ash on the floor and looked as if he was enjoying the questioning. His expression said, 'Ask what you like, pigs, you'll get nothing out of me!'

Frost scratched at his scar. 'The girl usually delivered your paper – the *Sun* – around eight o'clock?'

'Yes. But that day, she didn't turn up.'

'And you didn't get a paper?'

'Brilliant,' said Greenway, sarcastically.

Frost produced the copy of the *Sun* in its transparent cover. 'This is the paper you say wasn't delivered. And this . . .' He fluttered the forensic report, 'is scientific evidence which proves you are a lying bastard.'

Greenway snatched the report, his head moving from side to side as he skimmed through it. He gave a scoffing laugh and handed it back. 'A load of balls.'

Gilmore moved forward. 'Solid scientific evidence. The court will love it.'

Greenway smiled disarmingly. 'All right. Let's pretend it's genuine. So the newspaper was pushed through my letter-box and pulled out again. That doesn't prove the girl was in my house and it doesn't prove I bloody touched her.'

'We'll soon have all the proof we want,' said Frost. 'A Forensic team is going over your place inch by inch right now. One hair from her head . . . a thread of cotton from her clothes, and we've got you, you bastard.'

'Tell you what then,' smirked Greenway. 'If you find anything, I'll give you a full, sworn confession. Now I can't say fairer than that.'

Frost switched on his sweetest smile. 'We'll find it,' he said, trying to sound convincing. But he was worried. Greenway was too damned cock-sure. He looked up with irritation as the door opened and Wells beckoned.

The sergeant didn't look the bearer of good news. 'Just heard from the Forensic team, Jack. They've been all over the cottage and found nothing.'

Frost slumped against the wall. 'There's got to be something.'

'It's been over two months since she was there,' said Wells. 'Forensic are bringing in more men to go over the entire place again, but they're not optimistic. Are you getting anything from Greenway?'

'Only the bleeding run-around.'

Mullett's office door opened. He saw Frost and hurried towards him. 'What joy?' he asked eagerly.

'No joy, all bloody misery,' replied Frost. 'Unless Forensic can come up with something quick, the best I can charge Greenway with is dangerous driving.'

Mullet's smile flickered and spluttered out. 'I hope this is not going to be another of your foul-ups, Frost. I've really stuck my neck out with the Chief Constable on this one.' He spun on his heel and marched back to his office.

'Let's hope the bastard chops it off for you,' muttered Frost to the empty passage.

Back to the Interview Room where Greenway was making great play of nursing his injured hand. 'I'm in agony. I want medical treatment and I want to go home. You've got nothing to hold me on.'

'Lock the bastard up and get him a doctor,' said Frost. He felt tired and miserable and even more incompetent than usual.

His office was a hostile dung-heap of bulging files, snarling memos, and complicated-looking returns. Rain splattered against the window and drummed on the roof. He stared out to the rain-swept car-park, and was puzzled because he couldn't see his Cortina, then remembered it had been towed away for repairs after Greenway smashed into it. Gilmore poked his head round the door. He had his hat and coat on in the hope he could nip back home for an hour or so. He'd been on duty solidly since six and a busy night was still looming ahead. 'Greenway wants to know what's happening about his dog.'

'A dog-handler's on his way to pick it up and take it to kennels,' Frost told him. 'You off home then?'

'Yes . . . only for an hour . . . if it's all right with you.' Gilmore's tone implied that it had better be all right.

'Drop me off on the way, would you, son. I haven't got wheels.'

Gilmore readily agreed. It was only when he turned the car into the Market Square to take the short cut to the inspector's house that Frost broke the news that he wanted to be dropped off at Greenway's cottage. It was miles off Gilmore's route, but all right, he'd dump Frost off and then get the hell out of there. Frost could find his own way back.

Lights were spilling from every room of the cottage. From the back yard the dog kept up its monotonous yapping. The Forensic team were busy. Hardly any surface was free of fingerprint powder, small vacuum cleaners whirled gulping up dust, hairs and fibres for analysis, men crawled over the carpet with tweezers. Tony Harding, in charge of the team, looked up wearily as Frost entered. Gilmore hovered impatiently behind, scowling at the inspector who had said he would be a couple of minutes at the most and wanted a lift back.

'Still no joy,' said Harding, 'but we haven't finished yet.'

Frost received the news gloomily. 'Keep looking. Any clue – no matter how small. A pair of schoolgirl's knickers, a confession, a half-eaten chicken and mushroom pie.' He scuffed the carpet with his foot. 'At the moment, all we've got is the paint samples on the newspaper.'

'Ah,' said Harding, sounding shamefaced. 'I've been meaning to talk to you about that.' He took the inspector by the arm and led him to one side. 'The paint sample evidence might not be as conclusive as we first thought. It might not have come from this letter-box.'

A cold shiver of apprehension trickled down Frost's back. 'What do you mean? You did a spectrograph analysis. You told me it was conclusive.'

'Yes . . . well . . . it was . . . up to a point . . .'

Frost's shoulders slumped. 'Get to the bad bloody news. I don't want the death of a thousand cuts.'

'We did a spectrograph analysis of the paint sample from the newspaper. There were traces of three layers of paint, the bottom layer brown, the middle a grey undercoat, the top layer black. The spectrograph analysis of the sample taken from Greenway's letter-box showed three identical paint layers, same colours, same chemical composition.'

'Yes,' nodded Frost. 'That's the point in the story where I started believing Forensic weren't the big, useless twats I'd always thought them to be.'

Harding's faint smile accepted the rebuke. 'The test was fine as far as it went, but we should have tested other letter-boxes on the girl's delivery route. This I've now done.'

'And?' asked Frost, ready to wince, knowing he wasn't going to like the answer.

'Quite a few letter-boxes came up with identical spectrograph readings.'

'But how the hell . . . ?'

'Most of the properties on the girl's route are owned by the Denton Development Corporation. Every four years their maintenance department repaint exteriors . . . standard colours, standard specification. What I hadn't appreciated was that Greenway's cottage is also owned by the Development Corporation. They bought the land some twenty-five years ago for a new housing estate, but haven't yet found the money.'

'So it's received the same coats of identical paint every four years as all the other houses?'

Harding nodded. 'I'm afraid so. And that means that the girl could have pushed the newspaper through any of those letter-boxes by mistake, then tugged it out again. It doesn't have to be this cottage.'

'Thank you very much,' muttered Frost bitterly, knowing that Mullett would blame him for this. 'So unless you can find evidence that the girl has actually been inside here, we've got sod all to hold Greenway on?'

'Unfortunately, yes,' agreed Harding.

Frost wandered across to the window and looked out on to the puddled, muddy back yard where a black shape prowled up and down like a caged wolf. At the end of the garden a sorry-looking shed crouched under pouring rain. 'You done the shed yet?'

'Not with the Hound of the Baskervilles out there,' replied Harding. 'We're waiting for the dog-handler.'

As if answering his cue, the dog-handler's van drew up outside and a short stocky man wearing a padded jacket and thick leather gloves came in, swinging a muzzle and a leash. 'What sort of dog is it?'

'A bloody man-eater,' said Frost, leading him to the back door.

The dog-handler opened the door a fraction, squinted through the crack, then closed it firmly as the door bulged inwards when the dog hurled himself at it. He didn't look very happy. 'I hate Dobermanns. They're vicious sods.' He zipped up the padded jacket and pulled the gloves up over his wrists, then nodded. 'Right. Here goes.'

'Geronimo!' said Frost, opening the door just wide enough for the handler to squeeze through. He then shut it quickly and listened to the noises off – several minutes of ill-tempered barking and a lot of swearing.

'OK. I've got it!'

The bedraggled dog, muzzled and shaking with rage, snarled as it was pulled through by the leash. It charged at Gilmore then shook rain all over him as it was dragged off.

Frost beckoned to Gilmore who, frozen-faced, waited with ill-concealed impatience. 'Let's take a quick look in the shed, son.'

Shoulders hunched, they splashed to the end of the yard. The rusty padlock which secured the shed door yielded to the first key from Frost's bunch.

The torch beam danced over rubbish. The shed was stacked roof-high with junk. The dirt-encrusted frame of a deck-chair rested against a rusting lawn-mower. Twisting, crumbling remains of old chicken wire strangled sodden strips of mouldering carpeting, rotting fence posts and jagged-edged sheets of warped plywood. The torch beam bounced from item to item. Junk. Stacks of half-empty paint tins, torn bags spewing damp fertilizer. Useless, hoarded rubbish. Frost tugged at the deck-chair, but this caused paint tins to topple and he had to jump back quickly.

'Satisfied?' asked Gilmore, smugly.

Frost's shoulders drooped. 'Yes, I'm satisfied, son. A quick poke around the house, then we'll go.'

He really thought he had found something in the kitchen. On the work top, thawing from the freezer and ready to be popped into the microwave, was Greenway's planned evening meal. A box of microwave crinkle-cut chips and a chicken and mushroom pie. 'Stomach contents,' exclaimed Frost delightedly. He yelled for Harding, who listened and shook his head.

'They don't help us, Mr Frost.' He picked up one of the packets. 'Both common brands . . . the market leaders. Even if we could prove the girl's last meal was an identical product, the supermarkets sell tens of thousands of these every week.'

'Damn!' growled Frost.

'You ready to go yet?' asked Gilmore pointing yet again to his watch.

'A quick sniff around the bedroom and then you can get off to your conjugals,' Frost promised.

The bedroom reflected the state of the rest of the house with the bed and the floor strewn with dirty clothing and unwashed, food-congealed crockery. Was this where Greenway dragged her and raped her? Was this pigsty of a room the last thing that fifteen-year-old kid saw before he choked the life out of her?

One of the Forensic team pushed past him and began stripping the clothing from the bed. 'We're taking the bedclothes for further examination, Inspector, but I get the feeling they've been washed during the past four weeks or so.'

'I only wash mine once a year,' said Frost gloomily, 'whether they need it or not.'

Another long, deep, irritating sigh from Gilmore.

'All right, son,' said Frost. 'We're going now.'

In the hall, Harding looked even gloomier than Frost. 'We haven't come up with a thing, Inspector. There's no evidence at all that the girl was ever in the house.' He plucked a Dobermann hair from his jacket. 'There's dog's hairs all over the place. Would have been helpful if we'd found some on the girl, but we didn't.'

'Find me something, for Pete's sake,' pleaded Frost, 'otherwise I'm in the brown and squishy up to my ear-holes.'

Gilmore put his foot down hard on the drive back in case the inspector thought of some other outlandish spot to visit. Frost slumped miserably down in the passenger seat, stared at the rain-blurred windscreen, smoked and said nothing. Gilmore could almost feel sorry for him.

Then Frost sat up straight, pulled the cigarette from his mouth and rammed it into the ashtray. 'I'm a number one, Grade A twat!!' he announced.

Tell me something I don't know, thought Gilmore, slowing down at the traffic lights in the Market Square.

'Turn the car around,' ordered Frost. 'We're going back to the cottage.'

'You're kidding!' gasped Gilmore, looking at Frost whose face was bathed red by the traffic signal.

'Under my bloody nose and I missed it . . . All that junk in the shed. You'd expect it to be dry, but it was wet, dirty, muddy and rusty. It must have been out rotting in the open for months . . . so why gather it up and bung it in the shed?'

'Perhaps he just wanted to tidy up his garden,' said Gilmore.

'Do me a favour. His place is a rubbish tip, just like mine. I'd never tidy up my garden and neither would he. That junk was dumped in his shed to hide something . . . so let's go and find out what.' Frost's face was now bathed in green. Wearily, Gilmore spun the wheel round and headed back to the cottage.

The Forensic team had almost completed their work and Harding shook his head at them as they passed through. 'Nothing. We're now going to try the shed.'

'Then you can give us a hand,' Frost told him. 'Bring a torch.' Harding slipped on a plastic mac and followed them down to the bottom of the yard.

'This would be easier in the morning,' moaned Gilmore as rain trickled down his collar.

'Shouldn't take us long,' said Frost dragging out the deck-chair frame and flinging it into the dark of the garden.

It took nearly half an hour. As one item of useless junk was removed more and more was revealed.

'I can't think why he bothered to keep this,' grunted Harding, struggling with a muddy iron-framed bed-spring, heavily corroded with rust.

It was not until the shed was nearly empty that they found what Greenway had been hiding. Stacked high against the far end of the shed, white cardboard boxes, piled almost to the roof. Frost moved back to let Gilmore reach up and drag one down. He tore open the stapled lid. Inside, tightly packed, were cartons of Benson and Hedges Silk Cut cigarettes. Gilmore took out a carton and tossed it over to Frost who ripped off the wrapping. No 'Government Health Warning' on the side of the packets. These cigarettes were made for export.

Frost stared at the packets, feeling even more depressed. He wasn't sure what he was expecting to find, but certainly not this. This would effectively shoot his case against Greenway right up the anal passage. He went to the shed door and swore bitterly into the rain and the wind and the dark.

The Interview Room now reeked strongly of stale shag tobacco smoke and cheese and onion crisps. There was a spit-soaked, thin hand-rolled cigarette end in the ashtray. Someone else had been interviewed since Frost's questioning of Greenway.

'All right, all right. Stop shoving.' Greenway, rubbing the sleep from his eyes with a neatly bandaged hand, stumbled into the room, urged roughly from behind by a foul-tempered Gilmore. Frost waited until the man was sitting down, then he pulled a packet of Benson and Hedges from his pocket and pushed it across. Greenway stared at it for a while, turned the packet gingerly with a finger so he could confirm the absence of the health warning. 'You took your bloody time finding them,' he grunted.

Frost retrieved the packet and shook out a cigarette. He lit up and sucked in smoke. 'Feel like talking?'

Greenway helped himself to a cigarette and accepted a light from the inspector. 'I take it I'm no longer being charged with killing the school kid?'

'No. The bloke you coshed has identified your photograph.'

Greenway thought for a moment. 'All right. I'll give you a statement.'

But as Gilmore turned the pages of his notebook, Frost waved a hand for him to stop. 'This isn't our case. Detective Inspector Skinner from Shelwood Division is on his way over. You can give a statement to him.'

Gilmore snorted in exasperation. 'Would someone mind telling me what this is about?'

'Sorry, son,' apologized Frost. 'On the day Paula Bartlett went missing a van-load of Benson and Hedges king-size cigarettes for export was hijacked on its way to the docks. The driver was flagged down, coshed, and his load nicked. This happened on the motorway at Shelwood, miles outside Denton Division.'

'But Greenway told Inspector Allen he never went out that day,' protested Gilmore.

'I think he was lying,' said Frost. 'People don't always tell us the truth.'

'Of course I was lying,' said Greenway. 'The bloody van, full of nicked fags, was standing outside my house when the other inspector called that evening. I thought he was on to me, so when he asked me, I said I hadn't been out all day. But it was about the missing kid . . .'

'Can you help us at all about the girl?' asked Frost.

Greenway shook his head. 'I left home at six in the morning . . . didn't get back until nine o'clock at night. The paper hadn't arrived when I left and it wasn't there when I got back.'

A tap at the door. 'Detective Inspector Skinner is here,' announced Sergeant Wells.

Skinner, a burly man in a trench coat, looked exactly how a detective inspector should look, a contrast to the rag-bag Gilmore had to work with. His sergeant, lean and mean, looked like a detective sergeant who would always be in his boss's shadow, not how Gilmore intended to end up. 'Understand you've got a little present for us, Jack?' said Skinner, his eyes on the prisoner.

'He's all yours,' said Frost 'I can't solve any of my own cases, but I solve other people's.' He offered his cigarettes around and Skinner nearly choked when he was told he was smoking some of the stolen property.

Wells returned with papers to be signed for the transfer of the prisoner and whispered to Frost that Mr Mullett would like to see him in his office.

'Shit,' muttered Frost. 'It's been a rotten enough day already.'

In fact Mullett was hovering outside in the corridor and was full of charm and smiles for the two detectives from Shelwood. 'Delighted to have been able to help,' he smarmed. But as soon as they had gone, his smile froze to death. 'My office!' he hissed and spun on his heel away.

Frost was dead tired, but he kept his eyes open to pretend he was listening as Mullett droned angrily on. 'You've made me look a complete and utter fool in the eyes of the Chief Constable . . .'

He let his gaze drift around the old log cabin and noticed to his horror that there was a foil take-away food container, yellowed with cold curry sauce, poking from under Mullett's desk. He moved forward, looking very contrite, and nudged it out of sight with his toe.

'. . . and it wasn't even our case. We've improved Shelwood's crime figures, which made ours look sick anyway, and done nothing for our own. What on earth am I going to tell the Chief Constable?'

The drone of Mullett's voice roared and faded and Frost had to jerk his head up to keep awake. He fought back a yawn. This was all his life seemed to be lately, making balls-ups, getting bollockings from Mullett, and then sent out to make a fresh balls-up.

'. . . and, in any case, I had told you to concentrate on the senior citizen killings. So leave the Paula Bartlett case for Mr Allen and try and find that other suspect you let slip through your fingers. I want no more mess-ups.' He leant across his desk, his chin thrust out. 'Are you receiving me, Inspector?'

'Loud and clear,' said Frost. 'Loud and bloody clear.'

1.15 a.m. The lobby had a sour smell. A mixture of stale beer and spilt whisky. Wells was shouting at PC Jordan who, helped by young PC Collier, was struggling with a man in evening dress. The man's legs kept giving way and he seemed ready to collapse in the pool of vomit at his feet. At last they managed to sit him down safely on the bench.

'Anything in from the Met on Simon Bradbury?' asked Gilmore.

'How the hell do I know?' snapped Wells, irritably. 'I don't keep track of every bit of paper that comes in and out of this building. And another . . .' He stopped short and yelled, 'Take him outside! Quick!' The drunk was being sick again. Jordan and Collier grabbed him, but too late. More vomit pumped out and they jumped back just in time as it splattered on the lobby floor. Eyes squinting, the drunk tried to make out what the mess was at his feet.

'Bloody marvellous!' cried Wells, and he looked around for someone to vent his anger on. PC Collier decided this was a good time to take a refreshment break and sidled out towards the rest room, but didn't quite make it.

'And where do you think you're going, Collier?'

'Refreshment break, Sergeant.'

Wells consulted his watch and found, to his disappointment, that Collier was entitled to his break. 'Right. When you come back you can clean up this mess.'

'That's not my job, Sergeant,' Collier protested, firmly.

'Your job is to do what I bloody well tell you to do,' yelled Wells as Collier stamped out, slamming the door behind him. Red-faced Wells charged, fists clenched, after him. 'I'll have you, Collier.'

Frost cut across to bar his way. 'Hold it, Bill. Hold it,' he said, soothingly. 'We're all tired and overworked.' He poked a cigarette in the sergeant's mouth and led him back to the desk. 'Any chance of a cup of tea?'

'There's a kettle in the rest room,' said Wells. 'You might bring me one.'

The only occupant of the rest room was Collier who was huddled in a chair in front of a 14-inch colour TV set, warming his hands round a mug of instant coffee and brooding over the injustices of working under Sergeant Wells. On the screen, a young girl in pigtails who didn't look much older than twelve was sprawled naked on some grass, sunbathing. The camera moved to show a man with a riding crop watching from the cover of some bushes. Behind the man a board read *Trespassers Will Be Punished*.

'Where did you get that video?' demanded Gilmore, sharply.

Snatched too abruptly from his morose meditation, Collier started, spilling instant coffee down the front of his uniform. He reached out to switch off the set, but Frost grabbed his wrist. 'Leave it, son. Where did you get it?'

'We only borrowed it, Inspector. We were going to put it back.' He held up a video case which had the typed label *A Thrashing For Fiona*. It was one of the haul of pornographic videos removed from the newsagent's.

On the screen the naked girl was on her knees, pleading with the man who was slapping the riding crop against his leg.

'Go and fetch Sergeant Wells,' ordered Frost, dragging another chair in front of the set.

Collier registered dismay. It was unlike the inspector to report people. 'I only borrowed it, sir.'

Dragging his eyes from the TV set where the girl was across the man's knees, being thrashed with the riding crop, Frost gave a reassuring grin. 'Don't worry, son. I'll tell him I took it. Just send him in.'

Gilmore spooned instant coffee into three mugs and filled them with boiling water. He passed one to Frost and sat beside him in the chair vacated by Collier.

A clatter of footsteps up the passage and Wells came in. 'Look, Jack, I haven't got time . . .' He stopped dead as he caught sight of the screen. 'Bloody hell . . .!' He grabbed the other chair and sat down.

Engrossed, Frost gulped down his coffee, unaware that he hadn't added his usual three heaped teaspoons of sugar. The man was now using the riding crop to do something unspeakable. 'He caught her trespassing,' Frost told Wells, explaining the plot.

'Serves her bloody right,' said Wells. 'She'll think twice before she does it again.'

The video finished abruptly. Frost fed another one in. The title read *Animal Passions*. An interior scene this time. The same pigtailed girl, naked and with a dog, a large white and brown Great Dane with a torn left ear, its tail wagging furiously. The girl lay on her back. The dog, slowly and deliberately, was licking her.

'I bet he prefers that to Pedigree Chum,' croaked Wells.

'Who wouldn't,' said Frost.

Gilmore looked at his watch. Nearly two o'clock. He'd told Liz he'd try and pop in during the shift, even if it was only for half an hour. He tried to catch Frost's attention as the fool sat there, eyes bulging, like a schoolboy with a dirty book. 'Do you mind if I take a break, Inspector? About half an hour or so? I'd like to pop home.'

'Sure,' muttered Frost, his eyes glued to the screen where the dog, tongue lolling, whites of eyes showing, was coupling with the girl.

This was too much for Gilmore who turned away in disgust. As he reached for the door handle it was abruptly snatched away from him as the door opened and there, framed in the doorway like an avenging angel, stood a furious and angry Mullett.

The internal phone rang.

Gilmore stared at Mullett, open-mouthed. Bloody Frost had dropped him in it again. He was sure the Divisional Commander had gone home.

Frost and Wells, eyes fixed rigidly on the screen, were blissfully ignorant of this visitation and Gilmore could do nothing to alert them.

Mullett pushed Gilmore to one side and strode into the rest room. He stood between the two men and the TV set and glowered down at them, his face thunder black.

Wells nearly had a heart attack.

'Hello, Super. This is a pleasant surprise,' said Frost, managing an unconvincing grin.

The phone kept on ringing. Glad of something to do, Gilmore answered it. It was Collier warning them that the Divisional Commander was on his way in.

'Thank you,' hissed Gilmore through clenched teeth, 'but we know.'

'What the devil is going on here?' spluttered Mullett. 'I look in on my way back from a function and what do I find? The lobby floor plastered with vomit, a junior officer left on his own to cope and the station sergeant and other officers in the rest room, watching . . .' His eyes bulged as he looked over his shoulder to see just what they were watching, '. . . obscene, bestial videos.'

Wells was on his feet, his mouth opening and closing in the hope that his brain would provide him with something mitigating to say. Gilmore wished the ground would open and swallow him. At the first opportunity he would request an interview with Mullett to explain that he was not there from choice.

Frost didn't appear to be paying his Divisional Commander much attention, but leant forward to study the antics on the screen more closely.

252

Mullett's lips compressed as he bottled up his rage. This was the last straw. 'Would you please wait outside,' he asked the other two men. A mad scramble for the door as they raced to comply, leaving the inspector as hostage for the superintendent's fury.

Frost dragged his chair closer to the TV set. Angrily, Mullett pushed in front of him, blocking his view. 'If I might have your attention,' he began icily then nearly burst a blood vessel as Frost had the temerity, the brazen-faced insubordinate impudence, to reach out and push his Divisional Commander to one side.

'How dare you,' he spluttered when the words finally came.

Flapping a hand for Mullett to be quiet, Frost roared out, 'Gilmore . . . in here! Quick.'

The detective sergeant came back in the room, looking first at the purple-faced, rage-quivering Mullett, then at Frost who was on his knees operating the rewind button on the video recorder. Like a silent film in reverse, the naked girl and the dog moved jerkily backwards at high speed.

'Watch,' ordered Frost, releasing the rewind. The dog, panting with excitement, again approached and straddled the girl.

'For the last time, Inspector . . .' roared Mullett.

Curtly jerking his hand for silence, Frost jabbed the pause button. On the screen, in full close-up, the vacant face of the girl froze, quivering slightly as the video head passed over and over the same section of tape.

'The pigtails and blonde hair are a wig, son,' said Frost, his hands moving to block them out.

Gilmore stared hard at the girl's face, her lips slack, eyes glazed and unseeing, tiny flecks of sweat on the forehead.

'Recognize her, son?'

Gilmore nodded. Yes, he recognized her. The suicide. The Snoopy watch. The Mickey Mouse night-shirt. Fifteen-year-old Susan Bicknell. The marks of the beating were now explained.

Frost straightened up. 'Come on, son. I think we should ask her stepfather a few questions.'

'I demand to know what this is all about!' shrieked Mullett. But they were gone, the door slamming firmly shut behind them, leaving him alone in the room. Behind him the dog had worked itself up into a frenzy. He tried to switch it off, but none of the buttons seemed to work. He pushed the door open and thundered down the corridor. Tomorrow. He would see Frost tomorrow. And then it would be his turn. The lobby wall suddenly zipped upwards and the ceiling stared down at him as his back hit the floor. His feet had found a slippery patch of vomit.

'Whatever you do,' hissed Frost to Wells, just before he darted out to the car-park, 'don't laugh.'

A cold black night, made blacker by purple rain clouds that covered the face of the moon. They didn't have to drag anyone out of bed. A downstairs light was still on at the house and a shirt-sleeved Kenneth Duffy, tired and drawn, opened the door to them.

'Remember me, Mr Duffy?' asked Gilmore, showing his warrant card.

Duffy stared through the card and nodded.

'We'd like to come in, please,' said Gilmore. 'Just a couple of questions.'

Duffy twisted his head. 'It's for me, love,' he called, ushering the two detectives into an unheated lounge. 'I don't want my wife troubled,' he explained. 'She's broken up about this. We both are.' He dropped into a chair and stared at the drawn red curtains. He shivered. 'Sorry there's no heat.'

Frost sat down on the settee, facing Duffy. 'You're up late?'

'My wife can't sleep. I stay up with her. I don't like leaving her alone.'

Frost gave a sympathetic nod and looked up for his sergeant to start the questions.

'We're worried at the absence of a suicide note,' Gilmore said.

'Oh?' He tried to rub some warmth into a shirt-sleeved arm.

'You're quite sure there was no note?'

'Positive.'

Silence, broken only by the measured ticking of the clock on the mantelpiece. Then another sound. Frost had taken something from his mac pocket and was tapping it on his knee. It snatched Duffy's attention away from his study of the curtains.

The object was black, made of plastic, and Frost, a half-smile on his face, was tapping it slowly and regularly, again and again, on his knee.

At first Duffy couldn't make out what it was. Then his eyes widened and he sucked in air. It was a video cassette.

'Woof woof,' said Frost, and grinned.

'You bastard!' With a howl of rage Duffy hurled himself across the room at the inspector, his fists swinging wildly. Gilmore leapt forward to grab his wrists and fling him back into the chair.

'Was it something I said?' asked Frost in pretended puzzlement.

'You bastard,' repeated Duffy, this time near to tears. He shrank down into the chair and covered his face with his hands and his body convulsed with the sobbing he was no longer able to hold back. 'Don't tell my wife. It would kill her.' His voice was muffled by his hands.

Gilmore turned away. Raw emotion embarrassed him. Frost dribbled smoke and tried to look as if he knew more than he did.

Kenneth Duffy knuckled his eyes dry. 'What do you want to know?'

Frost waved the video. 'Tell me about it.'

Duffy bowed his head. 'I watched a few seconds – that was enough.'

'Where's the suicide note?'

The man shivered again and folded his arms around himself. 'I destroyed it.'

'Why?' snapped Gilmore who was standing behind him. 'Because it incriminated you?'

He twisted his head round and looked up at the sergeant. 'No. Because Susan asked me to. The note was addressed to me.'

Frost lit up a fresh cigarette from the stub of the old. 'What did it say?'

'It said, "The letter will explain. I can't face mum after what I've done. Please help me. Destroy this. She must never know."'

'Letter? What letter?'

'It was with Susan's note. An anonymous letter.'

Anonymous letter! Frost started, as did Gilmore. 'Tell us about it.'

Duffy paused to control his agitated breathing. 'It was addressed to my wife. Susan must have known it was coming so she waited for the postman. She opened it, read it and . . .' He shrugged as if referring to something trivial. '. . . and killed herself.'

'I want that letter,' said Frost grimly.

'I'm sorry. I haven't got it. I burnt it with the suicide note.'

'Shit!' said Frost vehemently. 'Describe it. The note-paper, the handwriting.'

'Is it important?' asked Duffy wearily.

'Yes, it bloody is.'

'Blue notepaper. Typed. Posted in Denton.'

Frost nodded grimly to Gilmore. 'What did it say?'

'What do you bloody think it said?' replied Duffy, again near to tears. 'It said, "Dear Mrs Duffy. Did you know that your dear darling, pure daughter Susan has taken part in depraved, bestial practices with men, with other women . . . even with animals, and is so proud of what she did that she allowed herself to be filmed. If you doubt me, I'm sending you a video."' He paused and listened to the clock tick.

'And did he send a video?' prompted Frost.

'Yes. It came the next morning . . . the day after Susan died. Imagine the effect on my wife if she'd received it. I waited for the postman, just like Susan must have done.' He shuddered. 'It was the one with the dog.'

All heads turned to the door as it clicked open. Mrs Duffy came in, a shrunken, stooped figure, face tired and lined, eyes red. Duffy rose from his chair. 'It's the police, love. Just asking a few questions.'

'Routine,' muttered Frost, avoiding her eyes. She'd have to know, but he wasn't going to be the one to tell her.

She forced a smile. 'I'll make some tea.'

'We can't stop, I'm afraid,' said Frost. 'Lots of things to do.'

'I won't be long, love,' said Duffy, helping his wife out of the room. 'You go in the warm.' When he came back he said, 'How old does she look? Sixty?' Not far short, thought Frost. 'She was forty last month and she never looked her age. Losing her only daughter was bad enough, but when this other business comes out, it'll kill her. You'll have another death on your hands.'

'You'll have to tell her,' said Frost.

'You bloody tell her,' said Duffy. He went to the sideboard and opened a drawer where he took out a small box. 'You see these?' He rattled it. 'The bloody doctor's put her back on the same tablets Susan took.'

Frost looked away. There was nothing to say.

Outside, in the car, Gilmore said, 'That video. Did you notice Susan's feet?'

'Her feet were the last thing I thought of looking at,' said Frost. 'Why?'

'The ground was rough so she was wearing shoes,' said Gilmore. 'Stark naked, but wearing shoes . . . just like Paula.'

Frost worried away at his scar, then shook his head. 'Coincidence, son. No-one would want to make a porn video with Paula. The poor little bitch didn't have the looks, or the figure.' He salvaged a decent-sized butt from the ashtray and lit up. 'The doc was right. He said that poison pen bastard would kill someone some day.' He huddled down in his seat, suddenly feeling cold. 'And I haven't the faintest idea how to go about catching the sod.'

Gilmore started up the engine. 'Where to?'

'Drop me off at the station, then go home, son. You'll be fit for sod all in the morning if you don't get some kip.'

Wednesday night shift (2)

Gilmore drew up outside the house and checked the windows. Despite the hour he half expected to see all the lights blazing and a still-smouldering Liz waiting for him. But the house seemed to be in darkness and he sighed with relief. He wasn't ready for another slanging match. But as he quietly clicked the front door shut behind him he heard mumbled voices and a slit of light showed from under the lounge door.

He tiptoed down the hall and turned the handle. An old black and white film was playing on the television and Liz was curled up in the armchair, a couple of empty tonic water bottles on the table and a bottle of vodka on the floor by her side. She turned and held up a brim-full glass in a mock toast. 'Home is the hunter!' In one gulp she swigged it down, waving the empty glass triumphantly aloft.

'It's gone four o'clock,' he said. 'What are you doing up?'

She pouted. 'You said you'd be in early. You promised me you'd be in bloody early.'

He shrugged off his jacket, loosened his tie and took a clean glass from the display cabinet. 'I said I'd try. It just wasn't possible.' He flopped wearily into the other armchair and reached for the vodka bottle. It was empty. He held it up accusingly. 'This was a full bottle on Saturday!'

'So I bloody drank it. What else is there to do in this stinking town, sitting in this lousy room, waiting for you and you never bloody come.'

He rubbed his hands over his face, trying to wipe away the fatigue. 'It won't be for long.' None too hopefully he pushed himself from the chair and foraged through the display cabinet, looking for something alcoholic amongst the half-empty bitter lemon and Coke bottles. Defeated, he poured himself a glass of Coke. It was warm and flat. On the television screen Humphrey Bogart was slapping Peter Lorre around. He relaxed, rested his head against the back of the armchair and tried to fight off sleep.

'You know what I thought,' slurred Liz in a husky whisper, putting her empty glass on the table. 'I thought I'd wait up for my randy, rampant, lover-boy husband and I thought we'd have some randy, rampant sex. How does that grab you, superstud?'

He was too tired. He wasn't in the mood and he didn't even think he was capable of making love. But he forced a grin. He didn't want a row, a hurtful, scratching row, all in hoarse angry whispers to avoid disturbing the neighbours. 'You're on,' he said, and held out his arms.

She slunk over and nestled in his lap. He kissed her. She tasted of vodka. Her body was hot and burning and her perfume was heady and erotic. Her hand crawled over him, tugging the shirt free from his trousers, her fingers exploring, caressing and lightly scratching his lower stomach. Then he wasn't faking any more. Then he was unbuttoning and easing off her dress. Then he was biting and licking and groaning.

And then, jarring like a dentist's drill, the door bell. A long, persistent ring. And someone banging on the door. And Frost's voice yelling for him to open up. This is a nightmare, he thought. A bloody nightmare.

'Sorry, son,' said Frost, barging in as he opened the front door. 'An emergency . . .' He stopped dead as he saw Liz smouldering in the armchair, her dress unbuttoned down to the waist, making no attempt to cover her naked breasts. Frost made no attempt to hide his gaping admiration.

Gilmore made the unnecessary introduction. 'My wife Liz.'

'Sorry about this, love,' apologized Frost. 'You must hate my guts.'

'Yes,' she said simply.

'I'm known as Coitus Interruptus in the trade,' added Frost, hoping to warm up the atmosphere, but neither of them responded.

'What do you want?' asked Gilmore curtly.

'Another arson attack at the Comptons'. I know it's your case, but I'll attend to it if you like.'

Gilmore hesitated.

'Bloody go,' snapped Liz. 'Bugger off and go!' The door slammed as she stormed out of the room.

'I'll wait outside,' said Frost. 'Be quick.'

'I'm coming now,' said Gilmore, grabbing his coat.

The rain had stopped, but a cold wind chased them to the car. 'Sorry if I sodded things up for you, son,' said Frost, settling into the passenger seat. Gilmore gave a noncommittal grunt and slammed the car into gear. He looked back at the house, half hoping Liz would be at the window so he could give her a wave. A forlorn hope.

The road was clear so Gilmore was able to ignore traffic signals and speed limits and drove with his foot jammed down hard while Frost briefly outlined what he knew. 'Compton phoned the station about half an hour ago. Someone was prowling about outside. A couple of minutes later the station alarm went off, so the prowler must have broken a window or forced a lock or something. Control sent an area car. It found the place in flames. The fire brigade's on its way. That's all I know so far.' As they left the town and climbed the hill to skirt the woods an orange glow throbbed in the sky ahead. 'Bloody hell, son,' said Frost. 'That's one hell of a fire.'

Soon they could see the flashing electric-blue beacons of the fire trucks and hear the deep-throated roar of the burning wooden structure fanned to a frenzy by the wind. The scorching heat hit them as they climbed out of the car and stumbled over a spaghetti confusion of hoses.

'Look out!' someone yelled.

A long-drawn-out creaking screech of agony as the supporting timbers of the mill gave way, then a slow rumbling as the roof collapsed and whooshed up a tongue of flame which licked the night sky with thousands of red, dancing sequins. Firemen in yellow oilskins turned their backs as the dragon's breath of scorched air and smoke blasted out at them.

With the roof down and the building open to the sky, the firemen were able to direct their hoses into the seething heart of the fire gradually damping down the flames and sending up clouds of steam and oily smoke.

'Inspector! Over here.' PC Jordan was waving to them from the side of a fire truck. There was something on the grass by his feet. Something covered by a crumpled sheet of grey plastic, dripping wet from the back-spray of the hoses.

'Shit,' said Frost. The plastic was draped over a dead body.

'The firemen found him in the lounge,' Jordan told them. 'He's burnt to buggery.'

Frost bent and carefully lifted the sheet, then turned his head away, but not before he had breathed in the sickening smell of burnt flesh. Gilmore, watching, felt his stomach start to churn. The dead face gawping up at him was blistered red raw and distorted by intense heat. Where the hair should have been was grey powdery ash.

'The firemen reckon he must have fallen into a pool of blazing petrol,' explained Jordan, staring straight ahead, determined not to look down. 'They dragged him out of the lounge.'

'Poor bastard,' muttered Frost. He pulled the plastic sheeting down further to see better. Welded into the bubbling black flesh, pieces of charred material. 'Looks like pyjamas.'

'Yes, sir. We presume he's the householder.'

Frost forced himself to bend again and study the face closer. If it was Mark Compton it would require medical and dental records for a positive identification. Slowly, he straightened up. 'So what happened?'

'The place was well alight when we got here. Simms radioed for the fire brigade. No way of getting in at the front, so I tried the rear and found Mrs Compton, in her night clothes, unconscious on the lawn just outside the back door.'

'Where is she now?'

'She's with someone in the village, I think.'

Frost nodded for him to continue.

'When the fire brigade got here they sent a couple of men with breathing apparatus into the house. The body was in the lounge. They dragged him out but he was already dead.'

'I thought the sprinklers were supposed to stop this sort of fire,' said Frost.

'They'd been put out of action, Inspector. The water supply was turned off at the mains.'

Gilmore thought it was about time he reminded everyone that this was his case. 'Radio through to Control,' he snapped. 'Tell all patrols that anyone out and about at this time of the morning, on foot or in a car, is a suspect and is to be detained for questioning.'

'And advise all hospitals, chemists and doctors that we want to know immediately about anyone requesting treatment for burns,' added Frost.

A car horn sounded and Dr Maltby's Vauxhall crept into the side road. Maltby, wrapped up against the cold in a thick overcoat, climbed out and surveyed the smouldering wreckage of the once beautiful house. He spotted Frost and made his way across, stepping with exaggerated care over the hose-pipes.

'He's drunk again,' hissed Gilmore.

'Then arrest him,' snapped Frost. 'We need the extra work. Over here, doc!'

The doctor lurched over. 'Terrible business, Jack.' He nodded at the sheeted shape. 'The husband?'

'All that's left of him, doc. He fell face first in some four star. What I want to know is, did he fall or was he pushed?'

Maltby pulled the sheet completely away from the body and arranged it over the wet grass so he could kneel down. He shook his head testily. 'He's too badly burnt. You'll need a proper post-mortem.' He lifted the head slightly, his fingers exploring the skull. 'Hello . . .' Carefully he moved the head so he could examine it more easily. 'The back of the skull's caved in.'

'Where?' asked Frost, squatting down beside the doctor. His nicotine-stained fingers probed. Yes, he could feel the pulpy fracture where the skull gave way under pressure. He wiped his hand on his mac and straightened up. 'Damn, damn and double damn!'

'Could it have happened when he fell?' asked Gilmore.

Frost shook his head. 'He fell face down, son . . . straight into the burning petrol.'

Maltby nodded his agreement. 'I'd say he was struck from behind . . . a heavy blow from a blunt instrument. If the blow didn't kill him outright, then the fire finished him off.'

Frost's shoulders sagged wearily. 'It's murder whichever way you look at it, doc.' He shook water from the plastic sheeting and jerked it back over the body. 'Where's the poor sod's wife?'

'Ada's looking after her,' said Maltby. He turned to watch the firemen. The Old Mill was now a skeleton of blackened, smoking timbers which had to be continually dampened down as a malevolent wind kept fanning sparks into flames. 'Get the bastard, Jack,' he said, as he stumbled back to his car.

'I'll try,' called Frost. He turned to Gilmore. 'Come on, son. Let's go and have a word with Old Mother Rigid Nipples.'

Gilmore exploded. He had had just about enough of Frost's callous crudeness for one day. 'Haven't you got any bloody feeling? A man's dead. His wife is a widow. Must everything be a cheap joke?'

Frost accepted the rebuke with a half-hearted shrug. 'I see so many rotten things, son. If I dwelt on them, I'd probably go and chuck myself under a bus, which might make Mullett happy, but wouldn't do the victim any good . . . so I joke. It makes the job a bit more tolerable . . . sorry if it upsets you, though.'

A concerned-looking Ada, a thick mouse-grey dressing gown over flannelette pyjamas, a man's cap covering her curlers, led them through to the bedroom where Jill

Compton, all respectable in one of Ada's passion-killing high-necked winceyette nightdresses, lay with eyes closed, on Ada's iron-framed single bed. Frost thought it was the most erotic sight he had ever seen and wished he wouldn't keep thinking dirty thoughts at inopportune moments. Jill's eyes fluttered, then opened wide in startled anxiety as Frost gently called her name. She sat up. 'Where's Mark? Is he all right?'

Frost groaned inwardly. He hadn't realized she hadn't been told. 'It's bad news, I'm afraid, Mrs Compton.'

She stared at him, then at Gilmore, her eyes pleading to be told that what she feared, what she dreaded, wasn't so. 'No . . . no . . . please . . .' And her head shook, rejecting what she knew they would tell her.

Frost knew of no way to deaden the hurt other than killing hope quickly. 'Your husband is dead, Mrs Compton. The firemen got him out, but it was too late.'

At first she looked angry, as if her refusal to accept what they were telling her would make it untrue. Then her body shook as she buried her face in her hands, tears streaming between her fingers. 'No . . .'

Ada pushed forward to comfort her. 'You'd better go now,' she ordered the two detectives.

'No,' said Frost, firmly. 'She's the only witness. The only person who can help us.'

Ada stood her ground, chin jutting defiantly, one arm protectively around her charge. 'I've told you to go. This is neither the time nor the place.'

But, sniffing back her tears and biting hard on her lower lip, Jill spoke quietly. 'It's all right. I want to help. What do you want to know?'

Signalling Gilmore to get out his notebook, Frost dragged a wicker-seated chair to the side of the bed. 'Tell us what happened.'

The detective sergeant gave a sharp cough and glared angrily. 'This is my case,' he reminded the inspector.

'Sorry, son,' said Frost mildly, moving his chair back a little.

Gilmore gave the woman a sympathetic smile. 'Tell us what happened, Mrs Compton.'

She fumbled under the pillow for a handkerchief, dabbed at her eyes, then, twisting the tiny scrap of cloth in her hands, related the course of events. 'We went to bed just before midnight. I woke up suddenly. Mark was using the phone by the bed. He was calling the police. He had heard someone prowling about outside.'

'Did you see who it was?' asked Gilmore.

'Not clearly. We looked out of the window and could see a shadow of someone moving about. Mark was angry. He grabbed a heavy torch and said he was going to teach whoever it was a lesson.'

'He was going to use the torch as a weapon?'

She nodded. 'I imagine so.'

'You didn't go downstairs with him?'

'No. He insisted I stayed in the bedroom with the door locked. I waited. Suddenly I heard shouting and crashing, as if there was a fight. Then it went quiet. I waited, hoping Mark would come back. I called him. No answer. Then I smelt burning so I unlocked the bedroom door. Thick black smoke. I could hardly see. I had to feel my way down the stairs. When I opened the lounge door, flames and smoke roared out. I could see Mark, face down on the floor. But the heat was intense. I couldn't get to him.'

She paused, her face drawn and pained as she relived the moment. Frost started to say something, but Gilmore brusquely signalled him to be quiet.

'I saw the lounge window was open, so I tried to get out into the garden through the back door. But the smoke

267

was so thick. I was choking. When I found the bolts, they wouldn't undo. I struggled and finally got them undone . . .' She looked at her broken nails, then hid her hands under the bedclothes. '. . . but I must have passed out. That's all I remember. There was a fireman . . . and then there was Ada.' The effort of talking had exhausted her. Her eyes closed and her head dropped back on the pillow. 'That's all I remember,' she repeated in a whisper.

'The firemen found you collapsed just outside the back door,' Gilmore told her. 'Did you see anything more of the person who broke in?'

Eyes still closed, she shook her head. 'No.' Her body trembled with the reaction and she tried to sit up. 'If only I could have got to Mark. He was so close. But the flames . . .'

Gilmore patted her arm. 'There was nothing you could have done, Mrs Compton. He was already dead when you first saw him.'

She raised her face to the sergeant. 'I pleaded with him to wait for the police. If only he had stayed with me . . .' And then she threw back her head and howled in anguish, her sobs racking her body . . .

With a belligerent stride Ada pushed in front of Gilmore. 'No more. She's had enough.'

Gilmore replaced the chair up against the forget-me-not patterned wallpaper. 'Thanks for your help, Mrs Compton. And I really am most sorry.'

Ada wrapped her dressing gown around her spare frame. 'I'll stay with her for a while. There's tea and biscuits in the kitchen if you want some.'

The kitchen, with the coal fire roaring away, was almost overpoweringly warm and Gilmore had to fight hard to keep his eyes open as he sipped Ada's hot, sweet tea. Frost had twitched back the curtains to reveal the early morning sky, part-streaked with smudges of smoke from the fire. He was sprawled in the chair by the kitchen table, using a saucer as an ashtray. He too was tired. He'd have given anything to be able to climb into bed, preferably with the naked Jill Compton whose tear-stained, unmade-up face seemed to hold an erotic attraction.

His foot twitched and made contact with something under the table, something that swayed, then toppled heavily with a glassy clunk. Yawning, he lifted the table-cloth. Nudging his foot lay a wine bottle on its side. One of Ada's home-made brews. There were about twenty or so more bottles of wine bunched together under the table. 'The stingy cow's hiding it from us,' he said, pulling the cork out with his teeth and taking a swig. The room shimmered, then jerked still. He replaced the cork and pushed the bottle back with the others under the table.

'You know what I've been thinking?' said Gilmore.

Frost shook his head to stop the fuzziness. 'If it's something rude, I'm all ears, son.'

'If that poison pen letter was sent to Mark Compton, then who is the woman he's been knocking off?'

'I wish I knew,' replied Frost. 'I'd love to get some of what he's been getting.'

'He's been going with another woman,' said Gilmore. 'There could be a jealous husband, or boyfriend.'

'A good point, son,' began Frost, then he stopped dead and looked under the table again as a nagging thought struck him. 'Why has she dumped the bottles there? She's usually so neat and tidy . . . everything in its place.'

'I don't know,' muttered Gilmore, his tone implying he didn't care either.

A wall cupboard in the corner caught Frost's eye. 'That's where she usually keeps her wine. Quick, son.

Take a look inside.' Gilmore showed his astonishment. 'It could be important, son.'

Anything to humour the old fool, thought Gilmore as he tugged at the handle. 'It's locked!'

'Catch!' Frost tossed him a bunch of keys. 'Try one of these.'

The first key didn't fit, so he tried another. 'We shouldn't be doing this without a search warrant.'

Frost raised his eyebrows in mock astonishment. 'You learn something new in this job every day. Someone was telling me you can't plant false evidence any more, but I'm not that gullible.' He lit up another cigarette. 'Hurry it up, son.'

Another key. Still no joy. But the next glided in smooth as silk and the lock clicked. Gilmore pulled open the door then whistled softly. Inside the cupboard was a battered old Olympia typewriter. He was carrying it over to the table when a door slammed and an angry voice shrilled, 'And just what do you think you're doing?'

'I tried to stop him, Ada,' said Frost, 'but he wouldn't take any notice.'

'I let you into my house. I give you tea. I give you biscuits . . .'

'But you don't give us your body, Ada. The one thing I've been lusting after.'

She wasn't listening to Frost. Angry eyes stabbed at Gilmore who was ripping a blank page from the back of his notebook and feeding it into the roller. Her voice, shaking with rage, rose an octave. 'Don't you dare touch that!' She plunged forward but Frost's arm shot out to restrain her.

'We've got to check it to make sure he hasn't broken it, Ada. I want you to get every penny of compensation.'

270

The page in to his satisfaction, Gilmore pecked out a test sentence. *The quick brown fox jumps over the lazy dog.* He snatched the paper from the machine and studied it carefully, a grin of triumph creeping across his face. 'The "s" and the "a" are out of alignment, Inspector. We've found the poison pen typewriter.'

Frost took the page from him and nodded. 'He's right, Ada. But I bet you've got a perfectly plausible explanation?' He waited expectantly.

She folded her arms stubbornly and compressed her lips.

'Can't quite hear you, Ada,' said Frost, cupping his hand to his ear.

Her eyes narrowed, but she remained silent.

Gilmore pushed himself between her and Frost. He was barely in control of himself. He kept seeing Susan Bicknell in her Mickey Mouse nightdress, stretched lifeless on the bed. 'You don't need to say anything, you evil-minded bitch. Because of you an old man tried to kill himself. Because of you a fifteen-year-old kid took her own life.'

She stared back at him, her eyes unflinching. 'Then you'd better arrest me, hadn't you?'

'Stop fighting, you two,' said Frost, flopping back in his chair. 'You never wrote those bloody letters, Ada. The longest note you ever wrote said "No milk today, please, the cat's got diarrhoea."' He shook an export Benson and Hedges from the packet. 'That's old Mr Wardley's typewriter, isn't it? He's the sod who's been sending the letters.'

Her expression didn't change.

'Wardley?' exclaimed Gilmore. 'That's impossible. He got one of the letters. He tried to kill himself.'

'He didn't try very hard, did he, son? He didn't try as hard as that poor cow Susan Bicknell.' He folded the piece of paper into a spill and lit his cigarette from the fire. 'I reckon Wardley didn't swallow more than a couple of those tablets.'

'The bottle was nearly empty,' said Gilmore.

'Only because he'd tipped most of the tablets out into the drawer of his bedside cabinet. He sent the poison pen letter to himself, then faked the suicide.' He puffed smoke towards the woman. 'I'm right, aren't I, Ada? You can caress any part of my body if I'm wrong.'

Her lips twisted into a tight, bitter smile then she moved across to the table and started stacking the dirty cups and saucers on a tray. 'How did you find out?'

'Guesswork mainly, Ada. But I was bloody suspicious of that unfranked poison pen letter Wardley was supposed to have received. Everyone else's letter went into juicy detail . . . every thrust, every withdrawal, each nibble of naked ear-hole all lovingly described. But there weren't any juicy bits at all in his own letter. It was almost polite. "What would the church say if I told them what you did to those boys!" Not a mention of dick anywhere.' He dragged hard at the cigarette. 'And then there was the missing suicide note. It didn't make sense you should destroy it. There was no point.'

Ada crossed the room to the sideboard. 'I didn't destroy it. I just didn't want you to see it.' From the drawer she took a sheet of blue notepaper. Frost glanced at it, then passed it over to Gilmore. ' "A"s and "s"s out of line, son. The silly sod used the same machine for the suicide note and the poison pen letters.'

'He thinks himself so clever, but he's not all there,' said Ada. 'I found out about him last year. I went in to do his cleaning and there he was, bashing away at the typewriter, so engrossed in one of his nasty letters he never heard me.'

'Then why didn't you inform the police?' asked Gilmore.

She dragged a chair to the fire and sat down. 'He's lived next door to me for years. I didn't want to get him into trouble.'

'So you just let him carry on writing his dirty letters?'

'I made him promise he'd stop. I thought he had stopped.' She stared into the fire then picked up the poker and shattered a lump of coal sending sparks shooting up the chimney.

'What brought things to a head?' asked Gilmore. 'Why the letter to himself and the faked suicide attempt?'

She rubbed her hands as if she was cold and held them to the fire to warm them. 'I was working up at The Mill when the post came. There was a letter addressed to Mr Compton. I recognized the blue envelope and the wonky typing right away, so I hid it in my pocket. I wasn't going to let him cause trouble with the Comptons.'

'Did you confront Wardley?' Frost asked.

'As soon as I finished work. I charged over to his cottage and told him I was going straight to the police. He said the police would never believe me. It would be his word against mine and he was a churchwarden and I was a charlady. Just then, in comes Dr Maltby with the sleeping tablets. I took the letter from my pocket and said, "Can I talk to you in private, doctor. I've got something to show you." Mr Wardley went as white as a sheet. Of course, when we got outside, I gave the doctor the letter and explained how I'd got hold of it, but I didn't tell him anything about Mr Wardley writing it. I only meant to frighten him. I can't tell you how I felt when I went back later and it looked as if he'd killed himself.'

'Like I said, he faked it to make you out a liar, Ada,' said Frost, pushing himself out of his chair.

Gilmore gathered up the typewriter and followed Frost out into the cold, damp morning air where the smell of smoke and burning clung to the wind.

The Old Mill was a depressing blackened shell, dripping water which plopped mournfully into soot-filmed, debris-choked pools. The ground squelched under foot as firemen in yellow oilskins and blackened faces rolled up hoses and stowed away equipment while others, helped by members of the Forensic team, were picking through the sodden wreckage. DC Burton in an anorak over a polo-necked sweater spotted their car as they pulled up and hurried to meet them. 'The pathologist has examined the body, Inspector. He thinks the blow on the head knocked Compton unconscious and death was due to smoke suffocation. He'll be doing the autopsy at eleven this morning.'

'I'll be there,' said Gilmore to remind everyone once again that this was his case.

'Any joy with petrol- and smoke-smelling suspects?' asked Frost.

'No, sir. Charlie Alpha picked up a tramp on the Bath Road, but what he smelt of isn't nice to say.'

'Forensic turned anything up?'

'Yes – those.' Burton pointed to three heat-distorted metal petrol cans, bagged up for laboratory examination. 'And this . . .' He picked up a plastic bag containing a blackened cylinder of metal, caved in at one end. 'They think this is the murder weapon.'

'Compton's torch!' said Frost. He told Gilmore to get Mrs Compton to identify it as soon as Forensic had finished their tests.

'That's what I intended doing,' hissed Gilmore through clenched teeth.

'What's the name of our one bloody suspect?' asked Frost. 'The one who picked the fight?'

'Bradbury,' Gilmore reminded him. The fool had a memory like a sieve.

'That's him! There's an all-forces bulletin out on him. Find out if he's been located yet.'

While Gilmore radioed through to the station, Frost peered through a smashed window at the remains of the lounge, which was now a miniature indoor lake of greasy water dotted with islands of ash and charred wood. He lit a cigarette, took one deep drag, then hurled it away. The smoke had the greasy taint of burnt flesh.

Gilmore returned, shaking his head. No joy yet on Bradbury. Frost took one last look round. Everyone seemed to be coping quite well without him. 'We're doing no good here, son,' he muttered. 'Let's go to the hospital.'

'The hospital?' echoed Gilmore. 'Why?' Now that he had committed himself to attending the autopsy in six hours' time, all he wanted to do was go home and get some sleep.

'To question Wardley,' explained Frost. 'You said Mark Compton's bit of spare might provide the motive for his death and Wardley knows who she is. I'll do it on my own if you like.'

No way! thought Gilmore, slamming the car into gear. No bloody way.

At that hour of the morning Denton Hospital was a place of uneasy, muffled noises, whispers, coughs and groans. The very young probationer nurse in sole charge of the wheezing, snuffling ward wasn't at all happy about

Frost waking up one of the patients, but Frost breezily assured her that he had permission.

Wardley, deep in a trouble-free sleep, was rudely awakened by a rough shaking of his shoulder. His eyes flickered open as he tried to focus on the two strangers looking grimly down at him. One of them he recognized immediately and his heart-beat faltered before thudding away. It was that detective inspector, back again, in the middle of the night. And the look on his face. God, they knew. They had found out. He closed his eyes tightly and feigned sleep, but the renewed shaking of his shoulder nearly jerked him out of bed. 'Yes?' he asked in a quavery, weak, old man's voice.

'Get dressed,' said Frost. 'I'm arresting you.'

'Arresting me?' He pulled himself up. 'It's that woman next door telling lies about me, isn't it? Don't you believe her . . . she's evil. She hates me.'

'Not as much as I bloody hate you,' said Frost. 'And the only lies Ada told us was when she was covering up for you, you sod. She even hid your typewriter – the one you used for your suicide note – and for your poison pen letters.'

'Poison pen?' He tried to sound indignant. 'The intention was to make people stop their filthy practices.'

'You made Susan Bicknell stop hers,' said Frost. 'The poor cow killed herself.'

The skin on the old man's knuckles stretched almost to blue transparency as he clutched at the sheet. 'I didn't mean that to happen. She over-reacted. I'm sorry.'

'Oh, you're sorry?' hissed Frost. 'That makes it all right. We'll dig the poor bitch up so you can apologize.' He dragged a chair across the floor with such a loud, teeth-setting squeak that half the ward stirred uneasily. 'Right,' he said wearily. 'I'm tired, my sergeant is tired, and we haven't got time to sod about. I'm going to ask you questions, and I want answers.'

'I'm saying nothing,' whimpered Wardley. 'I'm a sick man.'

The chair squeaked again as Frost stood up. 'Arrest the bastard, Sergeant.'

'Wait,' said Wardley. 'What do you want to know?'

Another squeak from the chair. Frost made himself comfortable, then shook the last export cigarette from the packet and lit up. 'Let's start with the pornographic video. Who's been making them?'

'A purveyor of filth. If I knew his name I'd tell you. I bought the video, Inspector. It wasn't for enjoyment. I have to do these things to ferret out evil. When I screened it, I recognized the girl. Her mother goes to our church. I've no idea who makes and distributes them.'

'Where did you buy it?' Gilmore asked.

'A newsagent's in Catherine Street. I don't know the name.'

'We do,' said Frost. 'We've already arrested him.' That part of Wardley's story checked out anyway. 'We'll leave that for the moment. You sent one of your well-meaning letters to Mark Compton?'

The old man pulled himself upright, his eyes wild, his expression intense. 'That lecher. All smug and high and mighty, but sneaking off behind his wife's back for disgusting perversions with a prostitute.'

'A prostitute?' said Gilmore, glumly. This ruined his theory. If Compton's bit of spare was a prostitute, a vengeful boyfriend or husband would have his work cut out.

'Never mind, son,' said Frost. 'We'll check her out anyway.' He asked Wardley where she lived.

'Where all these high-priced harlots live. In Queen's Court – those new flats at the back of the big supermarket . . . end flat, third floor.'

'If they were up on the third floor, how could you see through the bedroom window?'

Wardley smiled. 'The multi-storey car-park overlooks her flat. All you need is a strong pair of field-glasses.'

'And a dirty vicious bastard to use them,' said Frost.

PC Dave Simms tucked the area car into the lay-by off the Bath Road and reached for the thermos flask. His observer, PC Jordan, yawned and stretched his arms. 'I'll be damn glad when this shift is over,' he sniffed. 'I'm sure I've got this flu bug coming on.'

'Don't breathe over me then,' replied Simms, slopping steaming hot coffee into a plastic cup and passing it over.

Jordan sipped at the cup, then his eyes narrowed. 'Hello. What's this?'

Headlights approaching. Coming from the opposite direction to the fire, but they had been given instructions to stop everyone. Anyone out and about at this time of the morning was a potential suspect.

It was a small black van which slowed down and stopped as they sounded the siren and cut in front of it. The driver, a short, sharp-featured man with long greasy hair, in his late forties, eyed them warily. 'What's the trouble, officer?'

Simms asked to see the man's driving licence, his nose twitching, trying to detect the smell of smoke, or petrol, but smelling only fresh paint.

'I haven't got my licence with me. What's this all about?'

'Just routine, sir. Do you mind telling us what you are doing out at this time of night?'

Jordan was checking the van. The smell of new paint was strong. The vehicle had been freshly painted. A pretty ropey job, done with a paint brush, not a spray gun. He tried the rear doors. They opened.

'Leave them alone!' yelled the man, reaching forward to switch on the engine, but Simms' hand clamped round his wrist.

The beam of Jordan's torch found a stack of cardboard boxes. He pulled one forward and looked inside. Jewellery. Lots of jewellery. Mainly old-fashioned, but good quality – brooches, lockets, bangles, rings.

'Well, well, well,' smirked Jordan. 'And what is your perfectly reasonable explanation for these, sir?'

The hospital was slowly waking up as they clattered down the stone stairs past the first shift of cleaners with mops and buckets. They could hear the car radio as they crossed the pavement.

'Frost,' he yawned into the handset.

'We've got him, Jack,' reported Sergeant Wells triumphantly.

'You've got Bradbury?' asked Frost, unable to believe his luck. 'Is he dripping with petrol, smothered in blood and carrying a blunt instrument?'

'Not Bradbury,' replied Wells, testily. Frost was always joking at the wrong moment. 'No joy with him yet. But we've got Wally Manson. Jordan and Simms picked him up. His van's a bloody treasure trove – full of stolen gear from the senior citizen break-ins. Mr Mullett is cock-a-hoop.'

'What's that about Mr Mullett's cock?' asked Frost innocently. 'This is a very bad line.' He replaced the handset. 'The station, son.'

But Gilmore was already on the way.

279

Frost sank down in his seat again. He dug down in his pocket, but the Benson and Hedges packet was empty.

Thursday morning shift

A quarter to six in the morning and Mullett, freshly shaven, highly polished, and immaculately dressed in his best tailored uniform, emerged from his office, mentally rehearsing the speech he would make to the press and the television cameras after they had charged Manson with the 'Granny Ripper' killings. He waylaid the dishevelled Frost and Gilmore, both looking tired and edgy, on their way to the Interview Room. 'No doubts about the right man this time, Inspector. Hanlon has definitely identified an item of jewellery from Manson's van as belonging to one of the murder victims and there's a positive forensic report on those jeans.'

'Great!' muttered Frost, trying to share his commander's enthusiasm. He always got worried when things appeared to be going too well.

They looked in on the exhibits store where Arthur Hanlon, his nose red and sore from repeated blowing, was hovering over a collection of cardboard boxes, the spoils from Wally Manson's van. 'Mr Mullett tells me it's all cut and dried,' said Frost. 'Wally's confessed and hanged himself to spare the state the cost of a trial.'

'Not quite, Jack,' giggled Hanlon, blowing his nose with a sodden handkerchief. 'He's denying everything at the moment – you know what a slimy little sod he is.'

'Yes,' nodded Frost. 'I sometimes think he's Mr Mullett's illegitimate son. Anyway, what have we got?'

Hanlon pushed one of the boxes over and raised the flaps. 'This was a surprise, Jack.' The box was packed tight with pornographic videos. 'Forty-nine in all,' reported Hanlon. 'The same titles as we got from the newsagent's.' Frost grunted and pulled the next box towards him. This one held assorted house-breaking tools – screwdrivers, jemmies, hammers, glass cutters. The last box, the smallest of the lot, contained various small plastic supermarket bags. Selecting one at random, Frost looked inside, then handed it over to Gilmore. Jewellery. Gold rings, chains, lockets, crucifixes. Another bag held necklaces and ear-rings. Yet another, old-fashioned cameo brooches, and heavy dress jewellery.

'We've only positively identified this, so far,' Hanlon told them, fishing out a pearl-studded crucifix on a silver chain. 'But it's the one that matters. This belonged to Mrs Alice Ryder.'

Frost held the crucifix in his open hand. It looked like silver, but it wasn't and the pearls were false. It was worth a few pounds at the most and the old lady who fought to stop it being stolen had had her skull smashed in and had died in Denton Hospital. 'Mullett was yapping about positive forensic evidence?'

'The stains are definitely blood, the same group as the old lady, and there were small fragments of china which matched up to that vase he smashed getting through the window.'

'What have you told Manson?'

'I haven't told him anything. I've only questioned him about being in possession of stolen property.'

'You haven't mentioned the killings?'

'No.'

'Good. Let's keep the sod guessing. Bring him to Interview Room Number 1.' Frost patted his pockets and realized he was out of cigarettes. He sent Gilmore back to the office to fetch a packet from his desk drawer.

Gritty, tired and irritated at being treated as a messenger boy, Gilmore yanked the drawer open. Underneath the camouflage of two ancient files were a couple of packs, each containing 200 Benson and Hedges export only cigarettes. He paused. A way to get back into his Divisional Commander's good books. This was exactly the sort of thing Mullett had asked him to look out for. Evidence of Frost's dubious practices. A quiet word in Mullett's ear. 'I don't know if I ought to be saying this, sir, against a fellow officer, but . . .' He could already see the Cheshire cat grin spreading over the Divisional Commander's face. He stuffed a spare packet in his pocket as evidence. Then he noticed something protruding beneath one of the packs in the drawer. A battered, blue material-covered case. Something else Frost had helped himself to? He clicked it open. Snug on red plush a silver cross on a dark blue ribbon, the inscription in the centre reading *For Gallantry.* Frost's famous medal. The George Gross. The civilian equivalent to the VC. Gilmore stared at it, then quickly clicked the case shut and replaced it at the bottom of the drawer together with the spare pack from his pocket. Frost would never know it, but yet again his medal had got him out of possible trouble.

'Gentleman to see you, Inspector,' announced Hanlon, pushing Wally Manson into the Interview Room.

Manson blinked as his eyes adjusted to the bright light after the shaded bulb of his cell. Through a haze of blue smoke he could see the unwelcome sight of Detective Inspector Jack Frost sprawled untidily in a chair, a cigarette dangling from his lips. On the table in front of him were a couple of the boxes taken from his van.

'Nice of you to drop in, Wally,' said Frost, waving a hand at the other chair by the table. 'Sit down.' Behind the inspector, leaning against the wall under the tiny window, was a younger man he didn't recognize, in a smart suit. The younger man looked tired and frazzled and nasty.

Gilmore contemplated Manson with disgust. The man was a slob with his weasel-like face, lank greasy hair and eyes that kept shifting from side to side; a cornered rat looking for an escape route.

'I don't know what this is all about, Mr Frost,' Manson said, shrinking down into the offered chair. 'Like I told the other gentleman, I found those boxes dumped in a lay-by. I was on the way to the police station to hand them in when those two coppers picked me up.'

'I'm sorry to hear that, Wally,' said Frost, shaking ash all over the floor, 'I was hoping you were guilty, because we're going to frame you anyway.'

Wally grinned at the inspector's joke, but Frost didn't seem to be joking. He dipped into one of the cardboard boxes and pulled out a pearl crucifix which he swung by the chain under Wally's nose.

'She identified you, Wally.'

Manson jerked his head away. 'Like I told the other officer, Mr Frost, I found these boxes in a lay-by . . .'

'They'll find you in a bleedin' lay-by if you don't stop sodding me about, Wally. You've been identified, we know you did it and we're going to get a confession and a conviction by fair means or foul. So tell us about it.'

'If only I knew what you're talking about, Mr Frost,' said Manson, giving his unconvincing impression of puzzled innocence, then nearly jumping out of his chair as the young thug behind him suddenly bellowed in his ear, 'We're talking about the woman whose skull you fractured, you scum-bag.'

'There's no need to raise your voice, Sergeant,' re-proved Frost mildly. 'He's going to give us everything we want without bullying, aren't you, Wally?'

'I'll help you if I can,' said Manson, rubbing his ear.

Frost beamed a friendly smile that made the prisoner's blood run cold. 'Good. Then help me with Mrs Alice Ryder, the old lady from Clarendon Street who you put in hospital.' At this stage he wasn't going to let Manson know that she was dead.

Manson looked hurt. 'Not me, Mr Frost. That's not my style.'

Frost snorted a cloud of Benson and Hedges smoke. 'Style! You haven't got any bleeding style. If you're going to sod me about, I can sod you about. Notebook, Sergeant.'

Gilmore took out his notebook and flipped it open.

'Stand up,' snapped Frost to Manson.

Manson hesitated so Gilmore yanked him to his feet.

'Walter Richard Manson,' droned Frost, 'alias the Granny Ripper . . .'

'Granny Ripper?' croaked Manson, his astonishment sounding genuine this time.

'Shut up!' barked Gilmore.

'Alias the Granny Ripper,' continued Frost, 'I am arresting you on three counts of murder . . .' To Gilmore he said, 'Fill in the details – I forget the names and dates.' Gilmore nodded, his pencil scribbling furiously. 'You are not obliged to say anything – etc. etc., but anything you do say, blah, blah, blah. Take it as read, Wally – you know the words better than I do.'

'I am totally innocent of these preposterous charges,' said Manson smugly, twisting his head to make sure Gilmore was writing it all down.

Frost put his hand on Gilmore's notebook to stop him writing. 'Hold on, Sergeant. I'm sure we can do better than that.' He scratched his scar thoughtfully. 'Put . . . "The prisoner replied I didn't mean to kill them. I'm terribly sorry for what I did. I deserve to be punished."'

The man's jaw dropped. 'I never said that.'

Frost lit up another export only. 'What you actually said doesn't matter, Wally. It's what he puts down in his book that gets read out in court.'

Manson shrunk back in his chair. 'I shall deny saying it. I shall say it's all lies.'

'Of course you will, Wally. And it will be the word of a cheap slimy little crook with a record against a detective inspector with a medal. Courts seem to think that people with George Crosses are incapable of telling lies.'

'That's not fair,' said Manson, almost in tears.

'Life's not fair when some bastard breaks into your house and smashes your skull in,' snapped Frost.

Wally's tongue flicked snake-like across dried lips. 'You wouldn't perjure yourself, Mr Frost?' he pleaded, but the expression on the inspector's face said, 'Yes, I bloody well would.'

Frost leant his head back and treated the ceiling to a squirt of smoke. 'Not perjury, Wally – it's called oiling the wheels of justice. Take him away, Sergeant, and charge him. We'll have him in court first thing tomorrow.'

Hanlon stepped forward and took the man's arm, but Wally shook him off. 'What do I get if I co-operate?'

'My undying gratitude, Wally – and perhaps a whisper to the judge about how helpful you were.'

Manson hesitated. 'This old lady in Clarendon Street. You say she identified me?'

'She described you perfectly, Wally. She said her attacker was an ugly little bastard with bad breath and dandruff. We showed her some photographs and she picked you out right away.'

Manson gnawed at his lower lip. 'I didn't mean to hurt her, Mr Frost. She came at me like a bloody tiger.'

'An eighty-one-year-old tiger,' said Frost. 'What did she attack you with – her pension book?'

'A knife, Mr Frost . . . a flaming great knife.' He tugged the shirt from his trousers and lifted it to expose his stomach. 'Look what she did to me!' A thick pad of dirty red-mottled cotton wool, blood still weeping from the edges, was strapped to his stomach by strips of sticking plaster. 'She'd have killed me. I had to hit her to defend myself.' He fumbled at the dressing. 'Do you want to see what it's like underneath?'

Frost waved the offer away. 'No, thanks, Wally. It's a bit too near your dick and I haven't had my breakfast yet. I'll get the doctor to have a look at it.' He slid from his chair and went to the door, making a small jerk of his head to signal Hanlon to follow.

Outside in the passage, Frost closed the door firmly and lowered his voice. 'Here's a turn-up for the bleedin' book, Arthur. Did you check that knife to see if it matched up with any of the old girl's cutlery?'

'No, Jack. There were no prints on it and the damn thing had been honed razor sharp. I just assumed it came from her attacker.'

'She was terrified of burglars. She probably kept a sharpened knife to protect herself. Check it out now – and find out what blood group Wally is. It should be on his prison file.' He followed the worried-looking Hanlon down the corridor and asked Sergeant Wells to call the duty police surgeon.

*　　*　　*

The police surgeon dropped unused bandages into his bag and clicked it shut. 'I don't think there's any danger, but just to be on the safe side, the hospital should check him over.' He gave Frost his 'Payment Request' form to sign and checked it carefully before nodding his goodbye.

An agitated Arthur Hanlon was waiting outside the Interview Room. His shamefaced expression told Frost all.

'The knife came from her cutlery drawer,' Hanlon admitted. 'She's got a carving fork and a sharpening steel all in the same pattern to match. I'm sorry, Jack, I should have checked.'

'Never mind, Arthur,' said Frost. 'It makes me feel better to know I'm not the only twat in the force.'

'And Wally's blood group is O, the same as the dead woman's, so the blood on the knife could well have come from him.'

'Damn. The knife was the only thing that tied him to the other two killings and we haven't got that now. Never mind, let's do our best with what little we've got – as the bishop said to the actress.'

In the Interview Room, which now reeked of antiseptic, their prisoner was noisily drinking a cup of tea, watched by a sour-faced Gilmore. Frost dropped wearily into his chair. 'Right, Wally. The doctor says you're not going to die, but I've got over my disappointment. Tell me about the old dear at Clarendon Street – right from the beginning.' He pushed a cigarette across the table and lit it for the man. 'And cover up your stomach – it's wobbling like a bloody blancmange.'

Manson sucked gratefully at the cigarette. 'Thanks, Mr Frost.' He tucked his shirt back in and readjusted his belt. 'This was last Monday night – one of those nights when everything went wrong.'

Frost nodded in sympathy. He had many nights like that.

'The first house I tried I thought was going to be easy. Up on the dustbin and through the back window. I could hear the old boy talking to his wife downstairs, so I thought the coast was clear. Straight in the bedroom and there's this weird niff . . . I flashes my torch around and, bloody hell – there's a decomposing corpse grinning at me. I couldn't get out of there fast enough. I had to nip in the pub for some Dutch courage and who comes walking through the door but you and that bloke there with the fancy aftershave. This just ain't my bloody night, I thought. But I phoned you. I told you about the body.'

'I know, Wally,' nodded Frost. 'I recognized your voice.'

'I should have packed it in, but I needed some readies – I owed the bookie a couple of hundred and he was screaming for it. I'd already marked out this house in Clarendon Street. It looked easy and they said this old lady had cash all over the place. It must have been well bloody hidden – I never found it. The bedroom was empty. She was in the other room watching the telly, then, just my flaming luck, I knocks this vase over and the next thing I know she's charging in with the knife, slashing away. I lashed out in self-defence and she went out like a light.' He took another drag at his cigarette. 'It was all her fault, Mr Frost. I could have sued her for what she did to me. You know the law – you're only supposed to use reasonable force in ejecting a burglar, and gouging chunks out of his gut with a carving knife ain't reasonable force.'

'Neither is smashing someone's skull in,' barked Gilmore from behind him.

'A tap, Mr Frost, that's all I gave her. A tap with me jemmy, just to discourage her. The bloody knife was stuck in my stomach and I had to pull it out. I'd tore my rubber gloves in the struggle, so I wiped the handle clean in case my prints were on it, then grabbed up a few bits of jewellery and got the hell out of there. When I read in the paper next day she was in Intensive Care, it frightened the shit out of me – if you'll pardon the expression. I never did another job from that night to this. That's the honest, gospel truth.'

Frost shook another cigarette out of the packet and tapped it on the table. 'Tell me the honest gospel truth about the other poor cows, Wally. Did they all come at you with knives and then commit hara-kiri?' He watched the prisoner closely, but unless Manson was a brilliant actor, he didn't seem to know what Frost was talking about.

'Others? What are you trying to pin on me?'

Frost opened the file and spread out colour photographs of the two dead women showing their wounds in vivid close-up, his eyes still locked on Manson's face.

Wally shuddered and turned his head. 'Bloody hell, Mr Frost. That's horrible.' He fumbled for a grubby handkerchief to mop his brow. 'You ain't suggesting they're down to me? I've never killed anyone in my life.'

'Yes, you have, Wally,' said Frost, grimly. 'The old girl you discouraged by caving in her skull died in hospital.'

'Come off it, Inspector,' said Wally, grinning to show that he had seen through Frost's bluff. 'There's no way a little tap would . . .' And then he saw Frost's expression and knew he was serious. 'Oh my God!' The grin froze solid and his face drained of colour. 'Dead?'

Frost nodded.

'Bloody hell, Mr Frost. She came at me – with a knife. I had no choice – it was self-defence.'

'Were these self-defence?' asked Frost, smacking his hand on the photographs.

'You're not pinning them on me, Mr Frost. I'll cough to the old girl, but that's all.'

Frost gave him a disarming smile. 'Fair enough, Wally. Tell you what – as we're mates – cough to the others and I'll give you self-defence on the first one.'

'I never bleedin' did the others. How can I make you believe me?'

'I'd consider an alibi, Wally. Where were you Tuesday night?'

Manson looked appalled. 'I can't give you an alibi without incriminating myself. I was doing another job.'

'Don't be a twat, Wally. We're talking murder and you're talking petty burglary.'

Manson gave a hopeless shrug. 'I can't bloody win, can I? All right, on Tuesday night I did some cars over at Forest View – I got a CD player from one and a couple of cassette players from the others.'

'What about Sunday?'

'I did a house in Appleford Court. Got away with around £80. Then I tried a car round the back but the flaming alarm went off.'

Frost nodded. He knew about the Appleford Court burglary and he'd check on the cars. But this was Sunday night. Mary Haynes was killed in the afternoon. 'What about Sunday afternoon?'

'I stayed in. I had it away with Belle.'

'Let's say that took a minute – half a minute if you kept your boots on. What did you do with the rest of the time?'

'I stayed in until six – Belle will vouch for me.'

Frost gave a snort. 'She's as big a liar as you are. You've got no alibi for the time of the killing, and we've found a pair of your jeans soaked in blood.'

290

'That was my blood, Mr Frost . . .' Wally was almost in tears. 'You've got to believe me.'

'The court has got to believe you, Wally, not me.' Frost scratched his chin thoughtfully. 'Feel like doing a deal?'

Manson regarded Frost warily. 'What sort of a deal?'

'A bloody good one, Wally. We've got a whole stack of outstanding burglaries and car thefts on file. I want you to cough to every single one that's down to you . . .'

'Now hold on, Mr Frost,' Manson protested.

'Do yourself a favour and listen, Wally. Whatever sentences you get will run concurrently: one burglary or a hundred, you won't even feel it. In return, I'm prepared to tell the court how helpful you've been and to recommend to the DPP that we accept your plea of manslaughter in the case of Alice Ryder. To help you make up your mind, if you say no, we're going for murder.'

Manson chewed at his finger while he thought this over. 'What about them two?' He pointed to the photographs on the table.

'Call me a sentimental old sod, Wally, but providing nothing happens to make me change my mind, I'm prepared to give you the benefit of the doubt over them two.'

Wally sighed. 'All right, Mr Frost. You win.'

'Good boy,' smiled Frost, scooping the photographs back into the file and standing.

Behind the prisoner, Gilmore's eyes gleamed with satisfaction. The inspector had given almost nothing away – the DPP would probably have settled for manslaughter anyway – and in return a whole stack of outstandings would be cleared in one go and Denton's 'Crime Return' would start looking healthy again. Anxious to share the undoubted credit this would accrue, he dropped into Frost's vacated chair, ready to start taking

291

Manson's statements. His scowl deepened when Frost informed him that the little fat slob, Hanlon, would be taking over from now and it was with the greatest reluctance he vacated the chair.

At the door, Frost stopped and smote his forehead with his palm. He had almost forgotten the videos. 'Where did you get them?'

Wally hung his head. 'I nicked them from a car. Wouldn't have touched them had I known what they were like. Blimey, I like a bit of the old sex and violence as much as the next man, but I draw the line at dogs . . . they may be man's best friend, but that one was being too bloody friendly.'

'Details, Wally.'

'I'm driving in the van the Saturday night before last, about ten o'clock, and I spots this big flash motor parked round the back of the Market Square.'

'What sort of car?' Gilmore asked. 'What make?'

'I don't know. An expensive motor, all gleaming. Black, I think . . . the seats looked like real leather. Anyway, I wasn't there to admire it. I jemmied open the boot, grabbed this box and I'm back in my van before anyone spots me.'

Frost prodded Manson for more details, but there was nothing else he could tell them, only that it was an expensive set of wheels.

Outside in the corridor, Gilmore's anger boiled over. 'You're letting Hanlon take his statement? We get a confession on the Ryder murder and Manson is going to cough on all his other jobs. We do all the work and you're going to let Hanlon take all the credit!'

'I can't be sodded about with all that paperwork,' said Frost. 'We've got enough on our plates without having to take yards and yards of statement down.' He yawned. 'I don't know about you, son, but I'm going home for some kip.'

Gilmore, still angry, watched the old cretin shuffle off down the corridor. Just his lousy luck to be stuck with that apology for a policeman. He was being associated with Frost's many failures, but wasn't getting the chance to be involved with his all too few successes. Just because the fool had killed all his own promotion prospects, there was no need to deny them to everyone else. Damn and blast the stupid burk. He stormed off to the car-park.

As he was settling down in bed, Frost remembered he hadn't reported back to Mullett about Wally Manson. Ah well, he'd worry about that in the morning.

The jangling of a bell woke Gilmore up. He fumbled for the alarm, but the bell rang on. The bedside clock tried to tell him it was ten o'clock but he felt as if he had only been asleep a couple of minutes. The ringing went on and someone was banging at the front door. He pulled on his dressing gown and staggered downstairs.

A motor-cycle policeman holding a crash helmet asked him if he was Detective Sergeant Gilmore and told him to pick up Inspector Frost immediately.

There had been another Ripper killing.

'Why knock me up?' growled Gilmore. 'Haven't you heard of the telephone?'

'Haven't you heard of putting it back on the hook?' called the policeman, kick-starting his bike and roaring off.

Yes, the damn handset was off. Mentally cursing Liz, Gilmore replaced it and dashed into the bathroom for a quick cold shower which he hoped would jar him into consciousness. He had finished dressing when the front door slammed and Liz returned from shopping, the bottles clinking in her carrier bag.

'You're going out again?' she shrilled. 'Out all night and now you're going out again?'

He patted on aftershave, then knotted his tie and adjusted it in the bathroom mirror. 'I've got to. There's been another murder.' His head was aching from not enough sleep and he could have done without any more aggro.

She pushed past him, her face ugly, not saying a word.

He slipped on his camel-hair overcoat and made sure he had his car keys. 'I'll get back as soon as I can – I promise.'

'Don't bloody bother,' she snapped, slamming down the shopping. 'Don't bloody bother.'

Frost, looking as gritty and crumpled as he had done the night before, was waiting outside his house and he grunted thankfully as he slumped into the front passenger seat. 'Another old girl slashed,' he told Gilmore. 'Haven't got the full details yet.'

The address was Kitchener Mansions, a block of old people's flats. The lift, its wet floor smelling of pine disinfectant, juddered them up to the third floor. DC Burton, waiting for them outside flat number 311, looked shattered. 'It's a messy one, Inspector.'

'Tell me something new,' muttered Frost gloomily, following Burton into the flat.

They walked into a tiny passage, squeezing past a small table holding a telephone and a plastic piano-key index, then on to a small living-room which seemed to be full of people, all keeping well back from the object in the centre of the floor. 'Let the dog see the rabbit,' said Frost, barging through.

The old lady, fully dressed, sat in an armchair, her head back, empty eyes staring at the ceiling. Her neck grinned with the blood-gummed lips of a cut throat. Her stomach had been slashed open so that her intestines bulged out on to her lap. At her feet the grey-carpeted floor was sodden with the blood pumped out by her panic-stricken heart as the knife ripped and tore. The tiny room had the smell of an abattoir.

'Flaming hell!' muttered Frost. He backed away. He had seen enough.

Even Ted Roberts, the SOC officer, no stranger to violent death, was shaken and had difficulty in keeping his hands steady as he adjusted his camera lens for close-ups of the neck wound.

Gilmore pulled his eyes away from the corpse, and looked around the room. He recognized the uniformed constable, PC Simms, who had arrested Manson the night before. He also recognized the two men from Forensic who had been at Greenway's house. The duty police surgeon, a thin solemn-looking man busily engaged in filling in his Police Expense Claim form, he hadn't seen before.

A light oak sideboard stood against the far wall. On it a cut-glass fruit bowl held some apples and a black leather purse. Gilmore nudged Frost and pointed it out to him.

Carefully stepping wide to avoid the puddles of blood, Frost picked up the purse with his handkerchief. It bulged with the pension money the old lady had drawn from the main Denton post office the previous morning. He counted it quickly. Nearly one hundred pounds. Gloomily he pushed it back into the purse. 'How come the killer didn't take this?'

'Perhaps he was disturbed?' suggested Gilmore. 'He heard someone coming and legged it away.'

'Perhaps,' muttered Frost, who wasn't convinced. He nosed through the other compartments of the purse. An uncollected prescription for some sleeping tablets, a hospital appointment card, a membership card for the Reef Bingo Club, and some ancient raffle tickets. In the last compartment he found two Yale keys; one was for the front door, but the other was a maverick. He clicked the purse shut and returned it to the fruit bowl. 'What has been nicked?'

'Nothing, as far as we can tell,' answered Burton. 'Nothing seems to be disturbed.' He moved away so Frost could look into the bedroom where everything was as neat and tidy as the murdered woman had left it. Frost opened a couple of drawers. The contents clearly had not been touched.

'Like I said,' offered Gilmore, 'he heard someone coming and legged it before he could nick anything.'

'Perhaps,' muttered Frost, still doubtful. Back to Burton. 'All right, son. Let's have some details.'

Burton flipped open his notebook. 'Her name is Doris Watson, seventy-six. She's a widow and has a son living in Denton.'

'Anyone contacted him?' interrupted Frost.

Burton shook his head. 'We've been waiting for you, sir.'

Frost sent Gilmore to look the son up in the telephone index in the hall. 'Ring him. Ask if he can come over. Don't tell him what it's about.' He nodded for Burton to continue.

'Her neighbour, Mrs Proctor, in the next flat saw her at eight o'clock last night when she called here to borrow a *Daily Mirror* to read. A little before ten she knocked again to return it, but got no answer.'

'By ten, she was dead,' called the police surgeon, picking up his bag ready to leave.

'You're bloody precise all of a sudden,' commented Frost. 'You usually won't even pin yourself down to the

296

day of the week. Are you certain she was dead by ten?'

The doctor shrugged. Nothing was certain in determining the time of death. 'Give or take an hour each way,' he hedged.

'Thanks for sod all,' sniffed Frost as the doctor took his leave. He raised his eyebrows at Gilmore who had finished phoning.

'All I get is his answering machine,' Gilmore told him. 'I left a message for him to phone the station.'

Frost's eyes travelled round the room. No sign of forcible entry. The killer must have come in through the front door.

They moved through the hall to take a look at the door which had additional bolts fitted and also a security chain, but not a very strong one. There was a peephole lens so any caller could be verified before the door was opened. She was nervous of callers, but when someone knocked some time after eight o'clock at night she had drawn the bolts, unhooked the security chain and let them in. It had to be someone she knew. Someone she trusted.

'Her son?' offered Gilmore.

'He'll do for starters,' grunted Frost. 'Who found her?'

'The old dear in the next flat – Mrs Proctor,' Burton told him.

'OK. Burton and Jordan – knock on doors. Find out if anyone saw or heard anything. Gilmore, come with me. We'll chat up Old Mother Proctor.'

Mrs Proctor, her untidy grey hair in need of combing, squinted and blinked watery eyes at the warrant card held out for her inspection. 'I'll have to take you on trust,' she finally decided. 'My eyes aren't too good this time of the morning.' And to prove it, she bumped into the hall table as she unsteadily led them through to her untidy lounge. 'The old dear's pissed!' hissed Frost to Gilmore.

'Sit down,' she mumbled, breathing gin fumes all over them. Frost sat on something hard. An empty gin bottle. He carefully stood it on the floor. She flopped down in the chair opposite and tried unsuccessfully to stop her body swaying from side to side.

A messy room with dirty underwear draped over chairs and unwashed glasses in abundance. The gas-fire was going full blast and the room was hot and close.

She hiccuped gin fumes and fanned them away. 'Can I get you something to drink?' Thinking she meant tea, Frost nodded, but she slopped gin into two dirty cups and handed one each to the detectives. 'Get that down you!' Frost eyed the tea-coloured gin swilling about in the cup with tea-leaves floating on its surface. It was a bit early in the morning, but what the hell. He downed it in one gulp.

Mrs Proctor nodded her approval and topped up her own cup from the bottle. 'I don't usually indulge this time of the morning, but after seeing her, in that chair and all that blood . . .' The recollection required a quick swallow and a second helping.

Frost nodded sympathetically. He noticed a line of birthday cards on the mantelpiece. 'Someone's birthday?'

She suddenly burst into tears. 'Mine – and not a very happy one. A bloody fine present, finding your next-door neighbour butchered.' She dabbed her eyes. 'I'm sorry.' Tottering over to the mantelpiece she took down one of the cards with a picture of a basketful of kittens. 'This is her card. The very last card she ever sent me.'

'Very nice,' said Frost, unenthusiastically.

She sniffed derisively. 'I hate cats – they stink the bloody place out. Still, I expect she only bought it because it was cheap.' She leant forward confidentially.

'I know I shouldn't speak ill of the dead, but she really was a tight-fisted old cow.'

'You don't say!' said Frost.

'I do say. Her purse always looked as if it was pregnant . . . it was packed with notes, but you never saw her put her hand in her pocket to buy you a drink.'

Frost gave a disapproving shake of the head. Mrs Proctor started to say something else then burst into tears. 'Here am I running the poor woman down and she's lying dead in her chair.' She raised a tear-streaked face. 'It was awful . . . when I went in there and saw all that blood . . .'

'I know it's upsetting,' soothed Frost, 'so I'll get this over as soon as I can. You borrowed the *Daily Mirror* from her?'

'I borrowed it at eight o'clock. I went to return it at ten, but she wouldn't answer the door.'

'Was that unusual?' asked Gilmore, distastefully eyeing the gin slurping about in his sugar-encrusted cup.

'Bloody unusual. She was such a mean old bitch, she wouldn't have been able to sleep if I hadn't returned her paper . . . afraid I might run off with it. I banged at the door. No reply. So I went to bed.'

'Then what?'

'This morning I expected her to send Interpol round to arrest me for hanging on to her lousy paper, so I tried her door again. Still no reply. I thought she might be ill with that flu virus thing, so I let myself in.'

'How did you get into her flat?'

She fumbled in her apron pocket and produced a key. 'I've got the spare key to her flat and she's got the one to mine.'

Frost nodded. The maverick key explained.

'I didn't think I'd be able to get in with the key as she always put on the bolts and the chain. But it opened, and

I went in and . . .' Her body shook at the recollection.

He leant across and patted her hand. 'I know it's difficult, love. Just take your time.' At last, after several false starts, she managed to stem the flow and bravely nodded her willingness to continue. 'When you saw her last night to borrow the newspaper, did she say she was expecting anyone?'

'No. She just gave me the paper like she always did . . . bloody begrudgingly.'

'After that, did you hear anything?'

She blinked at him. 'Like what?'

Like a bloody woman being disembowelled, you stupid cow, thought Frost. 'Anything at all that might help us?' he asked sweetly.

'No – I had the telly on. I like to read the paper with the telly on – it gives me something to occupy my mind.' She shivered. 'Poor Doris was terrified of something like this happening ever since she heard about this Granny Ripper maniac. She was going to get a stronger chain put on her door, but she left it too late.'

'The chain wouldn't have helped her,' said Frost. 'She let this bloke in like an old friend. Did she have many friends?'

'Hardly any. She was such a tight-fisted cow, no-one liked her and she hardly ever went out – except to bingo and the club. The senior citizens' club – it's run by the church.'

'Did you go to her club?'

'No, but she used to get me to go to bingo with her – she was nervous of being out on her own – but I gave it up a year ago. I don't approve of gambling. Besides, I never bloody won anything.'

Frost shook his head both in sympathy and to keep himself awake. The gas-fire, aided by the gin, was strongly

300

soporific. 'She only went to the daytime bingo sessions, I suppose?'

'Yes. She didn't even like coming back in the dark late afternoon, but that nice driver used to bring her right to her door – leave his coach and escort her right up to the flat.'

Frost's drooping head suddenly snapped up. 'What driver?'

'Of the coach. They lay on this free coach for the bingo . . . picks you up in the town and brings you back.'

'Only back to the town centre, surely?' asked Frost.

'That's all they're supposed to do, but if you've got a nice driver and he passes your door, he'll drop you off. It's almost as good as getting a taxi.'

'And this nice driver . . . would he go with you to your door, wait until you got safely inside, help you get the key out from under the mat, or pull the string through the letter-box, or something?'

'Some of them do. Some just drop you off at the corner.'

'Hmm.' Frost spat out a tea-leaf. 'Mrs Watson was nervous, even of coming home late afternoons, and yet she let someone into her flat at night. Any ideas on who that might be?'

'The only person I can think of is her poncey son. He lives in Denton somewhere. He often came to see her.'

'What is he like?'

'A nasty piece of work. Do you know what he had the nerve to say to me? He said, "Why don't you buy your own *Daily Mirror* instead of scrounging one from my poor mother?"'

'Sounds a real right bastard,' Frost confided, rising from his chair. 'Thanks for your help. An officer will be along soon to take a written statement. If you think of anything else – anything – that might help, let the officer know.'

Gilmore pushed his untasted cup of gin to one side and followed him out.

In the murder flat they had to flatten themselves against the wall as the body was manhandled out on a stretcher by two ambulance men who had difficulty getting it round the tight bend to the front door, the corner of the stretcher ripping a section of the floral wallpaper in the process. Immediately following the stretcher came the pathologist, looking like an undertaker in his long black overcoat. 'I've given preliminary details to your detective constable. I'll phone your office with a time for the autopsy.'

In the lounge the Forensic team were packing up. The chair and the bloodstained carpet had been removed and the blood which had soaked through to the exposed floor-boards had been ringed in yellow chalk. The warm, sticky slaughterhouse smell still tainted the air. Moodily, Frost tore off the dangling strip of wallpaper. The poor cow. She'd have a fit if she saw the state of her little flat now.

From the bathroom door came grunting and a metallic clanging. He looked inside. Harding from Forensic was on his knees, swearing softly to himself as he tried to manoeuvre a long-handled spanner underneath the tiny wash-basin in an effort to remove the waste trap. 'Blimey,' Frost exclaimed, 'isn't there anything you won't pinch?'

Harding grinned. 'There's traces of blood in the sink waste, Inspector.'

Frost showed surprise. 'You mean he had a good wash afterwards?'

'The way he sliced her he'd have been splattered with blood. He couldn't go out like that.'

'What about his clothes?'

Sucking barked knuckles, Harding gave the spanner one final push and sighed his relief as he felt something give. He looked up at the inspector.

'I reckon his clothes are smothered in blood – unless he took them off before he butchered her.'

'Oh,' sniffed Frost. 'And what is she doing while he strips off? Staring hypnotized at his John Thomas?'

Harding grinned. 'Just a theory, Inspector.' He dropped the spanner and found he could now turn the large nut by hand.

Frost stuck his head out of the bathroom. 'Don't forget to check all dry-cleaners.'

'Already done!' replied Burton. A waste of time. This killer was too smart.

Back to the bathroom where Harding was easing off the waste trap. 'So, if he washed himself, the blood you're going to find in the waste trap will be the old girl's blood – right?'

'Yes, sir.'

'Do we need any more? We're nearly swimming in the bleeding stuff out there as it is.'

Harding shrugged. 'We've got to be thorough, sir.'

'Smile when you say that,' said Frost wandering out to the empty-looking lounge. 'I might think you're getting at me.' Gilmore watched him meander about aimlessly, picking up pieces of bric-a-brac and putting them down again. The old fool had no idea what to do next.

PC Jordan and another uniformed officer returned from their door-to-door enquiries to report no joy. As usual, everyone was shocked at what had happened, but no-one had heard or seen anything.

'This bloke's too bloody lucky.' Frost dropped his cigarette end on the floor and ground it underfoot. He felt tired, useless and inadequate. Mrs Proctor's gin was sloshing about in his stomach, he was beginning to feel sick and his head was starting to throb. He flopped into an armchair.

'What do you want us to do now?' asked Gilmore.

Just leave me alone, he wanted to answer, then sat up frowning at a burst of voices from outside. He groaned out loud as Mullett, bright and morning fresh, bounced into the room. He could have done without Hornrim Harry at this particular moment.

Mullett's lips tightened. Typical. A serious murder enquiry. Forensic busy and conscientious as always in the next room and here was Frost, sprawled in an armchair, and – Mullett's nose quivered to confirm his suspicion – reeking of drink. 'Another body, Inspector?' he said testily, his tone implying it was all Frost's fault.

'Where?' said Frost, jumping up and pretending to look around the room. 'I can't see it, Super.'

Teeth gritted, Mullett raised his eyes to the artex ceiling and sighed loudly. Frost never knew when it was the wrong time to act the fool. 'What progress have you made?'

'So far, sod all. This bloke's bloody lucky. No-one sees him, no-one hears him and he leaves no prints. Unless Forensic can come up with something spectacular we might have to wait for him to make a mistake. His bleeding luck's bound to run out sometime.'

A derisive snort. 'Wait? You mean until he kills again? No way! I want these killings stopped!'

'Oh?' muttered Frost. 'And how do we achieve that, Super?'

'By finding the killer and arresting him.'

'Oh! Make a note of that, Gilmore,' said Frost, the gin making him reckless. 'Any other bright ideas, sir – I'm always ready to learn.'

Mullett glared angrily, his jaw twitching. The man's insouciance always infuriated him. He jerked his head at Burton and Jordan. 'Wait outside, would you, please.' He waited until they had gone. 'You made a damn fool of me last night, Inspector.'

'Did I?' asked Frost, sounding very interested. 'How did I do that?' His tone implied he would mark it down for future reference.

'That Ripper suspect. You led me to believe you had a water-tight case against him, and I now understand that your big clue, the knife, belonged to the victim all the time.'

'I'm afraid so, Super,' agreed Frost, ruefully.

'And you left me dangling. You didn't even come in and tell me what had happened. I was waiting for your report and the Chief Constable was waiting for my report.'

'Sorry about that,' mumbled Frost. 'I forgot all about you.'

Mullett's mouth opened and closed. He was almost speechless. 'Forgot?' he spluttered. 'Forgot to inform your Divisional Commander about a suspect in a major murder investigation?'

'I have got a lot on my plate,' snapped Frost. 'We're going flat out, we're working double shifts and we get lots of stupid interruptions.' He hoped Mullett might take this subtle hint and go, but the superintendent hadn't finished yet.

'Detective Sergeant Hanlon works under the same conditions as you, Frost, but he managed to get results. He's obtained a murder confession from Manson and confessions on at least thirty burglaries. Excellent work that will put us right at the top of the league for crime rate figures this month. It's results that count,

Inspector, not excuses. It seems to me,' and here his glare of displeasure clearly included Gilmore, 'that you may not be up to the task, in which case I will have no hesitation in replacing you.' With that he spun on his heel and marched out, oblivious to the near-audible raspberry that followed him out.

Now it was Gilmore's turn to be angry. If he were to share in Frost's failures, he wanted to share in his few triumphs. 'Why didn't you tell him about Hanlon? He was the one who sodded up the knife and Manson was our collar, not his.'

'We're supposed to be a team, son,' said Frost, 'not all fighting for Brownie points.'

Gilmore's reply was stifled by the return of DC Burton and PC Jordan. But all right, he muttered to himself, if it takes Brownie points to get on, I'll give the bastard Brownie points.

Desmond Watson scooped up the post from the mat and closed the front door behind him. He dumped his brief-case by the hall stand and checked through the letters on his way through to the living-room. Two bills, a bank statement and a commission cheque from his firm. Watson was the Northern Area Sales Representative for a double-glazing company. In the living-room the little green light on his telephone answering machine told him there were messages waiting. He fast-forwarded on cue and review, his ear able to recognize from the high-pitched gabble the girl from his firm passing on sales leads which he would note down later, and then the familiar sound of his mother's voice. He released the button and listened as he opened up the envelope to check that his firm hadn't yet again made a mistake with his commission payment.

Hello, son. It's mother. You needn't worry any more about . . . *Just a moment, there's someone at the door* . . . A pause. A long pause. And then the automatic cut-off operated.

He raised his head from his checking of the commission payment and waited for the next message which should have been his mother phoning back. But it was a strange voice. A man's voice. It asked him to ring the Denton Police Station. The commission cheque fluttered from his fingers. His stomach churning with foreboding, he reached for the phone.

Thursday afternoon shift (1)

Gilmore spooned sugar into a cup of hot, strong tea and placed it in front of Watson who was still in a state of shock after formally identifying his mother's body. The cup clattered on the saucer as his shaking hand raised it to his mouth. He tried to concentrate on what the scruffy inspector was saying.

'I know it's been an awful shock, sir, but if you could answer one or two questions.'

The cup was rattling against his teeth. He lowered it back to the saucer, the tea untasted, and pushed it away. 'Yes . . . anything.'

'We've been listening to a tape from your answering machine, your mother's last message. You said she made the call at 9.35 p.m. If you weren't at home, how do you know that?'

'My answering machine logs the time and date of all calls.'

'I see, sir. And where were you at 9.35 last night?'

'Me?' His head jerked up 'You suspect me?'

'I'd be happy if I had anyone to suspect, sir,' said Frost, wearily. 'I just want to eliminate. Your mother was a nervous woman. She kept her front door chained and bolted and yet someone calls at 9.35 at night and she cheerfully lets them in. It had to be someone she knew and trusted . . . someone like you, sir. So where were you?'

'I was in Birmingham. The Queensway Hotel.' He pulled a receipt from his inside pocket and handed it across. 'You'll want to check, of course.'

Frost glanced at it and passed it to Gilmore who went out to phone.

'I'd like it back,' said Watson. 'I need it for my expenses claim.'

Frost nodded. He knew all about expenses claims. 'On the tape, sir, your mother starts by saying, "You needn't worry any more about . . ." Any idea what she meant by that?'

'I think she was referring to a new security chain. The one on her front door was inadequate. After hearing about those burglaries and then those two women killed, I'd been on to her to get a stronger one.'

'Can you think of anyone your mother would be happy to admit into her flat at 9.35 at night?'

'No-one. She was a very nervous woman.' He looked up as Gilmore returned with the receipt and murmured something in the inspector's ear.

'The hotel confirm your visit, sir.' Frost handed the receipt back and stood up. 'Thank you for your help. We'll let you know how our enquiries progress . . . and, of course, you have our deepest sympathy.' As the door closed behind Watson, Frost's solemn expression changed to a grin. 'So he had a double room and a woman and he asked the hotel for a single room receipt?'

'Yes,' confirmed Gilmore.

'The crafty bastard,' said Frost, shaking his head in admiration. 'He gets his firm to pay for his nookie. I wish I could wangle something like that. Anyway, Sonny Boy's in the clear.' He picked up the cassette from the answering machine. 'Let's find out if this can tell us what we want to know.'

The Murder Incident Room was swirled with a fog of duty-free cigarette smoke. Frost sat on the corner of the front desk watching Gilmore slot the tape into the Yamaha cassette deck. He clapped his hands for silence.

'Right. As you know, we've had another Ripper murder.' He held aloft some enlarged colour prints where red was the predominant colour. 'We've got photos of the victim, but unless you get a kick out of steaming entrails, I suggest you take them as read. The bastard almost disembowelled her.' He stood up, the cigarette waggling in his mouth as he spoke. 'The victim is a Mrs Doris Watson, aged seventy-six, a widow with one son. She rarely went out, except to the twice-weekly senior citizens' afternoon sessions at the Reef Bingo Club. The poor cow was terrified of being attacked so she had extra bolts, a spy-hole and a security chain fitted to her front door. Last night, at 9.35, she made a telephone call to her son. The son was out, but his answering machine picked up the call. This is it.' He nodded for Gilmore to start the tape.

A bleep. Then, *Hello, son. It's mother. You needn't worry any more about . . . Just a moment, there's someone at the door . . .* Vague sounds as the tape continued, then another bleep. Gilmore jammed down the Stop control.

The room was dead quiet.

'She put down the phone,' continued Frost, 'and went to the front door. She squints through the spy-hole, likes what she sees, so this nervous woman undoes the chain, draws the bolts and welcomes in the bastard who's going to rip out her intestines.' He took the cigarette from his mouth and spat out a shred of tobacco. 'You're all a lot smarter than I am, so let's have some brilliant suggestions. Come on – you're a nervous woman of seventy-six. Who would you let into your flat at night – apart from a toy-boy with his own teeth and a big dick?'

Burton raised his hand. 'Something we've never considered, sir. She'd never let in a man – but what if the Ripper was a woman?'

Frost chewed on his lip as he thought this over. 'It's possible, son. It would explain a lot, but my gut reaction is against it. We'll keep it in mind, though.'

WPC Jill Knight raised a hand. 'If she'd phoned for a doctor, she'd let him in.'

A buzz of excitement.

'You're right,' said Frost. 'She'd let a doctor in.'

'Or a priest,' added Gilmore. Purley was still his number one suspect.

'Or a priest,' agreed Frost. 'OK, son. You can check on the curate. We want to know where he was last night. And you, Jill. Find out who her doctor was. See if she asked him to call last night and even if she didn't, find out where he was at 9.35. Anything else?'

He waited. Nothing. He took out a fresh cigarette then threw the pack to Burton to offer around. 'I'll tell you something that worries me.' He struck a match on the table leg. 'This time he took no money. He didn't ransack the bedroom. Over a hundred quid in her purse in full view on the sideboard and it wasn't touched. Now Sergeant Gilmore suggests something disturbed the Ripper and he had to hoof it off before he could nick anything.' He blew out the match and let it drop to the floor. 'But stupid sod that I am, I can't buy that. This bloke is icy cold. Nothing panics him. I reckon money's never been his motive.'

'So what is his motive?' asked Gilmore.

'Killing,' said Frost. 'I reckon he gets his kicks out of cold, bloody killing.'

The room went quiet. Chillingly quiet. This had the ring of unpalatable truth.

'Right.' Frost slipped down from the desk. 'Let's play the tape again.'

It was played again, and again and again. Frost, smoking, chewing his knuckles, hunched in front of the loudspeaker. *Just a moment, there's someone at the door* . . . Vague sounds. A bleep. Gilmore's voice . . . *Mr Watson, this is Denton Police* . . .

'Again,' snapped Frost. There was something there. Something his subconscious had caught but which kept slipping away. 'This is no damn good,' he moaned. 'I want it louder.'

'It won't go any louder,' said Gilmore.

'We could use the hi-fi equipment in the rest room,' suggested Burton.

They crowded into the rest room. Gilmore slotted in the cassette and turned the amplifier up almost to its maximum. He pressed Play and the hiss of raw tape crackled from the twin speakers.

The bleep screamed out like an alarm signal. Tape hiss. *Hello, son. It's mother,* shouted the old lady, the sound almost hurting their ears.

311

'Leave it,' ordered Frost as Gilmore's hand moved to turn down the volume. *You needn't worry any more about* . . . Through the mush, a buzzing vibrating sound. Then another.

'The door bell,' muttered Frost. At ordinary volume level it was inaudible.

Just a moment, there's someone at the door . . . A rustling, then an echoing bang as if someone had hit a microphone. She had put the phone down. Fading footsteps as she padded up the hall to the front door, eager to let in her murderer. Now the tape background roar was paramount. Frost pressed his ear to the speaker. 'Nothing. I imagine she's giving him the eyeball through the peep-hole. Ah . . .' He moved back. Just about audible, the sound of bolts being drawn and the chink of the chain being removed. The lock clicked. The door opened. The woman said something, but it was so faint and the background so loud, they couldn't distinguish a word. Then a screaming bleep as the automatic cut-off operated.

'Let me have a go,' said Burton, elbowing Gilmore away and adjusting various controls on the hi-fi's graphic equalizer which could cut and boost individual frequencies. 'Now try it.'

By now, they almost knew every squeak, rustle and click off by heart. When the woman spoke after opening the door it was clearer, but tantalizingly not clear enough for them to make out a single word. 'Again,' ordered Frost. But Mrs Watson might have been talking in a foreign language for all the sense it made. God, thought Frost. She could be naming her killer – 'Come in, Mr Ripper of 19 High Street, Denton' – yet they couldn't understand what she was saying.

'Try the earphones,' said Burton.

The earphones were better, but still not good enough.

'Let me have a go,' said Jill Knight, adjusting the earphones over her tightly curled hair. She listened and frowned. 'Again,' she said. The frown was deeper, but this time her lips were moving as if she was repeating what she heard. She took off the earphones. 'She's saying, "Oh, it's you. I didn't expect you so soon."'

They played it again through the speaker. The WPC was right. *Oh, it's you. I didn't expect you so soon.* Frost's head bowed. He had been hoping for so much and this was nothing.

'She knew him,' said Burton.

'And he came sooner than expected,' muttered Frost. 'I think that's called premature ejaculation.' The resulting laughter lifted his depression. 'Let's hear it again.' He waved aside the moans that they knew it off by heart. 'Indulge an old man's whim. We might have missed something.'

Again they listened, but only half-heartedly. The tape had told them everything it could. There was nothing they had missed. *Oh, it's you. I didn't expect you so soon.* The thud of the door closing behind him, then the hiss and clanking as raw tape scraped past the replay heads when the automatic cut-out operated. A bleep . . .

Frost was sitting bolt upright in his chair, an unlit cigarette drooping in his mouth. 'Again – just the end bit – and the volume as high as you bloody well like.' Gilmore spun the volume control to its maximum. At first they didn't spot it. 'You must be stone bleeding deaf,' roared Frost. 'Again . . . and listen this time . . . There!' And this time they heard it. A fraction of a second before the message switched off. The closing of the front door. The hiss, roar and crackle as the tape bumped past the heads then . . . a boxy, metallic chink.

Burton scratched his head. 'Could be anything, Inspector. He could have bumped against the table as he came in.'

'Even if he did,' said Frost, 'there was nothing on the hall table that would chink. That is definitely a metallic sound.'

'There could have been something on the table – something valuable – but he took it away with him,' suggested Gilmore, who was feeling left out of things.

'I thought I heard something chinking as he came through the door,' said the WPC.

'Did you?' exclaimed Frost excitedly and he was up on his feet, jamming his finger on the Rewind button and playing the tape through again. 'Yes . . . there!' And through the mush, as the man stepped through the door, a faint metallic chinking sound . . . then another.

They didn't hear the door open. 'What's going on in here?'

'Piss off!' said Frost. 'Oh, sorry, Super . . . didn't know it was you.' He played the tape through yet again for Mullett who tried to look as if he knew what Frost was driving at, but obviously didn't.

'That noise, sir. At first we thought he'd bumped into the hall table and jolted something on it, but we now reckon that whatever it was, he brought it in with him and dumped it on the hall table.'

Mullett considered this. 'It might help if we knew what it was. But we don't.'

'I think I do,' said Frost. He looked around the room to make sure he had everyone's attention. 'What about a new security chain?'

Mullett frowned. 'A security chain?'

'Old Mother Watson had arranged to have a stronger one fitted,' Frost told him. 'And that's who she let in last

314

night with open arms . . . the man who was going to fit the new security chain . . . so she would be safe from attack.'

'It could be a chain,' said Mullett doubtfully, 'but we don't know for sure.'

'I know for bloody certain,' announced Frost. 'I've got a hunch.'

A thin smile from Mullett. 'Hunches are all very well,' he began, but Frost wasn't listening, he was giving instructions to his team.

'Knock on doors again. Go round to all the neighbours of the victims. Did the victims talk of having chains fitted? Has anyone been canvassing before, or since, offering to fit security chains? Don't cause a panic, but get what gen you can. I want someone to contact all the local security system firms. Do they send salesmen around canvassing? Have their salesmen found that some bloody amateur has been undercutting their prices? Mrs Watson was supposed to be a tight old sod, so this would have to be a cheap job. One last thing – Burton. Mrs Watson talked to the old biddy in the next-door flat about having a new security chain. Chat her up, see if she can come up with names. OK – on your bikes, everyone. Chop chop.'

As the team scurried out he flipped a cigarette from his packet and tried to catch it in his mouth. It missed. Scooping it up from the floor, he lit up and inhaled deeply. He felt happy. Things were now on the move. They were on the track of the killer, he felt sure of it.

The phone rang. Detective Sergeant Hanlon from the mortuary. 'The pathologist has completed the autopsy on Mark Compton, Jack. Definitely murder. A heavy blow to the head from behind. That didn't kill him, but the fire and the fumes finished him off – death from asphyxiation.' Frost pushed Mullett to one side so he could yell for

Gilmore, his voice echoing down the empty corridor.

Mullett cleared his throat pointedly. He wasn't used to being ignored.

'Sorry, Super,' grunted Frost. 'Be with you in a minute.' As Gilmore appeared in the doorway, he told him about the autopsy findings.

Gilmore checked his watch. He'd forgotten all about the damn autopsy. Frost's bad habits were contagious. 'How come Hanlon attended it?'

'I told him to, son. We're far too busy.'

'But it's my case.'

'Sorry, son, but we've too much work and not enough men to be able to specialize. It's everyone's case.'

But if I crack it, it's my bloody case, thought Gilmore. 'I want to see the woman that Compton was knocking off. She might know something.'

'Right, son. We'll do it now. Bring the car round to the front.' Back to Mullett. 'Anything I can do, Super . . . as long as it's quick?'

Huffily, the Divisional Commander produced the curt memo he had received from County. 'Still some discrepancy with your car expenses, Inspector. County are furious. They want an immediate reply.'

'They want stuffing,' corrected Frost, his mind elsewhere. 'Stick it on my desk as you go out, would you, sir? I'll deal with it later.' And he dashed out of the rest room to the car.

Mullett was halfway down the corridor before he realized that Frost had ordered him about like an office boy. But it was too late to go back and protest.

The flats behind the supermarket were owned by a firm of property agents and were usually let out on short leases. The Denton *Echo,* in one of its bouts of outraged crusading, had exposed several of these tenancies as being taken up by high-class call girls and for a while many of the apartments remained empty, but slowly, and more discreetly, many of the old tenants returned.

In the carpeted foyer a lift purred down and the door opened with a barely audible hiss. They stepped inside and Gilmore pressed the button for the third floor. So different from the disinfectant-masking urine smell of the lift in the senior citizens' flats, this lift was heady with the perfume of its previous passenger.

They walked over thick footstep-muffling grey carpet to the end flat. There was something outside the door. Four bulging rubbish sacks. Black plastic sacks, the sort Paula Bartlett's body was in. Frost peeped inside one. Assorted packets, cartons and jars as if someone had been clearing out a cupboard. He fished out a detergent packet. It had been opened, but was almost brim-full. 'The cow's done a bunk,' he said, jamming his thumb in the bell-push. He was surprised to hear footsteps from inside.

The woman who opened the door was around twenty-six years of age, and wore a tightly fitting knitted dress in emerald green. She was slightly plump, with red hennaed hair and breasts that could best be described as ample. Admiring their generosity, Frost had difficulty in locating his warrant card. Gilmore produced his.

'Police. May we come in?'

She stared at Gilmore's warrant card wide-eyed. 'Police? What's it about? That nosy old bitch downstairs hasn't been complaining again, has she?'

'Not to us,' answered Gilmore curtly. 'Can we come in?' Pre-empting her reply he pushed forward into the hall.

Bristling slightly at his tone, she led them through to the lounge, a comfortable room with pale blue carpeting and dark blue upholstered furniture. The light grey walls were hung with aluminium-framed abstract prints. Frost shuffled across to the large picture window and looked down on to the sprawl of the supermarket. 'Very nice,' he murmured. 'I bet you get a good view of the multi-storey car-park from your bedroom.'

Her lips shaped a brief, flat, non-understanding smile. 'This won't take long, will it? I'm in a hurry.'

'Mind if I sit down?' said Frost, sinking into one of the blue armchairs. He dug deep into his pocket for his cigarettes and frowned with disappointment. The packet was empty. He had been too generous in the Murder Incident Room. 'Do you mind telling us your name?'

'East. Jean East.' She studied her watch. 'Look – what is this all about?'

'A few questions,' said Frost, letting his eyes wander around the room. He imagined this was where clients waited while the bedroom was occupied. He straightened up. Two bulging suitcases stood side by side to the left of the lounge door. 'Moving out?'

'The lease is up. I can't afford to renew it. I'm going back to London.'

'Then we caught you just in time,' beamed Frost. 'Do you know a gentleman called Mark Compton?'

A barely perceptible pause. 'No. Why – what is this about?'

'He might not have told you his real name,' said Gilmore, moving in front of Frost to remind him that this was his case. He showed her a photograph.

She studied the colour print briefly, shook her head, and handed it back. 'Sorry. Never seen him before.'

'Perhaps you don't recognize him with his clothes on,' Frost suggested.

Her face tightened and her eyes blazed. 'You can get out right now.' She flung open the door dramatically, her breasts heaving, straining the woollen dress to the limits.

Frost heaved himself from the chair. 'We're going, love, but you're coming with us. Get her coat, Sergeant.'

She hesitated. 'Where are we going?'

'To the station. I want a policewoman to examine you.'

'Examine me? Why?'

'If you haven't got a little strawberry birthmark on your lower stomach, my apologies will bring tears to your eyes.'

She closed the door and turned slowly. 'How do you know about that?'

'You should keep your blinds closed when you're entertaining,' sneered Gilmore.

'You had an audience,' added Frost. 'An old boy with field-glasses watching from the car-park.'

Her hand covered her mouth. She looked horrified. 'Watching us?'

'From start to finish. And then he sent a poison pen letter to your client. It described you in graphic detail.'

Her face crimsoned to match her hair. 'Let's get one bloody thing straight. I'm not a tart. Yes, I knew Mark Compton. We were lovers. He came here and we made love and it was wonderful and if some dirty little snivelling shit in a filthy raincoat was watching, then sod him. I'm ashamed of nothing.'

'Eat your heart out, Mills and Boon,' said Frost. 'But you said you *knew* him. You *were* lovers. Past tense?'

'Yes – past tense, because the bastard threw me up last week. Came here, made love, then calmly told me it was all over. Look – what the hell is this all about?'

Gilmore raised his head from his notebook. He was content to let Frost ask the preliminary questions, but he would step in when the time was ripe. So she was a discarded lover. Not an uncommon motive for murder.

But Frost, digging fruitlessly through his pockets in the hope of finding a pinched-out butt, didn't seem to have realized the significance. 'Why did he chuck you?' He watched enviously as she took a cigarette from a black lacquered box on a side table and lit it with a tiny, initialled, blue and gold enamelled lighter.

'He was afraid his wife might find out.' She flung her head back and laughed bitterly. 'His bloody wife! He always told me he was going to divorce her and marry me . . . and like a fool I bloody believed him. Even when the bastard's cheques bounced, I believed him.'

'Cheques?' queried Frost, tapping his empty Lambert and Butler packet hopefully, but she didn't take the hint.

'He was always borrowing money, and when I asked him to pay me back, his cheques bounced.'

'How much money are we talking about?'

'Getting on for £500, which I could ill afford.'

Frost scratched his chin. 'He sounds a right charmer. How long have you known him?'

'A couple of months. We met in London.' She dropped down into the other chair and her breasts bounced like Mark Compton's cheques. Do that again, Frost pleaded silently.

'Does your husband know of this association?' asked Gilmore who, unlike Frost whose gaze was directed higher, had noticed the wedding ring on her finger.

She gave a tight smile and shook her head. 'No.'

'How can you be so sure?'

'My husband is a very violent and jealous man. That's why I left him.' Her hands travelled over her body and she

winced in remembrance. 'I could show you bruises . . .'
Yes please, pleaded Frost, again silently. 'I changed my
name so he couldn't trace me. If he ever found out that
Mark had been my lover, he would have killed us both.'

Frost's head jerked up. 'Changed your name?'

'East is my maiden name. My married name is Bradbury.
Mrs Jean Bradbury.'

Behind her, Gilmore choked back a gasp and slowly
expelled air. He felt a warm glow inside. The equation
was almost too good to be true . . . an unfaithful wife
plus a violent husband equals one dead lover. Now was
the time for him to take over. 'Are you aware that your
lover, Mark Compton, and his wife have been subjected
to verbal and written threats over the past few weeks and
that their property has been maliciously damaged?'

She seemed genuinely surprised. 'No, Sergeant. I was
not aware of that.'

'Are you aware there was a fire at The Old Mill last
night? The place was gutted.'

She couldn't disguise a malicious smile. 'I didn't know
that either, but serve the bastard right.'

'The bastard's dead, Mrs Bradbury,' said Frost, bluntly.
'He died in the fire. We think it was murder.'

The cigarette dropped from her fingers and she stared
unbelieving at the inspector. 'No! Oh no!' Then her
eyes widened in horror. 'And you think my husband
killed him . . .? Oh my God!' Her hands covered her
face.

'We've got to find him,' said Gilmore.

'If he's killed Mark, he'll kill me,' she said, scrabbling
for the cigarette which had burnt a black mark into the
landlord's carpet.

'We won't let that happen,' Frost assured her. 'Any
idea where he is?'

'I don't know and I don't care.' She studied the end of her cigarette, her full, pursed lips blowing it back to life.

God, thought Frost, squirming in his chair, you can blow me back to life any time you like, love. A muffled voice calling his name slowly caught his attention. His personal radio. He tugged it from his pocket. Johnny Johnson with some news. He moved away so the woman couldn't hear.

'We've located Simon Bradbury, Inspector.'

'Then grab him where it hurts and hold him,' said Frost, signalling for Gilmore to come over.

'No need, Jack. He's not going anywhere. He's at Risley Remand Centre . . . drunken driving, malicious damage and assaulting a police officer. He's been in custody for the past two weeks.'

'Damn!' Gilmore's foot lashed out at the waste bin in anger, spilling the contents over the floor. His one and only suspect now had a cast-iron alibi. They were back to square one.

There was no further point in staying. Frost rewound his scarf and began to button up his coat while Gilmore, on his knees, stuffed the spilt papers back into the bin.

'One last question,' said Gilmore. 'Do you own a car, Mrs Bradbury?' She nodded. 'And where were you last night?'

'Here. I did my packing and went to bed early.'

'No, you didn't,' smirked Gilmore. 'You drove over to Lexing to get your own back on your ex-boyfriend.'

She stared at him as if he were mad. 'I don't know what the hell you are talking about.'

'Don't you? Then I'll spell it out for you. Mark Compton chucked you up. You weren't going to let the bastard get away with it, so you made abusive phone calls and sent death threats.'

Her head moved slowly from side to side in disbelief. 'Death threats? I'd scratch his bleeding eyes out, but I wouldn't make threats.'

'You did more than scratch his eyes out,' continued Gilmore. 'You burnt his house down. But he caught you in the act, so you smashed his skull in and left him to burn to death.'

She looked in appeal to Frost who stared stoically back, hoping his own mystification didn't show.

'The death threat letters were made up of words cut from this month's *Reader's Digest*,' Gilmore continued. 'And what have we here?' With a triumphant flourish he waved under her nose a magazine he had retrieved from the waste bin. The current copy of *Reader's Digest*.

Frost slumped on to the arm of his chair. He thought Gilmore might have been on to something, but this was grabbing at straws.

'I've got news for you,' said the woman. 'They don't only print one copy. Lots of people buy it.'

'Oh, I agree, madam,' purred Gilmore. 'Lots of people read it. But how many people cut words out?' He thrust a scissor-slashed page under her nose, then flipped through and found another, and another. . .

Frost took the magazine. Gilmore was right. The death threat letters had been from this copy of the magazine. He looked up at the woman. 'Have you got anything to say?'

She stared at him, then at Gilmore, her face white. 'You're framing me, you bastards! I want a solicitor.'

'You can phone from the station,' said Gilmore. At the door holding her tightly by the arm, he called to Frost, 'You'd better bring her suitcases down. Forensic will want to examine her clothes.' He waited while she put on her coat before leading her out to the lift.

With a distinct feeling of being upstaged, Frost gathered up the cases. At the side table he paused and hopefully looked inside the black lacquered cigarette box. It was disappointingly empty. Not his lucky day. Shoulders drooped in resignation, he picked up the cases, kicked the door shut behind him, and left the flat.

The lift taking him down now smelt fleetingly of plump, jolly, hennaed-haired murderess, Jean Bradbury. Frost was vaguely worried. He had his own theories on the Compton killing and the woman didn't figure in them. But downstairs, with the woman locked safely in the car and glaring poisoned darts at them a smirking Gilmore called to him from one of the residents' garages.

'This is her garage,' said Gilmore as he squeezed past a beige-coloured Mini Cooper and pointed to patches of damp on the concrete floor. The pervading smell was petrol. 'This must be where she stored the petrol cans.'

Frost nodded gloomily. 'Well done, son.' He was forced to admit it. Gilmore was right and he was wrong.

'I'd better get my prisoner back to the station,' said Gilmore, leaving his inspector to close the garage doors.

The significance of 'my prisoner' instead of 'our prisoner' was not lost on Frost.

Police Superintendent Mullett sat to attention in his chair. He was on the phone to the Chief Constable. Opposite the satin mahogany desk stood a self-satisfied Detective Sergeant Gilmore, and a pale-looking Police Sergeant Wells who clutched a sodden handkerchief and kept interrupting the phone call by coughing and spluttering and noisily blowing his nose. If Wells thought he could wheedle his way on to the sick list, when they needed every man they could lay their hands on, he could think again.

'We're very much below strength,' he told the Chief Constable, staring at Wells as he said it, 'but I think you can rely on the Denton team to turn up trumps on Friday night.'

The door clicked open and Mullett looked up in annoyance as Frost shuffled in. Late again. 'Ah, Frost,' he said, putting his hand over the mouthpiece. 'The Chief Constable wishes to know what progress you have made with the Paula Bartlett case.'

'Bugger all,' said Frost, dragging a chair over to the desk and sitting down wearily. 'You told me to leave it for Wonder Boy's return.'

Mullett's smile flickered on and off like a dying neon tube. He held it unsteadily in place as he spoke into the phone. 'Detective Inspector Frost reports no further progress at present, sir. However things should improve when Mr Allen returns from the sick list.' He glared at Frost who, unabashed, seemed more intent on trying to read, upside down, a private and confidential memo in the superintendent's out-tray. Mullett pulled the tray towards him and turned the memo face down, then he flashed his gleaming white teeth into the receiver's mouthpiece. 'Yes, sir. Thank you, sir. You can depend on me, sir.' He grovelled his goodbyes, then replaced the phone.

He smoothed down his moustache. 'Trouble, gentlemen. County have been hearing rumours that those gypsies – or travellers as they prefer to be called – who were involved in the fighting in the town centre last Friday are out to seek their revenge on our Denton lager louts.

The Chief Constable wishes us to ensure that we have a sufficiently large police presence here on Friday night to nip any such trouble in the bud.'

'How many men is he sending us, then?' asked Wells, between coughs.

Mullett treated the sergeant to one of his thin, superior smiles. 'County are stretched to the limit, Wells.'

'And we're not, I suppose?' said Frost, flicking ash all over the carpet.

'Everyone's in the same boat,' snapped Mullett. 'I am not giving County the impression that we will go whining to them each time we have a minor problem. I want them to see that Denton can cope. So tomorrow, all leave will be cancelled. All off-duty men will be called in. And the sick list is closed.' He stared hard at Wells, letting him know that the last comment included him. 'I have assured the Chief Constable that the maintenance of public order will be our number one priority.'

'Priority even over our murder investigations?' asked Frost in his deceptively innocent voice.

'Of course a murder case takes precedence,' barked Mullett, 'but you will manage with the barest minimum.' He jerked his head away from Frost and gave Gilmore the full benefit of his white flashing smile. 'The Chief Constable was delighted when I told him of your success in the Compton case, Sergeant.' He beamed. 'There was some mention of him writing you a personal letter of commendation.' He noticed that Frost looked unhappy at this. Jealousy, of course. His assistant had succeeded where he had failed. 'That will be all, gentlemen.'

In the corridor outside, Frost grabbed Gilmore's arm. 'Has the Bradbury bird confessed yet, son?'

'No,' Gilmore told him. 'But we don't need a confession. The forensic evidence is overwhelming. The death threat letters definitely came from that magazine . . . they even confirm they were cut out by her own scissors. We've found identical notepaper and envelopes in her flat and the marks on the garage floor are definitely consistent with cans of petrol being stored there. We've got motive, opportunity and strong evidence. What more do we want?'

'I'm not happy about this one,' said Frost.

Gilmore bit back the urge to say 'tough'. 'If you'll excuse me, Inspector, I'm on my way to see Mrs Compton. I want to tell her the good news.'

'I'll come with you,' said Frost.

'Why?' asked Gilmore, icily. It was his case. He didn't want Frost along.

'Just for the ride, son. I haven't seen a decent pair of nipples all day.'

Ada Perkins wasn't very welcoming. Her vinegar expression and sharp sniff of disapproval showed them exactly what she thought of them barging in on her patient. She marched them into the living-room where a washed-out-looking Jill Compton in a thick towelling dressing gown sat staring into a roaring fire.

'Good to see you up and about,' said Frost, sinking into the other comfortable chair.

Gilmore dragged a hard kitchen chair over and sat opposite her. 'How are you feeling, Mrs Compton?'

'It hasn't really sunk in yet. Everyone's being so kind.'

Gilmore moved his chair closer. 'I've some news for you. We've arrested Mrs Jean Bradbury for the murder of your husband.'

She stared at him in total disbelief. 'Bradbury? You mean the wife of that man who tried to pick that fight with Mark?'

'Yes. She moved into Denton some weeks ago.'

'But why should she want to harm Mark?'

Gilmore looked at Frost, hoping the inspector would want to tell her of her late husband's infidelity, but, for a change, Frost seemed content to lean back and listen. He took a deep breath. 'Your husband was having an affair with her.'

She shrank back as if he had struck her, and stared wide-eyed, uncomprehending. 'No,' she whispered at last. 'Oh no!'

'I'm afraid it's a fact,' continued Gilmore doggedly. 'He even promised her he would divorce you and marry her. When he broke off the relationship, she began this hate campaign. Jean Bradbury started the fire last night. She killed your husband.'

Jill Compton shivered even though the room was sweltering. 'No,' she said firmly, as if trying to convince herself. 'I don't believe you. My husband would never look at another woman.' Then she covered her face with her hands and her body shook. 'This is more than I can stand. I've lost everything . . . my home . . . my husband . . . and now you tell me he was unfaithful.'

Gilmore turned his head away in embarrassment. He didn't know how to handle crying women. Frost leant forward to pat her arm sympathetically. 'There were lots of things your husband didn't tell you, Mrs Compton. This may come as a bit of a shock to you, but did he tell you that your business was bankrupt?'

Her expression was one of utter bewilderment. 'Bankrupt? That's nonsense. We had a thriving business.'

'It was thriving so much,' Frost told her, 'that your husband had to borrow small sums of money from his mistress . . . and then paid her back with cheques that bounced.'

She shook her head defiantly. 'You're wrong. We had no secrets. Mark would have told me.'

'I'm afraid I'm right.' Frost patted her arm again. 'I was in Bennington's Bank today. One of the cashiers there owes me a favour and he accidentally left your business file on his desk and then went out for a few minutes. He must have completely forgotten what a nosy bastard I am.' He dug deep in his pocket and fished out a crumpled scrap of paper. 'I've scribbled down the details. The Old Mill is in hock to the bank as security for unpaid loans, your current account is £17,000 in the red and creditors galore are breathing down your neck.' He stuffed the paper back in his pocket. 'My friend in the bank is a bit of a cynic. He said the only thing that could have saved your bacon was an insurance policy and a bloody good fire. Well, we've had the fire. Do you know the details of your insurance, Mrs Compton?' He offered her his cigarette packet.

'I know nothing of the financial side of the business. Mark handled all that.' Distractedly, she accepted a cigarette, looked at it in puzzlement and pushed it back in the packet.

'Then I can enlighten you,' said Frost, striking a match against the fire surround. 'A mate of mine works for your insurance company. He tells me that the building and the contents are insured against fire, theft, explosion, earthquakes and stampeding cattle for the sum of £350,000.'

Her eyes widened. 'I can't believe it.'

'Neither could I,' said Frost. 'I doubt if there was more than a couple of thousand pounds' worth of stock in the entire house . . . and even that wasn't paid for.' Again he patted her hand. 'You're a very lucky woman, Mrs Compton.'

'Do you think I give a damn about the money?' she asked incredulously. 'I want my husband. I want my home. That spiteful bitch of a woman . . .'

'I've got more bad news for you,' said Frost. 'That spiteful bitch had nothing to do with the fire.'

Jill Compton shifted her gaze from Frost to Gilmore who was seething in his chair. Why the hell was the swine undermining him like this?

'Your husband started the fire,' continued Frost. 'It was an insurance fiddle. One last throw to clear all the debts and make a dirty great profit. It was your husband who was sending all the death threats and the wreath and doing all the damage.'

'This is ridiculous. Why would he do that?'

'A providential fire, your business on the rocks and the sprinkler system turned off at the mains. No insurance company is going to pay out on that. So your husband had to invent this imaginary nutter who makes weird phone calls and death threats. He even involved the police to give it authenticity.' Frost shook his head in grudging admiration. 'Bloody clever. He almost deserved to get away with it.'

An ingenious theory, thought Gilmore, but where's your proof?

'I'm sorry,' said Jill, her chin thrust forward defiantly, 'but I won't believe a word against my husband. It was that damn woman . . .'

'We've got proof coming out of our ear-holes,' said Frost. 'He had the key to the girl's flat. The magazines he cut the messages from . . . his fingerprints are all over them . . .'

Gilmore stared down at the floor and tried to keep his expression impassive. He wanted no part of this. Forensic had found no prints other than the Bradbury woman's.

'Secondly,' Frost continued, 'we've a witness who saw your husband stacking petrol cans in Jean Bradbury's garage. But the clincher, the absolute clincher . . .' He scrabbled around in his mac pocket. 'I found these in the boot of your husband's car.' He opened his hand to show some bright green leaves nestling in his palm. 'Three different sorts of leaf. And not any old leaf. According to our Forensic Department they are identical to the leaves on that wreath which we found in your lounge. We've even traced the grave where your husband pinched it, haven't we, Sergeant?'

'Yes,' acknowledged Gilmore, curtly. That was the only part of Frost's tissue of lies that he was prepared to endorse.

She stared at the leaves and shook her head. 'This is too much. I just can't believe it.'

Carefully, Frost replaced the leaves in his pocket then gave her one of his disarming smiles. 'It shouldn't be too hard to believe, Mrs Compton. It wouldn't have worked if you weren't in it with him.'

She jerked back, her face white. 'How dare you!'

Ignoring her, Frost continued. 'You were his alibi, he was yours. When he was away, you vandalized the garden. You each claimed to have received the phone calls in the other's presence . . . and when the wreath was chucked through the window, you both claimed to have seen someone running away. Which was impossible, because your husband planted the wreath. Even a dim sod like me can see that you were in the fiddle with him.'

Her mouth opened and shut, then she thought for a while and finally took a deep breath. 'I was hoping this would never have to come out, Inspector. Everything you say is true. It was Mark's idea. I didn't want to go along with him, but he said things were desperate and this was the only way out. He was my husband and I loved him. I did what he asked. Any wife would have done the same.'

Frost nodded. 'But that still makes you an accessory, Mrs Compton.'

She gave the secret smile of a poker player holding a royal flush. 'An accessory to what, Inspector? I have no intention of making a claim on the insurance policy, and if I don't claim, then there is no conspiracy to defraud.'

Frost looked deflated. 'Law isn't my strong point, Mrs Compton. I suppose there's no law that says you can't destroy your own property. So who burnt it down – you or your husband?'

'Mark. I tried to stop him, but he did it.'

A match flared. Frost sucked at his cigarette. 'That only leaves one problem.' He flicked the match in the fire and slowly expelled a lungful of smoke. 'Who killed him?'

She frowned.

'I may be a bit slow on the uptake, Mrs Compton, but there was no mysterious nutter with a grudge . . . you and your husband invented him, so you couldn't have heard him breaking in last night. You must have gone downstairs with your husband . . . you wouldn't lie in bed while he was splashing petrol about. Only two people in the house and one of them is murdered. So who did it, Mrs Compton?'

Gilmore was watching the woman. God knows how Frost had stumbled on to the truth, but her expression was as good as a signed and sealed confession.

'Why did you do it, love?' asked Frost, his voice softening. 'Did you find out about him and the Bradbury woman?' Her reaction was barely perceptible, but he saw it.

She stared at him unblinking. 'I had no motive to kill my husband. I never knew about Mark and her.'

Frost pushed himself out of his chair. 'I think you did, love. You probably got a poison pen letter telling you all about it, but we can check on that.' He jerked his sleeve back to consult his wrist-watch. 'But here am I rambling away and it isn't even my case.' He gave an apologetic grin to Gilmore as he shuffled out. 'Sorry, son. I'll leave you to get on with it.'

Gilmore stood up and opened the bedroom door. 'Would you please get dressed, Mrs Compton. I'd like you to come to the station with me.' While he waited he was irritated to hear Ada's startled shriek from the kitchen, followed by the raucous roar of Frost's laughter and his cry of 'How's that for centre, Ada?' Stupid childish bloody fool, he thought.

Outside, Frost pulled the handful of leaves from his pocket and hurled them into the wind. There were plenty more on Ada's privet hedge where he had plucked them on his way in.

Thursday afternoon shift (2)

The Incident Room was buzzing with activity when Frost entered carrying a mug of tea and a corned beef sandwich from the canteen. Burton, eyes gleaming with excitement, hurried over to him.

'You look happy,' said Frost. 'Has Mr Mullett died?'

Burton grinned. 'It's better than that, sir.'

333

Frost sat on the edge of a desk and sank his teeth into his sandwich. 'Nothing could be better than that.'

'First of all,' Burton told him, 'we've checked all the local security firms. A couple of them send salesmen around cold calling to sell complete burglar alarm systems, but they leave chains and padlocks to the hardware stores.'

Frost washed down a mouthful of sandwich with a swig of tea. 'That doesn't send my pulse racing, son. What else?'

'We've knocked on as many doors as we can asking if any one-man-band outfits have been touting for custom in fitting security chains and locks. A complete blank.'

Frost chewed gloomily. 'Wake me up when you get to the good bit.'

'I called on Mrs Proctor as you asked . . .'

Burton paused for maximum effect. 'A couple of days ago Mrs Watson told her that one of the bingo coach drivers had offered to fit a stronger security chain on the cheap.'

Frost punched the air and whooped. 'Geronimo! Did she say which driver?'

'No, sir.'

'No matter, we can probably pin-point him. Now I want you to check all the coach companies . . .'

'Already done,' cut in Burton. 'The main bingo run contract is with Superswift Coaches, but they sub-contract the work out to other firms on a day-to-day basis. I've got details of the other firms.' He offered the typed list to Frost who warded it away with his sandwich. 'Each firm has a rota of drivers for its various runs, so you wouldn't necessarily get the same driver each time . . . additionally, most drivers are self-employed so the same driver could do work for different firms.'

Frost gave a weary shake of the head. 'All these details give me a headache. Skip the foreplay – go straight to the big bang!'

'Right, sir. Sally fed all the names and duty rotas through the computer so we could eliminate those who definitely weren't anywhere near Denton when the killings took place. We've come down to four possibles.' From a folder he pulled four typed A4 sheets with photographs clipped on them. 'We pulled the photographs from the firms' personnel files.'

Frost wiped his buttery fingers on his jacket and took the first page. The photograph showed a man in his late thirties, a podgy face, receding dark hair.

'David Allen Hardwicke,' recited Burton. 'Works for the Denton Creamline Coach Company. He's done a lot of bingo runs, but he's mainly used for coach parties from the clubs for West End shows and pantomimes. During the summer he does the outings to the seaside resorts.'

Frost stared down at Hardwicke's details. The man was thirty-eight, married with two children aged nine and ten. Frost poked at the typescript with the crust of his corned beef sandwich. 'He was away from Denton for two of the killings.'

Burton retrieved the sheet and shook off the breadcrumbs. 'Yes, but sometimes drivers swap turns with each other and don't let their firms know. That's one of the complications you didn't want to hear about. We're checking it out.'

Frost took one last bite, then hurled the remains of his sandwich in the general direction of the waste bin. It missed by a foot. He ambled over and tried to boot it in, but missed again. He picked it up and dropped it in. 'Who's next?'

The next was Thomas Riley, the photograph showing a thin, sharp-featured man, light hair plastered well back and well-spaced teeth. 'Riley runs a one-man business – Riley's Coaches,' said Burton. 'Forty-one years old, married, no children. Does the odd bingo and theatre run, but nowhere as many as Hardwicke.'

Frost drained his tea. He couldn't work up any enthusiasm about Riley.

'And he's got form,' announced Burton, waiting for the reaction.

'Form?' Frost snatched Riley's details and studied them again.

Burton's finger pointed out the information. 'Receiving stolen goods. Video recorders, TV sets, electronic gear.'

'Hmm.' Frost dumped his mug on a stack of computer print-outs and fished out his cigarettes.

Burton took one. 'And he beat up a night-watchman once.'

'Hardly beat him up,' corrected Frost, scraping a match down the side of the computer casing. 'Knocked the old boy over when he tried to stop him.' He turned to the continuation page. 'Anyway, Riley was out on a job last night. Didn't get back in until after the time of the murder.'

'He dropped his last passenger off at 9.15,' said Burton, leaning forward to share Frost's match, 'but didn't garage the coach until 9.45. Mrs Watson was killed around 9.35. He could just have done it.'

Frost snorted smoke. 'He'd have had to rush, and I can't see our Ripper rushing things. He likes to take his time.' He handed back the details. 'Next.'

Burton passed across another page and waited expectantly. If he had to put money on it, this was his nap selection. Robert Jefferson, thirty-three, married, one teenaged daughter. A thickset man with close-cropped black hair, he stared morosely from his photograph like a criminal having his mug-shot taken. Jefferson drove for Superswift Coaches, mainly long-distance and Continental work, but had done a couple of bingo runs from time to time. His off-duty schedule put him in Denton for every one of the Ripper killings. A man of violent temper, he had broken his wife's jaw and she was instigating divorce proceedings because of his cruelty.

Frost seemed unimpressed. 'I don't think so, son. I can't see Old Mother Watson inviting that thug into her flat. Bung him at the bottom of the pile.'

'You'd better like this one,' said Burton. 'He's the last. Ronald William Gauld, twenty-five, single, lives with his widowed mother. Does casual work as a relief driver for Clarke's Coaches – mainly bingo and old people's outings. He's supposed to be a ball of fun on the coach trips. All the old dears love him.'

'I'm beginning to hate him already,' said Frost, extending his hand for the details.

'He's only employed as a casual by Clarke's, so he could well work for other firms we haven't checked on yet . . . but Clarke's time-sheets have him off-duty on all the times and days of the Ripper killings.'

Frost glanced at the colour photo clipped to the sheet. Gauld, grinning with well-spaced teeth into the camera, looked more a boy than a man. His expression was frank and open, his brown eyes twinkled and his thick, light brown hair hung boyishly over his forehead. Excitement like static electricity crackled through Frost. Instinct. Gut reaction. He knew. He just knew. 'Bingo!' he yelled.

Everyone in the room looked up.

Frost waggled the photograph, then held it aloft. 'This is him. This is the Granny Ripper!'

Burton could only look puzzled. 'Why, sir?'

'Gut reaction, son. I'm very rarely right, but I am this time. Forget the rest . . . We go nap on Laughing Boy Gauld.' He slid down from the desk, rubbing his hands together and pacing backwards and forwards to discharge his nervous excitement. 'Put every available man on him. I want him watched twenty-four hours a day.'

Burton urged caution. 'Don't you think we should hedge our bets, sir?'

'No,' said Frost firmly. 'We go for broke.'

'He's only a possible suspect. We've got nothing on him.'

'So we find something on him. Show copies of his photograph to the victims' neighbours. Do they remember seeing this roguish little bastard hanging around? Find out if he's been offering to fit new security chains for any of the old dears who find him such a scream. Go back to Old Mother Proctor and ask her if Gauld was the name of the man who offered to fit Mrs Watson's chain. Check with Gauld's neighbours. Has he come home at night dripping with blood with a knife sticking out of his back pocket? Get everyone on it . . . even the girl on the computer.'

'Hold it, Inspector!' Detective Sergeant Arthur Hanlon, eyes watering, nose streaming, looking like death warmed up, had been standing by the door. 'You'd better hear what I've found out first.'

'If it's bad news, I don't want to know,' said Frost.

'You might have to look for another suspect, Jack. You asked me to check on the three murder victims. I did. The only one who went to bingo was Mrs Watson.'

'Rubbish, Arthur. The second old girl – Betty Winters. We found a Reef Bingo membership card in her purse.'

'She hadn't used it for five years. She was crippled with arthritis – never left the house except to go to hospital for treatment.'

'And the first one – Mrs Thingummy?'

'Mrs Haynes. Very prim and proper. Didn't believe in gambling. Wouldn't even play bingo down at the church club for packets of tea.'

Frost's shoulders slumped. 'Sod you, Arthur. Why must you be so flaming thorough?' He glanced down at the photograph of Gauld which seemed to be smirking smugly back at him. 'It's got to be Gauld. There's got to be some common factor that links him to all three.' He became aware that everyone in the Murder Incident Room was waiting for him to give them orders, to tell them what to do. And he didn't know. His one and only lead had gone down the pan. He stared through the window out at the miserable, depressing, rain-swept car-park, drawing deeply on his cigarette, punishing his lungs for his own inadequacy. As he pulled the cigarette from his mouth, a thought buzzed and screamed. 'You said Mrs Winters never left the house except to go to hospital for treatment. How did she get there – the poor cow couldn't walk?'

'She certainly didn't go by bingo coach,' said Hanlon.

'Very funny, Arthur – remind me to pee myself when I've got more time.' Frost's finger stabbed at Burton. 'Phone the hospital transport officer and find out.'

Burton reached for the phone, but he thought it was a waste of time. 'She'd have gone by ambulance, Inspector.'

'Not necessarily, son. Just phone and ask.' He paced the room impatiently as Burton held on, waiting for someone to fetch the transport officer from the canteen. And then he remembered something else. Mrs

Mary Haynes. The first victim. Her purse. There was a hospital appointment card in her purse. 'And ask about Mrs Mary Haynes,' he shouted.

Burton nodded, then held up a hand for silence. The transport officer was on the line. Burton put his questions and waited . . . and waited . . . There seemed to be a long delay with Frost hovering anxiously before the answers came through. 'Ambulances? I see. Do you have the drivers' names? I see. Thank you very much, you've been a great help.' He replaced the receiver and tried to look noncommittal as Frost hurried over. But he couldn't keep up the pretence.

'You bastard!' yelled Frost. 'We've hit the jackpot, haven't we?'

Burton grinned broadly. 'They have a pool of volunteer drivers who help out with their own cars when the ambulances are too busy to collect patients for treatment.'

'I know,' said Frost. 'A volunteer driver used to pick up my wife.'

Burton smiled sympathetically before adding, 'One of those volunteers is a Mr R.W. Gauld.'

Frost crashed down on a chair. 'Then we've got the bastard!'

'Not quite, Inspector. The hospital doesn't keep records of individual pick-ups – they handle hundreds of patients every day. All they can say is that Gauld was among the volunteer drivers on duty on the last two occasions when Mrs Winters and Mrs Haynes attended for treatment. He didn't collect them, but it's possible he took them back home afterwards.'

'And that's when he found out about the spare key under the mat and the string inside the letter-box,' said Frost, excitedly. 'Let's bring the bastard in.'

Hanlon was more cautious. 'We could blow it by acting too soon. Jack. We need some solid evidence.'

'All right. Go to the hospital, see if you can find anyone who saw Gauld take the old dears back home. Check with the neighbours in the hope someone saw Gauld deliver them back. Get details of his car – did anyone see it in the vicinity on the nights of the murders? You know the form – whatever I've forgotten, do it. Lastly, I want Gauld tailed. I want to know everything he does every minute of the day and night, and when he goes out on his next killing job, we grab him, and if he's got his bloody knife on him, that's all the proof I need.'

In the corridor, he collided with Detective Sergeant Gilmore who looked as happy as his inspector.

'We've got a full statement from Mrs Compton, Inspector.'

'Thank God for that, son. I was afraid I might have to perjure myself at her trial.'

'She admits everything, but says the husband's death was an accident.'

'How? Did she accidentally welt him round the head with one of her rigid nipples?'

A broad grin from Gilmore. Anything Frost said was funny today. 'Thanks for your help,' he added sincerely.

'All I did was tell a few lies,' demurred the inspector. 'Any self-respecting policeman would do the same.'

'And after your stunt with the leaves,' added Gilmore, 'I got Forensic to go over the boot of Mark Compton's car. We actually found a couple of leaves from the wreath.'

'That's what's known as nature imitating art,' said Frost. 'When you get a minute, see me in the office.

341

I'll update you on the Ripper case. We're nearly ready to nail the bastard.'

In the office, weighed down in the centre of his desk by a stapling machine, was the memo from County beefing about the balls-up with his car expenses. He screwed it into a tight ball, tossed it in the air and headed it towards the open goal of the waste bin. It dropped dead centre with a satisfying plonk. He beamed happily. Things were starting to go right.

Later, when everything blew up in his face, he would remember this brief moment of euphoria.

Thursday night shift (1)

The downstairs light went out. A pause, then the upstairs light came on and the silhouette of a man passed the window. Gilmore ducked down behind the steering wheel until the curtains were closed and the bedroom light went out. He shook Frost awake. 'He's gone to bed.'

Yawning heavily, Frost consulted his watch. A few minutes to midnight. They had been parked down the side turning for nearly two hours, since taking over from Burton. Gauld had collected a party of senior citizens from the Silver Star Bingo Club at nine o'clock, and had delivered them all safely back to their homes by 9.56. He had then driven his grey Vauxhall Astra back to his terraced house in Nelson Street and was indoors by 10.15.

Frost fidgeted and tried to get comfortable. He was tired and hungry and there was no chance of a relief until six a.m. His fault. He had forgotten to ask Mullett to authorize more overtime and Wells was playing it by the book. He smeared a gap in the misted windscreen with his cuff and peered out at the still, dark street. 'It's too late for him to murder anyone now,' he decided. 'Let's get ourselves something to eat. I know a place that's open all night.'

The 'place' Frost knew was a converted van selling hot dogs and hamburgers on a windswept stretch of waste ground near the cemetery. The stale greasy smell of frying onions slapped them round the face as they got out of the car. On the side of the van a drop-down flap provided a serving counter and a canvas awning sheltered the clientele from the worst of the weather. Behind the counter a tall, thin man with a melancholy face and a red, running nose sucked at a cigarette as he pushed some onion slices around the fat with a fork.

'Lord Lucan and party,' announced Frost. 'We did book.'

'Very funny,' said the man, pulling the cigarette from his mouth so he could cough all over the food. He banged two cups on the counter, dropped a tea-bag in each and filled them with hot water from a steam-belching urn.

They sipped the scalding tea while the man fried them two hamburgers in tired, spitting fat. It was a cold night with the wind flapping the canvas awning.

'You caught that girl's killer yet?' asked the owner, putting the burgers on a plate and sliding them over.

Frost lifted the top of his bun and peered suspiciously at the onion-topped meat sinking in a puddle of fat. 'We're on a different case, Harry. Suspect meat sold as hamburger filling.' He took a tentative bite and chewed cautiously. 'I hope yours comes from a legitimate source?'

Harry sucked nervously at his cigarette. 'Of course it does Mr Frost. That's top-class stuff, that is – minced steak.'

'Good,' said Frost. 'Only this dodgy outfit is importing so-called meat from the Continent . . . all sorts of rubbish – dead horses, cats, dogs, some of it even worse.'

'Worse?' asked Harry.

Frost leant forward confidentially and lowered his voice. 'Don't spread this around, Harry, it would cause a public outcry, but we've got evidence they're even buying unclaimed bodies from undertakers and putting them in the mincing machine.'

Harry pulled the cigarette from his mouth and flicked off the spit from the end. 'You're having me on, Mr Frost!'

'I wish I was,' answered Frost gravely. He took a bite at his hamburger, then pulled it from his mouth. 'Bloody hell!' He snatched the top from his bun and gaped in disbelief. Lying across the onion, drenched in a bloody pool of tomato ketchup, was a severed human finger.

Gilmore shuddered and dropped his on the counter. Harry's face went a greasy white and his head jerked back in horror, rattling the tins on the shelf behind him. 'Christ, Mr Frost! They told me it was good meat. They said it was prime beef steak . . .' His voice suddenly changed to outrage. 'You bastard!'

The severed finger was wiggling at him and Frost was convulsed with laughter as he pulled it free and wiped off the ketchup.

'It's not funny,' bellowed Harry. 'You nearly gave me a bloody heart attack.'

Frost wiped the tears from his eyes. 'I was going to put my dick in, Harry, but the buns were too small.'

'Bleeding funny!' snarled the man as they walked back to the car, Frost still convulsed at his joke. 'Pity you don't put your bloody energy into finding that poor kid's killer.'

Frost stopped laughing.

The cemetery was crawling past the car window. Frost asked Gilmore to stop. He lit a cigarette and stared moodily across white marble and granite. 'Harry was right, son. That bloody girl. I haven't the faintest idea what to do next.'

Gilmore said nothing. At the far end of the empty road he had spotted a man, dressed in black, crouching by the cemetery railings. Gilmore clicked off the headlights, then nudged Frost, who nodded. 'I see him, son.'

The man seemed to be doing something to the railings.

'What's he up to?' asked Gilmore.

'Whatever it is, let him get on with it,' muttered Frost, huddling down into his seat. 'I can't solve the cases I've got. I don't want any more.'

But Gilmore wanted more. Another arrest on top of the successful outcome of the Compton case would do his promotion chances a world of good. He wound down the window and stuck his head out, trying to make out what the man was doing. Frost shivered as the cold air rushed in. 'He's either got his dick stuck between the railings, or he's having a pee, son. Let's get back to the station.'

Suddenly the man seemed to push against the railings and was through to the cemetery where his black shape flitted briefly across the white of the headstones before being gulped up by darkness.

Gilmore was out of the car while Frost was still fumbling for his seat belt.

One of the cast iron railings had rusted away and could be lifted from its concrete base. Gilmore pulled it up and wriggled though, then held it so Frost could follow.

The cemetery was vast. Their man could have gone anywhere. 'We've lost the bugger, son.'

'Shh!' hissed Gilmore, squinting to focus his eyes. 'There!'

Frost's eyes followed Gilmore's finger. The moon pushed its way through a cloud and illuminated the cemetery in a cold blue light. Uncut grass twitched and shivered in the wind. Trees creaked and groaned. And then Frost saw him. About sixty yards away, zigzagging between the graves.

'Follow me!' ordered Gilmore, haring off in pursuit. Reluctantly, Frost stumbled after him. He couldn't see what Gilmore was getting all excited about. The man could simply be taking a short cut.

They jogged on, past angels and cherubs. The path veered to the right and there ahead of them was the Victorian crypt. 'Stop, son,' pleaded Frost, 'I've got to rest.' They paused alongside some new, raw graves, panting, sucking in air, looking left and right where the path split. Nothing but white headstones as far as the eye could see.

'We've lost him,' said Frost happily. 'Let's get back to the car.'

An irritated flap of Gilmore's hand hushed him to silence and pointed to the crypt. The man, his back to them, was bent over doing something to the padlock. A loud click, then a groaning of hinges as the door was pushed open. A torch flashed and the man disappeared inside the burial vault.

'Still taking a short cut?' scoffed Gilmore, smugly. He moved quietly round to the side of the building and squeezed through the railing by the tap, where Paula Bartlett's killer squeezed through with her body. Frost, slower, followed.

Round to the door where the newly fitted brass padlock still held the hasp firmly, but as before, the screws had been prised from the rotting door frame. Intermittent splashes of light spilled from inside. Echoing in the confined space, sounds of something heavy being dragged across the stone floor.

Gilmore and Frost looked at each other. What the hell was he doing?

Cautiously, Gilmore edged his head until he could see inside. Pitch black, then the man's torch clicked on again and lit up a scatter of something on the floor. Bones. Human bones. And on top of them, a grinning, yellow-toothed, human skull.

Gilmore's involuntary gasp was enough to make the man spin round, the glare of his torch hitting Gilmore straight in the eyes, momentarily blinding him. Then, with a yell, the man charged and Gilmore found himself flying through the air, his back, then his head hitting the stone floor with a teeth-jolting crack making pin-points of light dance in the blackness at the pain.

Crouching, ready to give him a second dose, the man moved forward.

'Stay where you are. Police!' yelled Frost, dragging his torch from his mac pocket and kicking bones out of the way as he advanced into the vault. The man blinked into the beam and Frost stopped in his tracks. Gilmore's assailant was wearing a clerical collar.

The curate gawped surprise at the sudden appearance. 'Mr Frost!'

Gilmore creaked open his eyes and saw a skull and a thigh bone within inches of his face. He sat up, gingerly touching the back of his head then studying the blood on his fingertips.

'I'm terribly sorry, Sergeant,' apologized the curate. 'I thought you were one of the vandals.' He helped Gilmore to his feet and examined the cut on his head. 'Only a graze, I think.'

With an angry jerk, Gilmore shook him off. 'Perhaps you'd care to explain what you're doing here at this time of night?' He picked up the torch and swept the stone floor with its beam. The lids of two coffins had been unscrewed open and the skeletal bodies inside tipped out with bones and pieces of shroud strewn all over the floor. 'And how do you propose to explain this?'

'I use the graveyard as a short cut to get back to the vicarage. I've been sitting with another sick parishioner. She died, I'm afraid – this terrible influenza epidemic.' He shook his head sadly. 'So many deaths.'

'Let's have the address of this sick old lady,' said Gilmore, pen poised over his notebook. He wrote down the details. 'Right. Now explain this.' He nodded at the mess.

'Does it need explaining?' said the curate bitterly. 'You're supposed to be protecting us against vandals. I passed the crypt and saw the door was open. I came in to investigate and found this.' He shook his head. 'Such pointless desecration. One tries to be forgiving, Sergeant, but this is sick.'

Gilmore snapped shut his notebook. 'All right, Mr Purley. That's all, for now.' He emphasized the 'for now'.

They followed him out and watched as he tried to make the door secure. 'You'll need a new door frame,' said Frost.

'Yes, Inspector. More expense.' Another sigh. 'I'll

come back tomorrow and try and fix it. I'll tidy up inside as well.' Round to the side of the building where they squeezed through the gap in the railing.

They watched him picking his way between the graves before veering off towards the vicarage.

'I don't trust him,' growled Gilmore. 'He's always out too late at night for my liking. If there's been another Ripper murder . . .' Frost was pinning his hopes on the coach driver, but Gilmore had serious doubts. 'Let's go. This place is giving me the creeps.'

'It must have given Paula Bartlett's killer the creeps, coming here at dead of night with a body in his arms.' Frost poked away at his scar and stared at the ranks of white headstones crowding in on the crypt. 'He knew how to find the crypt, son, and he knew he could get in.' He pushed his hands deep into his mac pockets and wandered along the railings, booting at pebbles in his path. 'So how did he know?'

'Perhaps he was someone who often used the graveyard as a short cut,' offered Gilmore, pointedly rubbing the back of his head.

Frost chewed his knuckles in thought, then took out his cigarette packet and shook it. One left. He poked it in his mouth and flung the empty packet into the long grass. A blast of cold wind cut across the cemetery, shaking the trees and making him shiver. 'Let's go.'

They walked on to the path where the first of the new graves encroached. Frost struck his match on a convenient headstone. The match flared. He saw the wording, but at first didn't take it in. Then he stared, open-mouthed, until the match burnt his fingers. 'Where the bloody hell did this come from?'

He struck another match so Gilmore could read the inscription.

In Loving Memory
Of
Rosemary Fleur Bell
April 3 1962 – September 10 1990
Adored Wife Of Edward Bell M.A.
R. I. P.

'The schoolmaster's wife! Her grave right on the bloody doorstep of the crypt and we haven't spotted it. We must be bleeding blind as well as stupid!'

'It's probably only just been put up,' said Gilmore, wondering what all the fuss was about. 'You have to wait ages for the grave to settle before you can erect a headstone.'

'That wispy-bearded bastard. I knew it was him all the time.' He turned and stared at the crypt.

'I don't follow you,' said Gilmore.

'You could spit on the flaming crypt from here,' said Frost. 'At the funeral Bell would have had a grandstand view of that fat-gutted plumber forcing open the door to get inside out of the rain. Later he needed somewhere to hide the kid's body. A crypt. Who'd look for a body in a Victorian crypt?'

'You're saying he killed her the very day of his wife's funeral?'

'Yes,' said Frost.

'But he was in the house all the time she was doing her paper round.'

'I don't know how he did it, I just know he did it.'

Gilmore swivelled his head towards the vault door with its solid brass lock hanging impotently. 'Even if you are right, how are you going to prove it?'

'Proof!' barked Frost. He took a long drag at his last

350

cigarette and dashed it to the ground half-smoked. 'Everyone's obsessed with bloody proof.' Then his shoulders slumped. Gilmore was right. Without proof, the bastard was going to get away with it.

Thursday night shift (2)

The minute hand on the lobby clock was quivering as it gathered its strength to claw up to two o'clock. The damn phones had been ringing non-stop and Wells was finding it hard to keep his voice sounding polite. 'I'm sorry, madam,' he told a caller who had phoned previously to complain that her neighbours were having a noisy row and were keeping her awake. 'We're short-staffed and we had to divert the car to a more important incident. We'll get someone there just as soon as we can.' Hardly had he replaced the phone and logged the call when there was an angry commotion outside, then a scowling, red-faced bull-frog of a man in an expensive black overcoat and a white silk scarf exploded into the lobby, closely followed by an anxious-looking PC Collier.

'Who's in charge?' the man bellowed, dumping a bulky briefcase on the floor. He reeked of whisky.

Wells put his pen down and sighed. He could do without this. 'I am, sir.'

The man looked disdainfully at Wells' sergeant's stripes and screwed his face into a sneer. 'I want someone in authority, not you. Not a bloody sergeant.'

'What's this all about?' Wells asked Collier.

The man barged between the two officers. 'Don't you damn well ignore me. *I'm* talking to you, Sergeant. You ask me, not him. Now get me someone in authority.' He fumbled in his pocket for a cigar.

'Would an inspector satisfy you, sir?' asked Wells, struggling to hold his temper in check.

'If that's all you've got, then he'll have to do,' snapped the man, clicking a gold Dunhill lighter and drawing on the cigar. Wells felt like pointing to the 'No Smoking' sign but wasn't in the mood for any more aggravation and the odds were that Frost would come slommocking out with a cigarette in his mouth. He used the internal phone and whilst the man glowered and puffed cigar smoke and whisky fumes all over him, asked Inspector Frost to come into the lobby.

'I'm Detective Inspector Frost. What's up?'

Frost, in his crumpled suit, greasy knotted tie and unpolished shoes, didn't look at all impressive and he certainly didn't impress the complainant who pulled the cigar from his mouth and stared contemptuously. 'Isn't there anyone else in charge?'

'No,' said Frost. 'So if you've anything to say, spit it out, I'm busy.'

'Not too busy to attend to me,' snarled the man. 'I'm making a complaint against that police officer.' His finger jabbed at Collier. 'He drove his car into me while I was stationary, then accused me of drunken driving.'

Frost wrinkled his nose and turned his head away from the whisky fumes. To Collier he said, 'Has he been breathalyzed?'

'No, Inspector. He refused.'

'Right,' said Frost to Wells. 'Get a police surgeon . . . one with warm hands. We'll have a urine sample.' Back to Collier. 'So what happened, Constable?'

'I've just told you what happened,' shouted the man, his face getting redder.

Frost pushed him away. 'Shut up. You're giving me a bleedin' headache.' Back to Collier.

'I was on patrol in the Bath Road when I saw this Bentley crawling along, swinging from one side of the road to the other. I signalled for the driver to stop. He pulled into the kerb. I drew up behind him. As I was getting out, he started up the engine. I think he was trying to get away, but he put it into reverse by mistake and rammed into me. He was obviously drunk – speech slurred, eyes glazed. He flatly refused to use the breathalyzer, and knocked it out of my hand, so I brought him in.'

'Well done,' nodded Frost. 'Book him.' As he turned to go, the man grabbed him by the shoulder and jerked him round.

'Do you know who I am?' he demanded, pushing his sweating face close to the inspector's.

'I know what you are,' replied Frost, shaking himself free. 'You're a drunken, boring prick. Take your sweaty paw off my suit.'

No-one heard the lobby door swing open. 'What's going on here?'

Frost groaned. Bloody Mullett had to choose this particular moment to do his rallying call act on the troops. A little touch of Mullett in the night. 'I'm handling it, sir,' he said firmly.

Mullett hesitated. He preferred not to get involved in anything unless he knew what it was about. Then his face lit up with recognition. 'Good lord! It's Councillor Knowles. What are you doing here?'

'I'm making an official complaint against this police officer,' said Knowles, 'and I'm being treated abominably. That man . . .' and his lip curled at Frost, 'has been incredibly rude. He has threatened me, sworn at me and made me the subject of a false charge.'

Mullett looked suitably shocked. His lips tightened. 'You'd better come to my office, councillor. I'm sure we can sort this out.' He glowered at Frost as he spun on his heel. 'Two coffees to my office at once, please, Sergeant.'

Frost jerked forked fingers to the door as it closed behind his Divisional Commander. 'Pompous git!' he bellowed impotently to the ceiling.

'Did you hear that? Two coffees!' croaked Wells. 'What does he think this is – an all-night flaming café?'

Young PC Collier was white-faced. 'What will happen, Sarge? It was a proper arrest. The man was drunk and he ran into me.'

'Go and make their coffee,' said Wells, 'and do one for me.'

The internal phone buzzed. Inspector Frost to report to the Divisional Commander . . . at once! 'When I'm ready,' said Frost, after he had hung up. Slowly he finished his cigarette, then ambled off to obey the summons. Mullett was waiting for him in the passage outside. He took Frost by the arm and drew him away, beaming a smile of smug satisfaction. Hello, thought Frost. What's the slimy sod been up to?

'I've managed to get the councillor to drop his complaint against Collier, Inspector.'

'What bloody complaint?' demanded Frost, his voice rising with anger. 'The drunken slob rammed into him then refused to take a breath test.'

Waving a hand for Frost to keep his voice down, Mullett led him away from the office door, then leaned forward to talk to Frost in his 'man to man' voice. 'Young Collier is inexperienced. Mr Knowles is a councillor. He is also on the Police Committee. It will be his word against Collier's. Who do you think will be believed?'

'Collier will be believed – especially when the urine test shows Fat-guts is as pissed as a newt.'

Mullett winced. He deplored Frost's too-frequent crudities. He carefully composed his face into a brittle smile and looked at the far wall across Frost's shoulder. 'Ah . . . there won't be a urine sample. We won't be proceeding with the charge . . .' His hand jerked up to silence Frost's explosion of outrage. 'Politics, Inspector. It pays to have a man of his influence on our side, instead of against us.'

Frost jerked his arm free from Mullett's grasp. 'You can have him on your bloody side. I don't want him on mine. And if I ever arrest the bastard for anything, I'll make the charge stick, politics or no bloody politics.'

The brittle smile slipped and shattered. 'There will be no vendettas,' hissed Mullett. 'And before you go, Inspector, there's one more thing. In order to persuade the councillor to drop his complaint against Collier, I agreed that you would personally apologize to him for your rudeness.'

'Up your shirt!' shouted Frost, ready to march back up the corridor.

Mullett's whole body was quivering with anger. 'That was not a request, Inspector. That was an order.'

'Very good, Super,' replied Frost, with an expression of such sweet reasonableness that Mullett was instantly uneasy.

Knowles was sprawled in one of Mullett's special visitor's chairs, his piggy eyes agleam at the prospect of Frost's impending humiliation. He looked up from his cup of Sergeant Wells' instant coffee in mock surprise as Frost entered, looking very contrite. 'Yes, Inspector?'

'I'd like to apologize', said Frost, 'for calling you a big, fat, ugly bastard.'

Knowles frowned and looked puzzled. 'I didn't hear you say that.'

'Oh, sorry,' said Frost innocently, sounding genuinely apologetic. 'It must have been what I was thinking.'

Knowles rose from his chair, eyes bulging, ready to erupt. Then he gave an evil smile. 'I shall remember this, Inspector.' As he spoke the threat, he swayed from side to side like a snake ready to strike.

'You're too kind,' cooed Frost.

With a furious, laser beam glare, Mullett ordered the inspector to wait for his return, then ushered his visitor out. Left alone in the old log cabin, Frost riffled through Mullett's in-tray, but found nothing of interest. He was delighted to discover that Mullett's cigarette box had been newly replenished for the recent visitor, so helped himself to a few, just managing to stuff them in his pocket and put on his contrite expression as the Divisional Commander stamped back, slamming the door behind him.

'That', said Mullett, 'was unforgivable. Mr Knowles is a councillor, a member of the Police Committee and a personal friend of mine.'

And a big, fat drunken bastard to boot, thought Frost. But he hung his head and tried to look ashamed of himself.

'Don't worry,' said Frost, trying to console a gloomy PC Collier with one of Mullett's cigarettes. 'You just misinterpreted the law. The law is that if you're a friend of Mr Mullett's, then you can get away with bloody murder.'

Collier squeezed out a smile, but was still upset. Frost inhaled deeply, then dribbled out smoke. Something propped against the desk caught his eye. He bent to examine it more closely. It was a brief-case. 'What's this?'

Sergeant Wells stretched over the desk to take a look and immediately panicked. 'Flaming heck, it could be a bomb.' His hand shot out for the phone.

'Hold on,' muttered Frost, crouching on his haunches to examine the object. 'Collier, did that fat sod have a brief-case with him when you brought him in?'

'Yes,' answered Collier, relieved to provide the explanation. 'He clung to it like grim death.'

With a grunt, Frost heaved it up on to the desk. 'I wonder if there's anything worth pinching inside.' He tried the catch. It was locked, so he produced his bunch of skeleton keys.

'You're not going to open it, are you?' asked Wells, his head anxiously flicking from side to side in case the Divisional Commander caught them in the act.

'Why not?' grunted Frost, trying to force a clearly unsuitable key to turn.

Wells backed away. 'I want nothing to do with it, Jack. Mullett's still in the building.'

'A suspected bomb,' said Frost, his concentration all on the lock. 'At great personal risk to life, limb and dick I am trying to defuse it . . . ah!' The lock yielded with a click. He lifted the flap and looked inside. His jaw dropped and he emitted a long, low whistle. 'Look what we've got here!' He produced a handful of banknotes. Dirty, creased, well-used banknotes of mixed denominations, fives, tens, twenties, fifties . . . The sort of money that rarely saw the inside of a bank, or was declared on an income tax return. He dived in and produced a second handful, then riffled his thumb through them. At a rough guess there was something in excess of £5,000. 'I wonder how much of this he gave to Mullett for letting him go? Right, let's share it out.' He proceeded to deal out the notes in three piles as if they were playing cards.

'Put them back, Jack,' pleaded Wells, now very agitated, his ears straining to catch the first sounds of Mullett's approaching footsteps.

'Why?' asked Frost. 'The sod's obviously been up to no good. This is crooked money. It sticks out a mile.'

'You've got no proof.'

'The man's a bastard, that's all the proof I need.' Reluctantly he stuffed the money back and let Wells lock the brief-case away for safe-keeping. A quick peep up the corridor. The light was still on in Mullett's office. 'Ah well. No-one will dare commit a crime while Hornrim Harry's still here, so I'm going off home.'

He poked his head round the door of his office where Gilmore was pecking away at a typewriter. 'Come on, son. You can surprise your wife in bed with the lodger. We're having an early night.'

Gilmore didn't really consider nearly three o'clock in the morning to be an early night, but he didn't argue. He scooped up his coat and hurried out after the inspector.

There were a few cars dotted about the station carpark. In its specially reserved parking space, sneering at Gilmore's Ford, stood Mullett's blue Jaguar. But making the Jaguar look like a poor relation was a gleaming black Bentley. Frost ambled over to it and peered through the tinted windows to the cream leather upholstery and polished figured walnut fascia. A jingle of keys and there was young Collier. 'Why didn't you tell me my new motor had arrived?' asked Frost.

Collier grinned. 'It's Councillor Knowles' car, sir. He went home by taxi. Mr Mullett wants me to drive it back for him.'

'How can that bastard afford to run a bloody car like this?' said Frost, walking around the vehicle and giving it his grudging admiration. He stopped in midstride.

'Gilmore!' Gilmore, waiting patiently by his own car, came reluctantly over. 'Remember how Wally Manson told us he nicked those porno videos from an expensive motor?'

Gilmore nodded wearily. There were lots of expensive motors about. He hoped Frost wasn't going to plunge head first in another of his wild, tenuous, proofless hunches.

'And you remember how Wally said he jemmied open the boot?' Frost pointed to the rear of the car. Gilmore moved forward to look. He had to agree. The boot had been forced open – and not too long ago.

'And the bastard's got a brief-case full of dirty money,' Frost continued. 'What's the betting he's been doing the rounds, flogging his dirty videos?' Frost held out his hand to Collier. 'Keys, son.' He took them and unlocked the driver's door. The aroma of rich leather and cigar smoke. He slid into the driver's seat and rummaged about in the dash compartment. He found a button to press and a concealed drawer glided open. Inside were a dozen or more of the familiar pornographic videos. Triumphantly he showed them to Gilmore. 'Proof enough for you?'

'It's a start,' agreed Gilmore, reluctantly. He didn't want to get involved. People like Councillor Knowles would always come out on top.

Frost told Collier to fetch the brief-case from Sergeant Wells. 'Tell him I'm going to kindly deliver it in person.'

'Are you sure you know what you're doing?' asked Gilmore.

'Yes,' said Frost. 'I'm risking my bloody job.'

Knowles lived in a large rambling house just north of the Bath Road on the outskirts of the town, standing in its own extensive grounds, completely hidden from the road by trees. Although it was well past three in the morning, lights still showed from the downstairs windows. They pulled up in front of a massive black oak door which was flanked by replica flaming torches lit by electric bulbs.

Up two stone steps, guarded on each side by stone watchdogs, to the door where the bell-pull, a heavy black iron ring on a chain, descended from the top of the porch. Frost tugged it and somewhere far in the bowels of the house a bell echoed. The ringing started a dog barking. A door slammed. Someone inside shouted angrily and the dog stopped in mid-bark.

Gilmore's agitation was showing. Not only were they barging into someone's house in the dead of night for the flimsiest of reasons, but it was the house of an important friend of the Divisional Commander who would have apoplexy if he knew they were there. Why the hell had Frost dragged him into this? Frost, striking a match on the rump of one of the stone dogs seemed blissfully unaware of the possible consequences of what he was doing.

They waited. Shuffling footsteps, then a light glowed through the coloured glass on either side of the door and a voice called, 'Who is it?'

'Police, Mr Knowles,' said Frost. 'You left your brief-case at the station.'

Bolts and chains clinked and the door opened wide enough for a hand to pass through. It closed round the handle of the brief-case. 'Tell Mr Mullett, thank you.' The brief-case vanished inside and the door jerked back. But it would not close. A scuffed, unpolished shoe prevented it.

'What the hell!' Knowles felt the door being pushed open. That damn, scruffy inspector, a cigarette drooping insolently from his mouth, was barging his way into the house.

'If we could come in for a moment, sir,' said Frost, kicking the front door shut behind him and snatching the brief-case back from Knowles who was clasping it tightly against a black and red silk dressing gown.

Knowles, the alcohol smell stronger than ever, quivered with rage and pointed dramatically to the front door. 'If you aren't out in thirty seconds I am getting on the phone to your Chief Constable.'

'I'm sorry, sir,' said Frost, not sounding it, 'but this is a very serious matter.' He opened the brief-case.

Knowles sobered up instantly. 'What right have you to open a locked brief-case?'

'No right at all,' replied Frost. 'It came open in the car and the contents fell out.'

Gilmore squeezed even further into the background, hoping Frost wouldn't seek his corroboration.

'In the brief-case was a large amount of money in used notes. Can you account for it, sir?'

Knowles took a red-banded cigar from his dressing gown pocket and lit it with a snap of his gold Dunhill. 'I can, but I have no intention of doing so. You have far exceeded your authority and you will very soon suffer the consequences.'

Ignoring the threat, and the mute pleading for caution from Gilmore, Frost ploughed on. 'We found a quantity of these in your car.' He held up two tapes. 'They are locally made, pornographic videos involving bestial and disgusting acts against children.'

'Just what are you insinuating?' asked Knowles, his voice soft and menacing.

'I'm insinuating sod all. I'm stating that you are involved with a pornographic vice ring. So get your clothes on. I'm taking you back to the station.'

With a chilling smile Knowles drew deeply on the

cigar, then flicked a cylinder of ash on to the carpet. 'I'll happily come to the station with you, Frost, and then you can kiss your career goodbye. Those videos were given to me by an outraged member of the public. If you check, you will find that I have already given notice that I intend raising this matter at the next meeting of the Denton Police Committee. I will also be raising the matter of your outrageous behaviour.'

Oh my God! thought Gilmore. This is it. The stupid fool's done it now. Well, he's not dragging me down with him. But he couldn't help feeling a pang of pity for the inspector who was shaken rigid and looked older, even more shabby and useless than usual.

With the cigar clenched in a gloating grin, Knowles retrieved the brief-case and quickly checked through the contents. 'I hope, for your sake, all the money is intact, Inspector. I suggest you leave now. I'll be speaking to your Chief Constable first thing in the morning.' He opened the front door. Outside it was raining again.

Defeated, Frost couldn't think of a thing to say. Mullett would demand his resignation and he would have to give it.

But luck, which all too often deserted him in his hour of need, suddenly remembered it owed him a favour. Somewhere at the end of the darkened passage, a door opened and a rectangle of light fell out. 'Is everything all right?' a woman called. Then a scamper of feet and she yelled sharply, 'No . . . come back!'

But the dog bounded up the passage towards its master, wagging its tail happily and whimpering. An enormous dog. A Great Dane. A brown and white Great Dane. Its left ear was torn.

Frost stared, then grinned happily in warm, sweat-trickling relief. He marched back into the house, closing

362

the front door firmly behind him. 'What a beautiful dog, Mr Knowles. He looks just like he did in the video.'

Dawn was scratching at the small window of the main interview room as Knowles and his wife were hustled in. They sat sullenly, refusing to say a word until their solicitor was roused from his bed. Outside, from a police van in the car-park, boxes and boxes of videos, raw tape, and video cameras were carted into the station.

The door opened and Frost slouched in and mumbled a few words to PC Collier who was guarding the prisoners. Collier nodded and left to stand watch outside, ready to warn the inspector of the solicitor's arrival.

Frost dragged a chair over and sat facing Knowles and his wife. 'Alone at last, Councillor.'

'I've nothing to say,' said Knowles in a flat voice. His wife, a superior-looking blonde some ten years his junior, stared aloofly ahead and wrapped her fur coat tighter around her. The early morning cold still clung to the room.

Slowly, Frost lit up a cigarette. A clatter of footsteps in the corridor outside made him look up in concern, but he relaxed as they passed on. He lowered his voice. 'I might be able to do a deal.'

Knowles' tiny eyes glinted. He was a pretty shrewd judge of character and he had this foul-mouthed tramp summed up as someone who could be bought right from the start. He leant forward. 'I'm listening.'

'The girl you filmed performing with your dog. Did you know she killed herself?'

Knowles lowered his gaze and found something on the floor that held his full attention. 'I heard something to that effect,' he said vaguely.

'It would do you a lot of good if we could stop it coming out in court,' said Frost.

'You could arrange that?' whispered Knowles.

'I can arrange for the videos of the girl and the dog to go missing. That part of the charge could not proceed and would not be mentioned in court – unless your side raised it, of course.'

'We're not likely to do that,' said Knowles, mentally working out how much this piece of good fortune was likely to cost him. 'Naturally, I would be extremely grateful if the tapes did go missing . . . extremely grateful. The death of the girl was unfortunate – nothing to do with me – but the court might not see it in that light.' He gave Frost a patronizing smile. 'Tell me how you would like me to express my gratitude?'

'You admit to all the other charges. Both of you. You don't dispute any of the facts. You plead guilty. You don't make us call any of the kids involved to give evidence. In return, the tapes go missing, which should knock at least three years off your sentence . . . and the girl's mother will never know what perverted things you pair of bastards made her daughter do.' He stood up and moved to the door. 'I want a "yes" or "no" right now, or the deal's off.'

Mullett strode up and down his office, pounding his fist, shaking his head in disbelief. 'You've lost a box of video tapes? Vital evidence in a serious case? I can't believe it. Even by your sloppy standards, this is disgraceful. I take it you've looked everywhere?'

'Everywhere,' mumbled the inspector, head bowed, looking very ashamed of himself.

'This entire operation was mismanaged from the start. You dashed into it, head first without any thought of he consequence should proof not be forthcoming.' He returned to his desk and looked again at the typed, signed statement on his desk. 'You can count yourself lucky that Knowles has decided to do the right thing and make a full confession of the other offences. It does show a certain amount of character. I'm sure it will count in his favour at court.'

'I'm sorry it turned out to be your personal friend, sir,' mumbled Frost, trying hard to suppress a grin of delight.

Mullett glared at him grim-faced. Two could lie if they wanted to. 'He's no friend of mine, Frost. I never trusted him from the start.'

Friday morning shift

Liz slammed the eggs and bacon on the table and stamped off back to the kitchen without a word. 'Thanks,' grunted Gilmore, eyeing with wary disfavour the flabby bacon floating in grease and the under-cooked eggs. He liked the bacon crisp and the eggs well done, but he held his tongue. She was spoiling for a fight and was just waiting for him to complain.

His knife sawed away at a tough chunk of meat which squeaked across the plate and defied all efforts to cut it. Liz returned with his tea. 'Anything wrong with the food?' she snapped.

'No, no – it's fine,' he lied. 'I'm not very hungry.' He risked a sip of the tea. Near-cold and milky when he liked it hot and strong. He replaced the cup on the saucer and made one more effort to restore peaceful relations. 'Look, Liz, I'm sorry.'

This was her chance. 'Sorry! I'm left on my own al night. You come in hours late, too tired to talk or d any bloody thing, then you tell me you've got to be ou again. I never bloody see you.'

'It won't be for long, love, then things will be different. He reached for her, but she shook him off.

'It's always *going* to be different, but it never blood well is. I'm sick of your job, I'm sick of this dead an alive town, I'm sick of everything.' The door slamme in an angry explosion behind her.

Gilmore sighed and took his plate to the kitchen wher he emptied it into the pedal bin. He hated to admit it t himself, but he was getting sick of Liz.

Frost wasn't feeling very happy either. That damn inven tory form had reappeared. Mullett must have quarrie deep into the filing tray in Allen's office where Fros had buried it and had transferred it to the top of hi in-tray with a large, block-capitalled inscription in re felt-tip yelling WHY HASN'T THIS GONE OFF? Because haven't bleeding sent it off, thought Frost, reading on MUST GO OFF TODAY WITHOUT FAIL. SCM – the OR ELS was implied.

Gilmore came in carrying a thick bacon sandwich an a mug of tea from the canteen. Frost brightened up unt he realized Gilmore intended it for himself. 'Doesn't tha wife of yours feed you?' he growled and was quite unpre pared for Gilmore's slashing expression of vehemence.

Burton broke the tension by coming in to report.

'What's the position with Gauld?'

'He left home at 8.56,' Burton told him, 'and drov straight to Denton Hospital. He's been ferrying ou patients backwards and forwards. We're keeping hir under surveillance.'

'Good,' nodded Frost. 'What have you found out about him?'

'Not much. He lives with his widowed mother. They moved to Denton some ten years ago from Birmingham. He's never had a permanent job – just temporary work, mainly driving. The neighbours like him. Apart from his hospital work, he helps out at the local Oxfam shop in his spare time.'

Frost gave a derisory snort. 'What else does he do? Cure the sick and raise the dead?' He thought for a while. 'Do the neighbours see him coming and going late at night?'

'Sometimes, sir. But you'd expect that with all the late-night coaches he drives.' Burton paused. 'I know you want to go for broke on him, Inspector, but it wouldn't hurt to keep a watch on some of the other coach drivers.'

'Then do it, son. As long as you don't let up on Gauld.'

'We could do with more men.'

'I could do with a new dick,' said Frost, 'but I've got to manage with what I've got.' He stared miserably at the inventory. 'You busy, son?' he asked Gilmore.

Gilmore backed towards the door. 'I'm due in court with Mrs Compton in twenty minutes.'

Frost flicked through the wad of information-demanding pages and shuddered. He chucked it back in his in-tray and reburied it. His internal phone buzzed. He scooped his mac from the hat-stand. 'Tell him I'm out,' he yelled from the corridor.

Burton picked up the phone. 'I'm afraid Mr Frost isn't here, sir,' he told the Divisional Commander.

The sound of the Westminster chimes reverberated inside the flat. A fat, motherly little woman in a green overall waddled into the hallway and opened the door. A shabbily dressed man twitched a shy smile. Not one of the regulars. She hadn't seen him before. 'I phoned,' he said.

She gave a welcoming smile to put him at ease. He looked so nervous. 'French lesson, isn't it? Miss Désirée's expecting you.' She led him through the hall into a dimly lit room with the curtains drawn. 'The gentleman who phoned,' she announced, then retired discreetly, closing the door with a gentle click behind her.

The woman sitting on the bed was in her late thirties and looked like a young Mae West. The loose-fitting red dressing gown she wore was carefully flapped open to display black bra, black knickers and black stockings which were held up by rosette, red garters. An over-brilliant smile clicked on automatically as she greeted her visitor. 'Don't be shy,' she purred in a thick French accent, 'I am Mademoiselle Désirée.'

'Hello, Doris,' said Frost, giving her a quick flash of his warrant card. 'How's your bunions?'

The smile withered and died with the French accent. 'Jack effing Frost! Well, you can piss off as soon as you like.'

'You can't get round me with sweet talk,' said Frost, helping himself to one of her cigarettes from a packet on the bed. He flopped into a chair and pulled a photograph from his pocket. 'Recognize him?'

She took the photograph and gave it a cursory glance. 'Can't place him,' she said, disdainfully handing it back.

'It's dark in here,' said Frost. 'Perhaps the light might be better down at the station.'

'All right. Haven't seen him for a while, but he used to be a regular. Every Wednesday just after five. His name's John Smith.'

'It's his John Thomas I'm interested in. What did he

pay for, Doris – straight sex, or did you have to tart it up, if you'll pardon the expression?'

'More or less straight sex – but I had to dress up.'

'As what?'

She crossed the room to a large fitted wardrobe and slid open the doors. Like the stock for a fancy dress ball, all sorts of bizarre costumes rustled and swung on hangers. On the floor of the wardrobe were whips, canes, a canvas strait-jacket, some handcuffs and various ropes, straps and chains. She selected a hanger and unhooked it from the rail. It held a black gym-slip, a white blouse, black knickers and thick dark stockings. 'He was kinky about schoolgirls,' she said. 'I had to wear this school uniform and act all bleeding coy. It didn't half get him excited.'

'It's getting me excited,' said Frost, standing up and stuffing the photograph of Bell back in his inside pocket. 'I only wish I had the time . . .'

Gilmore found Frost in the Murder Incident Room rummaging through the exhibits cupboard. 'You wanted me, Inspector?'

'Yes, son. Get the car. We're going to call on the schoolmaster.' He pulled out the plastic bag which held the shoes Paula Bartlett was wearing when they found her. He told Gilmore about his visit to the prostitute. 'That's clinched it for me, son. I'm going to nail the bastard.'

Gilmore hesitated. Frost's case was strong on suspicion, but pathetically weak on proof. 'How are you going to do that?'

'I might have to cheat a little,' said Frost, pushing the bag back into the exhibits cupboard, 'and if that doesn't work, I might have to cheat a lot.'

Bell led them through into his cold, cheerless lounge,

apologizing for the state of the place. 'I still haven't got over it.' He cleared some old newspapers from a chair, but they declined his invitation to sit.

'An official call, I'm afraid, sir,' said Frost, looking grim.

'Oh?' He straightened a few cushions and seemed more concerned at the state of the room than the unexpected visit of the two detectives.

'Probably nothing in it,' continued Frost. 'We get these crank calls all the time and we have to follow them up?

'Crank calls?' blinked Bell.

'Paula Bartlett, sir. We have a witness who claims he saw the girl in your house on the afternoon she went missing.'

'Here?' Bell frowned, finding the idea incredible. 'Oh no, Inspector, that's ridiculous.'

'I'm sure it's ridiculous,' continued Frost, 'but as I said, sir, we have to follow these things through. Just a formality, but do you mind if we have a look around the house?'

'Mind? Of course not. Look anywhere you like. It's all such a mess though, I'm afraid.'

'We're used to mess, sir,' Frost assured him. 'No need to come with us. We'll do it quicker on our own.' And he trotted up the stairs, Gilmore following close behind. The first door they tried led to the master bedroom, the unmade bed a shambles, discarded clothes everywhere. Frost grinned. 'This will do fine. Start searching.' He sat on the bed, smoking, as Gilmore poked around, dragging out the dressing table, peering behind the wardrobe.

'It would help,' grunted Gilmore, shouldering the wardrobe back into position, then climbing on a chair so he could look on the top, 'if I knew what I was supposed to be looking for.'

Frost puffed out three smoke rings then speared one with his finger. 'We're looking for proof the girl was in the house.'

Gilmore climbed down from the chair and rubbed the dust from his hands. 'We're never going to find it after two months.'

'I don't know,' said Frost, pushing himself up from the bed and wandering over to the dressing table. 'There's something poking out down there.'

He bent down and came up holding a shoe. A flat-heeled, lace-up brown shoe. Neatly written inside, in biro, the name 'Paula Bartlett'.

Gilmore stared in confusion. 'I looked there,' he said. 'I couldn't have missed it.' He snatched the shoe from Frost, his nose wrinkling in distaste as a clinging smell of decay floated up. 'This is one of the shoes we found on the body. You took it from the exhibits cupboard.'

'Keep your voice down,' hissed Frost.

'You're going to plant evidence?' croaked Gilmore. 'You fool! You'll never get away with it.' He thrust the shoe back into Frost's hand. 'You can forget it as far as I'm concerned. I want no part of it.'

'Play along with me,' pleaded Frost.

'No bloody way.' Gilmore's mind was racing. He couldn't wait to get back to the station. This was something Mullett had to be told about.

'Please!' said Frost.

The old twit looked so pathetic, Gilmore relented. 'Just don't involve me,' he said.

ell, slumped in a chair, straightened up as the two officers came back in. He forced out a smile which wasn't returned. The older detective's face was grim and gloom-laden. 'Is there anything the matter?'

Frost didn't answer. He just held out the shoe in mut
accusation.

Bell backed away, shaking his head in disbelief. 'I don
understand.'

'Paula was only wearing one shoe when we found he
sir. We kept this information from the press. In searchin
your bedroom we found this. It matches perfectly th
other shoe we found on the body.'

The schoolmaster's face was a picture of incredulit
'It's impossible. I don't understand . . .'

Frost felt the familiar, icy quiver of doubt. He was s
sure he had the killer that he hadn't fully considere
the serious consequences of what would happen if h
bluff failed. 'In your bedroom,' he repeated. 'There's n
way it could have got there by accident.' He was awar
of the irony even as he said it.

Still the man shook his head.

'I've had a chat with your prostitute friend, sir. Ver
interesting. Did your wife dress up in kinky schoolgi
clothes for you as well?'

Bell's head jerked back as if he had been struc'
He bit his lip tightly and shuddered, his face screwe
up as if on the verge of bursting into tears. He wer
through the pantomime of searching hopefully in th
empty cigarette box, then gratefully accepted one fro
Frost. 'We all do things we're ashamed of, Inspector.
was hurting no one. As I told you, my wife was incapab
of making love during the last months of her illness. I ha
to find an outlet somewhere.'

'And you found it in poor little Paula Bartlett? Yo
raped her.'

'No!' screamed Bell

'You strangled her, and rammed her in a sack like
much rubbish.'

'No! No, no, no.'

'So how did the shoe get in your bedroom?' asked Frost, hooking it on his finger and slowly swinging it from side to side.

Bell stared at Frost, his gaze unwavering. Because you put it there, you bastard, his expression seemed to say. Unflinching, Frost stared back. Gilmore's pen hovered over a page where nothing was written down.

Slowly, Bell pulled his eyes away from Frost, away from the shoe. He drew deeply on the cigarette, holding the smoke in his lungs, then gradually releasing it and watching the air currents catch it and tear it to shreds. Then he reached out a hand towards Frost. He wanted the shoe. He took it, turned it over slowly, then gave it back. 'You have a witness who saw her in the house?'

'Yes,' lied Frost.

He crushed out the cigarette in an ashtray and buried his face in his hands. 'I'd better tell you about it. Yes, Paula was here that day. I should never have kept quiet. It was stupid. But I was terrified you'd think I'd killed her. She was alive when she left here, I promise you.' Again he looked in the cigarette box, again seeming surprised to find it empty. Gratefully he accepted another from Frost.

'When I got back from the cemetery, I was soaked to the skin. There'd been a cloudburst during the funeral.'

Frost nodded. This part, at least, was true.

'To my surprise, Paula Bartlett was in the kitchen. All she was wearing was one of my dressing gowns and her shoes. She was putting her wet clothes in the tumble drier. She told me she'd been caught in the storm on her bike and had got absolutely drenched. She thought I wouldn't mind if she dried off in my house. I could have done without it that day of all days, but of course, I agreed.'

373

'How had she got in?' Frost asked.

'The back door wasn't locked.'

'Why was she out in the storm – she should have been at school?'

'She said she intended skipping the first lesson – she didn't like the relief teacher who was taking my place.'

'I see.' Frost signalled for him to continue.

'We had a meal from the deep freeze in the kitchen, then she went upstairs to put on her dry clothes. She left here shortly after one. I thought she was going straight to school. I last saw her pushing her bike up that path.' He pointed through the window. 'And that's the gospel truth, Inspector.'

'I don't think so, sir,' said Frost, shaking his head sadly and sounding genuinely sorry. 'You say she pedalled away into the sunset on her bike?'

'Yes!' insisted Bell.

'Wearing only one bloody shoe?' asked Frost, holding it accusingly under the man's nose.

Gilmore, his pen hovering, held his breath. Frost was pushing his luck. If the schoolmaster remembered both shoes were on the body, he'd realize that there was no way the other shoe could have been found in the bedroom and that Frost's case was built solely on a bluff.

But Frost's luck held. Bell was confused. His expression kept changing as various alternatives to his story flitted across his mind and were hastily discarded. His best bet would have been to keep quiet. To say nothing. To let the police do the proving. But he'd kept quiet for too long. He had to tell someone.

'The girl had sex before she died, sir,' Frost gently prompted. 'And we found her shoe in your bedroom.'

Bell shrank visibly, and stared down at the carpet. 'I'd like to make a statement.'

Concealing his relief, Frost gave the statutory caution and signalled for Gilmore to start a fresh page. 'When you're ready, sir.'

'We had lunch. I should have suspected something. Paula kept *"accidentally"* letting the dressing gown slip open. Then she went upstairs to get dressed. She called me. She was in our bedroom. Sitting on the bed. She was naked. She was wearing lipstick – thick lipstick. She looked like a child tart. The girl was offering herself to me.' He paused, then glared defiantly. 'What the hell! What the bloody hell! I suppose you think I'm some sort of animal?'

Frost said nothing.

The man's shoulders shook as he covered his face. 'When it comes down to it we're all bloody animals.' He stood up and stared out of the window. 'We made love. Half-way through she began to struggle. She yelled for me to stop. Then she started screaming rape. I panicked. I grabbed her by the throat to stop her screaming. We struggled. She wouldn't stop screaming. Suddenly she went still. I must have squeezed too hard. I didn't mean it . . . as God is my witness, I didn't mean it. I tried the kiss of life, I tried everything . . . but she was dead.'

'Did you think of sending for a doctor?' asked Frost.

'A doctor?' Bell frowned and his hand flicked away the question as futile. 'It would have been no use. She was dead.' He paused. The only sound in the room was the slight rustle as Gilmore turned the page of his notebook. Bell's head twisted to the sergeant, as if suddenly realizing that everything he was saying was being taken down. 'I didn't know what to do. I was so frightened . . . so appalled. I tried to think. I had to find somewhere to hide the body and I suddenly thought of that crypt. I thought it would at least be a Christian place of burial for

375

the poor child.' At this Frost gave an involuntary snort of derision, but Bell didn't care what Frost thought. This was the statement that would be read out in court, the statement the jury would hear. 'That night, I took the poor child's remains out to the car and drove to the cemetery. As reverently as possible I put her in the crypt. I said a prayer for her. I never meant to hurt her.'

'Before you did that, you reverently burnt the poor child with a blow-lamp,' said Frost. 'What sort of kindly, Christian act was that?'

He bowed his head. 'Genetic fingerprints. I'd read somewhere you could positively identify a sperm sample. I was trying to destroy the evidence.'

'The newspapers?' prompted Frost.

'I wanted it to look as if she hadn't finished her round, so I took the newspaper she had brought and put it in her bag, meaning to dump it somewhere with the bike. As I was passing Greenway's cottage, I noticed his paper sticking out of the letter-box, so I took that as well.' He waited until Gilmore's pen had finished writing this all down before adding, 'I bitterly regret the pain and anguish I caused Paula's family. It was an accident. I shall live with the scars for the rest of my life.'

Frost stood up and took him by the arm. 'So will the poor cow's parents, sir.' They helped him on with his coat and led him out to the car.

Mullett was angry. He paced up and down Frost's tiny office, shaking with rage. 'I've told you time and time again, Frost, catching the criminal isn't enough. We've got to be able to prove our case in court. What on earth did you think you were doing?'

'I thought I was solving a murder case,' answered

Frost. He didn't expect praise, but he was unprepared for Mullett's fury.

'By slipshod, unorthodox methods? By sneaking official evidence from the evidence cupboard? Planting it in a suspect's house? For heaven's sake, man, don't you realize the risk?'

'Risk?' asked Frost.

'What other solid evidence do you have against him apart from his own admission?'

'Nothing yet,' said Frost.

'Has he signed the statement he's given you?'

'Not yet. It's being typed now.' He nodded towards Gilmore who was typing at speed and pretending not to listen to Frost's bollocking. He ripped the last page from the machine and hurried from the room.

'What if he refuses to sign?' demanded Mullett. 'What if he decides to plead not guilty in court and claims that the statement was obtained by means of a trick . . . by the planting of false evidence? If this all blows up in our faces, Inspector, I'm distancing myself from the whole affair. It was done behind my back, against official instructions and contrary to my specific orders. Don't expect me to carry the can for your shortcomings. Don't expect me to stand by you.'

'I'd never expect that, sir,' said Frost, and he had never sounded more sincere. He looked up anxiously as Gilmore came back, the statement in his hand. 'Well?'

'He signed it,' said Gilmore, slipping the typescript in a folder.

'He can still retract it,' snapped Mullett, cutting short Frost's audible sigh of relief. 'And then we haven't got a shred of legitimate evidence against him.'

'We've got quite a bit, sir, actually,' said Gilmore.

'Forensic have just phoned an interim report. They've turned his house over and found strands of the girl's hair on the plush velvet headboard of the bed. Bell had changed and washed all the bedding, but there's definite traces of blood on the mattress corresponding to the girl's blood group.'

'Oh!' said Mullett, sounding almost disappointed. 'That's . . . good news. Perhaps more than you deserve, Inspector, but good news.' He took the statement from Gilmore and ran his eye over it.

'I almost feel sorry for the poor sod,' said Frost.

Mullett's eyebrows arched. 'You feel sorry?'

'A choice young naked piece of nooky offering herself. I wouldn't like to bet I'd have turned my nose up at it,' said Frost. 'Just his rotten luck she turned out to be a teaser.'

'That's just Bell's version. You surely don't believe it?'

'Yes, I do.' He turned to Gilmore. 'He said she'd put on lipstick. Do you remember when we searched Paula's room – in her wastepaper bin?'

Gilmore thought, then nodded. He remembered. 'An empty lipstick packet!'

'Plain little Paula never used make-up! The poor cow had a crush on him. She had it all planned in advance what she was going to do. And now she's dead, his life is ruined and when it all comes out in court it will break her parents' hearts. I thought I was going to enjoy bringing the bastard in on this one, but now . . .' He shrugged and pulled open his drawer for a packet of export only.

Mullett gave an uneasy smile. He didn't quite see what Frost was driving at. 'Another crime solved, and that's all that matters, Inspector.'

The phone rang. Gilmore answered it, then offered it to Mullett. 'For you, sir. The Chief Constable.'

Mullett tugged his uniform straight and stiffened as he

took the phone. 'Yes, sir . . . we've got him . . . and he's given us a full confession. And I modestly claim credit for our team work, sir. The good old Denton team have turned up trumps again.' He listened and smirked, oblivious to the faces Frost was pulling behind his back.

The other phone rang. Frost answered it. He listened and his face went grim. He snatched his mac from the hat-stand and jerked a thumb for Gilmore to follow. 'Another Ripper victim. An old lady. The bastard's nearly decapitated her.'

It was like seeing the same tired B-movie over and over again. The tiny over-furnished room. The smell, a mixture of blood and of too many people packed in too restricted a space. The atmosphere was frowsty with sweat, aftershave and tobacco smoke. 'Open a window,' yelled Frost. 'It stinks in here.'

Everyone was busy. The SOC officer, draped with an array of Japanese cameras and leather cylinders of lenses, blazing away with a Canon, the Forensic team, crawling over the carpet, the fingerprint man, whistling tunelessly to himself as he dusted away with his little brush, splashing white powder everywhere. Frost had almost to fight his way through to the corpse. 'Everyone outside,' he yelled. 'You can come back in when I've finished.' He waited while they shuffled out, then he approached the body.

She sat in the rust and grey armchair, her dull eyes fixed on an old 19-inch black and white television set which, encircled by a stockade of knick-knacks and framed photographs, stood on a rickety coffee table. Frost touched the set. It was still warm.

'It was still on when I got here,' said Detective Constable Burton. 'I switched it off.'

Frost nodded and haunched down to study the Ripper's

handiwork. A jagged gash on her neck had gouted blood which glinted stickily down the front of her brown floral dress. Blood from stab wounds in her stomach had leaked to form a puddle on her lap. Her left hand dangled down the side of the chair, the fist tightly clenched. His eyes travelled slowly up to her face, the wrinkled flesh bluish white against her sparse grey hair. He leaned closer to examine the hair, which was in untidy disarray. 'What do you make of that, son?' Gilmore crouched down beside him.

'He came on her from behind,' said a familiar voice and they looked up at the slightly swaying figure of Dr Maltby who had been waiting in the bedroom. He nodded a greeting, then prodded a finger at her hair. 'The killer came at her from behind, grabbed her hair and yanked up her head. Then he cut her throat. The head's only hanging by a thread of flesh at the back of the neck, so I wouldn't shake her if I were you.'

They backed gingerly away from the body, Frost carefully lowering himself into the matching armchair.

'When he cut her throat,' continued the doctor, 'he sliced through her vocal cords in the process, so she wouldn't have been able to scream, even if she wanted to.'

'I'm sure she bloody wanted to,' said Frost, poking a cigarette in his mouth and passing the packet around. 'I reckon the poor cow would have given her right arm to have been able to scream.'

Grunting his thanks, Maltby accepted a light and moved round to face the body. 'The killer then came round to here and stabbed her four times in the stomach.' He mimed four stabbing thrusts. 'That done, being a neat and tidy person, while she was still bleeding to death and drowning in her own blood, he wiped the knife blade clean, just there.' He indicated a wide smear on the skirt of the dress.

Frost took this all in with a sniff. 'I won't ask how you deduced all that, doc, because I don't suppose I'd understand a flaming word. Time of death?'

Gently, the doctor felt the woman's legs. 'Rigor's fully developed and she feels cold. It would need rectal temperature readings to be precise, but I shall leave that treat to our pathologist friend . . . he can be the one to have her head fall off in his lap. At a rough guess she's been dead fourteen to eighteen hours.' He jerked back his sleeve to read his watch. 'Say between nine o'clock last night and one o'clock this morning.'

Frost dropped to his knees and, very carefully, lifted the woman's left arm. 'Look at the way her fist is clenched.'

'Show me,' said Maltby, lowering himself, none too steadily and kneeling on the floor. He took the hand and focused his eyes with difficulty. 'Looks like a cadaveric spasm . . . you sometimes get it with violent death. Hello . . .' He looked closer. Something white. The corner of a piece of paper was protruding slightly. Frost snatched the hand and tried to force the cold fingers open.

Maltby stood up and distanced himself from the operation. 'Careful,' he said. 'You'll have her damn head off.'

Frost snapped his fingers at Gilmore. 'Hold her head, son.'

'Eh?' said Gilmore.

'She won't bloody bite you.'

Steeling himself, Gilmore took the head in his hands while Frost tugged at the tightly closed fingers. The head felt cold and as fragile as a blown egg. He gritted his teeth and willed the inspector to hurry.

'The pathologist won't like you interfering with his corpse,' warned Maltby gleefully.

'Sod the pathologist,' muttered Frost, grunting as the fingers opened and the hand suddenly went limp. Gilmore almost cried out as the body seemed to quiver and he swore he could feel the head parting from the trunk. Carefully and very slowly, like a man building a tottering house of cards, he took his hands away.

The piece of paper fluttered to the ground. It was a carefully folded £5 note. There was something else pressed tightly into the palm, leaving an impression in the flesh. Three pound coins.

Frost placed the coins in his open palm and stared at them. They told him nothing. He retrieved the banknote from the floor, pushed all the money back into the dead hand and tried to close the fist around it so the pathologist wouldn't know what he had done. But the dead hand remained limp and let the money drop.

'You've done it now,' called Maltby, moving quickly to the door. 'If you'd asked me I'd have told you that you couldn't put it back again.'

'I'll throw the bloody head at you if you don't hop it,' bellowed Frost as the door clicked shut.

Gathering up the money, he deposited it on the coffee table alongside the knick-knacks, then sank back in the chair. 'All right, Burton, let's have some details. I don't even know the poor cow's name.'

Burton flipped open his notebook. 'Mrs Julia Fussell, aged seventy-five, a widow, one son, married, two kids.'

Frost groaned. 'Don't tell me I've got to break the news to him.'

'He emigrated to Australia last year.'

Frost brightened up. 'Good for him. Carry on, son. Who found her?'

'Her next-door neighbour, Mrs Beatrice Stacey. She knocked to see if the old dear wanted any shopping, didn't get a reply, so let herself in with a spare key. I haven't got much sense out of her. She's having hysterics next door.'

'I'll see her in a minute,' said Frost.

'The pattern's the same as Mrs Watson, yesterday,' Burton went on. 'No sign of forcible entry, apparently nothing taken – the bedroom's undisturbed – and money left in her purse.'

A glum nod from Frost. He wandered over to the front door which was fitted with bolts top and bottom, and a security chain. 'As you say, son, exactly the same as that poor old cow yesterday. He comes late at night, but she lets him in and then she calmly sits down to watch the telly so he can creep up behind her and cut her bloody throat.' He examined the security chain. Quite a flimsy affair. 'You said her purse was untouched. Where is it?'

Burton walked over to a small walnut-veneered sideboard and tugged open a drawer. Using his handkerchief, he took out a worn red leather purse and handed it to the inspector. 'There's eighty-five quid in there.'

Holding it by the handkerchief, Frost flicked through the banknotes. All new £5 notes, crisp and consecutively numbered. The numbers tallied with the note taken from her hand. He chewed at a loose scrap of skin on his finger as he thought this over. 'Right. Try this out for size. It's the same pattern as yesterday. The Ripper's coming to fit a new security chain for her. She's waiting for him, the money all ready from her purse. She lets him in, sits down, holding the money tight in her hot little hand, and watches the telly while the nice man fits the chain for her. But the nice man just creeps up behind the poor cow and cuts her throat, then he stabs her in the stomach, wipes his knife on her dress and off he goes, all happy.'

'Then this puts Gauld in the clear,' said Gilmore. 'He was driving his coach until ten and we watched his house until past midnight.'

'He could have gone out again after we left,' said Frost, furious with himself for giving up the surveillance so early. 'If Doc Maltby is right the time of death could have been as late as one o'clock.'

'You don't call at one in the morning to fit a chain,' pointed out Gilmore. 'And old girls of seventy-five don't sit up all night watching television.'

Frost gave a rueful sniff. The sergeant was right. This was his star suspect flushed down the sewer. He pushed the money back into the purse, then noticed something else in the centre compartment. Membership cards for the Reef Bingo Club and for the All Saints Senior Citizens' Club.

'All Saints?' exclaimed Gilmore excitedly. Frost's suspect might be a non-runner, but his own one was fast coming up on the rails. 'That bloody curate comes from All Saints.'

The pathologist studied the rectal thermometer, gave it a shake, then wiped it clean before replacing it in his bag. His lips moved silently as he did a mental calculation. 'In my opinion death occurred between midnight and one o'clock this morning.'

Gilmore registered dismay. 'Not earlier?' They had seen the curate outside the cemetery just after midnight last night and it was over half an hour later that they left him to go on to the vicarage.

'If it was earlier,' sniffed the pathologist, snapping shut his bag, 'then I would have said so.' He shouted down the stairs for the mortuary attendants to come up and collect the body then shafted a glare of disapproval

384

at Frost who had come bounding back into the flat, grinning all over his face. 'I've relayed my preliminary findings to your sergeant.'

'Thanks, doc,' said Frost, not sounding very interested. He grabbed Gilmore by the arm and pulled him to one side.

'Autopsy at four,' called the pathologist, buttoning up his coat.

'Right,' said Frost. He wasn't interested in the autopsy. By four o'clock the killer should be behind bars.

But Gilmore got in with his own bad news first. 'Death occurred after midnight, so that clears the curate.' He waved away Frost's offered cigarette. 'So now we haven't got a single flaming suspect.'

'Yes, we have, son,' beamed Frost, sending his cigarette packet on a round tour of the room. 'Our luck had to change some time and now it's happened. I've been chatting up the old dear next door. First, the dead woman had a job getting off to sleep. She was always up watching television until three or four in the morning. Second, she'd told her neighbour she was going to have a stronger chain fitted and guess who was going to do it?'

'Gauld?'

'She didn't know his name but it was that nice young man who drove the mini-coach that took her to bingo.'

'Did she say when he was coming to do the job?'

'No, son. But he came last night. Late. After Joe Soap pulled off the bloody surveillance.'

'How do you know?'

'She didn't tell her neighbour *when* he was coming. But she told her how much he was going to charge her. Eight quid.'

Gilmore whistled. The £5 note and three pound coins in the dead hand. 'It sounds too good to be true.'

'You know my motto,' smirked Frost. 'Never kick a gift horse up the fundamental orifice.' He noticed Burton hovering. 'What is it, son?'

'Forensic have turned up a rogue fingerprint, sir. On the sideboard. Looks recent.'

Frost beamed. 'Luck could be running our way for once. I think the time has come to bring Gauld in.'

Friday afternoon shift

The coach drew up at the old lady's house. The driver sprang from his seat and opened the door, steadying her as she descended the steep step from the coach to the pavement. 'Can you manage all right from here, my love?' he asked. She nodded and waved her thanks and hobbled up to her front gate as the coach went on its way.

There was only one other passenger. A dishevelled individual hunched up in the rear seat, puffing away solidly on the journey back from the bingo hall. Gauld hadn't seen him before. He slowed down at the traffic lights. Damn. The scruffy man was making his way down the aisle. Not one of those chatty sods, he hoped. The seat behind him creaked as the man lowered himself down.

'Drop you off at the Market Square?' Gauld asked.

'Eagle Lane,' mumbled the man. 'Opposite the police station.'

As he turned into Eagle Lane he noticed in his rear-view mirror a police car close behind him. When he pulled up outside the police station, the car stopped even though it had plenty of room to pass. His passenger shuffled out, squeezing past two uniformed policemen who suddenly appeared at the coach door. 'Mr Ronald Gauld?' asked one of them. 'I wonder if you'd mind popping into the station for a couple of minutes.' The other policeman leant across and switched off the ignition.

They took him through to a small, functional room, sparsely furnished with a plain light oak table and three chairs. In the corner of the room a young thickset chap in a grey suit was sitting, a notebook open on his knee. Another man, whose scowl seemed permanent, was standing, leaning up against the wall. He pointed to a chair for Gauld to sit. The door opened as a third man came in. Gauld blinked in surprise. It was the scruffy passenger from his coach. 'Frost,' announced the man, 'Detective Inspector Jack Frost.'

The lino squealed as Frost dragged a chair over to sit opposite Gauld. He then laid out on the table a green folder, a pack of cigarettes, a box of matches and the large manila envelope containing the possessions the station sergeant had asked Gauld to empty from his pockets. This done, Frost smiled benevolently and helped himself to a cigarette.

Gauld wriggled in his chair. He cleared his throat and tried to keep his voice steady. 'What's this all about?'

Frost frowned. 'Haven't you been told?' He swung round to the man with the notebook. 'Didn't you tell him?' A headshake. Frost tutted with mock exasperation, then slowly took a match from the box and struck it on the table. 'It's about Mrs Fussell.'

Gauld frowned as if trying to remember. 'Never heard of her.'

'Oh dear,' exclaimed Frost, looking worried. He turned to the scowler. 'We might have the wrong man, Sergeant.' Looking puzzled, he scrabbled through the green folder and plucked out some typed pages. 'All these witnesses must be lying.' Back to Gauld. 'You'd swear on oath you don't know her, sir?' Before Gauld had a chance to answer, he added, 'What about Mrs Elizabeth Winters, Roman Road, Denton? Surely you're not going to tell us you don't know her?'

'I know lots of people. I'm a coach driver. I drive people about all the time. I don't necessarily know their names.'

'Then here's an easy one – Mary Haynes.'

'I've just told . . .' He blinked and stopped dead, his expression freezing as if he had just realized what the inspector was on about. 'Wait a minute! I've just twigged. Haynes . . . Winters! They were both murdered! Are you trying to pin them on me?'

'Yes,' replied Frost, simply. 'That's exactly what we're trying to do.' He shook out the contents of the manila envelope and raked through Gauld's possessions. There was a colour photograph of a grey-haired lady smiling doubtfully at the camera. He picked it up and studied it carefully. 'I don't recognize this one. When did you murder her?'

Gauld snatched up the photograph. 'That's my mother, you bastard!'

'Ah!' said Frost with an enlightened nod. He studied his notes. 'Father died when you were three, mother alive and well.'

'She's not well!' retorted Gauld. 'She's got a bad heart.'

'Sorry to hear that,' said Frost. 'Still, better a bad heart than having your throat cut. Any objection to our taking your fingerprints?'

'What happens if I object?'

'We'll take them anyway, so why cause bad feeling?'

A young uniformed officer was summoned to take the prints. Frost waited patiently until the task was completed, then whispered something to the officer who nodded and left.

'I ought to have a solicitor,' said Gauld.

Frost seemed astonished. 'You're innocent! What do you want a solicitor for?'

'Because I think you bastards are trying to frame me for something I haven't done, that's why.'

'Oh no.' Frost sounded hurt. 'I might frame you for something you had done, but not otherwise.'

The scowler moved forward. 'All the murder victims travelled on your coach.'

Gauld twisted in his chair to face the questioner. 'So what? Hundreds of people travel on my coach.'

'Where were you last Sunday afternoon?' barked the detective sergeant.

'I don't know,' smirked Gauld. 'Where were you?'

The door opened and the fingerprint man returned to murmur in the inspector's ear. Frost's eyes gleamed with satisfaction. 'All right, Gauld. You can stop the pretence. We've got you.'

'Have you really? he said cockily. 'I'm shaking with fright.'

'You'll be shitting yourself in a minute,' said Frost. 'You told me earlier you didn't know a Mrs Julia Fussell.'

'I said I didn't know the name.'

'You were going to fit a stronger security chain on her front door.'

Gauld leant back in his chair. 'Ah – now I'm with you. Little old dear – about seventy-five. Lives in Victoria Court.'

'So you do know her!' said Gilmore.

'I didn't know her name. I always call her Ma.' He

looked disturbed. 'What about her? Nothing's happened to her, has it?'

'You called on her late last night to fit the security chain.'

'No, I didn't. I was going to, but I felt tired, so I had an early night.'

Gilmore, standing directly behind him, bent down. 'You lying bastard. You went there and killed her.'

Gauld's knuckles whitened as he gripped the edge of his chair. 'Killed? You mean . . . she's dead? That poor old lady is dead?'

'Don't act the bloody innocent. You know damn well she's dead,' hissed Gilmore.

Gauld just stared straight ahead, slack-jawed, head moving from side to side in disbelief. Then his eyes narrowed. 'And you're accusing me of killing her?'

'That's right,' beamed Frost. 'You got careless this time. You left a fingerprint behind.'

'A fingerprint!' echoed Gauld, eyes wide open as if understanding for the first time. 'So that's why you think I'm the killer? Would you like me to give you a statement?'

'If you want to give us one, we'll take it down, sir,' said Frost, signalling to Burton who turned to a fresh page in his notebook. Frost was vaguely worried. The man was looking far too smug and self-assured. Could he possibly have made a mistake? No. His every instinct told him that this smirking little bastard had cut, slashed and mutilated.

When he saw Burton was ready, Gauld began. 'I am making this statement freely, without any inducements being offered, solely to help the police find the perpetrator of this terrible crime.' He paused to let Burton catch up with him. 'On 14th November, around ten o'clock in the evening, I was returning from the Reef Bingo Club with a party of senior citizens. Amongst my passengers was a lady I now know to be Mrs Julia Fussell, who expressed herself as being very nervous because of the killings of old people that were taking place and which the police seemed powerless to prevent. When we pulled up outside her destination, Victoria Court, I offered to escort her up to her flat. She accepted. At her door, she gave me her key. I opened the door, had a quick look around inside, and was able to assure her that all was well. I told her that her door chain was inadequate and suggested I fitted a stronger one when I got the chance. She accepted my offer. I then returned to my coach and continued dropping off my passengers. This may serve to explain why my fingerprints were found inside the flat and assist the police to eliminate me from their enquiries so they can concentrate on finding the real killer.'

A pause. The detectives shuffled their feet and cleared their throats. Gilmore shot a glance across to Frost who was looking very worried. 'You're saying that this happened on the 14th . . . the day before the killing?'

'That's right. I've got a coach-load of witnesses if you don't believe me.'

'We'll check them out,' said Frost, but he knew they would corroborate Gauld's story. This slimy sod was too clever by half and Frost wasn't anywhere near clever enough. He tugged the list of murder dates and times from the folder and began rattling them off one by one. 'Where were you on these dates?'

Gauld shrugged. 'I don't know. Probably at work, driving.'

'You weren't,' barked Gilmore. 'We've checked.'

Mockingly, Gauld knuckled his brow, then beamed. 'If

I wasn't at work, then I probably stayed in and kept my mother company. I'll ask her when I get home.'

'We can save you the trouble,' Frost told him. 'We've got a team searching your house now. One of my men is having a word with your dear old mum this very minute.' He jerked back as Gauld lunged forward, all composure gone.

'My mother's got a heart condition. If any harm comes to her, I'll kill you . . .'

'You know all about killing, don't you,' said Frost, getting in quickly while the man was rattled.

The only sound was Gauld's heavy breathing as he fought to control his temper. Then he smiled. 'I'm not taking any more of your insults, Inspector. You either charge me, or I'm walking straight out of that door.'

'You'll go when I say you can go,' snapped Frost, frowning as someone knocked. He didn't want to be disturbed. He wanted to get Gauld rattled again. The door opened. Detective Sergeant Hanlon, not looking like a man with good news to impart, beckoned him out. Hanlon had been leading the team searching Gauld's house.

'We tore the house apart,' reported Hanlon. 'We found nothing. No bank books, no money we can tie in with the killing, no sign of blood on his clothes or shoes . . . nothing!'

'There must be some bloodstains,' insisted Frost. 'The pathologist said he would have been swimming in the bleeding stuff.'

'Forensic have double-checked. Not a trace. And to make matters worse, his mother swears blind he was with her on each of the murder nights.'

'Then she's lying,' said Frost. 'He's as guilty as arse-holes.' He scuffed the brown lino moodily. 'What about his car? Did you check that for blood?'

Hanlon nodded. 'Forensic have given it the works – nothing.'

Frost treated the lino to an extra hard kick. Things were not working out. His heart sank as the brisk clatter of polished shoes announced the approach of the Divisional Commander, all eager for news of yet another triumph for the Denton team.

'We've hit a couple of minor snags,' Frost told him. 'We've found sod all clues and his mother's given him a watertight alibi.'

Mullett's jaw dropped. 'But you told me you had conclusive evidence. A fingerprint!'

'It wasn't so conclusive as we thought, Super. He explained it away.'

'The house search?'

'We found nothing,' said Hanlon.

Mullett switched his gaze from Hanlon to Frost. 'So what hard evidence have you got?'

Frost shuffled his feet. All he now had was a gut reaction. He knew Gauld was the Ripper. He couldn't prove it, but he knew.

'Your silence gives me the answer I expected,' snapped Mullett. 'You've blown this, Frost. You jumped in feet first without checking your facts. If he is the Ripper, which is by no means certain, all you've done is put him on his guard. Without evidence, there's no way we can hold him.' His lips tightened. 'Thank goodness Inspector Allen is coming back on Monday and we can start getting things done properly.' He spun on his heel and marched back up the corridor, pausing only to punch out one last below-the-belt blow. 'The inventory?'

'Almost done,' called Frost.

'I can tell County it will go off tonight?'

'Without fail,' Frost assured him. Tell the buggers what they want to hear, then make your excuses later was his philosophy. Absently, he pulled out his cigarettes, only to realize he was already smoking.

'What are you going to do?' asked Hanlon.

'I'm nipping round to see Gauld's mother and try and get her to change her story.'

'Be careful – she's got a weak heart,' Hanlon reminded him.

'And I've got a weak bladder, so that makes us quits.' Halfway down the corridor he turned and yelled, 'Probably a waste of time, but send someone down to check out the Oxfam shop where Gauld works.'

Gauld's house was just round the corner from Jubilee Terrace where they had found the mummified body all those weeks . . . no days . . . ago. A small cul-de-sac of older-type properties, jammed on both sides of the road with parked cars so Frost had to leave the station runabout round the corner.

The hinges of the black iron gate grated as he walked through. The woman who answered the door stepped back in alarm. She had been expecting the return of her son and here was this man in a dirty mac, a knitted maroon scarf trailing untidily from his neck. She was about to shut the door on him when he held up a piece of plastic with a coloured photograph on it. 'Detective Inspector Frost,' he announced.

She peered at the photograph, then at the man. There was a slight resemblance. 'I've had enough of police. Where's my son?'

He gave his reassuring smile. 'Ronnie's fine. He's having a cup of tea down at the station.'

'I've got his supper waiting,' she said.

Frost sniffed the savoury warm smell floating from inside the house. 'Lucky devil. I'd like a couple of words, if I may.'

She took another look at his warrant card. 'Are you *sure* you're a policeman?'

'Fairly sure,' said Frost, following her down the passage, 'although my boss has his doubts at times.'

The radio was mumbling away, just around the limit of audibility. The tiny kitchen was warm from the gas oven which breathed out sausage and onion. On the small table a red and white checked cloth was laid with knife and fork and HP sauce. One place only. Frost unwound his scarf, pulled the green file from his pocket and sat down. He sniffed again. 'Smells good.'

She opened the oven door and peeked inside. 'It'll spoil soon. When is he coming home?'

'Difficult to say,' Frost hedged. She moved a chair to the table and sat opposite him. Grey-haired, she was probably in her early sixties, but looked older. A nervous smile twitched on and off and her hands were constantly moving, plucking at her apron, smoothing out the table-cloth, straightening the knife and fork. A bag of nerves, he thought. He tried his smile out again. 'I'm not stopping you from making us both a cup of tea, am I?'

'You've got a cheek!' she said. But she filled the kettle from the sink. 'This isn't a restaurant, you know.' A plop as she lit the gas. 'Why are you still holding him?'

'Murder is a very serious charge, Mrs Gauld.' Her back stiffened as she reached for the tea caddy, but her face was composed and apparently unconcerned when she turned. From the hooks on the dresser she took two cups, her hands shaking a little as she set them down.

'He's a good boy,' she said flatly, 'a very good boy.'

A larger version of the photograph taken from Gauld's

wallet looked down from the top of the dresser. 'Does he miss his father?' asked Frost.

She frowned. 'His father died when Ronnie was three. He hardly remembers him.'

Frost 'tutted' sympathetically. 'He couldn't have been very old. How did he die?'

She looked away. 'He killed himself.' At Frost's start of surprise, she added, 'He used to get very depressed. He threw himself under a train at New Street station.'

'And you had to bring Ronnie up on your own?'

The tea in the pot was given a vigorous stir. 'I had to go to work. His gran brought him up.' She put the lid back on the teapot and filled the two cups. 'It wasn't a very happy time for him. She was very strict. She used to beat him. Poor little mite.' She pushed the tea across.

'I'm sorry to hear that.' He tried to conceal his excitement, but his hand wasn't steady as he spooned in the sugar. Whatever vague doubts he might have had about Gauld being the Ripper were now dispelled. He endeavoured to keep his voice casual. 'I suppose, being beaten by his granny made him hate old people?'

Her expression changed. 'What are you trying to make me say?'

'We both know what this is about, Mrs Gauld. He's your son and you want to protect him. I understand that. But he's killed four people. He could kill more.'

She thrust out her chin defiantly. 'Drink your tea and go!'

Frost took out the list of dates of the killings and waved it at her. 'You didn't tell my colleague the truth, Mrs Gauld. Ronnie wasn't with you on any of these nights. He was out killing old people. He gets a kick out of it.'

'I don't tell lies,' she said. He stared at her. She wouldn't meet his gaze and turned her head away.

He opened the green folder and dealt out the colour photographs of the victims. 'Look at these,' he ordered, jabbing the worst of them with his thumb. 'This is what your precious boy is doing to get his own back on granny.'

He heard her gasp with horror and then the gasp changed to an ominous choking sound. He looked up in alarm. Her face was contorted and blue and she was clutching at her chest. A heart attack! The old dear was suffering a heart attack. 'Where's your bloody tablets?' he shouted.

A gargling sound from her throat. Her finger shook weakly in the direction of the dresser.

By the time he had found them, she was slumped unconscious in her chair. He slipped the wafer thin tablet under her tongue, his other hand digging in his pocket for his radio. 'Frost to Control.' He paused. He couldn't remember the damned address. 'I'm at Gauld's place. Send a bloody ambulance quick.'

Mullett was feeling feverish. This wretched business with Gauld's mother couldn't have come at a worse time. The smoke from Frost's cigarette wafted across and made him cough, and when he coughed, his head ached. He fanned the smoke away pointedly. Frost took the cigarette from his mouth, flicked ash all over the carpet, then replaced it. The phone rang. Mullett snatched it up, his expression hardly changing as he listened. 'Thank you.' He hung up, then stared grimly across to Frost. 'That was the hospital. A very mild attack. They're keeping her in overnight for observation, but will probably send her home in the morning.'

Frost dropped down in the chair, almost sweating with relief. 'Thank God for that. I'll try her again tomorrow. I think I can bust the alibi story.'

Mullett took off his glasses and wearily rubbed his eyes. 'You're going nowhere near her. You've caused enough trouble. You knew she had a heart condition, yet you showed her those horrific photographs.'

'Of people butchered by her son. Don't worry, Super. I'll be gentle with her next time.'

'There's not going to be a next time,' said Mullett emphatically, thumping the desk and wincing as it made his head ache.

'I need to break his alibi,' insisted Frost.

'Even if you broke his alibi. Even if his mother confirmed he was out on each and every one of the murder nights, that simply means he *could* have killed the victims . . . you still don't have a shred of proof which says that he *did* kill them. I want proof, Frost, not suspicion, not gut reaction – good, old-fashioned solid proof.'

'Let me talk to her and I'll get your proof.'

'No!' Mullett's head was now throbbing constantly and he wished the inspector would accept the position and leave him alone.

'Without proof, I'll have to let Gauld go,' said Frost despairingly.

'That', said Mullett curtly, 'is your problem.' He winced as the door slammed behind Frost and set his headache roaring off again. He could feel the sweat beading his brow as he tugged open the drawer for the aspirins. It was this wretched virus, he knew it, but if he went down, then that would leave Frost as the senior officer. And there was no way he was letting Frost run the division.

Gilmore was waiting for him outside the interview room. 'Gauld's shut up like a clam. He's going to sue us for what we did to his mother and he's not saying another word unless we get him a solicitor.'

'We're letting him go,' said Frost. He filled the sergeant in on his interview with Mullett. 'But I still want him tailed twenty-four hours a day. At best we might get the bloody proof we want. At worst we can probably stop him killing another poor sod until Mr Allen returns on Monday and takes over the case.'

'Will I be transferring to him?' asked Gilmore, hopefully.

'I'm afraid so,' said Frost.

Gilmore tried to look disappointed.

'We haven't got the men to carry out a twenty-four hour surveillance,' said Johnny Johnson.

'You'll have to find them,' said Frost. 'Plain-clothes, uniformed, dog-handlers, walking wounded . . . I don't care. The important thing is we don't let the bastard out of our sight even for a second.'

'Are you sure he's the Ripper?' asked Johnson. 'A fine lot of fools we'd look with the entire force following the wrong man while the Ripper kills someone else.'

'Trust me,' said Frost.

'I've trusted you before, Jack, and you've dropped me right in the muck.' He sighed. 'But I'll see what I can do.'

The phone rang. Burton from the Oxfam shop. 'Can you come over, Inspector? There's a locked cupboard here full of stuff belonging to Gauld, and I can't get it open.'

'We're off to the Oxfam shop,' Frost called to Johnson.

'Buying another suit?' called Johnson after them.

* * *

The Oxfam shop used to be a carpeting and furniture retailers until the firm went broke. Pushing past racks of used clothing and stacks of kitchen utensils, Frost and Gilmore, hastily pursued by the manageress, a thin, angular woman in a green overall, followed Burton to the rear of the shop where he led them down a short flight of stone steps to the basement. There, Burton clicked a switch and an unshaded bulb lit up a small, stone-flagged room in which an old-fashioned solid fuel boiler, belching sulphurous fumes, clanked away, a heap of anthracite glittering at its side. To the left of the boiler was another door which took them into a narrow passage where six metal lockers, painted light grey, backed against one wall.

'That one is Gauld's.' Burton indicated the last locker in the row.

Frost examined the solid-looking padlock and fumbled in his pocket for his bunch of keys.

The manageress looked uneasy. 'I presume you've got a warrant?'

'Yes,' said Frost, curtly, staring back at her, defying her to ask to see it. The second key did the trick. He turned the handle. The manageress pushed forward, eyes goggling. 'You'd better keep back, madam. It might be a body.' Alarmed, she hopped back, stepping on Gilmore's toe as she did so.

'Abracadabra,' said Frost and pulled open the door.

The locker was crammed tight with men's clothing; jackets, trousers, shirts, assorted styles and colours. Some of the clothing was old and threadbare, some in reasonable condition, all second-hand.

The manageress gasped and stared open-mouthed.

'Looks as if he's been nicking your stock, madam,' suggested Frost.

'I can't understand it. Ronnie seemed such a nice boy. I'd have trusted him with my life.'

'Lots of people thought the same,' smiled Frost. 'What exactly did he do here?'

'He drove our little van – collected items that people wanted to give to Oxfam. And he would deliver some of the larger items that people bought. Oh, and he helped with the boiler . . . keeping it well stoked.'

'Sounds a little treasure,' said Frost. 'I wouldn't worry too much about the clothes. I'm sure he's got a good explanation.' He cocked his head to one side. 'I think I can hear a customer in the shop.' As soon as she had left he began examining the clothing. 'It's all about Gauld's size – he was taking it for himself.'

'So he's been pinching the stock,' sniffed Gilmore. 'Big deal.'

'You're missing the point, son.' Frost was getting excited. He held up a pair of torn and paint-splattered jeans. 'Much of this is rubbish. So why did he nick it?'

'I give up,' shrugged Gilmore, not sounding very interested.

'None of his own clothes were bloodstained. Supposing he kept a supply of old clothes that he could change into just for his Ripper jobs?'

Gilmore's eyes widened. 'And after each job he disposed of them in the boiler! It's so simple, it's almost brilliant.'

They went back to the boiler room. 'Any point shutting this thing down?' Gilmore asked. 'We could rake through the ashes. There'll be bits that don't burn . . . buckles . . . clips . . . zips.'

'It wouldn't prove anything,' said Burton. 'I was talking to the manageress before you arrived. They get lots of clothes offered to them that are verminous, or too dirty to sell . . . so they shove them in the boiler.'

'Damn.' Frost gave the boiler a kick. 'This bastard is either too clever or too lucky. If we want proof, we're going to have to catch him in the act.' He stretched his arms and yawned loudly. 'Come on, Gilmore, let's get some kip. I get the feeling we're going to have a busy night.'

The house was strangely still and quiet when Gilmore closed the front door behind him. Liz was either out, or had gone back to bed. He tiptoed up the passage so he wouldn't disturb the dormant fury. In the living-room the ticking of the clock seemed unnaturally loud. Or was it because the rest of the house was so quiet?

Her farewell note was tucked into the frame of the mirror above the mantelpiece. She'd used the expensive blue monogrammed notepaper he'd bought for her birthday, his name scrawled across the envelope in green ink. He read it, then dashed up to the bedroom to make sure. The unmade bed was empty, her clothes gone from the wardrobe. He crossed the passage. Her toilet things had been removed from the bathroom.

Back downstairs he read her note again, his free hand pouring out a drink. He tried to feel sad, but couldn't. He swilled down the remains of the drink, stuffed the note on top of the unpaid bills in the bureau and went upstairs to the empty bedroom.

Even as his head touched the pillow he was in a deep, dreamless, trouble-free sleep.

Police Sergeant Bill Wells shivered and turned the lobby thermostat up to full in the hope that it would encourage the radiator to belt out some more heat. A waste of time, because as soon as Mullett came in, he'd complain about the lobby being like a tropical greenhouse and would turn the thermostat right down again. It was all right for him, with his 3-kilowatt heater, but let him try working in this draughty lobby with the door opening every five minutes and that gale-force wind roaring through.

The lobby door slammed open, the wind roared through, and there was Jack Frost, his scarf wound round his face to cover his nose. He was unwrapping himself when Burton pushed through the swing doors carrying the sergeant's tea.

'What news on Ronnie boy?' asked Frost, warming his hands on the radiator.

'He drove to the hospital at 7.22 and brought his mother back home,' said Burton.

'His mother? I thought they were keeping her in overnight?'

'She couldn't have been as bad as they thought.'

'I knew the old cow was faking. So where's Gauld now?'

'Indoors. Collier's watching the house.'

The phone rang. Wells answered it, then pulled a face at the mouthpiece. The caller was Mullett. 'Mr Frost, sir?' Frost shook his head vigorously 'I'm afraid he's not here at the moment.'

'I won't be in until later,' said Mullett. 'I'm feeling a bit under the weather. What have we got on the menu?'

'There's this threatened gang violence when the pubs shut, sir. Can I call on other divisions for assistance if necessary?'

'It shouldn't be necessary,' replied Mullett. 'Put every available man on to it.'

'Mr Frost is going to need much of the available manpower to keep tracks on Gauld, sir,' persisted Wells.

'You must give Mr Frost every assistance possible, Sergeant. Both operations are top priority. I'm relying on you to ensure that each operation does not hamper the effects of the other.'

A click as he hung up, leaving Wells spluttering helplessly at the dead phone 'Both top priority and neither must hamper the success of the other! He knows it's flaming impossible, that's why the bastard's staying away. Why is it always me?' He swung indignantly round to Frost. 'You're the senior officer. You should have taken the call.'

'I wasn't here,' said Frost. 'I heard you tell him.' He hurried off to collect Gilmore, leaving Wells staring at an empty mug and slowly realizing that the inspector had drunk his tea.

PC Collier champed at the cheeseburger. He was parked at the end of the little cul-de-sac, tucked tightly behind a cream-coloured Ford Consul whose owner had decided it would look better in green, but had abandoned the idea after painting just the front wing. The car radio, on which he reported every fifteen minutes that there was nothing to report, was turned down low so that its stream of messages were not audible to passers-by. His eyes were fixed on the house in mid-terrace. Gauld's house. Parked opposite the house, but out of sight from Collier's position, was Gauld's Vauxhall Astra.

He twisted his wrist so he could see his watch. A quarter to ten. He'd been stuck down this side turning for some two hours. In mid-bite something made him pause. Movement reflected in the rear-view mirror. Two men, keeping tight to the wall, stealthily approaching, obviously up to no good. Collier sank down in his seat so his head was below the window and waited. Suddenly the car echoed like a drum as someone pounded a fist on the roof and jerked the door open.

'Are you playing peek-a-boo, Collier?'

He grinned sheepishly and kicked the yellow poly-styrene food container out of sight under the dash. It was Detective Inspector Jack Frost with the new chap, Gilmore. 'I spotted you coming, sir. Thought you were villains trying door handles.'

The car lurched as Frost and Gilmore climbed inside and settled themselves down on the back seat. 'What's happening?'

'Nothing, sir. He's still inside. Went in with his mother just after eight. Hasn't come out.'

Frost's nose began to twitch suspiciously. 'Can I smell cheeseburger?'

Collier blushed. 'Yes, I did have one, sir.'

'Did you cook it in the car,' asked Frost, innocently, 'or was it delivered?'

'Delivered?' frowned Collier, not sure what the inspec-tor was getting at.

'You didn't bloody go off watch to get it, did you?' barked Gilmore.

'I've had nothing to eat for hours. I wasn't gone more than five minutes.'

'Five minutes!' repeated Frost, sadly. 'A lot can happen

in five minutes. I could have five women in five minutes – on an off day. Is his car still there?'

Collier craned his neck, but the Ford Consul blocked his view. 'I think so,' he stammered.

'You *think* so?' exploded Gilmore. 'If you've blown this, Collier . . .'

'Nip out and see,' said Frost, trying not to let his anxiety show. Collier was soon back and Frost's heart nose-dived as he read the answer in the young constable's white face.

'His car's gone, sir. A couple of kids said he drove off about five minutes ago.'

'You stupid fool!' yelled Gilmore.

'It's my fault,' said Frost, 'I should have had two men in the car, not one.' He leant forward to grab the handset. 'Frost to Control, receiving?' He barked out his orders for all cars, all patrols, to be on the lookout for Gauld's Vauxhall and to report the sighting immediately.

Half-way back to the station, Frost smote his forehead with his palm. 'The Oxfam shop! He might try to burn the evidence there.' He radioed through to the station requesting a man on permanent watch at the Oxfam shop.

'I haven't got anyone to spare,' protested Wells.

'Just do it,' said Frost, switching off the set before Wells could reply.

As they roared past a public house they noticed a gang of youths pouring out of an old van and making for the public bar. They seemed to be spoiling for a fight.

He sat in Control, listening to the stream of radio messages, a mound of mangled corpses of half-smoked cigarettes in the ashtray at his side. He hardly looked up when Wells banged a cup of tea in front of him.

'Bloody Collier,' snarled Wells. 'He must choose the busiest flaming night of the week to sod things up.'

'I sodded it up,' said Frost, lighting another cigarette and offering the packet to Wells. 'Collier didn't have the experience and I shouldn't have left him on his own.'

PC Lambert, the officer on Control duty, twisted his head. 'Inspector! Punch up at the Denton Arms. A gang of yobbos smashing the place up. Can I send a couple of cars?'

'Send one,' said Frost. 'I need all the rest.'

'One won't be enough,' protested Lambert.

'It's better than sod all,' Frost told him. 'Tell it to drive with its sirens screaming full blast. With a bit of luck the pub will empty before they burst in.' He tossed his cigarette packet across to Lambert. 'And I want them back searching for Gauld's car as soon as they've mopped up the last drop of blood and guts from the sawdust.' He sipped his tea and shuddered at the taste while Control directed Charlie Able to the pub.

No sooner was that task completed than Control was in trouble again. 'Serious domestic at Vicarage Terrace. Neighbours report couple seem to be smashing the happy home up. They can hear kiddies crying. I'd like to send a car.'

'You're car-mad,' admonished Frost. 'Haven't you got a foot patrol who could handle it?'

'It will take a quarter of an hour for the foot patrol to get there. There's kiddies involved!' protested Control.

'The kids won't get their throats cut. Some senior citizen will if we don't find Gauld quickly. The bastard's going to try it on again tonight, I just know it.'

Anxious squawks from Control's headphones. Lambert turned a permanently worried face to Frost. 'The fight at the pub is getting out of hand, sir. It's sprawled into the street. Windows have been smashed and they're damaging cars now.'

Frost sighed. 'All right, son. You handle it. Send what you want.' His mouth felt stale and bitter. The last thing he wanted was another cigarette, but he lit one up. Nothing was going right.

It was Burton who saved the day. Control switched the call to the external loudspeaker.

'Have located Vauxhall Astra registration K, Kansas, X, X-Ray . . .'

'Sod the phonetic spelling, Burton,' yelled Frost, snatching the handset from Control. 'Where is the bastard?'

'He's parked half-way down Wedgewood Street. I only spotted him by chance.'

At Frost's raised eyebrows, Control indicated Wedgewood Street on the large-scale map. A derelict side street in an area scheduled for demolition. 'I can't think what he's doing down there, Inspector. All the houses are boarded up and empty.'

Frost nodded and went back to Burton. 'You got him in full view?'

'Yes, I'm parked right at the end with my lights off. I don't want him to see me.' A pause, then, 'Damn!'

'Now what?'

'He's turned his lights off. There's no street lamps down there. It's pitch black.'

Frost peered up at the wall map. 'He's got to pass you to come out.'

'Only if he stays in the car. If he goes on foot he can cut through any of the empty houses.'

'Right. We can't be sodded about any more. If he's still in the car, arrest him and bring him back here . . . parking without lights . . . any excuse you can think of. And hurry.' Frost drummed his fingers impatiently as he waited. Then a crackle from the loudspeaker.

'Have subject car in view.'

'But is the sodding subject in the sodding subject car?' demanded Frost.

A pause. Then, 'Subject car is empty . . . repeat empty.'

'Shit,' moaned Frost, 'repeat shit! I suppose he hasn't got out just to have a pee or something innocent like that?'

'No sign of him anywhere,' said Burton.

With a weary grunt, Frost flopped back in his chair. 'Right, son. This is what you do. You immobilize his car . . . wee in his petrol tank, let his tyres down, anything, just so he can't use it. We don't want him driving off the minute your back is turned.'

He waited nervously sucking at his cigarette until a blast of static from the loudspeaker announced Burton to report that he'd immobilized the car.

'Good boy. Still no sign of him?'

'No, sir. No sign of anything. It's a ghost street – just empty houses. Hold on . . .'

'What is it?' asked Frost excitedly.

'I thought I saw a light in one of the houses. It flickered like someone striking a match. I'll go and take a look.'

'Be careful,' ordered Frost. 'And keep in touch.' He lit a fresh cigarette and fidgeted in his chair as he waited. Gilmore came in with two more mugs of tea. 'Thanks, son.' He stirred it with a pencil, feeling vaguely worried. Why the hell was Burton taking so long? He hesitated about asking Control to call the detective constable. Burton might be stalking his prey and a police radio sounding could give the game away. He stared up at the big wall clock, just above Lambert's head. He'd give Burton another two minutes before asking Control to radio. But before fifty seconds were up he had one of his feelings . . . one of his icy cold fingers scraping the back of the spine feelings. 'Call him,' he barked. 'Now!'

'Control to Burton, come in, please . . .' Lambert flipped the switch to receive. A crackle of empty static from the loudspeaker. He tried again. 'Control to Burton . . . are you receiving . . . over?' More empty static. 'He doesn't seem to be responding, Inspector,' said Lambert, redundantly.

'Keep bloody trying,' yelled Frost from the door. 'Come on, Gilmore. Let's get over there.'

The traffic light changed to red and Gilmore slowed to a halt with Frost grunting his impatience as they waited. As soon as the cross-road was clear he ordered Gilmore to jump the lights. They passed a huge building site with skeleton tower blocks and giant cranes. Frost peered through the side window. 'Wedgewood Street should be along here somewhere . . .' They nearly missed it. 'There!'

Slamming on the brakes, Gilmore backed the car and turned into a dark side road. A dead street of empty windowless houses. Burton's car stood by the corner. Further down the road another car. A grey Vauxhall Astra.

At the top of his voice Frost repeatedly shouted, 'Burton!' The empty houses flung his words back.

'On the pavement – there!' Gilmore pointed to something black and rectangular.

They ran over. It was a police radio, its casing smashed and caved in as if it had been stamped on. When Frost picked it up his hand touched stickiness. He stared at his fingers. Blood, fresh and ruby red that glittered in the ray of Gilmore's torch. Frost yanked his own radio from his pocket and fumbled for the transmit button. He blurted out instructions to Control. 'I want every available officer to come immediately to Wedgewood Street.'

'There isn't anyone to send,' answered Control. 'They're all out. There's a near-riot at the Denton Arms.'

'Call them away and send them here . . . now! We've got an officer in trouble!' He switched off before Control could come up with any more stupid objections.

All of the houses had been boarded up with corrugated galvanized sheeting blanking out the windows and heavy planking nailed across the front doors. But on quite a few of the properties vandals had torn away the planking and kicked in the doors. Frost poked his torch beam tentatively into one of the houses and ventured inside. The passage was thick with debris and breathed a sour, mildewy smell. As he shuffled in, the debris moved as rats squealed and scuttled to safety. He lashed out his foot to hasten them on their way. Before he could proceed further the sound of a car, then the slamming of doors. Back to the street where PC Jordan and four other uniformed men were waiting with Gilmore. Five men! Was this all Control was sending?

'We're stretched to the limit,' Jordan told him. 'The pub fight is getting right out of hand.'

Frost stripped cellophane from a fresh packet of cigarettes and passed it around as he quickly briefed them. 'My guess is that Burton went in one of these empty houses after Gauld. The flooring's rotten, the stair treads and banisters are broken, so he could have fallen and hurt himself. But that doesn't explain his radio.' He held it up and showed it to them. 'We found it on the pavement, there, and it frightens the shit out of me. Anyway, sod the speculation until we find him. Take a house each and be careful . . . they're bloody death traps.'

He took the middle property himself, the one nearest to where they had found the smashed radio. It reeked of damp and decay. His torch beam blinked feebly into the blackness, picking out rotting floorboards and slimy rubbish. A door to his right was closed. Warily he turned the handle and pushed. A groaning creak as it swung back on to an empty, dead, urine-smelling room. He moved on, things rustling and scurrying in front of him. To his left, stairs with broken jagged banisters lurching outwards. Another door in front of him. He kicked it open. The kitchen, piled high with rubbish and smelling of bad drains and cats and rotting food.

Back to the hall and up the stairs, testing each tread carefully before putting his weight on it. Half-way up he stopped and held his breath as he listened. A creaking. There was someone up there. There it was again. The soft creak of a floorboard. 'Burton?' He waited. Silence. No! A rustling, then another floorboard creaked. His torch kept flickering. The beam shuddered and died. He gave the casing a welt with the flat of his hand which frightened it into brief life again before it died finally a second time.

He waited to let his eyes adjust to the darkness and took another step. Then he froze. Something. He stopped dead, ears sharply focused for the slightest sound. Silence. Silence that screamed in the blackness. But there was something . . . someone up there. 'Burton?' If it was Burton, why the hell didn't he answer?

He rammed the useless torch in his pocket and fished out his matches. Up the stairs to the landing. The match burnt his fingers. Swearing softly, he shook it out and struck another. A door, slightly ajar, to his right. He nudged it open with his foot, then poked the hand with the match inside. He nearly dropped the match. On the floor, in the flicker of the flame, a face. Another match. God, it was Burton, his face a sweat-soaked dirty white, his lips mumbling incoherently.

Frost dropped to his knees on to a puddle of something wet which soaked his trousers. Another match. He was kneeling in a pool of blood. Burton's hands were clasped round his stomach. A red trickle oozed from between slippery, red fingers. He was trying to say something. Frost brought his head down to Burton's lips. 'Gauld. The bastard stabbed me.' His eyelids flickered and closed.

'Up here!' yelled Frost at the top of his voice. He tugged out his radio. 'Control. Burton's been stabbed. Get an ambulance over to Wedgewood Street . . . now!'

The ambulance men adjusted the strap around the red-blanketed Burton, then wheeled the trolley up into the ambulance. One of the uniformed men hopped in the back with it.

'Got a stack of your chaps in Casualty,' the ambulance driver told Frost cheerfully as he climbed into his seat. 'Blood and broken noses everywhere. A bunch of yobbos breaking up a pub or something.'

Oh, sod! thought Frost. I'd forgotten all about that. He radioed through to the station.

'We're being massacred,' Wells told him. 'Things are getting out of control and bloody Mullett's not answering his phone in case he should have to make a decision.'

Gilmore tugged at Frost's sleeve. 'Gauld's been spotted. He's got into that building site.' He pointed in the direction of the giant crane.

'Damn,' said Frost. There were a hundred places Gauld could hide in in the sprawl of the building site. Back to the radio. 'We know where Gauld is. Without more men we'll lose him. Pull more people out from the pub.'

'I can't,' insisted Wells.

'Just bloody do it. Then phone County and get re-inforcements from other divisions,' said Frost.

'Mullett won't like that. He'll do his nut.'

'Sod Mullett. Just do it.'

Wells hesitated. 'If it blows up in our face, will you take the can back, Jack?'

'Don't I always?' said Frost.

The building site covered almost twenty acres and would eventually house a hypermarket, shops, and two tower office blocks which, at the moment, were skeletons of scaffolding and girders. The car picked its way along a muddy, temporary road to the main gates.

Chain link fencing encircled the area. A notice in red warned *Keep Out. Guard Dogs Loose On This Site*. The main gates were locked and chained, but there was a smaller gate to one side which sagged where it had been kicked in. Beyond the gate a brown and white shape twitched and whimpered in the mud. The knife-ripped guard dog.

Gilmore's radio reported the arrival of reinforcements. Three pub-battle-scarred warriors were in position at the back entrance of the site, ready to move in from there. 'It's not enough,' said Gilmore.

'As the bishop said to the actress, son, it may not be much, but it's all I've got.' He took the radio and warned the newcomers to be careful. Gauld had a knife and was prepared to use it. 'Right. Let's go in.'

Near the entrance stood a green-coloured Portakabin. Frost tried the handle. Locked. He flashed a torch through a window. Desks, phones and drawing boards.

Other torches bobbed in the distance as the rest of his thinly stretched team carried out the search. The site was littered with hills and mountains of building materials; earthenware drainage pipes, concrete blocks, bricks on pallets covered with polythene sheeting, bag after bag of cement. And then there was machinery. Bulldozers, earth-moving equipment, cranes, and overshadowing everything, a giant skyscraper of a crane on its tower of scaffolding. The muddy ground had been churned into a Somme battlefield by the wheels of countless lorries.

It was a slow, laboured search. Heavy items had to be man-handled out of the way, planking covering drainage trenches removed, builders' huts forced open and searched, canvas and polythene sheeting stripped away. They squeezed between stacks of splintery timber shuttering, crawled under wooden sheds and, finally, mud-caked, dishevelled and disheartened, there was nowhere else to look and Gilmore was wearing his 'I told you so' smirk.

They gathered round Frost who was dishing out cigarettes, forming a tight circle as he struck a match to stop the rising wind from blowing it out. 'Now what?' asked Gilmore.

'We go back and search again, son.'

'He could be miles away.'

Frost's chin poked out stubbornly. 'No. He's here. Laughing at us. I know it.' He held up a hand. 'I thought I heard something.' Someone's radio was burbling away about casualties and ambulances and shortage of manpower. 'Turn that thing off.' The offending radio was silenced. 'Now listen.'

They listened. The wind, working itself up into a paddy, rattled chain link fencing, flapped polythene sheeting, and made the temporary overhead telephone wires sing and hum. Almost 200 feet above them, the jib arm of the giant crane, with its warning light on the far end, creaked and groaned and shrieked as if in pain.

A sudden clatter. All heads turned. Jordan grinned sheepishly. He had knocked over a stack of empty lubricating oil drums.

Frost shook his head. Whatever he thought he'd heard wasn't going to repeat itself. Then he clicked his fingers. 'The crane. We haven't looked up there!' Heads turned up and up and up. The distant warning light, a pin-prick of bright against the night sky, seemed almost another star.

'It's bloody high,' croaked Jordan.

'Yes,' agreed Frost, now wishing he hadn't suggested it. The damn thing seemed to go up and up and up for ever.

A yell from Gilmore. 'Someone's up there!' And as the moon elbowed through black clouds, there was Gauld, on the ladder, nearly 100 feet up, clinging for dear life and looking down at them.

Making a megaphone with his hands, Frost yelled up into the night sky. 'You can't get away now, Gauld. We've got you. Come on down.'

The wind fielded Gauld's defiant reply and hurled it away.

'He's coming down,' exclaimed Jordan.

'He's not,' said Frost. 'He's going higher.'

Necks craned, they watched until he was swallowed by blackness. 'Let's have some lights,' Frost ordered.

With much difficulty an area car zigzagged, bumped and slid its way towards the crane, and then a powerful spotlight sliced upwards, cutting a steamy white swathe in the night sky and picking out the doll-man as he climbed up and up.

Gauld was nearly at the top of the ladder and could see the platform of the driver's cab just above his head. He gripped the rungs tightly with hands that the wind was trying to tear loose. Above him the jib groaned and whined and shuddered. He heaved himself up on to the small platform outside the cab. The protective metal handrail seemed flimsy and inadequate and he kept well back as he looked down, eyes squinting against the blinding spotlight beam. The police were still staring up at him, the one in the dirty mac yelling something which any fool should realize couldn't be heard at this height. One of the uniformed men was running from a car with something in his hand. A loud-hailer.

'Be sensible, Gauld. You can't go anywhere. Come on down.'

Pointless shouting. They wouldn't hear him. But the cop was right. He couldn't go anywhere. They had him trapped. God, how had it all gone wrong?

'Come on down, Gauld.'

The fool was yelling again. Come on down? He ventured another look over the edge. Just looking made him dizzy and he pressed back against the cab, his hands scrabbling for something to hold on to. If they wanted him, they'd have to bring him down.

Above him the jib gave another tortured scream of pain, then another sound pierced the night. A two-tone siren.

The fire engine halted outside the gate and a bearded fireman made his way across to the inspector. He looked angry. 'You called a vet for that dog? It's still alive, you know.'

'He's on his way,' snapped Frost, annoyed with himself for not attending to it. He signalled to Jordan who moved out of earshot and radioed through to Control. Frost pointed to the crane platform. 'We want to get up there. Would your turntable ladder reach?'

The fireman squinted up, then shook his head. 'You'd need a bleeding helicopter to get up there.' He moved to the ladder lashed to the scaffolding and gave it a shake. It didn't seem very firm. 'That's the only way up.'

'Sod that for a lark,' said Frost. 'Take me up on your turntable ladder as far as it goes. I'll see if I can't sweet-talk the bastard down.'

The turntable platform gave a jerk, then the ground suddenly hurtled down and Frost had to grab the rail to steady himself as the ladder zoomed upwards. Briefly he chanced a look down, then quickly pulled his eyes away and concentrated on staring straight ahead at the bolts and nuts and rusted metal of the scaffolding as they zipped past.

After what seemed ages, the ladder slowed and juddered to a halt and the fire officer tugged Frost's sleeve. 'As far as we go.'

Frost looked down. Toy cars, tiny people, miles and miles away. He looked up. Lots more scaffolding roaring up to the sky and the white blob of Gauld's face staring down at him. 'There's nowhere to run,' shouted Frost. 'Chuck your knife and we'll bring you down.'

Gauld yelled something, but the wind snatched and tore the words to shreds. Then the blob of his face withdrew and they couldn't see him any more.

'Now what?' asked the fire officer.

Frost's neck was aching from craning upwards. He lowered his head. In front of him was the flimsy metal ladder which Gauld had climbed. It didn't look very safe and was rattling in the wind. He shivered. 'If we both went up, we could overpower him.'

418

'Not our job to overpower nutters with knives,' said the fire officer, firmly. 'Disarm him and you can have as many of my men as you like. Until then, you're on your own.'

Sod it, thought Frost. Let's pack it in and starve the bastard into submission. But he'd come this far. He wanted to get it over and done with. Fumbling at the buckle, he released the safety belt. 'Help me across to the other ladder.'

The fireman looked doubtful. 'Are you sure you know what you're doing?'

'I never know what I'm bleeding doing,' said Frost.

The gap between the platform and the scaffold ladder grew markedly wider as he looked at it. Before common sense made his nerve fail he ducked quickly under the rail, holding it tight with one hand, and plunged forward in the blind hope his other hand would find something to hang on to. He managed to find one of the ladder rungs and squeezed it to death as he released his grip on the guard rail and grabbed at the same rung. He was now hanging over the gap, feet on the platform, hands on the ladder rungs and definitely at the point of no return.

'You're doing fine,' called the fireman unconvincingly. 'Now hold tight and swing your feet forward.'

He didn't need to be told to hold tight. The skin over his knuckles was paper thin and the bones threatened to burst through. He swung forward, his feet kicking about as they tried to find the rungs. They found only space . . . pulling, plunging space. He was hanging by sweat-slippery hands, kicking wildly and he was terrified. Then he felt hands grabbing his ankles and placing his feet on a narrow rung. He managed to croak a word of thanks to the fireman and froze to the ladder, heart hammering, his face pressed against the cold metal, not wanting to look up or down or left or right, just wanting to be back on the ground, looking up at some silly sod doing what he was doing and telling everyone what a prat the man was.

'Anything wrong?' The fireman sounded anxious.

'No,' lied Frost. 'Just catching my breath.' He forced one hand to release its grip and move further up the rail. Then the other. One leg lifted and found the next rung. This was easy. As long as he didn't look down, this was easy. It was just like climbing a ladder a couple of feet off the ground. But confidence cloaked near-disaster and he almost screamed when his foot slipped from the rung and he had to hug the ladder, shaking, feeling the ladder rattle like chattering teeth against the scaffolding. He forced himself to press on, rung by rung, his body stiff and rigid, leg muscles aching with the effort. 'I'll be fit for sod all when I get up there,' he kept telling himself, trying to erase the mental picture of himself sprawled on the gantry, gasping for breath, while Gauld slowly hacked away at his windpipe. But even that prospect was currently preferable to going down, which meant moving backwards, descending the ladder in reverse. God, he was never going to get down again.

'You're doing fine!'

The voice seemed to come from a long way down. He risked a glance and saw the top of the man's helmet floating in space below his feet. With an effort he forced himself on.

There was one frightening section which required him to swap from one ladder to another, holding with one hand to the first and reaching out for the next and swinging across. But not far now, thank God. He must be near the top. The teeth-setting grinding and squealing of the jib, like a giant fingernail scratching down a blackboard, screamed in his ears.

The ladder stopped and his sweat-blurred eyes were

level with a wooden platform. His hands seemed fused to the ladder, but he tore them free and flung himself forward on to the gantry where he rolled across to huddle up tight to the side of the cab, keeping as far from the edge as possible.

'Are you all right?' A faint voice calling from a hundred miles down.

'I'm fine,' he yelled, not feeling it. A quick fumble through his pocket for a cigarette, turning his back to the hurricane force wind which, at this height, was making everything shake violently. Far away to his left were the winking dots of light from the Lego town of Denton. His radio squawked.

'Inspector!' It was Gilmore from the smug safety of the firm ground. 'Gauld's round the other side of the gantry to you. Just seems to be standing there.'

'Not much else the poor sod can do,' he answered. He'd almost forgotten about Gauld, the whole purpose of this nightmare climb. Another squawk from the radio. Gilmore back again. 'Mr Mullett is here, Inspector. He'd like a word.' Mullett! Trust Hornrim Harry to be in at the kill. All ready to take the credit should the operation prove a success, and to dissociate himself from it in the more likely event of failure. The thought of realizing a long-held ambition to defecate on Mullett from a great height flashed across his mind as he waited.

'What's the position, Inspector?'

'I'm just about to go round and talk him down.'

'Good. Let's tie this up neat and tidy. Bring him down safely, and do it by the book.'

Stupid sod. How the hell do you get a knife-wielding mass-murderer down from a 200-foot crane by the book? He stuck the radio back in his mac and dragged himself to his feet. The wooden platform creaked and gave slightly under his weight, then the whole structure lurched and the stars danced in the sky as the wind pounded the jib. Through the cracks between the planks he could see straight down to the swaying, yawning black of the bottomless drop. One last drag of his cigarette before he flipped it away. The wind caught it and hurled it over the side where it nose-dived down to oblivion, spitting red sparks.

He inched round to the other side, keeping tightly to the solid reassurance of the driver's cab. And there was Gauld, his back to the rail, hair streaming, legs braced against the force of the pummelling wind. 'Keep away from me!' In his upraised hand something bright reflected the twinkling blood gobs of the warning light at the end of the jib.

Frost leant against the cab and wearily shook his head. 'It's all over, son. You've got nowhere to go.' He waited for a response, eyeing the man warily. If Gauld decided to put up a fight, there wasn't much he could do. There was hardly room for a punch-up on this barely 2-foot-wide platform. They'd probably both end up over the edge, splashing blood, brains and guts all over Mullett's patent leather shoes.

Gauld moved forward, the arm with the knife still raised, a manic grin clicking on and off. Then his face crumpled and tears streamed. 'Why didn't you leave me alone?'

Shit, thought Frost. Don't make me start feeling sorry for you, you murdering bastard. He kept his eye firmly on the blade and edged forward a fraction. Gauld, the guard rail pressing into his back, couldn't retreat. He could only move forward.

'The knife!' said Frost firmly, optimistically holding out his hand.

422

Again the flickering, manic grin. Gauld scrubbed at his face with the back of his hand to wipe off the tears. His eyes glinted slyly and the knife-hand shook. 'You want the knife? You want the bloody knife?' He held it out. 'Here it is. Take it.'

'Don't try anything,' warned Frost, 'or I'll push you over the bloody edge.'

Gauld raised the knife higher, then, as Frost steeled himself, flung it far out into the night where it spun and glinted before vanishing into the void. 'It was only a penknife. You couldn't cut bloody butter with it.'

A cold trickle of relief, but Frost moved warily towards Gauld who looked as if he still had a few aces hidden up his sleeve. Tugging out his radio he let the firemen know it was safe for them to come up and give him a hand.

'You've got him?' cried Mullett's excited voice. 'What's the position?'

'Later,' snapped Frost. 'I'll tell you bloody later.' He clicked off the set and felt for the handcuffs, still watching Gauld like a hawk.

'I panicked,' said Gauld, suddenly. 'I had the knife in my hand and I panicked.' He glared at Frost. 'It was your fault. Why didn't you leave me alone?'

Frost frowned. What the hell was the man talking about? 'My fault?' He now had the handcuffs and reached for Gauld's arm.

'Of course it was your flaming fault,' yelled Gauld, snatching his arm away. 'You hounded me. You frightened the shit out of my mother. That's why it happened.'

Frost's mind raced, trying to make sense of all this, but then the wind suddenly wailed and hit the crane jib with a tremendous punch, wrenching the gantry round until the anchor chains braked it with a shuddering jerk. Frost was flung to the floor of the gantry, the stars zip-panning across the sky. And through the creakings and squeals and resounding clangs, the sound of a man screaming.

In an instant he was up on his feet, trying to regain his balance on the shaking platform. Gauld. Where was Gauld? The guard rail where he had been standing was broken and a section dangled down. Still that screaming. And yells from below as firemen clambered up the ladder.

'Help me!'

Frost leaned over the edge. A spotlight from the fire appliance on the ground blinded him. He shielded his eyes with his arm. Someone on the ground saw what was happening and yelled for the beam to be directed downwards. It slid down and locked on to a screaming, pleading Gauld who was clinging by his fingertips to the protruding edge of a girder just below the platform, feet kicking wildly in a futile effort to find a foothold before his fingers gave way.

'Hold on!' roared Frost. A stupid thing to say. What else could the poor bastard do? He flung himself down on the gantry, kicking into a gap in the planking to wedge in the toes of his shoes. With the platform cutting into his stomach he leant out over the edge and reached down.

Below him, the white, upturned face of the dangling man who was whimpering with terror. It didn't seem possible that Frost could reach him. The thudding of firemen's feet on the ladder over on the far side was getting louder. He prayed that they would hurry. Way, way below, tiny dolls held out a circular white canvas, only part of which protruded from an overhanging section of the scaffolding. A tiny, inadequate, very missable target.

He groped and stretched. The bitter, cutting wind stung his cheeks, roared pain into his scar, and gradually sucked the feeling from his bare hands. He gritted his teeth and stretched further. Something. Cold flesh. Icy cold knuckles gripping raw-edged metal scaffolding.

'Take my hand!'

Gauld moaned and gave a feeble shake of the head. 'I can't.'

'Don't sod me about,' shouted Frost. 'Take the bloody thing!'

Gauld's hand fluttered, then snatched. Frost grabbed at wet, blood-slippery fingers, cut by the saw-edge of the metal. It was not a secure grip, but the first fireman was now up on the platform and could take over. As long as Gauld didn't release his other hand, Frost could sustain him. 'Wait,' he yelled down.

But Gauld wasn't going to wait. He wanted to be pulled to safety. He let go of the girder and snatched up at Frost, but he couldn't reach and his body started to swing and his fingertips just brushed the hand Frost was straining out to him and his life depended on Frost holding on to his cut and bleeding fingers.

Frost could feel him going. He gripped tighter, but this squeezed more blood from Gauld's torn hand. Slippery blood. The fireman flung himself alongside Frost, but even as he did so, Gauld was screaming. Frost, free arm flailing, desperately tried to find something to hold. Gauld's hair raced through his fingers and the white terrified face grew smaller, smaller, smaller, still screaming. He screamed as he fell. He screamed as he hit and bounced off the protruding girder which broke his back. He screamed as he smashed into the ground. After he was dead, after his heart stopped pumping blood out of his broken body, his screams still rang and rang round and round the building site.

Friday night shift (2)

The ambulance took away the pulp in a body bag and the firemen hosed away the mess. Frost, white and shaken, greedily sucked at a cigarette and was hardly listening to what Mullett was saying.

'You're absolutely certain Gauld was the Ripper?'

Frost took one last gloomy drag then chucked the cigarette away. Up until half an hour ago he was positive but now the shrill, insistent nagging voice of doubt kept raising the terrible possibility that he might have hounded an innocent man to his death. 'Yes, I'm certain,' he said without conviction.

'Did he admit it?' persisted Mullett. 'We're a little short of solid proof and it would make things neat and tidy if I could tell the Chief Constable that we got a verbal confession.'

Admit it? It was those last words of Gauld that triggered the doubts. 'It was your fault,' Gauld had said, 'You hounded me . . . that's why it happened.' That sounded more like an apology for stabbing Burton, not an admission that he was the Ripper. 'No, he didn't admit anything.' He searched for his cigarette packet.

Mullett gave a deep sigh. Couldn't Frost take the smallest hint? Gauld was dead. No-one would know whether he had actually admitted guilt or not, and if Frost was certain Gauld was the Ripper, then where was the harm in a little white lie? 'Are you *sure* he admitted nothing?' he asked, slowly and deliberately, giving the inspector the chance to amend his answer.

'Of course I'm bloody sure,' snapped Frost, turning his back on his Divisional Commander.

Mullett's lips tightened. But he wouldn't create a scene here. Just wait until he got Frost back to the office. 'By the way,' he hurled at Frost's back, 'the hospital called. Burton is quite comfortable . . . all he required was a few stitches. His wounds were quite superficial.'

'Good,' grunted Frost, his mind whirling, his doubts multiplying. Superficial! None of the Ripper's other victims had superficial wounds. That poor cow with her head hanging off – that wasn't superficial. The canker of doubt gnawed and chewed and got bigger and bigger. But it had to be Gauld. It just had to be. Only vaguely was he aware of Gilmore answering a radio call in the car, then hastening across to Mullett and murmuring something in his car.

'What?' Mullett couldn't believe what he had been told. He listened, open-mouthed, as Gilmore repeated it, then spun round to Frost, his whole body shaking with uncontrollable anger. 'You were so damn sure!! While you were chasing Gauld with his Boy Scout's penknife, the real Ripper has struck again.'

Frost went cold. Icy, shivery cold. He could only gape at Mullett. He looked pleadingly at Gilmore, willing him to say it was all a mistake.

'Elderly lady,' said Gilmore. 'Slashed to ribbons. They've rushed her to Denton Hospital.'

Hospital! Then she was still alive. He almost knocked Mullett over as he dashed for the car.

'Come here, Frost,' choked Mullett. 'I haven't finished with you yet . . .' Doors slammed and the car roared off. 'My office!' screamed Mullett to the dwindling red lights. 'I want you in my office . . . now!!' Panting with fury, he gasped for breath, then was aware of someone at his side. A stocky figure in a dark blue anorak poking a miniature cassette recorder at him.

'Mr Mullett, I'm from the Denton *Echo*. Is it true you've caught the Ripper?'

Hunched over the steering wheel, dragging savagely at a cigarette he didn't want, he went over the night's events again and again. Could he have saved Gauld if he had tried that much harder to reach out and grab him? Was it his stubborn certainty that Gauld was the Ripper that stopped him from trying harder? And now, it seemed, Gauld was innocent.

He lurched to one side as the car spun into the main hospital access road. Out of the corner of his eye he was vaguely aware of an ambulance parked outside the mortuary and the stretchered body-bag being carried in.

The car had barely stopped when Frost was running up the steps and barging through the swing doors. A uniformed constable seated on a wooden bench by the night porter's cubicle snatched the cigarette from his mouth. 'She's in Intensive Care, Inspector.'

His running footsteps clattered and echoed along the empty corridors. The night sister in Intensive Care looked up angrily as they barged into her domain and was completely unimpressed with the warrant card Frost flashed at her.

'One minute, that's all I'm giving you.' She led him across to a bed where liquid-filled plastic bags dripped through tubes into the veins of a barely breathing woman who was swathed in white bandages through which blood seeped. The nurse adjusted the flow of one of the drips and gave the plastic bag a squeeze.

'Will she live?' asked Frost.

The nurse shrugged. 'Cut throat . . . slashed abdomen.

She's barely alive now. She regained consciousness for a couple of minutes, then drifted off in a coma again.'

'Did she say anything?'

'She tried to. It was all garbled. Something about her son. She said he did it.'

Her son? Frost pushed the nurse to one side and bent close to look at the face. Shrivelled and sunken with her dentures removed, she looked a hundred years older than when he last saw her.

It was the mother. It was Mrs Gauld.

Her eyelids quivered, then fluttered open to reveal watery colourless eyes. She didn't seem surprised to see the blurred face of Frost hovering over her. Her lips moved and her voice was so weak he had to press his ear close to her mouth and feel the hot rasp of her breath on his cheek. 'I told him it had to stop or I'd tell the police. That made him angry. He always had a temper.' With a strain of effort that made the nurse look worried, she lifted her head from the pillow and stared pleadingly at Frost. 'He didn't mean it. Not his own mother.'

'Of course not,' whispered Frost.

'You won't hurt him?'

'No,' said Frost. 'Of course we won't hurt him.'

She managed the ghost of a smile as her head dropped back.

He sat with her until she died.

So it was Gauld?' Mullett's mind was racing. Frost had dropped him in the mire yet again. The phone on his desk was still warm from his call to the Chief Constable, explaining that Frost had screwed up and Gauld wasn't the Ripper. Having dumped the blame for the debacle on Frost, it was going to be difficult to claw back any credit for himself.

'Yes, Super,' said Frost, dragging the visitor's chair across the carpet and flopping wearily into it. 'Those photographs of the victims I showed his mother apparently did the trick. She told him she was going to shop him, so he knifed her. Then he panicked and went on the run.'

'I see.' Mullett pointedly fanned away the smoke which drifted across from the cigarette Frost was puffing at without permission. 'Well, somehow or other you seem to have muddled through to a correct result on this one.'

'Thank you, Super.' He pushed himself out of the chair and brushed away the cigarette ash that was all over the front of his coat. It snowed down all over the blue Wilton carpet. Making no attempt to cover his mouth, he gave a loud yawn and moved towards the door. 'If there's nothing else, I'm going home.'

Mullett looked down at the long list of casualties from the pub fight. The men returning from sick leave would not make up the deficiency and the manning level would be worse than before. Damn Frost. Why did he have to be saddled with such an incompetent? His eyes glinted malevolently. He'd almost forgotten. He'd poked through Frost's in-tray earlier that evening and, to his fury, had found the inventory return, completely untouched. 'Oh.' He tried to keep his voice casual. 'Before you go, Frost, I'd like you to drop in the completed inventory return. I've promised County they'll get it tonight.'

'Sure, Super,' muttered Frost. He pulled the door shut behind him and felt his shoulders slump. How the hell was he going to get out of this one?

Back in his office, watched by Bill Wells, he retrieved the bulky wad of blank forms from the depths of his in-tray and thumbed through them despairingly. 'The bastard,' he moaned. 'He knows damn well I haven't done it.'

'But you told him you'd finished them,' said Wells.

'He knew I was lying,' said Frost. His eyes skimmed round the room. 'Two desks, two chairs and a filing cabinet.' He flipped through the pages and scribbled in the figures.

'You've missed out the hat-stand, the typewriter, the filing trays, the telephones, the stationery stocks. You'll never do it, Jack.'

The cigarette packet was generously proffered. 'But if you helped me, Bill.'

'If I did, it would cost more than a lousy cigarette. There's no way you're going to get it done tonight, Jack, even if we all pitched in. It used to take Mr Allen the best part of a week with three people to help him.'

Frost admitted defeat. He dragged his scarf from the hat-stand and wound it round his neck. 'I'll give the bastard the blank form and tell him to stick it up his arse. He can only sack me. Then I'm going home. I think I've got a dose of flu coming on. With luck, it'll kill me.'

He shuffled along the corridor to the Murder Incident Room to collect Gilmore. The detective sergeant, anxious to take advantage of his new-found freedom, was chatting up Jill Knight, the red-headed WPC who operated the computer. She didn't appear very interested.

'I'm off home,' announced Frost.

'Message just in from Birmingham Police,' Gilmore told him. 'They traced a copper who remembers something about Gauld. Apparently, when he was twelve he attacked his grandmother with a knife but she wouldn't press charges, so the case never went to court.'

'Wouldn't have hurt to have had that earlier,' sniffed

Frost. He pulled the inventory from his pocket. Now to face Mullett.

A cry of recognition from Jill Knight. 'So that's where it's been. I've been looking for it everywhere.'

Frost could only watch and wonder as she took the blank inventory return from him and began pounding the computer keyboard. At her side, the dot-matrix printer clunked, then the print-head screeched as it shuttled back and forth, hammering out columns of figures on continuous stationery.

'Inspector Allen put the inventory details on computer before he went off sick,' she explained. 'I've been hunting high and low for that return.'

Frost pulled out his cigarettes and poked one in her mouth. 'Will it take long?'

She leant forward to receive a light. 'You can have it now.' She tore the sheets from the printer, clipped them together and handed them over.

Frost wound the scarf round his neck and buttoned up his mac. 'I don't know whether to kiss you or the bloody computer.'

With a happy, off-key whistle hampered by the cigarette in his mouth, Detective Inspector Jack Frost sashayed up the corridor. Gilmore, a thin look of contempt on his face, watched him go. Thank heaven Inspector Allen would be back on Monday and he'd be working with a real copper for a change.

THE END